#2 in The Heaven's Pond Trilogy

The Soldier's Return

Laura Libricz

Blue Heron Book Works, LLC
Allentown, Pennsylvania

Blue Heron Book Works, LLC
Allentown, Pennsylvania 18104
www.blueheronbookworks.com

DEDICATION

Let us honor those unnamed men and women wrongly accused of witchcraft, exposed to unthinkable human horrors and subjected to torturous deaths.

CONTENTS

ACKNOWLEDGMENTS

There are times writers must remind themselves why they began a project. I only wanted to read a historical novel about the Thirty Years War in Germany in English. That was almost ten years ago. I always dreamed about writing but I never imagined I would finish one book, let alone two, with a third waiting to be finished. I'd like to thank those who have continued to make this journey possible: Bathsheba Monk, whose influence has made this work what it is; Graham Stockley, the keeper of the keys; Pam Boyer, brilliant editor; Kay Thomas, well-read nit-picker extraordinaire; Betsy Souders, BFF; Nicole Weber, my right arm; Jan and Yvonne, all-round wonderful people; and those readers who have taken the time to support me and my work.

Part 1

Prologue

Excerpt from the Journal of Sebald Tucher
March 1626

With this entry I mark the end of a decade here at my farm, Sichardtshof. I have allowed the last ten years to race by light-heartedly. The fear that my time here is about to be violently and abruptly terminated haunts me with each echo of war. Rumors of mercenary movement and of the villages they reduce to ash-piles are delivered with every message we receive from any fleeing source that passes through.

Although I want to make public my observations, print this journal like a celebrated littérateur and impart my wisdom onto others, I share this book reluctantly. If my knowledge is the only thing I grace the world with before I die, it is my hope that someone may learn from it. These musings may be the only thing my children inherit from me. But among these musings are private thoughts and they must remain private until I die. My views could get me into trouble as well as those who possess this book. There are many who die on the fire because what they say and write is contrary to the accepted opinion.

What is the accepted opinion? That is a throw of the dice. Sichardtshof lays on a tract of land where the villages are mostly Protestant. My beloved Heimat, Nuremberg, is not only Protestant but also the strongest city in South Germany and there are forces that would like to bring Nuremberg to its knees. But we are interjected with strongholds of the Roman Catholics—Höchstadt, Herzogenaurach and Bamberg; Bamberg posing a formidable and oppressive presence together with Würzburg. This ongoing animosity between the Catholics and the Protestants has turned into an excuse to destroy much of the landscape here in the German territories situated between France, Italy and Denmark. It has fueled the ruthless greed and charred egos of the princes and the warlords. And, under the rule of Emperor Ferdinand II of the Holy Roman Empire, the German cities and villages are left to not only fund this savage war, but the villagers are also expected to wring their existence from muddy, trampled, burned or ravished homelands, often destroyed by the troops that are supposedly freeing them.

Naturally, other stronger powers sense an opportunity to gorge themselves, taking everything, leaving us broken and scarred behind, if we are lucky to be alive. What better way to do this than with underpaid, starving, sick, desperate mercenary soldiers? In my opinion, we could be building ships, bridges, transportation for trade routes. But the rights to these channels, routes, means and ends are exactly what the powers are fighting about.

Now, after much deliberation and endless discussions with my mother, my Uncle Paul has come to a conclusion and I have no choice but to collect my wife and two boys from Nuremberg and bring them here to the Sichardtshof farm to live. I am willing to remain at Sichardtshof and wait for the devil to come stake his claim. But the decision to bring my children here is difficult. In Nuremberg they are protected behind the city walls. There is enough money and ammunition and weapons to keep them safe. But others have this impression too, and the city steadily fills with all sorts: refugees seeking religious sanction, homeless who have lost everything because of the fighting, fortune seekers and undesirables who want to earn from others' sufferings. And with the masses comes the plague.

My wife wants to go to London and we are awaiting word if passage is possible. She tries to convince Paul to allow her to travel, take the boys and go abroad. She doesn't want to live at Sichardtshof any more than I want her here.

Here at the Sichardtshof farm, my muse, my elation, my pearl in the Aisch River valley, my paradise on earth, here Katarina and I are free. When I first met her, Katarina was a boisterous installation at the Stork's Nest tavern. I had to have her; to cage her and hold her close, clip her wings so she would be mine to adore. Yet when I found I did have her, I could not cage her as would have been my first desire. She is a creature that needs nurturing, as I myself am. She needs to be close, she needs to be cared for, as much as she needs to care for someone. I enjoy when that someone is me. Why do I love her so? She listens to me, that is what it is. I can pull her in my arms and I find myself freely expounding on everything that troubles me, no matter how banal it seems. Katarina understands. She does not try to better me or to even resolve the situation. She listens. And together we have found many a solution to the affairs that cause me duress.

Together we have made this farm what it is today.

But this freedom comes with a high price. Troops are moving along the Aisch River valley at regular intervals. We have erected fences of spiked logs, we are armed and we have secured the animals as best we can. We've hidden our valuables—buried many things in the forest or in the fields. Much of our food is hidden or buried. I must say, honestly, and no one knows this except Uncle Paul, I am so badly in debt that there is no money to bribe the regiments to continue on their way and leave us in peace.

Over the years I have tried to keep up correspondence with Pieter van Diemen, the son of my dear friend the Dutch merchant. After the year Pieter worked for me at Sichardshof and left the farm, I heard both father and son had mixed in some risky arms commerce. That, along with van Diemen the Elder's failing health, had sped the old man's demise. After the father's death, Pieter wanted to return here. Because he'd made himself indispensable and showed himself to be a major asset to my people, I sent him a sum of money to travel. He never found his way back. That was five years ago. I wrote several letters after that but had no reply. I fear he may have taken advantage of my gullible nature. With the war in Holland I can only hope he fares well and will soon return. Tanner and the other farm hands could only benefit with a man like Pieter, strong stature and ready to fight, working here on the farm with us. Any extra manpower is desperately needed now.

There was problem enough when the first mercenary troops came in 1621. They were insulted with the small amounts of food and drink we had to spare. The last five years, the size of the troops has doubled, quadrupled, multiplied into horrendous numbers. And the depths that these men can sink to was demonstrated by the wreckage of their last visit.

They came last November right before St. Martin's Day, just when I had thought all soldiers were long in their winter quarters and we were safe to move around. Katarina and I were settled for the evening. Isabeau, who was nine years old at the time, was in bed. We never heard them coming. Upon waking the next day, a camp had been erected all around the farm. They had set up a barricade with watchmen and we could not get out of the farmyard. At first I was not too worried. The troop was comparatively small, thirty men; a roughish-looking band of misfits. But then they began to slaughter sheep and were preparing meat, getting more and more drunk on our wine. They insisted Katarina bring them more and then they insisted that Katarina and the maids, Anna, Sara and Elsbeth, join them in their merrymaking.

I, as the master, protested. The soldiers knocked me out cold. They tied the rest of the men together and locked us all in the barn. I heard this all from Tanner when I came to because I was out for the good part of an hour. The soldiers told the women that they would burn us men alive in there if they did not join in the soldiers' party. At some point Katarina decided to stand up for herself. She grabbed a knife from one soldier as he ate. The other women, except Elsbeth, grabbed weapons and decided to fight. The men overpowered the three of them and beat them horribly and raped them for the better part of an hour. We men could do nothing but sit tied together and listen to the men defile our women.

This moral degradation, the vile, numbing cruelty and the callous savagery was, at one point in my life, unfathomable. But now, the disgust I feel at the readiness of one human being to invoke complete ruin on another makes me so incoherently angry that I am afraid of the damage I could do to another given the chance. As I analyze my own anger, I think about where these soldiers come from. They have watched as others raped their mothers, wives, daughters. They have witnessed the destruction of their own villages and homes. In front of their eyes, loved ones have been slaughtered. And then I wonder, why do these soldiers, these victimized, tortured people, follow the same route? Why not band together and fight against those in power who send them on this route of humiliation, loss, and fear? I then come to the conclusion that we have all been lowered to the ranks of savages and we are no more than cattle, Nutztiere, *allowing ourselves to be herded from one paddock to the next. We accept what the soldiers do with us because of our fear of imminent slaughter.*

The soldiers themselves have no idea of what they are fighting for, nor do they care. These are farmers without farms, people without homes, men without a country. So, with having nothing to appease these brutes with, I am afraid these desperates will relieve us of all our belongings, take the men and myself as necessary manpower for their march, abuse our women into insanity, burn the buildings to the ground and then just kill us all in the end.

My choice is not an easy one. Do I allow my children to rot in the rancid city until we secure passage to London? Or do I subject them to realizing their worst nightmares at the hands of roguish soldiers? They are my first responsibility now. I have not even mentioned the responsibility I have towards my loyal counterparts here on the farm. But the worst dilemma of all: can I allow my wife to come to Sichardtshof, my heart's only refuge, and risk ruining the only thing of value I have left—my relationship with Katarina?

Chapter 1

Pieter van Diemen
March 1626

Pieter van Diemen fidgeted with the chains binding his arms. Dull and thudding, they rattled against the wooden floor of his compartment in the ship's hull. The only light permeating the dark hole came through a small split in two boards. Every so often a spray of salt water made its way through the split, into his prison, to dampen his face and lips with brine. Today was the first day he sensed subtle changes signaling the ship neared Europe. The clime had cooled, at first gradually. Now, finally, the stifling southern heat was replaced with a cold, damp smell reminding him of the English Channel, the North Sea; lush and budding like spring in Europe. Home.

His first ocean crossing was the journey to Batavia in the East Indies. That must have been in 1620; over five years ago. This homecoming from Batavia was only Pieter's second voyage. He swore this would be the last time he boarded a ship. This ship, the *Vrijheid*, a Dutch-built, wide-bottomed fluyt, had set sail from Batavia right after Christmas and the journey with the slow, heavily-laden vessel was to last three months. In the hold, a treasure chest of spice, namely nutmeg from the Spice Islands, headed for Amsterdam. Along with the precious cargo, they carried trunks upon trunks of documents and paperwork for those reporting to the Gentleman Seventeen, the directors of the Dutch East India Company.

His present predicament, incarcerated and chained, was representative of his whole East Indies career. He had spent most of his time in the east locked up in prison. Each time, alcohol and his wagging tongue were to blame. Still, this last and longest imprisonment had been in a cell with men they still needed. He'd heard the men they didn't need were locked in holes beneath the privy. But Pieter could read and write. That had gotten him out of more scrapes than he could tell. They used him as a scribe and locked him up again. Until he'd been ordered back to Amsterdam, in chains, to face his ongoing imprisonment there.

The journey home began uneventful enough. When half of the crew took ill, the *Vrijheid*'s captain decided to give Pieter a chance, unchain him and allow him to be part of the crew. The captain simply needed someone of Pieter's size to get home. Pieter, seeing no reason to exercise discipline, had exchanged strong words with the first mate; a soft, spoiled merchant's son who the executives of the Dutch East India Company had assigned to the *Vrijheid*. He challenged Pieter, insisting he was the better wrestler and Pieter showed him he was wrong. In his drunken state, Pieter not only insulted the man but also pinned him to the narrow upper deck in front of a jeering group of German soldiers. And the captain. Pieter thought he'd killed the weakling and was grateful when the man began to breathe again. The captain saw no other alternative but to keep the unruly, drunken Pieter locked up.

There Pieter remained, chained into this compartment in the hull of the *Vrijheid*. As they crossed the equator, the hull of the ship was a deathly hot and stifling place. With nothing more than a cup of bad water a day and wormy biscuits to eat, he spent most of the time in a daze. Time passed at an eerie pace and he had a strange feeling of being unborn, suspended. He spent his waking hours piecing together all that had happened since he left to go abroad. It bothered him that he could not organize his memories. He would have to try to write it down sometime.

He smelled the change in the air as they neared the North Sea, his hometown, wonderful Amsterdam. They were almost there. Maybe he should accept his fate and give himself over to the Dutch authorities. Prison was becoming more and more comfortable, familiar, soothing, as if his spirit was truly broken.

Pieter now felt the ship knocking against wood, like they were docking. An array of sounds, gulls, cheering and yelling, made him picture the Amsterdam he remembered. He heard someone approaching. He knew the guards would come and expect him to go quietly. On second thought, he would not give himself up to the Dutch authorities. Pieter had also devised a plan of escape. All he could think about now was jumping into the water, no matter how cold, to rinse the filth from his clothes, his body, his mind. None of the guards would expect him to go into the water. Most of the seafarers could not swim. He crouched and awaited the *click!* of the lock being opened. The door swung open. Pieter squinted against the brutal light. One small soldier reached for his chains. The other inserted a key and released the irons that bound him. Pieter readied himself for a fight. He crawled out of the compartment and the two men stood aside.

"Oh ho, Friend, what a stench you give off," the one man said. He backed up and held both hands high to signal his peaceful intent.

"They're waiting for you on the dock," the other said. "You know the way."

"Don't you want to chain me?" Pieter said. "I might get away."

"That's what we're hoping, Friend," the first man said. "I'm not going to touch you!"

Pieter looked at himself in the light. What little he could defecate was in his clothing. He looked and smelled like an animal who had rolled in his own excrement, soaked in salty urine and sour sweat. As he climbed the ladder from the under deck and stuck his head through the main deck, he smiled at the fresh and tasty salt-tang of the northern air and the gulls' *yeow-ha-ha-ha*. No one expected a prisoner to jump into the freezing water of the bay. No one paid him any attention at all! He could easily slip off the ship and into the cool water, a welcome relief. He moved towards the weather side, took one look out and jumped overboard.

The freezing March water took his breath away. He stifled a scream, his mouth opened wide to pull air into his shocked lungs. He gulped and gulped, desperate for air until he could focus his strength and mind to calm this frantic reflex. His arms and legs stiffened like frozen fish and he forced himself to move, to tread water and to breathe. Slowly the feeling returned to his limbs and he struggled towards an abandoned stack of beams on the shore away from the bustle of the unloading ship. He crawled out of the water, up a sandy path strewn with rotting wood and staggered into a dark alleyway. A vagrant man teetered and reeled, blocking his path. Pieter's first instinct was to bash him over the head and take his dry clothes but the man was quicker.

"Touch me, boy and I'll slit you," the man said in Dutch, his scraggly red, brown and gray beard bobbing as he chewed something. He was a head smaller than Pieter but built like a stone pillar, with short limbs and hands the size of frying pans. One of those hands was around Pieter's throat, the other held a small blade.

"I need clothes," Pieter said through chattering teeth. "I fell into the water."

"Someone looking for you?" the man asked.

"Don't be silly," Pieter said. "I was on my way home and stepped too close to the water. I was just having a pee."

"Come with me," the man said. "I have a dry place to sleep. Johannes, that's my name."

Johannes led Pieter farther down the narrow mud path between two wooden buildings resembling warehouses. Pieter smelled a hint of pepper behind a strong reek of urine and excrement. They slipped through a wooden door on the right, through the warehouse and into a small room. It looked like a chamber where dock workers slept.

"I've been in and out of here the last two weeks," Johannes said. "They work during the day and I sleep here. I leave when they come back. I can also hide and listen to what they say."

Johannes handed Pieter brown linen breeches, a light tunic with a string tie at the neck and a leather buff coat. Pieter found two discarded *Kuhmaul* shoes with holes and linen stockings and pulled them over his bare feet.

The authorities were looking for Johannes in his home town, he told Pieter, because he'd killed two Spanish soldiers who slaughtered his wife and two children. Pieter listened to Johannes' story about how he came up north to Amsterdam, fleeing in front of the Spanish troops who sacked village after village in the southern Low Countries. Pieter trusted him.

"I had a house here in Amsterdam," Pieter said. "I've been away since my father died. Come with me. The house will be better than this hovel."

"If the authorities find me, they will kill me." Johannes scratched his beard. "I can't be roaming around town. Until I find a way out, I have a nice warm room here."

"We can go have a look round in the night," Pieter said. "Nothing will happen to us."

"How long have you been away boy?"

"I left, I think it was 1620. The journey to Batavia was my way out. I had a bit of trouble in the East, though." Pieter picked and chose a story to tell Johannes, if only to establish a camaraderie.

"There are so many people here now," Johannes said. "If your house was empty then it isn't now. There are refugees from all over Holland. Business is booming but there are a lot of very, very poor people here, too.

And these Company men, they aren't going to let you get away with this. Don't you realize they will execute you for what you've done? Crimes against The Company are punishable by death!"

"I've no 'crimes against The Company.'"

"You do realize insulting an officer when you're drunk is enough to get you killed. They have it all documented."

"How do you know so much?"

"I've been hiding in this warehouse for two weeks now," Johannes said. "I've heard quite a bit. You're not the first sailor to pass through here who The Company wants to hang."

"I'm going anyway. I'll be back in a few hours."

Pieter had to see for himself that his life in Amsterdam was over. He did not believe anyone would catch him, let alone hang him. Under dark, threatening clouds, he left the waterfront and walked towards the new canals, towards the Singel, where his father's house was. He loved this part of town, the slim townhouses standing watch over the canal, their slight lean forward imposing a careful, watching eye. The smells reminded him of the carefree lack of discipline that was Amsterdam: sour, damp-earth smoke of burning peat; brackish water; human waste. But there was more desperation here than last time. Streets teemed with errant families of more colors and languages than he remembered. Sad, dirty children flocked around sad, dirty adults and Pieter wondered if they all lived on the streets. He walked back and forth in front of a new house under construction. He had been sure this was where his house had been. An emptiness and sense of loss saddened him. What had he expected to find here? His family?

Further along the canal, a soldiery-looking fellow with a small child emerged from what seemed to be a makeshift tent. At first Pieter was afraid for the child but then he saw the soldier doting over the child like it was his own. He saw the way the child looked at the soldier and the bond the look conveyed. He was struck with a longing and wished for his father, for his mother. He wished for the relationship he never had with his family. The child clung to the man and Pieter found himself wishing for this undying love relationship. He'd searched for it in all his relationships, especially with his mother, who wanted nothing of the sort. With their housekeeper Trydje, who was only out to corrupt him. She would do things to arouse him and then do things to relieve him and he found himself unwilling to picture those moments, guilt-ridden and repulsed he had enjoyed those encounters.

Turning his back on the soldier and the child, he walked back towards the waterfront. He surrendered to the most comfortable conclusion: the fated approach. Love in that respect did not exist for him. Maybe for other people but not for him. He was not destined to find someone who would give him children. He meandered through the buildings by the waterfront, into the warehouse and found Johannes sitting on an upturned crate sipping at a ceramic cup.

"I'm ready to leave this God-awful place," Pieter said. "What do you suggest?"

"Is there any place you want to go?" Johannes said. "Any safe place? An old sweetheart?"

"I lived at a farm in Germany ten years ago," Pieter said and pulled up another crate, the thought of getting back to Sichardtshof the last idea in his sack of schemes. "I've been in contact with the patrician there. He was like my father."

Johannes shook his head. "There's a war on in Germany."

"All of Germany?" Pieter suddenly felt his heart sink. He had only lived there the year but he loved the farm and the seclusion. Katarina would keep him away from the drink. He would chop wood and be left alone. Tanner was a strict overseer and Pieter, needing that sort of discipline in his life, could work with him. Without it he would end up in chains or dead. Johannes was still talking.

"Maybe we should go there," Johannes said. "They are rallying troops to send to Germany. They pay money. They also take anyone."

"I'm finished fighting," Pieter said.

"You don't have to fight," Johannes said. "We need to get there and then you can desert. Everyone is traveling with these troops. There is food and women, I heard from some English men. They land here now and they are all going to the continent to fight. They go there, loot and pillage, make their fortune and go back to England. They have rank in the military and enough money to start a family. That's the only hope for men like us." Johannes lit a candle. "We don't have long before the dock workers come back. Here, boy…"

Johannes produced a bottle. Pieter had only just noticed how dark it had become. He took the bottle, dreading what would happen when alcohol had its way with him. He swallowed the first sip and the warm, burning sensation felt like coming home. He gulped a second and wondered why he ever worried about drinking. It made his soul sing.

The dock workers returned and greeted Pieter and Johannes like they were old friends, handing around their own bottles and lighting tobacco pipes. The men reveled late into the night until one after another they dropped off to sleep. Pieter and Johannes drained each bottle still on the table, conspiring ways to make money, ways to escape tyranny and ways to save the world. They formed their plan and decided to walk, first sign of light, towards Germany, to Ascherleben, to Halberstadt.

"That's where they are recruiting," Johannes said. "We'll make our way there."

Chapter 2

Katarina
March 1626

Katarina poked at the fire and threw two logs on the embers. Sparks sailed up the flue and the flames revived. Twice last night she'd been to the kitchen to keep this fire burning. Fire was the sustainer of life, the taker as well. She lit a tallow lamp, opened the door to the low-vaulted stable adjoining the kitchen and hung the lamp on a hook rammed into the sandstone. The two cows lowed and her goat yawned. Their water was empty, the troughs too. She crossed the hay-strewn stone stable floor and opened the door leading out to the paddock. Bleating sheep, more than the paddock could accommodate, threatened to break through the wooden fencing.

Strange rumblings groaned and swelled underground, traveling towards the Sichardtshof farm along the Aisch River. Katarina imagined some heavy, tethered beasts grumbling while pulling slow-rolling burdens. She brushed aside the memories of the last visits from the mercenaries like she was clearing sticky cobwebs from the rafters. The past was not to be relived, Herr Tucher told her. Rise above it or it will destroy you, he said.

She took her overcoat down from the peg on the wall, shrugged into it, grabbed a bucket and hurried back through the kitchen and up the few steps to the house's main entrance. She pulled on one of the double doors. In the winter the wood door swelled and stuck in the frame, squealing on the stone floor as she pulled it open.

She rushed past the half-timbered barn and the adjoining stable that dominated the other outbuildings forming the oval farmyard. A lamp burned somewhere inside. Tanner the Elder was awake, tending the horses. Distinctive sounds rose above the rumblings now: men's shouts and whistles, the clank of chains from animals' harnesses. Katarina startled as a flock of waterfowl squawked into flight from the ponds that lined the lowest point of the hollow called the Edelgraben. The water reflected the eerie, pink light of the dawn. The hills that protected the farm on either side of the hollow were shrouded in mist. But the hills never stopped the soldiers from coming before. The men knew the Sichardtshof farm was here and what it had to offer.

It was too early in the year for soldiers to be traveling. The nights were still frozen and dark. *Friert's am 40-Ritter-Tag, so kommen noch 40 Fröste nach.* Because there was frost today, March 10, the day of Forty Martyrs, the farmers said forty more days of frost would fall upon the land. But Katarina smelled a slight turn in the air, as if the emerging vegetation let off a scent to attract and entice—a lush, green smell. Buds developed on the low bushes surrounding the square stone well and when the leaves filled in, the bushes made a good hiding place for the children. After such a long, cold, dark winter, these inklings of spring should afford some comfort. But Katarina took more comfort in the fact that in the winter, the soldiers moved into winter quarters and stayed away. This past winter was peaceful and Katarina had almost forgotten the rest of the world, the troubled world beyond the farm.

Katarina's trembling hand grabbed time and time again for the rope and finally pulled the bucket up out of the well, craning her neck to look over the bushes back to the crooked little workers' house. Covered in bramble bushes, she could just make out the glow of a fire through the tiny kitchen window. A figure passed by inside. The Tanner family and the other workers must be awake too. Katarina set the full bucket down by a small surplus of buckets next to the well and ran back to the house. Brambles snagged on her trousers as she softly rapped on the door.

"Who is it?" a man's voice growled.

"It's me, Tanner, let me in."

The door to the workers' house creaked open. Tanner's large frame filled out the doorway. Behind him, ceramic mugs clinked, water boiled, a baby cried, men spoke in low tones and a woman coughed. Tanner looked over Katarina's head and sighed, running a hand through his short, dark-blond hair. His cheeks were flushed with the heat of the fire.

"Listen," Katarina said.

He nodded, understanding. "Wake the master."

Katarina turned and ran back to the well, filled a second bucket and slopped icy water as she hurried back to the main house. She ran past the paddock jammed with sheep to the front door she'd left ajar and back down to the kitchen. Wanting to act as if it was a normal morning, she filled a pot with water and set it on the tripod over the fire to heat. She thought better of this and moved the pot away from the flame. She would not be back in the kitchen today.

Katarina climbed the steps and opened Herr Tucher's bedroom door. The room took on the chilly, pink light as the sun rose. He wanted no more than his bed, a matching chair and a small dark table with a pitcher and basin in his bedroom. And Katarina. As of late they spent their nights entwined in each other's arms like two lost children dispelling one another's deepest fears. Katarina counted Herr Tucher's contented puffs exhaling in quiet, peaceful intervals. He finally slept after a fitful night of disturbing dreams. She paced her breathing with his.

Katarina wanted to allow him this peace, just a little while longer. He so seldom had the luxury. She opened the window. Above the dull rumbling, faint drum beats kept the cadence of marching feet. She'd lost count of the regiments that had passed through the valley on their way north or west. But she would never forget the last attack they had suffered. A band of strays had appeared right before St. Martin's Day. Katarina made up her mind, this time she would stand up to the men and fight against them. But there were too many and they overpowered her. The other women, Sara and Anna, suffered for her foolery. The only blessing was after the soldiers had 'taught those nags a lesson,' satisfied at the way they'd beaten and abused them, they'd left and forgot to take their share of the plunder. Katarina's wounds had healed. The scars she carried were all internal now.

Katarina shut the window and crept towards Herr Tucher's bed. "I wish things would be like they once were," she whispered.

Even her memories of the simple pleasures did nothing to soothe the rising dread of what would come today. She wished she could curl up next to him and listen to him sleep. She wished she could let him sleep but the brick-red woven rug did nothing to dampen the echo of the creaking floorboards. Herr Tucher had bought the rug to match the plastered panels of the half-timbered walls. Together, Katarina and Herr Tucher had painted the panels pale brick red and the beams themselves they'd stained dark brown. She remembered how she had worried the colors might clash but they went together perfectly. As an accent, they painted grapevines full of juicy grapes in the same dark red color around the windows, the door and all around the upper edge of the room. These memories were fragile and fleeting and slipping away from her like a silky stream of smoke.

Herr Tucher stirred and whispered, "Where are you going?"

She sat on the bed and kissed his cheek. "They're coming."

He pulled her under his feather quilt and wrapped his arms around her. "We need to be strong. For the girl. Rise above this."

"I wish I could. Teach me how." She touched his cheek. "We live simply here. Why must they take everything away from us?"

"I promise it will get better, my dear Katarina. We will do our best to make it through the day, shall we?"

As she tried to pull out of his embrace, he tightened his grip and pulled her close. She settled into that space next to his heart, a space she fit into perfectly and the one where he'd held her so closely for the past ten years. This was her favorite place in the world: in his arms. These first few years of living with Herr Tucher at the farm had been much too comfortable. They prospered here, no matter how modestly. What a little family they'd become, Katarina, Isabeau and Herr Tucher; almost like a real family. The three shared Herr Tucher's far-fetched philosophies and enjoyed his easy wit, he most of all—the same things Katarina had resented early on in their relationship. Oh, if only the three were a real family and they could move far away from his war.

He whispered how he loved her more than his own life and kissed the top of her head. She savored the moment, afraid it could be the last they would share. She inhaled his scent, reluctantly wriggled free and rolled off the bed.

The pressures of society had overlooked Herr Tucher and Katarina out here in the country. The master and his maid needed no proper courtship and it was an arrangement no authorities questioned. The particulars of his arranged marriage to a wife who remained in Nuremberg were intact and respected, businesses ran smoothly and nothing was publicly out of the ordinary. Herr Tucher and Katarina lived the first few years contentedly as if in a dream until the regular delivery of those new printed newspapers began. When Katarina first moved to Sichardtshof, a courier or messenger bringing word was a seldom occurrence and always had an ominous air. Now they came regularly, once a week, with the news of the latest disaster from Nuremberg and further abroad.

Herr Tucher dressed hastily. He pulled his hair back and secured it behind his head with a tattered black ribbon, prominent gray strands straining against his temples. "I only regret we didn't get the fencing finished yesterday. There are still sections that are decayed."

"The fencing never held them back," Katarina said.

"Yes, but it does slow them down," he said. "Get the girl up, go back to Tanner's and get into the cellar with the other women. Send Tanner here to me, please. We will do everything we can to deter these men. I promise."

Katarina scaled the new, light-colored chicken ladder to the garret rooms above like a panicked cat, her breathing shallow and scared. The sound of the ladder creaking resonated through the house. The fresh, balsamic smell of spruce resin made her sneeze. The old steps had to be replaced after Isabeau broke through last autumn. The child had fallen one whole story and landed on her back. Remembering that incident with such fondness made her snort at the paradox of memory. All life's trifle tragedies had been easily surmountable compared to what this day might bring.

Katarina opened the door to Isabeau's garret room. Wooden boards now covered the slanted ceiling where once the roof tiles were exposed. This added a bit of warmth to the frozen space. Isabeau's few books lay open and stacked over one another on the tiny table. A shock of white-blonde hair stuck out from under her feather quilt on the simple wooden bed that was getting too small for her. Katarina crossed to the bed and pulled the quilt away from her bare feet. She felt around under Isabeau's bed for her slippers and pulled them onto her feet.

Katarina put her hand on Isabeau's shoulder and gently roused her. "We're going back to Tanner's house. You can see Albin."

"Oh, Kata, leave me for just a little while longer," Isabeau said through a yawn.

Katarina threw the quilt aside and sat her up. "Hurry, Isabeau…"

"I'm so tired…"

Isabeau seemed to grow overnight, every night. She was now nine years old and already as tall as Katarina; her frame willowy and fine. Katarina touched Isabeau's chiseled chin and ran her finger over her sharp cheek bones. They must have come from her mother. The curve of her mouth, the rounded tip of her nose and those indignant blue eyes she had inherited from her father Hans-Wolfgang—her hoarse voice and that barking laugh, too.

"Hurry, Isabeau."

They met Herr Tucher on the landing outside his rooms. He stood aside and allowed Isabeau and Katarina to pass by. Katarina pulled the double front doors open. The cold wandered through the doors and curled around their legs. Isabeau shivered, dressed only in a night shirt and felt slippers. She threw her coat over Isabeau's shoulders and pulled her close. All too near the farm now, men's calls driving animals to pull heavy objects interspersed with drum beats and clanking weapons evoked the unmistakable reality of trampling horses, rolling canons, and marching mercenaries.

Isabeau and Katarina rushed across the farmyard past the barn and the stable. Isabeau stopped and tugged at Katarina's arm when she heard the horses in the stable neighing to each other, the approaching troops making them restless.

"Isabeau, no, we need to take cover. Your horse will be safe," Katarina lied.

They ran back past the well to the workers' house. Straightening his jacket, Tanner came towards the two and passed them by without a word. Tanner's wife Sara stood in the slightly lopsided doorway waiting for them. Her light-brown hair hung open underneath a hastily-donned white blouse. She dried her hands on the white apron that hung over her brown skirt.

"I don't like the sound of this," Sara said as she backed into the kitchen.

Isabeau started up the ladder leading to the upper floor, an open space under the roof where the farmhands, the women and the children slept.

"Isabeau, he's down in the cellar," Sara said. "Albin," she quietly called into the open trap in the kitchen floor.

Albin looked up out of the cellar. A young lad of eight years, he resembled his father in so many ways, cheeks flushed pink and his short dark-blond hair tousled.

"Take Isabeau down there with you for breakfast," Sara said.

She handed Katarina two pitchers filled with drinks. Katarina smelled beer and peppermint tea.

"I already took some bread, milk and eggs down into the cellar. Anna and Elsbeth gathered the chickens before sunup and they are in the cellar, too. Smells awful, but I don't want to lose them."

"I latched the stable door from the inside," Katarina said. "If they want the cows, they'll have to break the door down." Katarina frowned. That was exactly what they would do if they wanted the cows. "But all the sheep are still out in the paddock. We have no time to bring them away."

"That they are marching now surprises me. Tanner thought they would wait until it got warmer." Sara wiped her hands on her apron. "He says they are heading towards the Low Countries."

The front door burst opened and the two women squealed.

"Sorry ladies," Tanner's father said.

He shook his head, removed his hat, smoothed his white hair back and replaced his hat all with one fluid motion. These Tanner men looked so similar but the Elder's coloring had paled with age and his skin had a touch of gray. He squeezed past Sara and grabbed one of the scythes standing in the corner next to the fire. The blade had been modified, sticking straight out like a pike.

"We're no match for these scoundrel mercenaries," he said. "Maybe we can satisfy them with sheep. But the numbers are dwindling. What are we going to do when we have none left?"

"Let's just pray that this conflict is almost over." Sara handed Tanner the Elder a chunk of bread. "We're going in the cellar. Would you please cover the trap door with the rug when we're in?"

"We'll come get you when they've gone," Tanner the Elder said.

"Take care of yourselves," Katarina said.

"Don't you worry about us. Just stay in there and stay quiet," he said.

Sara ducked her head and walked down the stone steps. Katarina followed. The light from above slowly faded and the trap door closed. Katarina wasn't sure who she feared for more: for their men or for her own life and the lives of her friends and their children. The soldiers didn't differentiate. Men were either to be killed or tortured until they gave up every last asset. If the men were dressed well, the soldiers assumed the men were rich, worth kidnapping and held for ransom. Women were treated like loot, even better than wine or food because the soldiers could use them again and again. Women and children could also be traded for a good price. Or they would just be killed in the ruckus like livestock.

The few chickens in wooden cages clucked. Katarina's nose wrinkled, filled with the sharp scent of chicken droppings and the acrid smoke from the burning tallow lamps. This cellar was too small to store the provisions they needed for the winter and even though they'd used most of the supplies, there was still not enough room to hide the women and the children. Elsbeth complained as she settled on the dirt floor. Anna reprimanded her in whispered tones as she sat down cross-legged in front of a row of small barrels and pulled Elsbeth's tiny daughter onto her lap. Anna's hair had grayed and thinned like an old crone's this past year. Her crooked and knotted fingers shook as she bit off a bit of bread. Elsbeth leaned back against the dirt wall, shoved her baby under her shirt and attached him to her breast. She turned her head away from Katarina with a haughty toss of brown hair and tried to slap one of her two elder sons who wrestled next to her.

Anna had been at the farm the last ten years as well as Katarina and Sara and the three women made a great team. They all had the same goal in mind and had become loyal friends. Elsbeth, on the other hand, had come to them last summer from a neighboring village. After Elsbeth's husband died of dysentry and the village had been visited by the mercenaries, she'd lost her house. Katarina found the very pregnant Elsbeth in the woods behind Sichardtshof with her three children. Katarina convinced Herr Tucher to take her in and thought Elsbeth could show some gratitude. Instead Elsbeth needed to be prodded like a lazy ox to do any work.

Elsbeth's boys scuffled and cursed.

"Stay quiet, boys," Katarina hissed. "The soldiers will hear you!"

"Don't speak to my boy like that," Elsbeth said and slapped the younger boy. "I'm the only one he listens to."

"If the soldiers hear us and find us here," Anna said, "they'll eat your boys for breakfast. And you, Elsbeth."

"They seem to like the master's tight mistress better than a stretched out mother like me," Elsbeth sneered. "They leave me and my saggy tits alone."

"They haven't left you alone," Anna said. "You don't have to be ashamed. They've hurt us all."

"No one has ever hurt me," Elsbeth said. "I'm not like you women."

Katarina had heard that speech numerous times before. Elsbeth was not like the rest of them. She must have been the daughter of a rich farmer and was used to having a maid take care of her since she was a young girl. Those days were over. Katarina showed Isabeau and Albin to a spot where they should sit down. While poking and kicking at each other, Elsbeth's two sons stuffed food into their mouths. The larger of the two sons, a black-haired devil named David, grabbed an egg away from the smaller blond boy. The blond boy, Fredrick, slammed him, *crack!*, on the ear with his fist.

Elsbeth sneered and shook her head.

Katarina wished she had a window to see outside, to see what was happening. When the troops started moving along the river about six years ago, the Sichardtshof farm was still undiscovered. The regiments would just pass by and leave them alone. But once the farm was found out, it became a popular stop. Sichardtshof had, in the beginning, something to offer: sheep, grain, wine and, of course, women.

Der Krieg ernährt den Krieg. Herr Tucher said the weekly newspapers reported how 'the war fed the war': that meant the troops had no money or support from the princes or the regent or whoever had hired and rented them out. The land was supposed to feed the troops. That also meant they were allowed to take whatever they wanted from the villages. The war was supposed to be between the Catholics and the Protestants, but it didn't matter what religion each village was. If the village was situated in the warpath, it was fair game.

As the years passed by, the true nature of this war became more and more muddled. It seemed to Katarina the war was simply troops and their leaders out of control, with nowhere to go should the war end and the troops disband. The troops were now an ever-feeding, ever-growing *mechanisma* that needed to destroy to sustain itself.

The boys scuffled behind the barrels, their squeals and oaths rising in pitch. Katarina heard the door upstairs open. Men's boot-falls rang through the floorboards. The boys fell silent. Katarina stiffened and listened, holding her breath, hoping it was Tanner the Elder. Shuffling feet prowled the workers' kitchen but they heard no voices. Katarina counted maybe three or four pairs of feet. Hannah sniffed and Anna put her hand over the child's mouth. A ceramic mug shattered. And another.

Katarina knew they'd been found out.

Sara grabbed a hold of Albin's wrist and dragged him behind the barrels. Katarina pushed Isabeau in behind them. Elsbeth slowly stood, hugging her baby tight to her breast. She stared and seemed incapable of moving. Anna panicked and shook her head, waiting for instructions from Katarina. Katarina grabbed Hannah, shoved her behind the barrels, wrenched the baby from Elsbeth's grasp and pushed the baby into Sara's waiting hands. There was no more room in the crawl space for the remaining three women.

The trap door to the cellar flew back against the wall with a bang. Katarina shielded her eyes from the light with one hand. Anna grabbed Katarina's upraised arm and Elsbeth grabbed onto the other.

"We're done for," Anna whispered.

"Be quiet," Katarina said.

Two soldiers came into the cellar, daggers drawn. The blond soldier grabbed Anna as he elbowed Elsbeth. He held his dagger to Anna's face and pressed her tightly against the wall. The dark-haired one fixed his gaze on Katarina and took a handful of her hair. His dagger poked Katarina's side and he pushed her towards the steps. His leather jerkin squeaked with every movement and he smelled of disease and alcohol. Without looking back, Katarina climbed the steps. Many men shouted and cursed out in the farmyard, the mix of voices a dissonance of anger and violence. Katarina tried to look beyond the soldier blocking the doorway to see what was happening outside. No shots fired but the noise rioted, rose and fell.

The few soldiers filling the kitchen looked to the dark-haired one and seemed to wait for his command. He tightened his grip on Katarina's hair. He bent her over the table and held her there with his hand around the back of her neck. Her cheek pressed firmly to the table as she watched a blond soldier, dressed in a sorry array of torn garments of an unidentifiable color that neither fit him nor fit together, sorting through the shelf under the ladder leading to the upper floor. He held a bed sheet tied together like a sack and he and another man examined a metal mug and whispered. The blond soldier nodded approval and threw the mug into the sack.

A small soldier wearing a black hat with a large red feather sticking out of it came out of the partitioned space behind the tiled wood stove where Tanner and Sara slept. He held a bed sheet as well.

"Food," he said to the dark-haired soldier that detained Katarina.

Katarina pointed out the door towards the farmyard. He pointed into the cellar. Katarina tried to shake her head. They only stored a portion of their food here. The rest of the root vegetables and grains were buried in the forest. She wanted to lead them away from the house and away from children. Even those scant stores would not be enough for these brutes but she must try to send them away from the farm. The dark-haired soldier grabbed Katarina's hair, pulled her off the table and spun her around to face him. He grabbed her around the throat.

"What's in those barrels down there, angel? Get us something to drink."

"We store our food and drink in the forest," Katarina said.

He released Katarina and shoved her towards the cellar. "Get me those barrels."

She climbed back down the steps and pulled a small barrel of beer off the top of the stack. Sara and the children made no sound. Katarina handed it up the steps to the small man with the black hat and he handed it on to another comrade. The three loaves of two-day old bread on the shelf fell to the cellar floor. Katarina bent, picked them up and handed them over one after another.

"Get us a second barrel," he said. "It's going to be a long day."

One other man took the second barrel. The dark-haired soldier jumped down the steps, into the cellar, grabbed Katarina by the hair and dragged her up the steps into the kitchen. Two other soldiers pushed Anna and Elsbeth out of the house.

Katarina smelled fire. She tried again to see past the soldier in the doorway. None of the buildings seemed to be burning. As the soldiers led Anna and Elsbeth away from the workers' house, Katarina saw the bonfire the soldiers had made. The dark-haired one prodded Katarina with his fist and pushed her out the door to follow the other women.

They approached the oval farmyard. Other soldiers threw planks of wood onto a raging fire. Someone had opened the paddock. Sheep were running all over the yard. One soldier grabbed a sheep and two others held it still while the soldier slit its throat. Katarina made to follow Anna and Elsbeth but someone grabbed her hair from behind.

"No you don't, angel. You're coming with me."

He pushed Katarina towards the barn. Her knees wobbled as she walked. Just as they came around the corner of the barn, Herr Tucher stumbled out of the barn door hanging half ripped away from the barn's wooden wall. His hands were bound behind his back. He was arguing with what seemed to be the troop's captain, judging by the quality of the man's extravagant slit sleeves and trousers and the red plume in his wide-brimmed hat.

"Take as many sheep as you want," Herr Tucher said. "Take all of these. For the love of God, just take what you need and get on your way."

"Thank you for the suggestion," said the captain. He pushed Herr

Tucher down on his knees and struck his face. "But first we will accept your hospitality. We are going to roast a meal and drink your wine and beer. Then we'll get on our way. You should be glad you can serve our troop. Others might not be so generous and would take everything including your life."

Katarina walked slower and tried to steer herself towards Herr Tucher. She wriggled her arm and tried to pull free but the soldier held her tight in his grip and led her away. A quick visual survey showed Katarina the soldier had a dagger on his belt, close to her detained arm. He carried no musket but as he walked, the wooden powder apostles hanging from his chest clattered like teeth. What looked like a dagger handle rose from his boot top.

She looked over her shoulder and saw Herr Tucher: his face solemn and sad, apologetic and loving. His expression was begging Katarina to be strong. He'd told her to remember she was no match for these men. He despised this all but if she fought and got herself killed, he couldn't live without her. If she did fight and kill this man, if she thought she could kill a man, what about the other soldiers? They would never let her live. With Herr Tucher bound and possibly the rest of their men held prisoner, all would suffer. They all paid the last time she fought.

The dark-haired soldier shoved Katarina into the barn and pulled on the door that hung away from the wall. His fist slammed against her chest and she flew onto her back on the hay. She reeled and panicked, heated from fear as if she ran from a racing fire. Her brain jammed as incoherent thoughts flashed at a ridiculous pace. Before she could catch her breath, he was on top of her. His knife cut the seam of her trousers in one slick swipe, his fingers prodding between her legs. His hot breath blew into Katarina's ear and the smell of alcohol made her heave. He fumbled with his trousers.

"Hey, this one's easy," he said to no one in particular. "Doesn't even try to fight. You may have lots of company today, angel."

Katarina's cheeks tingled with fear and rage. She closed her eyes and listened to the ringing in her head. Tears seared the back of her face. The soldier's huffing dampened Katarina's hair as he defiled her. She heard the voices of other soldiers that had come into the barn and waited. Looking past the beast on top of her, she saw five. She knew there was a choice: to allow the soldiers this and try to accept it and get on with her life; or to fight them, be tortured and killed, and endanger everyone else here on the farm. She gritted her teeth together. Her face hardened into a solid mask and she tried to retreat into a sacred state.

Her desperate petition was to *Holla*, the spirit of mother nature her grandmother Frau Kuni was known to call on: "*Please accept my sacrifice: let them hurt me, but take care of the children and spare Isabeau this corruption and the lifelong scars no one will ever see.*"

Katarina remembered one instance when she'd hid here in this barn as a child. Farmer Hanson had chased her after she knocked over a bushel of apples. He was drunk. He was angry. He had a strap. She hid in the farthest corner under the horse cart. He couldn't bend down and see her because his knees were so bad. Alone in the barn she felt protected. Daylight came in through a small hole in the wooden wall, close to the ground, and lit her refuge. She imagined she could disappear into the eerie light. She was small and invisible inside that cloud of sparkling dust together with the spirits protecting her. The spirits of the smoke from Frau Kuni's incense. Frau Kuni said such men would be banished by their own stupidity. Katarina had to learn to forgive. Could she forgive? Forgiveness was something she was not capable of. She meditated on the spirit of forgiveness. Right now, Katarina's only strength, her power, was her ability to sacrifice.

"*Dear Holla, please teach me how to forgive. Please accept my sacrifice and save those that mean the most to me. By destroying me you are making me whole. This is my worldly body and the scars will disappear when I move from this world to the next. I am not these bones that bind me to this earthly realm. I am much more than this. I am fire and earth. I am wind and water. These men are but puppets made of wood. Wood is weak, wood can burn, wood can rot when it is damp. Damp wood. Rotting wood…*The wood wall of the barn."

Katarina opened her eyes. Back in the corner of the barn under that old, broken-down horse cart, she saw the light shining through the same hole in the wooden wall. Katarina focused on that one point of light. The hole was larger than she remembered. Maybe she could just squeeze through it. She would just have to wait for the chance to get away. She turned and saw the face of the blond soldier. He was slight and undernourished judging by his weight. She sneaked a glance over his shoulder and saw they were alone. She had been defiled by them all, then. Her thoughts drifted again. She tried to concentrate on the sounds that seemed so far away: men reveling, drunken laughter, tortured animals, scuffling and metal on metal. The blond man must have finished because he stood, did up his trousers and walked towards the barn door. He swayed, held onto the wall and walked out. She was alone.

Katarina got up on her knees and swooned. Her bladder emptied of its own accord, burning and stinging. She swallowed a scream, forced herself to keep conscious. She had to get out of sight. The corners of the barn were draped in shadows, except for that small, eerie light. She crawled under the cart towards the light. The hole in the rotted wood was too small to fit through but if she dug a bit in the packed earth…

"Hey, where is she?" said a drunken voice by the door.

A wave of heat rushed through Katarina's body and her hands dug with the fury of a starving dog chasing a mouse down a hole.

"You said she was in here," a second voice said.

Katarina stopped digging and held her breath.

"Don't worry, we have two more bitches over here, you can have one of these," someone yelled from outside.

"Where's my angel?" came a third, drunken, unmistakable voice. Straw crunched under his feet as he walked into the barn. "Come here, my angel, I have something for you."

Katarina dug frantically now. The dirt pushed up under her fingernails. She dug harder and harder. The packed earth tore her nails away from the skin of her fingertips. The pain made her feel real and she embraced it. Tears streamed down her cheeks. She dug until the pain became almost unbearable and stuck her head through the hole which was just large enough for her to get her shoulders through.

The afternoon March sky was heavy and dull. Katarina heard a fire roaring and crackling and the soldiers' songs echoing from the other side of the barn. But in the midst of the undergrowth covering the North Hill, Katarina heard voices whispering, like wind rustling the trees. Shapes ran back and forth between the trunks, like sneaking children, people on the run. The silhouettes were not those of soldiers. Fright and panic rendered her motionless. Katarina pulled her head back into the barn.

"Where's my angel?" he said. Farm implements crashed in the opposite corner, like he had fallen against them.

Katarina decided whatever was out there was not as bad as this soldier here. She squeezed out of the hole and stood, steadying herself on the outside wall. Where could she go? Her legs gave out and her back slid down the wooden barn wall. She slumped with a puff of air like a punctured bellows, drew her knees up to her chest and buried her head in her lap covered in her torn, soiled and wet trousers. Then the tears came. She swallowed the heavy sobs but they took possession of her body. She heaved and heaved and could not stop.

"Katarina?" a voice whispered.

She held her breath.

"Katarina?"

The voice was closer now. She caught a scent of lavender like the oil Herr Tucher used. He touched her shoulder. She covered her head with her filthy hands.

"Thank God, you are alive." Herr Tucher put an arm around Katarina's shoulder, sat down beside her and pulled her close.

She breathed in his scent, a hint of lavender behind the mixture of pitch, soot, sweat and blood. From the other side of the barn, soldiers' yells, a muddle of singing and fighting, the din of a hundred drunken men, rose and fell with the breeze.

"Come, we need to get away from here," Herr Tucher said.

He stood and grabbed both Katarina's battered hands and pulled her up onto her feet. She could not meet his gaze. The shame of what had happened made her sink to her knees.

"Go on without me. Just leave me here," she said.

"Oh, no, I will not leave you here," he said. "We will go together. I love you."

"How could you love me, when you know where I've been?"

"My fate has not been better," he said. "I feel I have failed you. I should be able to protect you and the others here. Instead I allow myself to be tortured like a common criminal. My shame is as deep as yours."

"But those men," Katarina spluttered. "Those men…"

Herr Tucher silenced her with a finger placed softly on her lips. "They are behind us. It is behind us. We are alive. We are together. I am grateful."

He wrapped his jacket around her shoulders and led her towards the North Hill, away from the farm, her home, her family, her safe harbor that had become a place of horror and desecration. They climbed the hill in silence. Twigs snapped and Katarina had the distinct feeling someone watched them pass. Ethereal sounds hushed around them and Katarina could see people flitting between the trees like ghosts. Herr Tucher tugged at her arm.

"Here is the spot," he whispered. "We will remain here for the rest of the afternoon and maybe the whole night."

"There's someone out there," Katarina said.

He pulled her into a protected cluster of bushes forming a sort of hut with a roof over their heads. They sat and he wrapped her in his arms.

"Who are they?" Katarina whispered.

"A lot of strays I would assume," Herr Tucher said. "I never really get to see any faces, but many displaced folk have taken to the forest. Even more so now the soldiers are here. Could be those following the troops looking for leftovers. Or those villagers afraid to return to their houses." He snorted ever so quietly. "Much like the two of us."

Katarina drifted in and out of sleep. Each time she awoke shivering with cold, Herr Tucher pulled her in even closer. She settled her cheek against his chest. It was late evening and night was coming. She listened to his beating heart, grateful they were together. She remembered the nun who had taught her to read and a bedtime prayer she had said:

Schütze alle, die ich lieb,
alles Böse mir vergib.
Kommt der helle Sonnenschein,
lass mich wieder fröhlich sein.

"Protect all of those I love…" She felt herself drifting back to sleep, together, their happy little family. Suddenly, Katarina jolted awake and sat straight up. "Oh dear God in Heaven!" she cried.

"Quiet!" Herr Tucher whispered. He gripped her arm, his body tense.

"The children!" Tears crawled down Katarina's cheeks. "And Sara. They must still be in the cellar."

"We must wait until we are sure the soldiers are gone. We cannot give away Sara's position. There is another spot over there where we can watch the farm unobserved by those in the farmyard. But we must stay here the night. Tomorrow morning—God willing the soldiers move on—we can return. We must stay together no matter what. Only then can we manage through this. Promise me you will stay with me."

"I will never leave you," she said.

Chapter 3

Ralf
March 1626

Father Ralf gathered his notes together on the pulpit. The door to the small lecture room on the ground floor of the *Collegium Ernestinum* slammed open and closed and his parchment rustled in the draft. Theology students rushed out of the classroom, babbling and gesturing, a continuation of the lively discussion Ralf had led. Even though he had great satisfaction from these invigorating talks, he was relieved when they were over and he no longer stood in front of the class under their scrutiny.

His lecture had been a strenuous debate of the writings of Anton Praetorius, a well-known critic of witch trials. Praetorius' writings were used to criticize Ralf's preferred methods, those used in Bamberg, to drive the devil from the damned. Ralf re-read his notes as he packed them into his leather satchel, recalling phrases he had used during his lecture. Praetorius had stated he was against the use of the *peinliche Befragung*, torture and flagellation, because the devil did not feel the pain of torture and was not driven from those he had hold of. Ralf disputed this and other of Praetorius's theories with the newest publication by Friedrich Förner, their own Bishop here in Bamberg. Bishop Förner's writings described how they needed to use all the weapons God had given them to drive the demons from the flock and torture belonged to these weapons.

Had Praetorius still been alive, Ralf argued, he would have been shocked at the hold the devil had over Bamberg and seen the need for the *peinliche Befragung*. There was real evil in Bamberg and it needed to be hit hard. This new wave of witchcraft was not the ordinary potion-mixers and fortune tellers, like in Praetorius' time. There was genuine evil at work here and the Catholic faith was in danger of extinction; succumbing to Lutheran teachings being the least of their worries.

Förner's writings were the transcripts of the series of sermons he had been giving at mass. The man had an oratory talent and people listened to him. His case for the re-catholicization of the Franconian area was a strong one and people were standing up and listening. Ralf was envious of the way the man could talk and sway people. That was why Ralf put the extra effort into his lectures. The preparation alone took him hours and he labored late into the night.

But no one seemed to heed Ralf the way they did Förner, even though Ralf thought his lectures and writings were better versed than Förner's. Ralf noticed his themes would conveniently show up in Förner's sermons, too. Ralf should be the one delivering those sermons! But it made no difference to him, he tried to console himself. Ralf was not looking for fame or position. He was down here every day with these boys and he knew what real challenges they faced. Bishop Förner, in contrast, sipped tea with the Prince Bishop and didn't have the connection to the students like Ralf did.

Ralf always watched the boys carefully to see how they reacted to his teachings. There were pious ones who were the perfect vessels for soaking up the word of God. These boys prayed the Divine Office and accepted the challenges a life of God put in their paths. They would go on to the seminary and ordination. Then there were those boys who were here because they were forced by their rich parents. That was a life Ralf would never know, never understand and never condone. But there were none so dangerous as the boys who were already in the clutches of evil. Though not noticeable at first, hints something was amiss with some boys would slowly surface: they had no control over their carnal lusts; they showed weaknesses even after Ralf tried everything to teach them how to combat these weaknesses with prayer and confession; they were fascinated by the devil in a most unsavory manner.

Ralf shoved the last of his parchment into his satchel. Two boys approached his pulpit.

"Father, may we have a word?" the fatty, unkempt boy asked.

"A word, yes," Ralf answered. "After which I will tell you exactly how I feel about the way you took part in the lecture, which was not at all. And then we will discuss why you need to be asking questions afterward. If you had paid attention instead of conversing with your neighbor."

The boy's fleshy companion stifled a grin and turned away. Ralf swung his leather satchel over his shoulder, gave an impatient exhale and prepared himself for the boys' silly comments. These boys were those who were put here by well-to-do Bamberg citizens. They not only had an unhealthy fascination with the methods used to drive the devil from the damned, they seemed sympathetic with the damned themselves. They seemed to take a certain pleasure in the more base matters of humanity. The apple doesn't fall far from the tree, Ralf thought. The fatty boy's father was a strict opponent of the witch hunts.

"We want to ask you," the fatty boy continued. "We know you say that Praetorius had the theory that: *Zauberei kann für uns im Grunde gar nicht existieren, weil sie über menschlich Vermögen und wider die natürliche Ordnung Gottes ist.*"

"Like I said, Praetorius felt witchcraft was against God's natural order." Ralf laid his satchel back on the pulpit. "To say that because of this, it doesn't exist is well, folly, and while you are at it, please refer back to the ninth sermon in Bishop Förner's book about how curiosity in magic is the lure of the devil. You must arm yourselves with God's weapons! These passages are on the reading list. Instead of asking silly questions, you should both now go reflect on this passage."

"But what does that mean for us?" the boy continued like a raincloud. "What does that mean for the rest of Bamberg? My father says the city council leans more towards a philosophy like Praetorius too but you say it is wrong. Who are we supposed to believe?"

"The real authority here is God. God's earthly representative is the Prince Bishop and next to the Prince Bishop is Bishop Friedrich Förner. They have the real authority here. The city council is made up of so many bleeding hearts. They should busy themselves with market days and arranging to have dung transported and fixing the schedule of the city watch. But in the matter of who takes care of your soul, that will always be the function of the church! The city council should never forget that."

"But I just heard Burgermeister Junius say that..."

"If you want to believe the heresy of the Burgermeister and his city council, then you are in the same league as they are! I will end this conversation here."

The boy squared his shoulders, oblivious to Ralf's lack of enthusiasm and harried expression. "We know a woman on the market. She fits all the things you say about these witches. She has a red streak in her hair. We've seen her beyond the city walls in the river and she had a *Hexenmal* on her back..."

"On her back?"

The other boy stood tall to his friend's defense. "We saw all of them in the Hauptmoorwald."

"You followed her into the Hauptmoorwald?"

"We wanted to see where she was going."

Ralf knew exactly who the boys were talking about. Klara, Widow Braun's niece. She worked on a market stand on Wednesdays. Today was Wednesday. Maybe he would see her today when he crossed the square. Ralf thought she lived in a village beyond the wall but she often stayed with Widow Braun on the Kaulberg.

"What were you doing near the Hauptmoorwald?" Ralf wanted to shake these boys.

"We wanted to be sure they were meeting there before we said anything," the boy said.

This was the sort of danger Ralf was worried about. Those who were fascinated by the witches and their meetings beyond the city walls in the infamous forest, the Hauptmoorwald. Those charmed by the dark ways of the world. He'd been to the witch interrogations. The women would be stripped naked and inspected for *Hexenmale*, the witch's marks. They would have their heads and private parts shaved and city officials inspected every last nook and cranny. Many officials reveled in this practice. They had no desire to suppress their carnal impulses. Ralf feared they were all overrun with devilish drives.

Like now, Ralf felt the boys' lusty sickness. Their tainted thoughts seeped towards him. One day these boys would rot in a hole with the witches.

"I will report this to Dr. Fuchs and the witch commission. You boys need not think any more about this situation. And stay away from her. These devilish acts are meant to pull in boys such as yourself. Look at yourselves. You must chastise and cleanse. Go to the chapel and recite the Office. Don't just read them. You recite them, together. And don't pay other students to do it. Yes, I know you do that. I have heard about the two of you! Meet me in the Obere Pfarrer before sun-up tomorrow. I will hear your confession. Think long and hard about why this is so enticing."

"No one said anything about enticing," the boy spluttered.

Ralf grabbed his satchel and felt his face turn red as he hurried out of the classroom without further comment. Past younger, weak, fat boys whose sloppy forms could not rival his own youthful physique, Ralf hurried away. Today, Ralf himself would do more than recite the Office. He would march out into the flood plain until he could no longer march and then chastise himself until he drove the boys' tainted thoughts from his body. He nodded to students as he marched past, wondering how many of these boys actually believed the lessons the Catholic Church taught them. How many of them teemed with devilish thoughts?

Ralf's lip stretched dry and taut across his upper row of teeth. A drop of condensation hung from his nostril and he wiped it on his black sleeve. He was afraid the devil had infiltrated this most holy of establishments, through these boys. He had to make sure this infiltration was stopped.

Back in his simple chamber, a small cell on the top floor, four stone walls and a sleeping pallet, he dropped his satchel onto the bare stone floor, got on his knees and prayed for strength. Fear was a lack of faith and he had faith. By God! He had faith! The churning in that area behind his loins unnerved him. It was fear and fear could be scrubbed from his body. He'd recently discovered Glauber's salt, a new preparation from a man by the name of Glauber. Mixed with water, the solution purified him, leaving him clean. The lighter he was, the more relieved he felt. The emptiness after the cleansing made him feel less empty, if that made sense. He mixed the solution and drank it on an already empty stomach.

Ralf left his chamber and the sandstone residence, heading towards the market square. The March air was still damp and chilly, like early this morning, and he was grateful for the cool air to soothe his burning face. He loved living in the city of Bamberg. When Ralf arrived in Bamberg ten years ago, he feared he had lost the battle all together. His travels and his life at Upper Eierhofen had drained him spiritually and theologically and intellectually. His charge and student, Andra-Angela, had not heeded him and fell from grace, losing her life. He carried the guilt of having been entrusted with her care and education and he could not save her from herself. After the estate fell into the hands of Hans-Wolfgang, he came to Bamberg, a broken soul. His mentor and most trusted confidant, Father Marius, had allowed Ralf refuge in his chambers here at the *Collegium Ernestinum*. Marius fell ill, could no longer teach at the school and needed a replacement quickly. Father Ralf covered one of the lectures, using Marius's lecture script.

Together Ralf and Marius prepared the lectures and Ralf continued to take over the lessons, winning approval from the *Collegium* fathers and the students. He'd found his place at long last, a proper Jesuit educator, his purpose to educate these boys to save their own souls.

The *Collegium*, the way the Jesuits ran the school and their teaching methods not only stimulated his wisdom but also gave him something he had lacked: a real sense of belonging. And he would defend this life to the last if he had to. This was reinforced when the new Prince-Bishop Johann Fuchs von Dornheim came to power in 1622. Together with Bishop Förner, Bamberg was finally willing to accept the truth: the real war was happening here, at home. Bamberg was the front of the war against heretics and would lead the fight against evil.

But as conflicting problems with the witches arose, Ralf found his way of life and his belief system under fire. He took his role as an educator and a bringer of the word seriously, his goal to make those people listen to him before they drove the whole world to ruin!

Providentially, Ralf had been blessed with the ability to assemble a special troop of boys at the Jesuit school, together with Father Marius, God rest his soul. These boys were the most important thing to him now, a group of thirty strong, young men. To his surprise, he also produced his elite group of four. His Soldiers of God.

As Ralf passed the edge of the market square, he observed the farmers as they displayed their wares for sale. Next to the stand by the bridge, Ralf recognized Widow Braun and the girl, Klara. Klara wore a green full skirt that hung just so around her hips. Her fresh, feisty face and devilish grin gave her an appealing look. Ralf knew why his students would talk about her. All the boys whispered things about this girl. Ralf could only pity her for it.

Klara scrutinized Ralf as he passed by. She held up a dark red winter apple and smiled. Her taunts evoked a churning in his stomach and he feared he would not hold his excrement. What was this devil's work? Her gaze alone caused him to lose his faculties. He walked closer to the stand. The apple she held was shriveled and looked like it had been stored in the cellar.

"Apple, Father?" she said and bit into the apple.

"My child, are you well?" he said.

Klara reminded him of Andra-Angela. She had taunted him, too, but he had been younger and less equipped to fight it. He had loved Andra-

Angela dearly and feared Klara would come to a similar end.

"Could be better, Father," Klara said. "You look pale today. Is something wrong?"

"I am fine," he said.

Ralf moved to the next stand. Klara handed an apple to the fabric salesman tending the stand with two other market women. Aside the table strewn with bolts of green and brown linen, stood a table full of straw figures, bits of wood, stones hanging from leather cords and what looked like bits of bone.

The market woman at the stand shouted to Ralf: "The end is near! Protect yourself from the end of the world with this talisman!"

Ralf crossed himself. "I will pray for you all, you poor lost lambs."

He scurried out of the market and marched beyond the city wall. He feared not only for Klara but for all of them. The repercussions of their heathen practices would bring them all eternal destruction! He desperately wanted to save her but even more so wanted to save himself.

He knew what he needed to do. Shine like a beacon in the night. Teach them, all of them, the way. Convince them his way was the right way. By saving them, all of them, he would save himself. He would make them listen. He stopped by an oak tree, knelt down and prayed for divine intervention. Consumed with the spirit, he swooned and fell to his side.

Chapter 4

Pieter van Diemen

Rain dripped from Pieter van Diemen's hat. The drums had stopped long ago. His marching feet kept no rhythm but instinctively maneuvered one in front of the other, through the mud, avoiding the ruts made by wagon wheels. This was the first day he and Johannes had marched with their *Fähnlein*, their banner, the 400-man segment of a larger regiment. Spring came reluctantly to this damp land. Chunks of ice floated in the flat river bed of the Elbe. A rancid smell came from the water: rotting fish and human refuse.

The horses and the wagons up ahead stopped. Muttering and broken bits of conversation resonated through the ranks of the banner. The foot soldiers around Pieter stopped as well. The constant rain muffled their words. Certain sounds were discernible though. Wonderful words that meant they would finally halt here for the night.

"I think we'll reach the castle tomorrow," Johannes said. "Then we can see some action."

"Then we have to work," Pieter said.

"Lazy man, would you rather march? I'd rather fight."

"I'm not a fighter," Pieter said.

"You're not a lover either, are you Pieter?" He scratched his scraggly beard. "You're too good for this soldier's life, aren't you? Well, we need food, we need coins, we need drink. When was the last time we got paid?" Johannes punched Pieter on the shoulder and almost sent him reeling. "Come on, let's go look for a pool of mud to set up camp in." He laughed and gave Pieter a brotherly wink.

Pieter and Johannes never made it to Ascherleben. They'd secretly followed some Scottish soldiers who wanted to fight with General Mansfeld's army and they joined up as well. Pieter wondered if it mattered who they fought for. He wasn't even sure *what* they were fighting for anymore. They supposedly fought for the Dutch against Spain. Pieter's other comrade, an Englishman named Howard, said Mansfeld's funding came from the English crown and the enlistment of the English regiments were meant to support the Protestants and reinstate the displaced Bohemian Queen, who was English. But now King James had died and the new king was his son Charles. Wasn't Charles going to marry the Catholic Spanish Infanta? Were the English fighting against Spain now? Or they were fighting for France against the Catholic Holy Roman Empire? Weren't the French Catholic as well?

They were heading south along the Elbe River towards Rögatz Castle. Then on to Magdeburg, from what Pieter had heard. General Mansfeld had said he wanted to do something for himself: *"für mich Selbsten etwass thun."* So this march was really the mission of one man looking for personal gains. Rumor had it they would soon conflict with the troops of General Wallenstein's unthinkably huge army. Wallenstein's Imperial army was in service to the Catholics and the Holy Roman Emperor and Bavaria. Pieter heard Wallenstein was really in service to himself as well.

Although Mansfeld's army was supposed to be 20,000-men strong, the possibilities of them being mashed like straws of wheat in a field were more real than speculation. But Pieter was not going to Magdeburg. He was going to do something for himself too. He would desert as soon as he could. Time was running out. All he needed was a horse. And some clean clothes. And dry boots.

Johannes muttered something about the damned rain, no food, no beer. Pieter rammed his pike shaft into the mud. He pulled off his dirty, tattered hat, wiped a soiled rag over his smeared face, blew his nose into the rag and threw it aside. Shouldering his pike again, he slapped Johannes on the shoulder.

"May I show you to your room, Your Royal Highness?" Pieter said.

"Follow me, Dutchman," Johannes said and stomped up a slight slope towards an open field.

Their boots squish-squished in the mud. They slipped and slid and followed Howard towards the hedgerow. Howard leaned his pike against a taller tree and threw his pack onto the muddy grass. Pieter took Johannes's pike and leaned both of them next to Howard's. Howard opened his pack and unrolled a soggy once-white bed sheet. He threw it to Pieter who secured two corners to two trees. Together, Pieter and Johannes rammed two axe shafts into the sodden earth, fixed the other two corners to them and made a sort of tent. All along the hedgerow, similar shoddy shelters fluttered in the wind.

Howard sunk down on the ground with a huff. Pieter poked Johannes and pointed at Howard as he pulled his boots off, undid the rags around his feet and produced more from his pack. Dry ones nonetheless.

"Where did you get those?" Johannes said to him. "One of those market girls?"

"We fulfill each other's needs," Howard said.

"Can't you get her to give me and Pieter here something to drink?" Johannes said.

"I am thirsty as a bear," Pieter said.

Howard smiled wide. "I'll see what I can do. We're going to look for anything that resembles meat." He bound his feet up and pulled his boots back on.

Pieter could imagine having warm, dry feet, as he coaxed his meager fire to burn. His feet were cold and numb. Rather numb than when he could feel them—sore, hot and throbbing. That feeling would come back later when he tried to sleep.

Johannes slid his dagger from the sheath on his belt. *"Ik ben zo terug,"* he said and followed Howard.

Pieter and Johannes had covered a lot of ground since they left Amsterdam. They'd started off the following day at dawn, on foot, for Germany. The first day they met various travelers who told sensational war stories. Various printed flyers were circulating throughout the German-speaking areas—conflicting accounts of war and terror, derogatory caricatures of the Pope and of Martin Luther, all sorts of propaganda. They spent an overnight in a village where the people recounted how General Mansfeld and his sons-of-whores had ransacked the place. Then Pieter and Johannes stole the villagers' last two horses and continued on their way towards Bremen.

En route to Bremen, they followed a group of Scots who in turn stole the horses and led them to the *Musterplatz,* Mansfeld's recruiting area, and they signed up. The few coins they received upon enlisting were long gone, spent on food and their chosen weapon—the pike—having had to pay for the pikes themselves. The soldiers were then encouraged to pry whatever else they needed to survive from the surrounding villages. Pieter learned quickly that hunger could drive a man to do things he wouldn't normally do.

Johannes approached, his muttered Dutch-laden German causing Pieter to break a sort of smile.

"No bread, no beer, just these sick old rats," Johannes muttered. "And no cheese for the Dutchmen."

He threw the two rats at Pieter's feet. "I get so angry sometimes." A low growl formed in Johannes' throat. "I had a house, a lovely wife, a beautiful farm and a comfortable life. I hate everything about this war. I hate the men involved in it. I hate the rain. I hate…" Johannes slowly shook his head and laughed. "Howard met up with his girlfriend. Says he'll get us something to drink and some bread."

"Wonderful." Pieter sliced one of the rats open, threw the innards behind the tree and threw Johannes the other rat. "Skin this bastard, why don't you."

"You don't belong here boy," Johannes said. "You need to find a nice merchant's daughter. Get her pregnant and marry her and share the family's wealth."

"That life isn't in the cards, is it?" Pieter said. "Or can you see me, in front of the fire, reading a story to the eldest, the wife sending the other children to bed and then warming the bed for me?"

"Pieter?" Johannes said.

"Wrapping her arms around me, her lips touching mine…" Pieter said.

Johannes boomed. "*Hey*! Do you have any coins left?"

"No. Nothing." Pieter wiped rat blood off his hands in the grass and grabbed his pack. "Look, nothing."

"Damn…"

"How far is the next town?" Pieter asked.

"Tomorrow's foot march away. We'll be reaching the castle tomorrow evening, they said." Johannes turned his back to Pieter and slit the rat open.

Johannes and Pieter skewered their rats and held them over the little fire. The smell of singed hair and burning, rotten meat caused Pieter to turn his head but his stomach rumbled in joyful anticipation. Other fires had sprung up along the hedgerow and the men's laughter and conversations rose like the smoke. Footsteps approached in the mud. Howard walked into the light of the fire holding two ceramic bottles.

"Something strong to ward off a chill," Howard said. "Sorry, there's no bread."

The three men shared the rat meat and swallowed the schnapps in no time. Schnapps filled a belly just the same as bread. It also drowned the gamey, muddy taste of the sinewy rat meat. Pieter leaned back against the tree, adjusted his baldric so he could rest his hand on the hilt of his sword and settled in to get some rest.

In what seemed like only moments, gray light on the horizon woke him. It was a sad excuse for dawn but at least the rain had stopped. Pieter shook himself from his dreamless, unrestful sleep. He ran his fingers through his hair and then the itching began. He scratched his scalp and chunks of dark-blond curls came out with the scabs. He didn't want to think what his skin looked like under these filthy, lice-filled, constantly-wet rags. He inherited this uniform from some poor sod—sleeves and hose slashed with the once red-gold colors of some regiment or another, unmatched to any of the other men here. He stretched and sat up. Mornings he could always feel his feet. The throbbing was enough for him to fear removing his boots. Pieter could not bear to see what they looked like. If he found a man his size, he would kill him for dry boots.

The three men grabbed their pikes and joined the ranks. Pieter marched, his feet instinctively maneuvering one in front of the other. At least his feet went cold and numb on the march. Their banner had ceased to keep any sort of formation. Maybe in the front where the officers were but here at the rear, the men plodded along the river bank, four in a row, sometimes two in a row or single file, depending on how dense the vegetation grew. This section of the Elbe was wide and flat, the current calm. One of the men had said it was deceptive and to be careful not to fall in. The water was deep.

In the afternoon, they stopped at a once-intact village. They weren't the first band of marauders to come through here. The men were free to look for lodgings and loot, whatever they liked amongst the burnt ruins. The war should fund the war, the important men said. That should ease any guilt a decent man might feel, Pieter thought. The soldiers needed everything to help sustain them through the day: bread, wine, beer, maids. Pieter was mostly interested in boots.

Johannes and Pieter approached a small farm. Soldiers from earlier campaigns had already desecrated the sad family. The half-burnt house still smoldered and smoked. A mother and her maid sat huddled together in the open barn on a bed of dirty straw. A man lay face down next to the women. Flies buzzed around his open, crusted wounds.

As they approached the women, they only wept, tears streaking their soot-covered faces. "We have no gold!" the one woman ranted over and over, a chant of suffering.

Johannes knelt down next to them and spoke in soothing tones like a father would. Pieter left him to pry whatever he could out of the broken women.

Pieter sneaked around the back of a cluster of houses and came to a seemingly-empty barn. He heard a tell-tale sound—a hoof impatiently scraping the ground. He walked around the barn and found no way in. The building was completely boarded up and there was no door. On his second round, he found a weak spot in this construction behind some bushes—a few loose boards nailed shut from the inside. They easily gave way when Pieter pushed on them, creating a hole big enough for a horse to pass through. He drew the dagger from his belt with his left hand and entered the dark barn. A horse snorted. And another. The smell of their sweet sweat mixed with the scent of dry hay brought a whispered Hallelujah across his lips. Were Pieter's ghosts smiling on him today?

He felt his way around in the dark. Slivers of dusty light showed through the barn's wooden walls. He heard a man's quiet whispers. So this was a hiding place. It wasn't the first time villagers tried to hide their valuables from the *soldateska*. Pieter felt his way towards the sounds of the animals.

Straw crunched under moving feet. Someone grunted. From behind, something heavy struck Pieter on the shoulder. He faltered and regained his balance as something wooden smacked him in the face. His hat flew from his head and landed with a whisper in the straw. He tasted blood in his mouth. He lunged at the dark object standing in front of him with his dagger out first. A low release of air hissed when the point of the dagger entered something soft. Warm liquid flowed over Pieter's hand.

"God, make your people stop fighting me!" Pieter pleaded.

A figure moved, rustling in the straw. Pieter drew his sword with his right hand. "I won't hurt you," Pieter whispered. "Give me a horse and I will leave."

A woman whimpered. "You killed my husband."

"It takes more than one stab wound to kill a man," Pieter said and re-sheathed his sword.

A shadow lunged with a swish of air. Her soft, warm body collided with Pieter's and the surprise knocked him onto his back. His dagger flew from his hand. Pieter smelled her sour, panting breath and her fearful sweat. She jumped on top of him, her hands swinging, trying to hurt him in some way. Pieter held her tight, rolled the two of them over and now sat on top of her, her arms pinned down in the scratchy straw. The horse snorted.

She growled low and mean like a cornered dog.

"I don't want to hurt you!" Pieter said. "Give me a horse and I will leave."

Her body thrashed and she managed to free her arm. Her fist slammed into his cheek and she wriggled her body free from under his thighs. Before she could crawl away, Pieter grabbed her skirt and it tore. He pushed her down on her back and sat on top of her again. A sliver of light fell across half of her face, illuminating her panicked fear, her young skin gray and pale, her hair tattered and caked with blood.

Her chest rose and fell and Pieter tore the fabric away from her tiny, shriveled breasts. So this young creature had already suckled a child with these breasts. She heaved her hips and tried to dislodge him. He weighed three times as much as her.

Pieter reached his hand under her skirt and found her folds to be hot and wet. He laid his weight on top of her squirming little body, undid his breeches, spread her legs and entered her. She tried to bite his neck. He covered her mouth with his hand and pressed her head back down into the straw.

Pieter finished quickly and sat back. Straw rustled as she scurried away. He was not going to wait for her to come back with a weapon. In the straw he found his hat and his dagger. He stuck that in his belt, put the hat on his head, stood up and straightened his breeches. A horse snorted, groaned and shifted his weight from one side to the other. A hoof scraped along the dirt floor.

In the dim, dark light Pieter made his way towards the sounds and felt the warmth of living animals. His hand stroked the haunches of a burly horse, covered with a blanket. Under the blanket his fur was still thick from the winter. His fingers grasped the rope twisted around the horse's head as a halter. The horse tossed his head. Pieter stroked his mane to calm him and loosened the knot that bound him to the barn wall. After a few soft words of praise and thanks, the horse was calm. Pieter slung the rope around his neck and fixed it on the other side of his head to make some sort of reins. He felt his way to the horse's side, shoved the blanket up around the horse's shoulders, leaped up once and got on his muscled back. The horse chose his path carefully and headed towards the opening in the back of the barn. Pieter ducked down as they passed out into the open.

The late-afternoon air had a vile smell of death and fire and destruction. The setting sun struggled through the gray clouds and Pieter heard the usual sounds of pillaging: some crying; some wailing; some laughing; some destruction. A small group of soldiers fought over a barrel of beer. One of them yelled and pointed at Pieter on top of this burly black horse. Another small group close by turned as a whole.

Johannes emerged from the group. He walked towards Pieter, his face an expression of puzzlement, slowly shaking his head to indicate his confusion. He stood still and tilted his head to the side. A slight smile crossed his lips and he nodded. A silent understanding. Pieter had found a way out of this horrible company, out of this horrible life. Johannes raised his hand in a salute of farewell.

Pieter kicked the horse's flanks and he burst into motion.

Chapter 5

Katarina

It was late morning when Katarina saw the last soldier leave. A small group of mounted, official-looking soldiers had ridden up the path after sunrise and roused the men out of their drunken stupor. Katarina could only imagine the state Sara and the children would be in. As the last of the men staggered off around the bend, Katarina ran down to the workers' house.

"Sara?" Katarina whispered, not wanting to scare her. She pulled the cellar trap open. "Sara!"

Sara ran up the steps, embraced Katarina and then stared in horror at Katarina's state. Katarina's hair was matted, her trousers cut. She was filthy and violated.

"Dear God…" Sara began. "Are you…?"

"I'm alive. And Herr Tucher. We need to gather the others. I haven't even started to look."

David and Friedrich rushed out of the cellar and ran out of the house. Isabeau and Albin crawled out behind them and sat at the table.

"Those boys are impossible," Sara said. "They will be the death of us. We have to think of something."

"Let's look for Elsbeth," Katarina said. "It's the fault of those boys that we were found out. She's responsible for this."

"One moment," Sara said and disappeared into her sleeping space. She came back with a skirt and a blouse much too small for her. "The soldiers missed this. I had it under the floorboards. I'll get you a bucket of water and you wash yourself first. You'll feel better."

Katarina pulled her tattered clothes off and let them fall to the floor. She stood right there in the middle of the kitchen, in front of the children and Sara while she washed, dried and dressed. She was beyond modesty and shame. "Come, you two, and help me look for something to eat."

Isabeau and Albin ran out ahead of Katarina and headed for the stable.

Isabeau was no doubt going to check on her horse. Katarina passed by the well. Tanner the Elder filled water buckets for the animals. That meant there were still animals, then. Herr Tucher joined him, washed his hands in one of the buckets and dried them on his trousers.

Katarina found Anna in the stable. Anna pushed her gray hair out of her face. "I finally got away and into the cellar here," Anna said. "It was already dark."

Anna had obviously suffered at the hands of the soldiers. Bald scalp showed where tufts had been pulled out. Her cheeks were blackened and her neck and arms were bruised. Blood was caked in her hair and around her mouth. Katarina tried to get close to Anna in order to inspect her injuries but Anna shied away.

"You're hurt!" Katarina said and tried to touch Anna.

Anna pulled away. "There is no need for sympathy. We have work to do."

Katarina laid her hand on Anna's shoulder, but Anna shrugged her off. Katarina needed the warmth of her friends to digest this last attack. She would drown if she had to swallow all this rage and sadness. This was the hardest part of all the abuse. But with Anna there could be no discussion, no emotion, no reflection.

"Where's Elsbeth?" Anna asked.

"I never saw her once we were out of the house," Katarina said.

"We still have her children to take care of," Anna said. "There are onions and other roots in this cellar. I found them when I fell over them. I knocked a whole stack of crates over in the dark."

Together they collected the root vegetable from the toppled stack of crates and brought some back to the workers' house. Katarina sifted through the crate, pulled out the parsnips they had stored over the winter and shook the sand from the shriveled roots. Anna threw them into an empty crate and carried them outside to wash them. When she returned, Katarina noticed she had washed the blood from her face and hair.

Katarina chopped onions, feeling uncomfortable in the silence. Anna plunked her crate on the table. Hannah sucked her thumb. Metal scraped on stone as Sara cleared ash off the hearth into a wooden bucket. David and Friedrich pushed the front door open, slamming it against the wall. They pounded up the ladder and then down. Up the ladder, down the ladder. Up the ladder. The boys screeched and the floorboards creaked as they jumped on the straw mattresses in the sleeping spaces upstairs. Katarina flinched as a crash upstairs caused dust from the ceiling to rain down onto the table and the vegetables she chopped. Anna growled. She climbed up the ladder and Katarina heard one *crack*! Then another *crack*! The two boys moaned and cried.

"One more sound and I'll hammer you both again," Anna hollered up at the boys as she climbed back down the ladder. "I'll leave bruises worse than either one of you would."

Elsbeth's baby cried from Sara's bed behind the ceramic-tiled stove. Above their heads, another wailing scream went off like that from a slaughtered beast. Anna flew up the ladder again. The ceiling rumbled and more dust fell through the cracks onto the table. The boys sniveled; a pathetic, muffled whimpering.

Anna climbed back down the ladder. "Now I had to tear the two apart. I have had it with those boys."

"Do you think we should search for Elsbeth?" Katarina asked.

Anna sighed, grabbed her mug and took a large gulp of beer. Sara just shook her head.

"I don't think she's coming back," Katarina said.

Anna and Sara turned away and went about their business.

"I don't think she ran away," Katarina said. "Don't you both think…?"

Judging from the look on her two friends' faces, the discussion about Elsbeth, the soldiers and the war had just ended. Anna grumbled something about having to take care of herself, grabbed an axe, hacked viciously at some bones and threw them into the pot over the fire. This was how she would cope. The smell of browning flesh filled the kitchen. Anna doused the sizzling bones with water and a cloud of steam rose up the flue.

Sara put a pot of water on a tripod over some embers and grabbed a ceramic pot of valerian and poppy down from the shelf. Katarina wondered if this was how some could 'rise above it.' Children had to be fed, animals had to be tended. Life had to go on. There was no place to go to escape this. This farm was their home and their families were here. One swallowed the sorrow and buried the dead and thanked whatever force had kept them alive. Those who did not survive could be grateful for not having to relive the horrors, even if it was only in their minds and their dreams, day after day, night after night.

Isabeau and Albin quietly climbed down the ladder. They had been up there the whole time.

"I want to check if they found my horse," Isabeau said.

Sara shook her head. "Nobody is going outside. The Tanners will round up the horses. You are sleeping in the cellar again tonight."

Anna gave the children some bread and then soaked bits of bread in the poppy tea and fed the baby. As the others ate, Sara and Katarina made beds for the children in the cellar. The kitchen darkened, the oil lamp on the table spluttered and Anna took all the children down for the night. She came back up, handed Katarina two bottles and went back down. Katarina closed the trap door and covered it with the carpet. Sara pulled two sacks of wool from her room. She clunked four single-row wool combs on the table. Katarina refilled and relit the lamp.

"We must finish the spinning," she said. "We have so much work. This is really holding us up."

The men had sheared the sheep early this year. They desperately needed the wool and the money they could earn by selling it. Sara squeezed into her chair behind the table and searched around the small room like she was looking for something. Sparks rose up from the fireplace into the open flue above. She pushed herself up out of her chair and almost tripped over a bucket as she stepped over to the shelves hanging on the small space behind the ladder to the garret room above.

"Where are those damned spindles? If those boys took those spindles…"

Katarina spotted the two hand spindles under the table. "Here they are. I thought I saw those two devil-children poking each other with them."

She pulled a handful of wool out of the sack, held the wool comb with its single row of tines sticking up and began to pull the wool gently through the comb, her fingers removing bits of dirt left after washing. Sara poured two mugs full of wine and they drank in silence. Her face strained and tired, she pulled the fibers longer and longer until she had one long swatch of combed wool for Katarina to spin. No sounds came from the cellar below.

"Is everything in order with you Katarina?" Sara asked with a serious look on her face.

"Everything is fine, just fine," Katarina said, drained her mug and refilled it, emptying the wine bottle.

Sara yawned, stretched her back and left the room. Bottles clinked. She came back with more wine.

Katarina put her spindle down after the third skein. "Sleep if you want to. I certainly can't."

Sara combed the rest of the sack of wool. She rolled the combed wool into neat packages and stuffed it back into the sack.

"I may just lie down for a few minutes," Sara said. "My back is aching."

Katarina drained the rest of the wine from her mug and put her head down on the table. The wood was cool on her cheek. She tried to conjure up some joyful thoughts, a story to soothe her aching head.

A shout echoing from the yard woke Katarina. She jolted upright in the quiet, dark room. The sun had not yet risen and the fire was but an orange glow. Sara's feet pounded out of her room. Outside, a commotion rose and fell on the early morning breeze. Both women froze in the dark, listening. Shouts and stomping feet and swearing resonated somewhere in the farmyard. Arguing voices shot back and forth, a volley of insults. Wood splintered, bodies scuffled as if engaged in a fight. Metal on metal. Then quiet.

Sara crossed the room and grabbed the door handle. Katarina jumped to her side and gripped her shoulder, her face flushed with heat as she pushed Sara up against the door.

"No!" Katarina hissed. "Don't open the door."

Sara froze. Katarina thought she looked more frightened of Katarina than what was outside.

Katarina took a deep breath and released her. "Please wait until our men come for us. If anything has happened to them, who knows what the soldiers will do to us. And to the children."

They stood next to the door, listening. Finally, a knock sounded.

"Katarina?" Herr Tucher said.

She opened the door. The early morning air was crisp and carried a scent of blood.

"They have gone, all of them. I am sure of it," Herr Tucher said. "It was only a small group, maybe ten or fifteen men. But still more than we can deal with."

He came through the doorway and Katarina closed the door. "Nobody is hurt but I am afraid they took more than I would have liked," he said.

Katarina handed him a mug of wine. He drained it in one gulp.

"The cows are gone and they slaughtered your goat," he said. "They took the carcass with them as well. But none of us are hurt." He laid a hand on Katarina's shoulder. "Please stay here with the other women until they clear out of the area altogether."

Katarina nodded. He grabbed the door handle and rushed out of the house. She shut the door behind him. They stayed indoors all day again, another day cooped up with those boys. By late afternoon, Katarina had enough of them. She wanted to take Isabeau back to the main house and sleep in their own rooms tonight. She climbed the ladder to the sleeping spaces upstairs. The white linens waved in the draft. They hung at angles to create some sense of privacy in this open, sloped space. Katarina pushed one aside and found Isabeau and Albin with a pair of mice they had lured into a small wooden box.

"Let's go, *Schatzi*," Katarina said. "Let the mice go."

"I want to keep them," Albin said.

"I have enough mice in my house," Katarina said.

Isabeau stood and they climbed down the ladder. Sara ladled a small pot full of hot broth, covered it and handed it to Katarina along with the last hunk of bread. Katarina hugged her and whispered her thanks.

"For what?" Sara said.

"Just so."

Katarina and Isabeau hurried to the well, picked up two empty buckets and filled them. The afternoon sky was cloudy and rain threatened. As they walked to the main house, the wind picked up and rustled along Katarina's skirt. Her ears attuned to every sound the wind carried, she heard muted murmurings and wondered if fear amplified hearing. Isabeau set her full buckets down among the planks of wood that once were the paddock doors. Katarina set the pot down and together they cleared the planks to the side. A puddle of shiny-black blood stained the floor in the low-vaulted stable where the goat had been.

Herr Tucher walked from the kitchen into the stable. He took Katarina by the hand. "Bjarne sneaked up the North Hill," he said. "He came back and told us the soldiers were still camping on the other side and did not seem to be preparing to leave. We must remain cautious." He led her into the kitchen. "Do you really want to stay in the house tonight? Would you rather stay with Sara?"

Isabeau pushed by and sat down at the table holding a sheet of birch bark and a piece of charcoal.

"I don't think it really makes a bit of difference where we sleep," Katarina said. "If they're coming, we can't hide."

"Well, then, the decision is yours. Bjarne told us about a man in Lonnerstadt who went missing. They found him in the moat by the small castle where my acquaintances live. There must be 1500 soldiers camped there. They have dumped barrels of beer, stolen anything they could get their hands on. What they do not steal, they destroy. A man in Gremsdorf was so badly knocked about he died."

"Elsbeth is missing," Katarina said. "None of us have seen her."

"I have not either, I am sorry to say."

He passed behind Isabeau. He smoothed his hand over her hair and she smiled up at him. He admired the picture she was drawing on the birch bark.

"A horse," he said. "Lovely likeness. Oh yes, Bjarne brought your horse back."

Isabeau smiled to herself and looked to Katarina.

"Tomorrow, child," Katarina said. "You stay in now."

Katarina wished the three of them were far, far away. She put the last hunk of bread into a basket on the table, alongside the pot of salty broth. Isabeau shoved her picture aside, dipped the bread into the broth and ate. Herr Tucher patted the girl on the shoulder turned to leave.

"We are very lucky," he said. "We can rise above this."

Katarina nodded and smiled. She wanted to assure him she could, yes, rise above this. And she would. They were not seriously injured. They were together. She had pondered enough about the implications of the last few days and she was exhausted. Like the other women, she would retreat into repetitive activity. Katarina dragged a sack of wool out from the alcove, pulled it over to the low stool next to the fire, took the wool combs down from the hook on the wall and combed wool. Isabeau got up from the table.

"Where are you going?" Katarina said.

"To bed," she said and left the room.

The front doors scraped as they opened and shut again. Katarina's heart leapt. Isabeau had gone out to the stable. Did she not understand what these soldiers were capable of? What they would do to Isabeau if they got a hold of her? How could she make that girl understand the danger?

She was too exhausted to run after her. Isabeau would hide in the stable to make sure her horse was safe. Katarina wouldn't be able to find her anyway. She set the wool combs aside and walked into the little alcove next to the kitchen where she had slept as a child; the tiny space usually meant for storing wood. In the corner stood a wooden box the size of a baby's bed. She opened the well-oiled latch and a heavy, musky-flowery scent rose out of the box. Herr Tucher had brought oils back from Amsterdam and this one seemed to have leaked out and soaked into the wood. She rummaged through old swatches of fabric and odd mementos she had collected over the years and found a little ceramic flask stopped with a cork. She opened it and downed a vile gulp of bitter laudanum.

Chapter 6

Ralf

Ralf closed the black leather-bound Roman Breviary, concluding his morning hour of praying the Divine Office. Father Marius had given him this breviary on the day of his ordination. In Bamberg, many parish priests and some of Ralf's teacher colleagues met to recite the Office in choir, but Ralf learned from Marius and the Jesuits to pray in private. The words and the movements of his lips when he said them gave Ralf peace. *"God come to my assistance, Lord make haste to help me."* Morning praise prepared him for the work he needed to do each day—to labor strenuously for his religion; his service, to teach and spread the word of God.

He left the Obere Pfarre, his favorite church in Bamberg. The sky lightened and a cool mist hung over the cobbled street descending away from the Kaulberg. He'd slept fitfully and was still sleepy, even after reciting his morning prayers. The walk in the chilly morning air did little to refresh him. He walked past Widow Braun's still-shuttered house towards the river and his stomach rumbled. He would allow himself some water but food must wait. His body was empty and his thoughts were buoyant, drifting on the lightness that prayer, lack of sleep and lack of food gave him. It was a place he liked to start the day, from this unburdened, redeemed feeling; ready to be filled with the challenges the day brought him.

Ralf worried about Klara and would pray for guidance on how he should confront her with his fears regarding the heathen talismans they sold on the market and her involvement in that practice. He had just read Friedrich Förner's sermon concerning this for the third time, the main theme being: *arm yourself with the weapons of God, in order to resist the bait of the Devil!* These talismans they sold on the market were just that: bait of the devil. Because the city council allowed them to sell these 'things' made them as much at fault as the marketeers themselves. The only weapon of God people could count on were the *Agni Dei*, the lambs of God made from wax

53

and properly blessed by clergy, as instructed by the Pope.

As he approached the market, the first few farmers from beyond the city wall shuffled across the market schlepping barrows and baskets, the odd cow-drawn cart laboring along the cobbled road. He instinctively looked for Klara and her full green skirt.

A man followed by two women carrying fully-laden baskets pulled a two-wheeled wagon towards the market square. Ralf recognized him as the fabric salesman Klara was so friendly with. Ralf walked around the outside boundary of the market and slowed to observe. The fabric salesman oversaw the two women, directing them as they set up their tables and dressed them with wares. These were the women who sold the talismans. As Ralf approached the stand, a shout and scuffling drew his attention to a narrow passage between two run-down timbered houses. There a young boy, maybe ten years of age argued with an older boy who carried a sickly, tatty-looking girl who was no more than five. He was drawn towards the children.

The young boy waved his hands around, trying to make a point. "I told you if we got here early enough, we could probably get some for nothing."

"I'm not going there with her," the older boy said.

"If we take her, they'll feel sorry for us," the younger boy said.

The older boy set the girl down. "You carry her. She's sick."

The girl was beyond protesting. She slumped onto the ground. She was full of disease and malaise, her skin a tinge of yellow.

Ralf watched the whole exchange as if they were specimens on a table, with a sort of distant regard for the human condition. "Bring her to the poor house," he said to the boys.

Both boys shot Ralf a look that said he was interfering until the younger one obviously had an idea.

"Say, Father," the younger boy said. "We need alms for the poor. We need to get some food for our sister here. Can you help us? We need some money."

"Is the girl sick? Why don't you go to the Liebfrauen-Siechhaus? There is certainly someone who will help you there. You have a right as God's children to some help."

"We have a right?" the older boy said. "We have rights when we have money to pay for it. Otherwise they will try to sell us to the passing troops.

They don't care what happens to us."

"You need to pray to God, it is the faith in God that will heal you. God gives us the trial and tribulations in order to test our faith. We should be grateful for these trials he sets in our way. We are grateful and take on the hardships with joy. This is what brings us closer to God. And if God decides it is time to take us from this earthly realm, we shall pray to be admitted into His heavenly kingdom."

"We need money to get her some medicine," the older boy said. "We need money for medicine for our Oma as well."

"But paying for medicines from so-called quacks and poison-mixers is not the correct way, boys. This is the way of the devil. Don't you listen to Bishop Förner in church?"

"What, listen to what they say in church?" the older boy said. "We can't understand anything they say. And they all want money too. They say our parents are dead and in purgatory. If we want to save our parents' souls, we need money. What are we supposed to do? We have nothing to eat, she's sick and we should pay to save their souls?"

The boy heaved the sickly girl back up and set her on his hip, like a mother. She clung to his shoulder and coughed.

"You need money, you say?" Ralf asked the older boy. "I have something you could do for me. It's worth a chicken, I would say." Ralf had their interest now. "There's a woman on the Kaulberg. Widow Braun…"

"We know her. She knows our Oma," the younger boy said.

"Here's two bits, boy. Go to Widow Braun and buy what you need."

Before Ralf had a chance to change his mind, the two boys rushed off, grumbling in that horrible Franconian dialect Ralf detested. He'd been in this area for years now; fifteen years or more. And after ten years in Bamberg, he still couldn't understand the Franconians, muttering their lazy, half-chewed words. Ralf walked behind the boys, watching them turn away from the market and hurry up the Kaulberg towards Widow Braun's. He continued towards the fabric stand, now open for business and manned by the two women and the fabric salesman.

They were busy with other customers so Ralf took the opportunity to have an undisturbed look at their wares. One table was loaded with bolts of fabric—natural-colored linens, browns and greens, and a few swatches of black. Ralf ran his finger over the scratchy, stiff linen. They smelled earthy, like the dyes used to color them, and fresh from hanging in the breeze, like the laundry his mother had hung out to dry. Another table was covered with horse brushes and hair brushes, combs made of bone, brooms for the floor. The next table was piled with dried, bundled herbs. Alongside that stood ceramic bowls filled with dried leaves, powders, dried blossoms, bottles of colored liquids. Elixirs, by the look of it. Ralf fingered some dark chips that looked like oak bark. He'd been noticed by the toothless woman who traveled with the fabric salesman.

She attended to Ralf in the spirit of a true hawker. "Oak was the holy tree of the Germanic people for a long time and its properties are well known."

Ralf said, "Devilish deception and pagan poison-mixing."

The fabric salesman laughed. "Wait until you have a sore bottom and see how well it helps. And oak bark tea when drunk will sooth that sour stomach of yours. I can tell by your pained face and by the way you smell that your stomach is sour and giving you problems."

The woman said, "Have you ever tried this wormwood tea? A bitter drink would soothe you. You do smell sour. Do you have diarrhea? Do you have the flux? Let me see your eyes. Let me see your hands. You know, I can tell your fortune."

Ralf felt how damp his hand was when she grasped his with her own cool, dry hand. He snatched his back and backed away. "No, thank you. I am fine!"

What sort of devil's work was this? Telling the future, divination. He feared what would happen if he even had a diviner in his midst! Oh, again this fear. Where was his faith? Words he had once read shouted in his head: *God said, whoever goes to a magician or a fortune teller: I will turn my face to him and extinguish him from the middle of my people. One should stone them.* He needed to properly arm himself against these people if he intended to fight against them. The destruction they bring to this town, to this land, to this world! He had to stop this heresy from spreading.

Ralf rushed from the market and headed back towards the school, back to the residence, to his chamber. As he approached the stone staircase, his four best and most trusted students came towards him as if they'd waited for him: the two brothers Konrad and Karl, the older and more serious boys in the group who had taken to wearing the black monks' robes and cowls of the Jesuits; Martin and Michel, two orphan brothers who had recently shown themselves as eager to learn, willing to obey and ready to live for service to the Society of Jesus.

"Father, we have brought you bread," Konrad said. "Come and eat with us."

Chapter 7

Pieter van Diemen

Pieter had no money, no food. He was alone. He rode south and needed to stay away from the main roads, away from the rivers, away from the routes the troops were marching on. Dressed in that makeshift uniform—the soiled, damp fabric stinking of sweat, mold and sickness—he looked like a solider. If caught, and it didn't matter by whom, he would be hanged; for deserting, for being a soldier, for being Dutch, for being alone. If only he could get to Sichardtshof, he'd be safe. He wondered if Herr Tucher would still receive him. With war waging, he wondered if the farm was still there at all.

After Pieter's father died, all those years ago, the Amsterdam authorities sent in collection thugs to claim everything van Diemen the Elder had owned. Whether his father really had debts or not, Pieter never found out. It sure gave Pieter an excuse to drink until he dropped, which he did right next to the Singel Canal. When he regained consciousness, one of those thugs was floating face-down in the canal. Pieter was going to be hanged for the man's murder! Trydje agreed to hide him and Pieter wrote to Herr Tucher, begging to come back to Sichardtshof. Herr Tucher arranged for money for Pieter to travel. But Pieter and Trydje wasted the money on wine. So, what else could he do but sneak off, sign up and sail from Amsterdam to Batavia? Pieter sent one last message to Herr Tucher, telling him he was sailing East. After that, Pieter had no further contact with him.

Then there was Katarina. He had thought about her often. Quite simply, if he could get back to the farm, she would take care of him. That was the underlying reason he wanted to get back to Sichardtshof. He could do her chores, mindless work that quieted his mind, and she would let him alone. And maybe she could cure this nagging problem he had with the drink. She always had a tea or an herbal concoction. Maybe she could rid him of this demon that came out every time he drank schnapps. Other men weren't like this. Then again, many were.

But right now he had no schnapps. He rode along the top of a hill, observing the fields on both sides, and headed for a tree line in the distance. Below, a brook flowed in a hollow towards the same line of trees. The brook flowed southward judging by where the sun was setting. As he rode into the forest, the trees absorbed what was left of the daylight. He dismounted his horse and led him down through the thick underbrush towards the babbling brook, a shallow but clear flowing water. The undergrowth crunched under their steps. The forest floor was still frozen.

Pieter had ridden the horse hard. The horse needed food and he as well. The horse stopped instinctively and dipped his head to drink. He drank and drank. Pieter knelt next to him and slurped the cold, sweet water. It ran down his neck, causing a shiver, and he splashed his face and head. His thoughts cleared.

He heard something. He stopped splashing water long enough to listen. The wind carried a beacon in the evening, a tolling bell in the distance, one meant to call farmers back to their village. Strange to hear a bell: so many bells had been plundered to be melted down for the metal, ammunition, canons. And no village wanted to draw attention to itself these days. Down in this hollow it was impossible to tell where it was coming from. Pieter tethered the horse to a tree and climbed the hill to the top. The bell echoed from all over. He looked for any sign of life, like smoke rising from a chimney.

The sky darkened. The full moon was rising. What wasn't full was his stomach. Katarina had called the March full moon the crow moon. A crow would taste fine now, if he had one. Pieter needed to get anything to help him still his complaining, cramping stomach. He pulled a handful of last year's growth from a fir tree and munched on that. He slid back down to the brook, untied the horse and led him around the forest. The horse nosed around the forest floor. His strong upper lip searched through fallen leaves and he nibbled at whatever he was finding. At this rate it would take a long time for the horse to fill his belly. Pieter looked closer at the ground. Something else had been grubbing through the fallen leaves and the acorns. The soil was overturned, plowed through.

The sounds of the dark forest took on a life of their own: flapping wings in the treetops; water splashing over smooth rocks; tree boughs creaking and moaning in the slight breeze that couldn't force its way to the forest floor. Something rustled in the underbrush. Every sound made Pieter jump and catch his breath. He chastised himself: he was afraid! Shadows began to take shape and he wondered if he should camp in the clearing on the hill above the hollow. Pieter grabbed the rope around the horse's head and held his breath. One drop of sweat ran down his spine. Then the pounding of a charging animal forced him to hop on the horse's back and kick him into motion. The horse's powerful flanks pushed the two of them up out of the hollow. When Pieter stood in the clear he looked back to see what it was.

Shadows moved down where the brook left the edge of the trees. A wild sow strolled out from under the trees and three of her young circled her. They bounded back under cover of the forest. An idyllic image for one who knew not the violence such a creature could inflict. Still, Pieter's mouth watered and he could almost smell roasting meat. But he wouldn't dare approach the sow with young. Maybe with more men and a bow and arrow but not alone with a horse, a dagger and a sword. The sow, too, disappeared into the shadows.

All along the top of the hill, a hedgerow accented the dark sky with the silhouette of the stark bushes; sloe and elder still too early in the year to bloom. Pieter tethered the horse once more and sat close to him in the open space. He grabbed the blanket off the horse's back, pulled it tight around himself and tried to think warm thoughts. He wondered if he was better off in the regiment instead of here, out in the middle of nowhere, completely alone. Anything was better than starving to death alone.

Pieter woke to the sound of that single bell tolling. The sun rose and a few rays warmed his stiff and frigid body. He scratched his head and listened to the bell. On this clear morning, he could hear distinctly that it was coming from the south. A small pillar of smoke rose from just beyond the next line of trees atop the opposite hill. The village must lie on the banks of the brook an hour's ride from here. He would follow the water's edge until he reached the village and try to beg a bit of food for him and his horse.

Pieter rode south. The rising sun warmed his back. He could tell the village was near. These fields had once been cultivated. The crop of grain from last year lay unharvested and trampled. A cat ran down the beaten track that led around a bend, away from the brook. He followed the cat past a large sandstone cross standing lopsided at the side of the track, dismounting where the path bent back towards the water. A cluster of houses and a few outbuildings stood in the clearing. Smoke rose from the chimney of what looked like a community baking oven.

He approached the first house. A woman's voice rose above the clucking of chickens. A child hummed; a boy digging a hole in the front garden with a stick. He stopped when he saw Pieter. Like a little chick, the boy peeped and ran through the open door into the house. The smell of wood smoke and manure hung in the air. The village was comprised of a few other run-down houses and the small village center with a bread oven. The ground was muddy and indented with human and animal prints. He searched the area for other signs of life, mainly signs of men working. Signs of men at all. Pieter saw and heard none.

Out of the house shot a harried woman with a pitchfork. "What do you want," she barked.

"I need food for myself and forage for my horse," Pieter said.

"I have nothing to give you," she said.

Her thin face looked tired, almost haunted, but dangerous and mean. Her dress hung as if she had recently been ill and lost a lot of weight.

"Please, I am alone," Pieter said. "I will work for whatever you can give me. Anything."

"I have nothing to spare." She held the pitchfork straight towards Pieter but did not advance. "Get going."

Pieter took two steps towards her. "Fetch your husband, woman. I am strong and can help him work."

The boy peeked around the door jamb. "Mama…"

"Get back in the house, you fool…" she sneered at the boy.

Pieter took two more steps towards her. "Please…"

She appraised Pieter up and down. He knew he could soften her up. The condition of the house divulged her need. Wooden shutters hung away from the windows. Planks were missing from the door. Pieter's ears strained, searching for signs that anyone else still lived in this village besides this woman and her boy.

"Are there no other villagers besides you?" Pieter asked.

"You look like a soldier," she said.

"I am fleeing from the war. My family was killed in Holland and I am looking for work."

The pitchfork sagged in her hand and the prongs landed in the mud.

"I can fix the door," Pieter said. "I can chop wood."

She turned her back and walked towards the house. She had a slight limp in her left leg. Pieter followed.

"I need forage for my horse," Pieter said.

She pointed to the barn. Pieter led the horse towards the run-down barn and carefully opened the door. The hinges threatened to come away from the rotting wood. What little hay was left Pieter scraped together into a pile with his foot. The horse sunk his head greedily into it.

Pieter left the horse in the barn and leaned the door against the frame. The woman stood next to the front door. She went into the house, setting the pitchfork along the wall out of sight. Pieter had to duck his head as he went in behind her. The little hallway was dark and smelled moldy. Pieter followed her down the hall and turned into a tiny kitchen with a small table, two chairs and a cold open fireplace.

"I need wood," she said, took a bottle and a ceramic cup down from the shelf next to the crooked wooden door and set it on the table. "Drink."

Pieter sat on the chair and poured a mouthful of bad-smelling schnapps. It tasted as bad as it smelled and burned from his throat down into his gut.

"I will try to gather something to eat," she said. "Look for wood."

Pieter poured himself another mouthful of schnapps, downed it and stood to leave. Firewood. Purposeful work. He found an old axe in the barn and a cache of logs hidden in a narrow space behind a fake wooden wall. He would have missed it if he wasn't looking. It was a clever construction, leaving just enough space to hide something long and slim, maybe the mother and her boy. Pieter's mind quieted as his body engaged in the simple repetitive work. The woman finally came for him late evening.

She brought him to the kitchen, set a plate with some mashed root vegetable and peeled acorn on the table in front of Pieter, set one down for herself and sat on the chair opposite. The fire atop the open fireplace warmed this damp, moldy space. She filled Pieter's cup with more of that schnapps. She told Pieter her name was Hilde and her husband had died of dysentery. Most of the younger men had gone off with the soldiers, leaving the few women here alone. The village had all but died out from disease. Hilde smiled now, warmed by the fire, the food and the drink. She was much younger than Pieter thought. The boy was her only child.

"I feel so much safer now that I can latch the door from the inside,"

Hilde said. "Tomorrow we can get at the barn door. Then my neighbor needs some work done too. We can't pay you but we will take care of you."

She left the room and came back holding a ceramic flask. She stopped behind Pieter and picked through his hair. "I have a columbine tincture to get rid of the lice."

A strange bitter smell accompanied the cold, burning sensation on Pieter's scalp as she dribbled the liquid onto his head. Her fingers combed through his tangled hair and she gently worked the solution through his curls. One finger traced the scar over his right eye and then the one under it. Pieter nodded off until he felt her tug at his worn boots. He yelped and startled her.

"I could soak your feet and get the foot rags off," Hilde said. "And give you some fresh clothes. I still have all my husband's clothes."

She knelt beside Pieter and took his hands. Pieter surveyed this woman, her situation and felt her desperation. She would surely die here alone, either at the hands of the mercenaries or from disease or hunger. She kissed Pieter's hands and laid her head in his lap. She stroked his thigh and looked up at him, smiling. Pieter knew this look of a desperate woman: she begged him to find her attractive. He'd seen this look all too often.

Hilde was sweet in an innocent, simple way, like a kitten without a mother. She needed a man to help her keep house. Certainly there were strong women somewhere who would fight and take care of a household. Pieter had just never met one. Certainly not his mother. He remembered Katarina and her feigned iron will, but even she lacked that extra something that would make her strong and independent. They were, after all, just women.

Hilde stood and slowly pulled the shirt over Pieter's head. She soaked a rag with the tincture and applied it on the back of his neck and under his arms. His open, sore skin burned but the tincture numbed and soothed. Hilde pulled Pieter to his feet, unlaced his trousers and they fell around his ankles. Pieter was obviously aroused. He sat back down and she treated his groin with the tincture.

Hilde threw her dress over her head and stood for a minute. She eased herself onto Pieter's lap and allowed him to enter her. She stroked his thighs, his hips and was skilled at giving a man pleasure. Pieter began to consider the arrangement here. If he stayed, it would win him time and he could hide. Pieter watched her face and imagined his life should he stay. It would be a hard life but that was the least of his worries. Sitting here, helpless, until the next wave of troops came to visit was the real problem. The troops would kill him or take him with them. That was exactly what he did not want.

He had no intention of staying here. Her situation was sad, yes, but he could not save the world. He had to save himself and to do that he had to keep moving. He now had what he needed from this woman. And, yes, he was leaving in the night.

Pieter allowed himself to climax. Hilde relaxed, her head on his chest. He could smell a mixture of sex, sweat and columbine tincture.

"I'll take care of you," she said and kissed Pieter's hand. "You can stay here with me. I'm going to lie down."

"I'll be in in a moment," Pieter said. "I need to check on my horse."

Hilde went into the room where the boy was sleeping. Pieter sat for a while until he heard them both breathing low and peaceful. He sneaked out in the middle of the night, got his horse and rode off under the light of the waning but still bright moon.

Chapter 8

Katarina

"Have you seen Isabeau?" Katarina asked.

Herr Tucher walked up to the front step of the farmhouse and put his hands on her shoulders. "Bjarne and Lasse finally rounded up the rest of the horses. With Isabeau's help. The soldiers did not catch any of them. Either they stopped looking for them or the horses were faster. After Isabeau helped the boys she went for a ride."

"And nobody stopped her?" Katarina said.

Isabeau rode into the yard through the open gate, dismounted and led her sorrel mare to the front of the stable. Katarina would let her know it was unacceptable to be out and about in the countryside! Katarina jumped off the front step, prepared to chastise the girl, but Herr Tucher held her back.

"A fine young lady," he said. "See the way she lands on her feet? Like a kitten. Nimble…"

"She's not a young lady!" Katarina said. "She's a child. She needs to be protected from herself!"

"Other girls are being betrothed and sent away to their marriage beds," he said.

"That is so unfair," Katarina said. "They are still children."

"What were you doing at that age?" he asked.

Katarina gave a little start at the question. When she was a child, nobody considered her feelings. She was only the child of the farm maid. Her mother had left and her grandmother raised her. And, yes, at that age nobody watched over Katarina and she was left to fend for herself on most occasions.

"No one cared what I did," Katarina said. "But there weren't murderous soldiers hiding at every roadside. And Isabeau is different. She…"

"She is different," Herr Tucher said. "There is something about her."

"Yes, she's different." Katarina was torn between being proud of the girl's strength and independence and fearing for the girl's life. "She's too young to be out on her own. She doesn't know any better. We have to be so careful."

"The difference is she matters. Her life matters to you as it does to me. Is this what you want to say? We care about her. That is just how we should feel about our children."

"I wonder if the problem is she's not my child," Katarina said. "She knows that and I think it undermines any authority I could have. She won't listen to me!"

"You're the only mother she's ever known. It is normal to worry about her. And it is normal for her to fight your authority. Think about yourself in her position."

Katarina fought against her grandmother all the time. A twinge of guilt nagged Katarina as she thought about the time she ran away to Nuremberg with a young traveling weaver named Willi Prutt. She'd exchanged harsh words with her grandmother.

"We need to build the confidence in these children," Herr Tucher said. "Try to have some faith in her. It's like allowing a child to climb. A child will only climb as far as they trust themselves to go. Allow her to climb as high as she feels she can go. If she falls, she will learn. If you coddle her, she will become weak."

"If she falls, she may die," Katarina said.

"You must let her go," he said. "Have a little faith. Faith is all that is left to us. Live for today and rise above the rest. We are together. Make the day count."

"How can I let her ride free through the countryside when there is so much danger out there?"

"The child is better-equipped to handle this situation than you think."

"You have so much faith in her prowess," she said.

"I know what she is capable of. She is a thinker. She is clever. She knows this area better than you or I."

"What happens if they find her?" Katarina said. "What will they do to her?"

"Sometimes we have to believe we are safe. We cannot live in constant terror."

"Are you playing the brave soldier for my benefit?" Katarina said in jest. "I am not convinced."

Herr Tucher smiled. "Katarina, I have searched my whole life for some semblance of peace and purpose. I have found it, funnily enough, in this farm, in you, and in my relationship with this child. Isabeau has been the tether grounding you and I and our little family. My easy relationship with Isabeau has helped me to forge a relationship with my own children I would not have had. As sketchy as that relationship is."

"I fear for Isabeau like I have never feared for myself." Danger seemed to roll off Isabeau's back, Katarina thought, as she watched her clean her mare's hooves.

"That is what it is like, having children. I fear for my children too. This is something I must address. I have to think of my children."

"Why don't you bring them out here for the summer again?" Katarina thought about the soldiers coming and going. "I am sorry. I see the dilemma. I would understand if you felt you had to go back to the city."

"This dilemma plagues me the whole time. And I would only leave here with you. We, you and I, Katarina, and Isabeau, must give this some serious thought. It is not something we want to think about but we may have to look into it. Though I hate to give up our freedom, if freedom is being attacked every other week."

Isabeau slung her mare's reins over her shoulder and walked towards them. Katarina was again torn. The girl was rash and compulsive but she admired the girl's casual indifference. Katarina was also envious, of Isabeau's youth, of her courage and her determination.

"*Sonntagskind*," Katarina said. "Lucky child always seems to land on her feet. Like a kitten, you say?"

"I thought she was born on a Monday," Herr Tucher said. "She possesses a sort of greatness. I expect her to do something remarkable in her life."

Isabeau passed by and went into the house. Katarina could only see a headstrong child, too reckless and daring. If that was greatness, it was better kept under wraps. Now that she was older, she'd perfected the indignant stare of her father, as well as his gruff manner. Being a young girl, Katarina thought Isabeau should keep her head down and away from the eye of the community.

Isabeau still didn't know Hans-Wolfgang von Untereierhofen was her father. He had visited the farm sporadically over the years but had never confronted her or even talked to her directly. Katarina tried to remember when she saw Hans-Wolfgang last. Had the soldiers sacked the Eierhofen estate? Was he even still in the area? She didn't even know if he was alive. She would ask one of the farm hands if they knew anything.

Last spring, Hans-Wolfgang gave Isabeau a three-year-old sorrel mare much like the stallion he rode. Hans-Wolfgang had given Isabeau anonymous presents through Katarina before. He'd felt the time had come for Isabeau to have her own horse. She named the mare Crone, loved her more than any other being and spent most of her time taking care of her, when she wasn't in the lessons Herr Tucher insisted on giving her. Tanner the Elder helped her to train Crone. She'd begun to ride and the more she learned the scope of her physical strength, the more risks she was willing to take. Katarina had trouble holding her down. She was only nine!

The sound of hooves pounding up the track made both Herr Tucher and Katarina turn and look towards the approaching rider. Katarina recognized the messenger who frequently delivered news from Nuremberg. Herr Tucher went to meet the messenger. Herr Tucher would sort out the world and she would sort out that child.

Chapter 9

Ralf

Ralf leaned his weight up against the whitewashed wall outside Widow Braun's kitchen window. Lime rubbed off the wall and onto his black monk's robe. He cursed as he pushed away from the wall and tried to brush the white, oily substance from his shoulder. The bells from the Obere Pfarre sounded the midday hour. From his standpoint outside Widow Braun's house, he could see the bell tower. The bells of Bamberg's Cathedral joined in now too. The voices in Widow Braun's kitchen rose over the pealing bells and Ralf honed in on the conversation.

"Here, Eva, drink this," Widow Braun said, her voice scratchy. "This will fix you right up."

Ralf heard the little girl he had met on the market as she coughed.

"We need something for our Oma as well." Ralf recognized the older boy's voice. "Her cough is worse than Eva's."

"How much money do you have?" Widow Braun asked. "How is your Oma's belly? Did you give her the tea I sent last week? Look at this, I bet your Oma wants one of these too."

Ralf would wager his evening portion of dry bread and water that Widow Braun's 'one-of-these' was a talisman the widow wanted to sell to the boy along with those witch's brews she made of herbs and God-knows-what-else. He strained to look through the window and remain hidden. The bells of St. Stephan's added their opinion on the matter, as if they protested the widow's actions. Her heathen transactions, conducted under the shadow of these mighty churches, mocked this sacred ground. This district of Bamberg was under the immunity of the church and outside the authority of the town proper. And all the properties in these immune districts were coveted by those who wanted to escape the town's tax laws, as well as by the church fathers for their favorites. Ralf promised the commission he would get Widow Braun out of this house and off this land.

69

Chairs scraped on the wooden floor of Widow Braun's kitchen. Chatter between the diverse voices signaled the meeting was breaking up and they would be coming out now. Ralf was waiting for them along with his four black-robed comrades, his Soldiers of God. Ralf motioned to them to prepare for the onslaught. The door opened. The house began to empty. Ralf's students pounced.

The first three to exit Widow Braun's house were the two boys and the girl who looked tattier than before. They fell into the arms of Ralf's two sturdy students, the brothers Karl and Konrad. Karl struggled to keep the three squirming children together and Konrad had them quickly under control. The two students tied the children's hands and then bound them to one another. Ralf pushed his way past the throbbing entity and entered the house. The place smelled of peppermint and anise. A figure bolted from the kitchen and ran to the steps. A rush of excitement filled him as he recognized the green skirt swishing around the stairwell.

"I'll get her, Father," Martin said.

"Leave my Klara alone!" Widow Braun cried.

"She is just as guilty," Michel said and ran after her up the steps.

Ralf heard Michel stomping along the upstairs rooms and scuffling. Klara squealed.

"Bring her down and tie her with the others," Konrad hollered up the steps.

The two scuffled down the steps and Konrad grabbed her. "Ow, she bit me!" Konrad said and shook Klara as he led her out of the house.

Ralf had hoped Klara would not be here today. He wanted to save Klara, not arrest her, confine her to the Old Court or denounce her.

Ralf rounded on Widow Braun in the kitchen. "I will personally take care of you, Widow Braun. What happens to Klara is your fault. You should have tried to lead her down a more chaste path."

Widow Braun stammered and crossed herself. "Father Ralf, please, you know you are mistaken."

Ralf appraised the kitchen and looked out the window. "And you profess to being a Christian. We cannot have you selling herbs and talismans under the guise of helping these children, Widow Braun. The first and best defense against sickness is a thorough and extensive confession. The second is to attend mass! Their hope must lie alone with God in order to fight this evil."

"These children are sick, not evil!" Widow Braun looked up at him. "Eva, her brothers and their Oma. Klara and I want to help them! That cough, the lice. Their Oma was almost dead because of the bloody flux. Those teas, they're herbs. The devil would never teach us to use herbs to heal. They help us."

"The devil knows all about those herbs and their effects. He uses your bodies to further damage your souls." Ralf pitied the woman for her gullible nature. He laid his hand on her shoulder like an understanding brother. "You do see you are the one prolonging these maladies. You cannot fight against the Demon. We have evidence to the fact you have been seen in the Hauptmoorwald forest at certain festivities with Satan. With your neighbor, Frau Schüster. She told us everything. You lead those three children, and Klara, to ruin. I feel you have lost your way and lead the others astray."

"I've done nothing," she said.

"Frau Schüster told us everything. She told us those boys were playing the flutes. She told us what you all ate and drank. She watched you have intercourse with Satan after which you forced Klara to engage in sodomy with him."

Ralf crossed himself and walked out of the kitchen. As much as he wanted to educate these people, he feared his path would lead him to a futile war on heresy and evil, a fight with no end. These simple, susceptible souls were easily tempted by the devil and they needed cleansing. He wanted to help these poor, thick-brained farmers and peasants and those women! There were simpletons who were seduced by the path of sin and debauchery, even though the Bishop Friedrich Förner offered instruction on how to heal their devilish diseases in his fiery, informative and sincere sermons. But some refused to heal themselves. They lacked faith. When the day of judgment came upon them, they would go weeping into the fire! The righteous would shine like the sun.

But what if the day of judgment came and the devil prevailed? What if the devil viewed all of Bamberg as his realm; the whole of Franconia, guilty? Ralf could not let that happen. He would save these people from themselves. The only way to do that was for men like Ralf to drive the devil from those fallen souls. With force. With fire.

He nodded to his Soldiers of God. "Get the widow. Take them all to the Old Court. I must report this arrest to Dr. Fuchs. He wants to question them himself. We will meet you there."

Ralf hastened down the hill away from the Domplatz, across the left arm of the river Regnitz towards the Schloss Geyerworth, the residence of his Princely Grace, the Prince-Bishop Fuchs von Dornheim. Together, Bishop Förner and Prince-Bishop von Dornheim would stop this pestilence of evil; together with prudent men like Ralf and his students of the Jesuit school.

Ralf broke into a run when he saw Dr. Fuchs outside the Schloss Geyerworth. Dr. Fuchs conversed in pleasant discourse with a group of men of his standing, all of them dressed in black. He hailed Ralf towards the group.

"Father Ralf, good day to you." Dr. Fuchs extended his hand.

Ralf took Dr. Fuchs' hand, nodded his greeting and scrutinized the group. Two younger men who belonged to the witch commission congregated around Dr. Fuchs with three other unfamiliar men. The ruffled collars they wore were haughty and uncalled for, Ralf thought, and then he softened his stare. They were all on the same side, interested in one goal.

"Ralf, these are our visitors from Ingolstadt," Dr. Fuchs said. "Dr. Stoltz and Dr. Haas…" The men nodded. "…and from Eichstätt, Dr. Schwarzkonz. They are to help us with those poor souls detained in Zeil. We have pressed the Prince-Bishop to allow us to process them quicker. The towers in Zeil are filling, every inch of the place has been converted to prison cells to detain these people. Why is the devil so active in Bamberg?"

"Surely all of Europe is suffering," Ralf said. "Only in Bamberg we have taken the challenge and we are fighting back!"

"Eichstätt is also full of witches," Dr. Schwarzkonz said. "We shall work more closely with the Prince-Bishop."

"We have now the permission to build here in Bamberg," Dr. Fuchs said. "As you and I were discussing, Ralf. Bishop Förner and His Grace Prince-Bishop von Dornheim have agreed to give us the land to build a witches' jail. Down by the city wall; the shooting range where the marksmen practice. Then we will have enough room for our *Drudenhaus*. We will show the devil he cannot win this war."

"Ah, yes, I have just arrested a new group who need to be seen to…" Father Ralf began.

Dr. Fuchs cut him off in mid-sentence. "Yes, our visitors can watch us work," he whispered. "We will join you as soon as we dismiss those soft-hearted city council members."

Dr. Fuchs nodded towards two men Ralf recognized from the city council who stood apart from the others, took his leave by clapping Ralf on the shoulders and returned to his visitors. Ralf pulled his black hood over his head and hurried across the bridge. He climbed the cobbled hill leading to the cathedral and crossed the Domplatz towards the Alte Hofhaltung, the Old Court, where his students had taken Widow Braun and the others. As he passed through the ornate stone gateway directly adjacent to the cathedral, into the Old Court's courtyard, the sound of Widow Braun's whimpering croaks and mutterings, punctuated by a man's shouts, filled his heart with purpose.

"That is the sound of a poor sinner who has not the strength or will to fight," Ralf said. "We shall free you."

Ralf swallowed an oath as he stepped in an apple of horse manure. Soft, warm and juicy, it squished in through the sole of his leaky boot. Karl and Konrad stood up straight when they saw Ralf marching across the courtyard. The other two students, Martin and Michel, approached after exiting the Old Court building from a side door.

"The commission will see us now, Father Ralf," Martin said.

Martin and Michel undid the chain that held the four prisoners to the wall. They led the four, their hands bound behind their backs and then bound together in a single file, towards the door they had just exited. Konrad led the widow by herself. As long as Ralf knew her, the widow was a well-to-do woman. One could even say a rich one. She was also known to sleep late on Sundays and often missed mass or came too late. This behavior was the breeding ground for misguidance.

Widow Braun lowered her head. Her legs wobbled and gave out. Konrad pulled the rope upward in an attempt to help her regain her footing but her legs were too weak. The widow hung suspended in the air, her arms wrenched at an unnatural angle behind her back. Ralf yanked on her tied hands but this only raised the painful angle of her arms. She screamed in agony.

Ralf bent to speak into the woman's ear. "Now old woman, we are only trying to help you. Stand now, the time is here for us to drive that devil out of you. Revel in the joy that you will be doing a great service for yourself and your community."

Ralf grabbed her under the arms, set her on her feet and they all entered the cool stone hallway. Their shuffling feet echoed off the walls and they stopped outside the interrogation room. The prisoners were made to stand along the wall between two tallow lamps hanging from hooks in the wall. Ralf's students took their leave.

"All the children did was come by and drink some tea and have a bit of bread," Widow Braun said, her whispers echoing. "I wanted them to help me beat my rugs out."

"Frau Schüster said you gave the children an elixir and she saw Satan himself come through the chimney," Ralf said.

The older boy spat, "You sent me there to buy those herbs. You never gave me the chicken even though I did what you told me."

Ralf smiled. "And you agreed wholeheartedly which shows me where your loyalties lie!"

"You told me this was to help my Oma," the younger boy said. "You told us we would get the Old Widow to give us tea and then we could all leave. All this talk about the devil is a laugh. Nobody believes it. Just a laugh."

"The devil is no laughing matter," Ralf said.

"There is no devil," Klara said. "You are the evil one, Father."

"I will attend to you alone, Klara," Ralf said. "After we deal with the widow, I will see you tonight."

"You just want the widow's property," Klara said. "That's what everyone around St. Stephan's is saying."

"Oh, are they now?" Ralf said. "Who is 'everyone' then? I'll get those names out of you. By the end of the day I'll have all those heretics in the St. Stephan's district. They will burn right alongside the widow!" Ralf would cleanse this city of nonbelievers and misguided lost lambs along with the heathen city council that surrounded them.

All of them entered the musty, damp interrogation room. Klara and the three children she was tied to were instructed to stand against the wall. Light came from one grated window close to the ceiling and a single lantern on a long, dark wooden table. Behind the table sat Dr. Fuchs, Dr. Schwartzkonz, Dr. Stoltz, the two men from the Witch Commission and an old man with a quill—the town's scribe. Ralf positioned himself next to the prisoners. He must watch them. He'd seen the violence when those possessed finally broke down and confessed they had consorted with the devil.

The executioner entered the interrogation room and stood next to a table with the tools of his trade, the instruments he would use in the *peinliche Befragung*. He showed the prisoners the instruments, thumb screws, the candle, and explained if they would not confess he would have to force them to speak by squeezing their thumbs until the blood oozed out from under the nails or by holding the burning candle under their arms. The winch with the rope, installed on the ceiling of the interrogation room, was used for reverse hanging. Ralf knew as soon as the winch was used on the old woman, they would all talk, especially Klara. Widow Braun was positioned in the middle of the room in front of the wooden table.

"Fredrike Braun, you have been denounced by the witch named Schüsterin," Dr. Fuchs announced. "She named you as one of the group at a fest with the devil in the Hauptmoorwald. Name the other participants and you will be allowed to repent your sins before your execution."

"None of this is true," Widow Braun said.

"Satan has you full in his grip, my dear woman," Dr. Fuchs said. "We are prepared to break that grip. Executioner, show her the winch."

The executioner demonstrated how he intended to attach her bound hands to the rope and pull her arms behind her back, towards the ceiling, causing her shoulders to dislocate. Ralf had seen him pull prisoners up to the ceiling and allow them to drop.

"There is no devil," Widow Braun said. "This is all wrong."

"I have no time for this," Dr. Fuchs said and motioned to the executioner.

Widow Braun whimpered. "It wasn't me. That woman who was here selling cloth. She came with a man from Herzogenaurach."

"Yes? And who was he? The devil himself?" Dr. Schwarzkonz said. "We detained a traveling merchant in Eichstätt who sold cursed artifacts and mandrake root, fabrics that smelled of sulfur."

"Did you buy fabrics from this man?" Dr. Fuchs asked. "What else did you buy?"

"Search her house!" Ralf said. "We will take everything we can find."

"And you were engaged in this feast with these people and the devil in the Hauptmoorwald?" Dr. Fuchs continued.

Klara fought against her restraints. "This is ridiculous! Do you men hear yourselves?"

"Silence that witch!" Dr. Fuchs said. "Say it, Widow Braun. Was that man a messenger of Satan? Tell us your true persuasion. Slowly, so we all can hear you."

Widow Braun lowered her head. Klara cursed, a whisper that sounded like a sneeze. Dr. Fuchs nodded to the executioner. He attached the rope to Widow Braun's tied hands. He turned the handle of the winch and her arms were pulled behind her back and upward.

"Stop!" Klara yelled.

Widow Braun's legs gave out again as her arms were pulled towards the ceiling. Her shoulders responded with a snap and a pop. A shiver shook Ralf and he crossed himself, wary of any spiritual onslaught.

"Are you consorting with the devil?" Ralf yelled.

"Please stop," Widow Braun croaked.

"Enough!" Klara yelled.

"It was those women," Widow Braun whispered.

"Tell me everything," Ralf said.

"Please let me down," whimpered Widow Braun.

"Tell me!" Ralf hollered.

"At the market. They were here with the cloth trader," Widow Braun said. "That man who was here last week. A man called Ziegler. He came from Herzogenaurach. He stopped by Höchstadt first, then they brought their wares here."

"We need to check the clergy out there in the province," Dr. Fuchs said. "I've had my doubts about them. Who is that *Amtmann* who is in league with the Protestant heretics? We need to keep an eye on him as well."

"Von Seckendorff," the scribe said.

"Who else came to the fest besides this Ziegler and his women?" Dr. Fuchs screamed. "Was it von Seckendorff?"

The widow whispered something and nodded her head to the affirmative. Ralf rushed to her side and held his ear to her mouth. Her breath smelled sour with a twinge of alcohol.

"She said she is a witch and was with the Amtmann von Seckendorff."

Dr. Fuchs nodded, satisfied. "Ralf, you must travel there and find this cloth trader. And plan on staying a few days. Pay the *Amtmann* a visit."

"I'd thought these areas were void of witchcraft. But, yes, we will travel there. That area is very vulnerable, so close to Nuremberg. My men and I will go to Herzogenaurach."

Chapter 10

Pieter van Diemen

Pieter rode through the Thuringian Forest in what he hoped was a southernly direction. These last days of the journey, the fog was so thick he'd lost his orientation. Navigating this landscape of hills and valleys was difficult as it was. Lost, frustrated and thirsty, he resigned to follow a downward path through the trees, hoping the splashing he heard was a river. He dismounted and led the horse over exposed roots down the steep, muddy path. Pieter also heard voices. On the bank of a wide river, a road-worn band of stragglers refreshed themselves. The water swirled and burbled. Pieter and the horse gratefully sunk their heads and slurped the cold, fresh water.

"Heading west, young man?" the largest man in the band said.

"South," Pieter said, wary and cautious.

"You've gone too far east. This is the Saale river," the man said. "Come with us. We'll set you on the right road."

Pieter walked beside the horse for a spell and talked with the stragglers. The man pointed Pieter towards the old pilgrims' road called Via Regia, leading south-west and to Erfurt.

"Be careful not to head north on this road," the man said. "You'll only end up back in Magdeburg. In this fog, it's easy to lose your way!"

"Thank you for your trouble," Pieter said, remembering his manners.

"Why you would want to go south?" the man asked. "We came from the south, from the war. South Germany is flat and perfect for marching soldiers and rolling canons. It's a great place to wage war but not a good place to travel these days."

Pieter took his leave and rode on the Via Regia fast and hard. It was dark by the time he reached Erfurt so he rode close behind some travelers. Two coaches of noisy merchants led him to an inn. He fell in with their group and they invited him to join them for a late meal. They asked him if he was caught up in the unrest around Magdeburg. Pieter smiled and shook his head, feigning ignorance, allowing the chatty men to talk. They were generous with their wine and as they drank, they became increasingly careless. The merchants argued about the blasphemous heretics, the bleeding papists and laughed about the latest printed caricatures of Pope Urban VIII and the Elector of Bavaria, Maximillian I. They traded stories about the Generals Wallenstein and Mansfeld. The two great generals were both lovers of astrology and the merchants doubted the stars would save their lives. As the night wore on, the drunk merchants took bets as to where the two generals would clash; Dessau Bridge being the most strategic location, in their opinions.

Pieter thanked his ghosts he had left his banner before the slaughter began. And a slaughter it would be. In a battle of this magnitude, there was never a winner. He observed the men, keeping quiet, barely sipping his wine, waiting for them to completely lose their facilities.

Having drunk no more than a few sips of wine paid off in the end. One by one, the merchants laid their heads on the table of the inn's common room, snoring contentedly, bellies full of roast boar and red wine, their faces flush from the crackling fire. Their purses and their bodies unattended, Pieter made his rounds and helped himself to a small donation from each man. He lifted just enough coins to pay for the inn and then some and left Erfurt as the first light appeared.

He chose the main southerly road he'd heard would take him to Coburg and then on to Nuremberg. There was some unrest in Franconia, the merchants had said, but a broad-shouldered *Kerl* like him shouldn't be worried. He noticed the road took a distinct decline out of the mountains. The air warmed as he descended to milder elevations. At least it wasn't raining. Approaching the Protestant city of Coburg from the north, he could see the Veste, the castle on top of the mountain. Wanting to stay under cover, he again took to the trees.

Before he saw them, he recognized the sound of the troops, cutting through the peace of the forest like a slow-moving devil of destruction. The muttered speech of marching men; grunting, coughing and swearing; the clang of metal; creaking, rolling wheels of disaster. Pieter slowed, judging them to be directly ahead on the road to Coburg. Wanting to get away from the troops as fast as he could, he kicked his horse into motion and took a turn down a narrow path that led him away in a westerly direction. He cursed when the clear creek he rode next to ended in the middle of a swampy patch of trees. The sun was setting and the sky was overcast with heavy clouds. Between the tree trunks, eerie plays of light and dark unnerved him. Pieter had lost his orientation again and was lost.

Distinct voices echoed up ahead among the trees. He saw bobbing lanterns and slowed the horse to a walk. Just on the other side of the swampy patch, squeaky wagon wheels plodded along the path and the sound of a man's '*Brrr*' meant someone just brought a horse to a halt. These were no soldiers. Chains clanked against wood as the wheels of the *Fuhrwerk* came to a standstill. Pieter smelled wood smoke and cooking onions. Firelight illuminated a clearing. He dismounted and picked a path around the boggy vegetation, towards the sound. There must be an inn or a private home in that clearing. Maybe he should stop and ask where he was and how far away he was from Nuremberg. He hoped he could beg some food and maybe even find parchment and someone who would deliver a letter.

These long rides offered the opportunity to compose letters in his head. Pieter thought about Johannes and what he would like to tell him about his journey. Johannes was a good man but he was not willing to risk deserting with Pieter. He said he'd found his place and he wanted to die in battle. Johannes said he was happy with a drink and a bite of bread, maybe some meat. Pieter also thought about what he would say to Herr Tucher. Pieter felt he should pen him a letter to warn him he was on his way. He hoped he would be welcome if and when he appeared at Sichardtshof. Herr Tucher might reprimand him but he would not stay angry.

Pieter hid behind a tree just out of the light from the small fire. He could see the front of the house and the small traveling party prepared to disembark from the *Fuhrwerk*. A man dressed in black conversed with the cart driver who sat on the coach box huddled in a heavy brown cloak. The man in black then helped a young woman and a younger girl climb down from the cart. The little girl was covered in a brown blanket and shivered in the chilly night air. She yammered about sitting on the back of the open wagon and being cold. Pieter kept to the trees and waited until they went into the house.

He tied his horse to a tree and walked around the house. It was a private house by the way it looked. He could smell other types of smoke now, sage and lavender. Amulets and odd figurines hung from the trees and around the front door and the tiny windows. He wondered if this was maybe the house of a healer, of a holy person or a witch.

He checked the barn and it was locked. His choices were to break into the barn and have a rest, to sit out here all night with his horse or to knock on the door and see if he could beg some food. He decided on the latter, swallowed his pride and knocked on the door. The conversation inside diminished to whispers and he heard the swishing of uncertain movements, as if someone tried to cover up what they were doing.

"Hey there, I am a lone traveler who seeks refuge for the night," Pieter said at a low level. "Please allow me to beg some food. I am fit to do some work to pay for my keep."

The door opened and the man dressed in brown, the cart driver, surveyed Pieter. "You're not from around here?"

"No, I've been driven away from my home in Holland and I've ended up here."

"He looks like a solider," the man in black said.

"He means no harm." An old woman appeared from behind them. "He's trouble but not for us. He's someone else's trouble."

"Where am I?" Pieter asked.

"We are close to Zeil," the old woman said. "Much too close to Bamberg, I am afraid."

"Ah, I made good time today," Pieter said.

The cart driver stood aside. Pieter had to duck to enter the hut. The old woman sat down by the fire and tended the little girl. She was sickly thin and coughing, her skin a greenish-yellow pallor. The other woman stood by with the concerned look of a mother. The two men took their places at a tiny table and got down to spooning thin, lumpy, oniony-smelling gruel from wooden bowls. The ceiling was so low Pieter had to slump. Together, the fireplace, the small table, shelves with ceramic clay pots, bundles of drying herbs hanging to dry and five people filled out the room. A door led away from the main room and Pieter assumed there were sleeping quarters in there. The cart driver in brown finished eating, stood and offered Pieter his seat. The concerned mother filled a bowl for Pieter and set it down in front of him.

"I can help you in the morning, old woman. I can chop wood," Pieter said, between mouthfuls. This was the best onion gruel he had ever eaten.

"You can help me tonight. There is enough light in the barn with a lantern to chop wood. You can sleep there tonight as well."

Pieter held his bowl up, the mother filled it again and he emptied it in a few mouthfuls. The old woman lit a lantern and nodded for him to follow her. She led him out to the tiny barn, hung the lantern on a hook and handed him the axe. Pieter began to split logs. After he'd made good progress, he heard voices coming from the woods. Under cover, Pieter watched three men on foot approach the house. One man carried a torch. The other led a horse and tethered him to a tree. They made no secret of their ill intentions.

The third man bashed on the door. "Open I say! Let us in!"

Pieter peeked around the corner of the house. The man with the torch waited by the door while the other two thugs entered the house.

"Fräulein Ursula Wagenpfeil," the man boomed from inside the house. "You are to be detained for the crime of Witchcraft."

The old woman raised her voice and said two words: "Get out!"

Pieter could hear the man's voice, nasty and muffled, clear and menacing. "Witch commission…from Zeil. That little girl…devil's daughter…denounce…evil…"

The front door closed and some arguing ensued. Pieter felt his anger rising. These men had no right to barge in here. He hated what they stood for. The old woman and her people had been nice to Pieter. He sneaked around to the tethered horse and pinched his flanks. The horse squealed and jumped to the side. Being on a short tether, this further irritated the horse because he couldn't get away from Pieter. The torch holder moved towards the horse but the burning torch further agitated the animal. The man laid the torch by the small fire and returned to the horse. Pieter grabbed the man, dragged him out of the firelight into the swampy patch of trees. A short burst of regret for what he was about to do made Pieter shake his head at what the world was coming to. He pulled his dagger from its sheath, turned the man to face away from him and cut the man's throat. He booted the man away and walked towards the house.

The door flung open and the two thugs struggled with the squirming Fräulein Wagenpfeil. Pieter wondered how those two thugs could possibly get away with detaining the young girl. His two dinner companions hung back, unable or unwilling to fight. Pieter sensed they needed someone to take control of the situation. Seeing how he was the largest of the men, a delight rose in him, one he'd not felt in a long time. He grabbed the one thug and punched him—he was to pay for every time Pieter had been wronged. He felt a twinge of guilt as the man's nose crumbled under the impact. Pieter grabbed the second man, dragged him to where he'd dealt with the torch holder and took care of him in the same manner. He then returned to the house, pulled the man with the broken nose outside, finished him off and let him lay where he fell.

He faced his two dinner companions. "There's a bog back there. Bind their bodies and sink them with stones. I'll take their horse and you can have mine. No one will be the wiser. I'm going to get some sleep."

"We should thank you," Fräulein Wagenpfeil's mother said.

"I need to pen a letter," Pieter said. "If you could deliver it for me, I would be grateful."

Chapter 11

Katarina

After days of sitting in the house, Katarina finished combing the next to the last sack of wool. The dull daylight in the kitchen had faded to a dark gray and she found herself in darkness. Pulling her shawl around her shoulders, she walked to the fire. The door from the paddock to the stable was still missing. As she stirred the embers she could hear Herr Tucher quietly conversing with Tanner the Elder. The two men said their good nights.

Katarina dragged the combed sack of wool back into the alcove, pulled out the next sack of raw wool, dragged that back to the kitchen and let it fall by the table. Shadows leaped and turned as she lit a tallow lamp and walked towards the now-empty stable. Lamp light flickered off the low-vaulted ceiling. Cold, damp March air streamed into the kitchen and the lamp almost blew out. She hung the lamp on the hook by the stable door. Katarina was sorry about the goat. Her name was Blume and Katarina had her for four years now. Blume was smarter than any of those soldiers and had not deserved such a demise.

Katarina closed the flimsy, provisional door from the kitchen to the stable. At least it held back the draft. Herr Tucher's light footsteps sounded down the stone stairs. He entered the kitchen holding a crate filled with books. These last few weeks had etched deep frown lines on his brow. His trouser leg was torn at the knee and his boots were muddy. He set the crate down next to the hearth and rubbed his face with dirty, scraped and bleeding hands.

"Even though our meager possessions are buried, here are a few things I was waiting to put away. I do not want anyone getting their hands on these, Katarina. You must promise me, if anything happens to me, you will burn my journal. There is too much information. If in the wrong hands…"

"It's all personal notes," Katarina said. "Why would that be of interest to anyone?"

"I do not want to be the link to my family. I have noted many of my business dealings in the journal. And I am not ready for my personal affairs to be public knowledge."

Katarina fetched a rag, dipped it in the warm pot of washing water that stood behind the fire and dribbled some tincture from a ceramic flask onto it. She took his hands and cleaned the blood from his palms.

"Many of the views I have expressed in that book over the years are not popular opinion," he said. "Maybe we should burn this at once."

She finished cleaning his hands and let them fall. Herr Tucher rubbed them together, kissed Katarina on the cheek and whispered his thanks. He grabbed the journal from the top of the crate, sat down at the table and opened the book. Katarina took the bottle of wine from the table and filled two cups. She handed him one and she sipped at the sour wine. Isabeau came back into the kitchen, dressed in breeches and an outdoor woolen smock. She kicked her boots off under the table as Katarina handed her a cup of tea.

"Is your horse snug for the night?" Herr Tucher asked her.

Without a word, Isabeau sat on her chair, set the cup down, grabbed her boots from under the table and pulled them on.

"Where are you going child?" Katarina said.

"I'm going out to Crone," Isabeau said.

"Oh no, you're not!" Katarina said. "You're staying inside tonight."

"No, I'm sleeping with my horse. I don't want anyone to take her again." She marched towards the stable door.

Katarina reached the door first and blocked her path. They stood eye to eye. In a few years Isabeau would tower over her.

"Let me by," Isabeau growled. She grabbed the ceramic cup of wine out of Katarina's hand and smashed it on the ground. She slipped under Katarina's arm, threw the flimsy door open and rushed out of the kitchen, into the stable and out into the yard.

"I'm sorry, Katarina," Herr Tucher said. "That was my fault."

Katarina sighed as she closed the door again. "What am I supposed to do with her?"

"She does not mean any harm," he said. "Don't take her too seriously."

"She's exhausting, that child."

"Be happy you have her here with you." He tore some bread from the loaf and shoved a small bit into his mouth. "I'm worried about my children."

"Have you decided what to do with them?" Katarina said.

He swallowed his bread. "I am not so sure where the best place for any of us is. I'm worried about the hordes of people coming from all over and pushing their way into Nuremberg. The religious tolerance of the city drives them there. There is not enough to feed them all. And the diseases they bring are running rampant."

"Maybe it is time to leave here," Katarina said.

"I cannot say if we would be any safer if we traveled abroad. The way is filled with as many dangers. I intend to stay here, until we are forced to leave at a moment's notice. For myself, the right decision." He closed the journal. "I don't have the heart to burn this. It is the story of our decade. May I leave the decision with you?" He stood and looked towards the door, an uncomfortable expression on his face, like he struggled with something. Without turning back, he said, "Yes, I have decided. The children will come from Nuremberg. To stay for a longer period this time. There may be more people coming this time as well."

His uncle Paul had come many times and stayed. He was a good man and popular with the other workers. He could drink with the best of the men and he could sing. Thankfully, Herr Tucher's wife would not want to come here. She had accompanied Herr Tucher's two boys on their yearly journey to Sichardtshof and left them here so they could stay longer. The older boy, Christoph, who was the same age as Isabeau, had spent whole summers at Sichardtshof. Frau Tucher hated the country, she'd said that much, and thought she deserved to be at court in Paris or London or someplace similarly noble. On the very few occasions she spent a few nights here, she needed to be waited on hand and foot.

"Katarina, it may be a bit of a squeeze in the house, but we should manage," Herr Tucher said. "I'm trying to decide on the best time to move them so they don't meet any hostile troops."

Herr Tucher walked through the doorway, his light footsteps climbing the stairs. Katarina took another ceramic cup off the shelf and poured it full of wine. She took a sip and bent to pick up the shards of ceramic laying on the stone floor. Should she go out, confront that child, bring her back here and send her to bed? She dropped the shards into an empty bucket and they thudded on the wooden bottom. She threw a log on the fire with a bit too much fervor. Sparks crackled and flew up in a cloud of black smoke. She grabbed her cup, the journal and another little book from the top of the crate. Exhausted, she sat down by the fire, sipped the wine and her body slumped.

Katarina recognized both books. She riffled through the pages of the little book Herr Tucher scribbled his notes into. It contained a messy, almost indiscernible smear of letters, drawings and dates, numbers. Katarina set it aside and opened the journal. Turning to the first page, she read the title: *The Journal of Sebaldus Novellus*. She thumbed through the pages filled with his fine-flowing script. Katarina had only looked in here once before. The entries were all uniformly spaced with few corrections. She turned to the last page. This entry was new, from the day before the soldiers came this last time. The book was now full.

Katarina paged back through the book, slowly now. She saw her name. Often. She flipped backwards again, towards the beginning. Tanner. Falk. Pieter. Another name came up. Isabeau. He seemed to enjoy teaching the girl to read. She was a bright child and soaked up facts and verse like a dry towel.

"She's in the barn again, Katarina," Tanner the Elder said.

Katarina jumped, not having heard him come into the kitchen. She closed the journal, leaving her finger in between the pages to mark her spot.

He took off his hat and smoothed his graying hair. "Would you like me to bring her back in?"

"Yes, please." Katarina attempted a weary smile.

She opened the journal again and read his thoughts about Isabeau. He mentioned the strange look Isabeau had in her eyes, like she saw unfocused images they could not. As a small child, she had a habit of looking through them in a disregarding way. Back then, she was an uncomplicated child, cooperative, quiet and helpful, even loving in her own composed manner.

Isabeau came in the door with a sour look on her face.

"I'm hungry," she said.

"Stay here tonight, Isabeau, it's not safe out there. Tanner's father will be in the barn. He has an eye on the horses."

She nodded and pulled a hunk of bread off the round loaf and stuffed it in her mouth. Katarina spooned some thick soured milk into a wooden bowl, set it on the table in front of her and sunk a spoon in the creamy mass.

"This is the last of the milk. You have it."

Isabeau spooned the thick milk into her mouth and dunked the bread into the bowl with the other hand.

"We're getting more visitors," Katarina said.

Isabeau bit off a mouthful of bread.

Katarina sipped her wine. "Christoph is coming to live here."

"He's mean to me. I don't like him," Isabeau said, chewing and swallowing at the same time. She filled her mouth with thick milk and stared into her bowl with a scowl on her face. When she had finished, she stood and said, "Good night."

"Night," Katarina said.

Isabeau's feet padded on the stairs. The chicken ladder creaked as she climbed up to the garret rooms. Katarina walked into the little alcove, bent over the little wooden box, heaved it onto the straw sack mattress and opened the latch. She inhaled the heavy, musky-flowery scent and laid the little book with notes inside. It fit easily but the journal would not.

She rummaged in the box until she found the comb made of engraved bone from Herr Tucher. She pulled the leather cord holding her hair in a tight bun and combed through the knots. The last warm drops of oil dribbled into her hand as she tipped the flask. Herr Tucher told her this strange-smelling oil from some far-off land would ward the moths off the wool. She loved this smell and worked the dark, musky scent through her hair.

The aroma of the strange flower brought Katarina clarity and calm. She counted her blessings. Isabeau was in the house and in her bed. Katarina could rest assured, at least this evening, knowing the child was safe. Herr Tucher had gone to his room. She would join him in a moment. This night could be their last one. How long could they survive this madness? She poured some more wine, took the journal and sat by the fire. The journal opened and she read a passage Herr Tucher had written about how he hated to sleep for fear of wasting what little time he had.

Katarina, too, wanted to fill every moment she had. There was no insurance, no guarantee. Life was a roll of the dice. And there was nothing she could do to change that. The need to reminisce all the twists and turns of the last ten years saddened her. She wished she had appreciated the moments as they came and suddenly realized the worth, no, the pricelessness of this journal. She turned the page and read an entry from 1618:

May 1618

Today marks the second anniversary of my life at the Sichardtshof farm. And what a fine time of year to be in the countryside. I sit next to the open window and play a guessing game: identify the smells wafting on the May breeze. I can smell, of course, manure, but there are different types of that too. I can smell sheep and I can smell horse and cow. They all smell different.

Two elder bushes grow outside my window. They have just begun to bloom and they are quite early. We had some unseasonably warm days in April. After a cold bitter winter, any warmth is welcome. The perfume from the delicate blossoms makes my heart soar. Soon every drink and meal will be augmented with the scent and the flavor. Outside the window, a slight breeze rearranges dry straw into piles along the walls of the outbuildings. A horse snorts. A blackbird sings. Isabeau cries.

She is now two years old, that is to say she was abandoned here two years ago. I am by no means an authority on judging a youngling's age. But a strange child she is. She speaks with two and three-word sentences but her choice of words is interesting. Isabeau is not what I expect from a baby girl. She walks and runs and is underway around the farm much of the day. She can climb and my heart stands still to see how high she tries to go. She will also sit for long periods in the barn with the horses and play with straw. She has no fear of the animals and they accept her there like a welcome colleague. What can she say? 'Ride horse.' 'Shear sheep.' 'Feed dog.' 'Kata come here. Kata do this. Kata do that. Kata Kata Kata! Hold me. Carry me.'

I have never been so close to a growing baby before. My son is reared by the nursemaid and my wife keeps herself and the child contained to her wing of the house. I spend little time at the Nuremberg house as it is. I assume that is the accepted practice. I barely knew my father. He had little part in my upbringing and just as little in my mother's life.

When Uncle Paul first brought my intended wife to meet me, he referred to her as the impeccable Fräulein Imhoff, daughter of the powerful Nuremberg merchant, the family made rich from the saffron trade. Paul does try to humor me still with wine and money because I agreed to the arranged marriage with this impeccable young woman. The wonderful connections we sealed by uniting these two families! The opportunities it has brought to the Tucher family! And we have a son! My work, complete, like that of a prize stallion.

The impeccable woman was expected for an extended visit to Sichardtshof this month for the first time. She arrived last week. She exited her carriage with a flourish. I greeted her with a kiss on the cheek. She took one look around the farm, pressed Christoph's hand in mine. (He is only one and a half years old and just beginning to walk securely. Now that I think about it, not at all comparable to the deft and developed Isabeau.) My impeccable wife climbed back into her coach and signaled to the driver she was ready to leave. Away they went, leaving the boy and myself, staring, mouths agape!

Katarina came out and took the boy into the kitchen and made honey cakes with him, taught him to milk the goat and kept him happy all day.

Paul informed me that a long-standing acquaintance and business partner of his from Venice has offered his home to those of the Tucher family that travel abroad. He has a residence in Venice as well as London and would open his home at any time to us. I make the note here so as not to forget it. I spent time in London last year for a short period and I believe London would better suit my wife's tastes. I hope this is accepted practice. I have no understanding of the accepted practices for many things. My mind retains such unnecessary thoughts unwillingly. Those dictated codes of conduct and secret unspoken laws of behavior elude me.

I received a letter from Pieter van Diemen just the other day. Heavy my heart, his father has died. Long were we business partners, acquaintances, friends. What a good man. Pieter is preparing for a voyage to the far east. Slowly the world becomes smaller. Uncharted waters are no longer a mystery. Where we only before got word of other parts of the world, we now have settlements. Where we only had word of mouth, we now have regular post and newspapers. Where we could only rely on the church for information, we have the documents of noted thinkers and intellectuals. Though we must dispute the reliability of the content in all these documents, no matter who they come from.

Paul's hired men have been moved out to help with the unrest in and around Prague. The Holy Roman Empire is being challenged by the forces that would like to see the Catholic Church and its immorality and its decadent ways reformed. What began with the Czech scholar Jan Hus in the fifteenth century, an attempt to reform the Catholic Church, ended in his being burned at the stake. Martin Luther continued in the sixteenth century and ignited a spiritual fire in the German territories of the Empire. Nuremberg has been Protestant since 1535 and we were the first city-state in the Empire to declare ourselves Protestant. The Emperor wants to force us back into Catholicism. But that will never happen. Nuremberg is too great a city!

What started out as a bit of a struggle with doctrine will become a full fledged war. Catholicism is no longer a religious decision but a political one. Others in my circles do not believe me or do not want to see it. I stand accused the forever pessimist! Troops are congregating. Troops are moving and seem civil but how long will they be? The

Landsknecht Landsknecht *and their tradition and honor has long ceased to be the standard. Mercenary soldiers are poor and starving; badly trained men who have nothing to lose. They are blood thirsty and eager to get their hands on the spoils no matter what they do for it.*

And the meek shall suffer. I must protect what little I cherish. My meager farm. My dearest Katarina. I am unsure of the accepted practice (again!) but every man in my family has had a beloved. A woman who has truly stood by their sides, albeit in the shadows. I will always be completely unified with Katarina. All I want to do is walk up behind her in the kitchen, push her hair to the side and kiss her neck. I want to take her in my arms and hold her there forever. I want to kiss her until she is breathless. Love her until she is exhausted. She lives under my skin. I smell her scent on my skin all the time. I hear her voice when the wind blows. My greatest fear? That she will one day see through me for who I really am, a simple man not worthy of her love.

Chapter 12

Ralf

Ralf and his four Soldiers of God rolled their blankets together and covered all traces of their camp. They'd traveled yesterday from Bamberg on the way to Herzogenaurach and stopped when it became dark, spending the night in the woods outside Höchstadt, the half-distance point between Bamberg and Herzogenaurach. Höchstadt was not only an important Catholic outpost belonging to Bamberg but also close to the Upper Eierhofen estate Ralf had shared with Andra-Angela and her father all those years ago.

Konrad and Karl jumped up on the coach box. Ralf, Michel and Martin settled back onto the cart's wooden bed and Ralf pulled out his leather-bound travelling prayer book. Konrad snapped the reins, the old nag jerked into motion and the wagon creaked along. Ralf allowed the emotion to swell as the landscape of the region became more familiar. This area had been his home ten years earlier and he had not been back since. A chill ran up his spine when he thought about Andra-Angela. There'd been a baby. He wondered if the baby was still alive and living at Sichardtshof. She would be about ten years old now.

"I'd like to ask you something, Father." Michel shifted his position, obviously uncomfortable on the hard, wooden cart. "I've never spoken about this because I thought I was too young, but I'd like to ask. How old do we have to be to continue onto priesthood?"

Ralf was pleased the boy was interested. "I was barely twenty years old when I took the vows of the Jesuits. After I was found by Father Marius, God rest his soul, when I was fourteen, I studied at an accelerated pace. I know of no other who accomplished that. You need to complete your studies. There is a certain amount of years but that can be shortened with diligence and discipline. You and your brother are on the right road."

Michel fidgeted in his seat. "I never met Father Marius."

91

"He was a great man," Ralf said. "He was Brother Marius back then. He found me the day after my parents died. Brother Marius was poor, his cowl torn, his face dirty. He shared his last bread with me and took me to Würzburg, to the Jesuit monastery. They took me in and admitted me to the school there. I was younger than many of the other students but I studied harder than anyone. I owe everything to the Jesuits."

Bumbling along this road in this creaky old cart reminded him of his years at the Upper Eierhofen estate. He wanted to caution the boys against striving for personal gain. His own downfall had been the need for power and property. When he lived at the estate, he was young and dumb and was convinced that taking over the property was his destiny. He'd been self-centered, power hungry and suffered greatly for his lack of understanding. Yes, he would love to see the Upper Eierhofen estate again but it held a bittersweet memory. Andra-Angela was his charge, he let her die and his mishandling of the situation led to his ruin. But it was precisely this ruin that brought him to his life in Bamberg.

"And I have made mistakes," Ralf continued. "I hope you can benefit from my experiences. Although one should never question what God has in store for us. God knows what we need and we should be grateful for every drawback we come up against. These drawbacks are a test of our faith. It's God's way of seeing if we have faith at all."

Ralf wondered if he would ever live down the mistakes he made as a young man. What he would give to speak to Marius again. Marius would know what to say. He chastised himself for even wishing such things. There was no room for this senseless sentiment. Any amount of lamenting the past or wishing for a different future would only bring him eternal damnation. He would be no better than those who were mixing magic potions and burning herbs and dancing in the moonlight, praying to the devil to save their sorry souls.

His conviction was unwavering. His faith was steadfast. He had argued on many occasions with those who fought to prove their opinion because they had no real conviction. Because he resolutely believed in what he was doing, he had no need to defend his position. There was only his position. He was right.

"Allow me," Ralf said, opened his prayer book at random and read in Latin. "Plug your ears so you cannot hear the voice of the magician. Pay no attention to the siren song of the devil! The hatred of those women who make magic potions to try to heal people; they do this in God's name! God gave life and will take it away. However it pleases Him, so shall it be, praise the Lord!"

The cart gave a jerk and the nag danced to the side. Something had frightened the old gelding.

"*Ruhig*," Konrad whispered trying to calm the horse.

From the forest, another horse gave a whinny. The nag returned the call.

"Someone's coming," Karl said.

Ralf heard unshod hooves padding toward them at a lively tempo. A sorrel horse came into view. Atop the sorrel horse was a girl no older than ten years. Their presence on the road startled the girl, as if she'd not expected to see them. She pulled back on the reins and her horse jumped to a stop. The horse turned in a circle one time, the girl clicked her tongue and they shot away again into the forest. What a beautiful girl, Ralf thought, fair hair, stunning face, a ghost of Andra-Angela. His heart rose and fell in a crescendo that scared and intrigued him.

He would find out who that was.

Chapter 13

Pieter van Diemen

Pieter had lost count of the days. He'd left the old woman's house, got away from Zeil without further incident and headed south, hoping to reach Sichardtshof during the day. Because there were more comings and goings on the main thoroughfares and he was afraid of meeting up with more of those types he met in Zeil, he kept to the forest and the narrow footpaths. The disadvantage was he'd lost his bearings yet again. Today he would follow a wider road continuing south. As the terrain flattened, nothing looked familiar. He feared he'd gone too far south.

The air was noticeably warmer and now that the evening darkened, it started to rain. He needed to find cover. Pulling his hat down over his forehead, he slowed the horse to a walk. They were both exhausted from the day's ride, a lack of food and the rain. He should stay off such a main thoroughfare but tonight he hoped he could reach another town, maybe rob a passing merchant and sleep in a stable. He would not risk sleeping in a tavern.

The days were still too short for traveling. It was impossible to see with the rain blurring the already dark surroundings. He dipped his head and tried to concentrate on his way, looking from side to side for any place to take cover. The rain pounded even heavier. A muffled cracking sound and a shout caused the horse to grunt, toss his head and prance backwards. Pieter's weight slipped on the horse's wet hair.

Pieter regained his balance but with one jerk, the reins were torn from his grip. The surprise overwhelmed him. Pieter saw two, no, four men holding the reins and his reactions jammed. The men steered him away from the road. Without a word, they pulled Pieter off the horse. One man grabbed his sword. The other pulled the dagger from his belt. Two men led the horse away. The other two men bound Pieter's hands behind his back.

Pieter struggled against the restraints. His arm was forced into a painful angle. He bent forward, trying to throw the assailants off. His hat fell into the mud. Some blunt object slammed into Pieter's lower back. He blew out a great oath and turned his head, determined to see who restrained him. The two scruffy men with scraggly hair and tattered black hats, wearing mismatched bits of clothing decorated with colorful strips of cloth, seemed unsure of how to manage Pieter's large stature. He could further unnerve them with threats, he was sure.

"I'm going to kill you when I get out of this," Pieter said.

"That's why you're not getting out of this," the one fellow said in a strange northern German dialect. His black hat had a long red plume hanging down his back. Pieter's hair was pulled and he straightened. Rain splashed his face and his hair dripped water under his collar.

"Where are we going?" Pieter said.

"You're going to the Hauptmann," the man wearing the black hat with the red plume said.

The two men walked Pieter through the hedgerow into a camp set up in a circular fashion. The camp's outer circle was protected by musketeers standing watch behind heavy muskets supported on forks rammed into the earth. Other watchmen congregated next to spluttering torches and underneath shelters made of canvas sheets hung with bellies of water. Covered wagons with canvas sheets tied to them provided some shelter for the horses. Strong wooden wagons with provisions were watched by women and men in an array of colorful clothing. They passed by shabby tents that most undoubtedly housed the common foot soldiers; the entrances to the tents adorned with pikes and halberds.

Heads turned as they walked through the common center of the camp. Canvas sheets hung over a gaming area. Underneath the shelters, men sitting at tables rolled dice and tittered as Pieter walked by. Fires burned all around the main area. Pieter should have seen the fires from the road.

The two scruffy men took Pieter to a large tent standing on a high, celebrated area of the camp. Next to it, the company flag fluttered at the entrance of a lesser tent. Must be where the flag bearer slept. A fire burned outside in a pit and an iron tripod holding a heavy metal pot stood among the flames. Two men in official looking uniforms flanked the entrance to the tent. One threw a flap back and the two scruffy men pushed Pieter inside.

A man, almost as tall as Pieter, stood before him, straight and proud.

The man's face held an iron expression and small, strenuous dark-gray eyes. He took a long draught from a tin cup. A huff of breath ruffled his long, brown mustache, showing his full lips glistening with red wine. His cheeks were clean shaven except for the point of brown hair around his chin.

"Where are you coming from, young man?" said the man who Pieter assumed was the Hauptmann. He slammed the tin cup onto the table. "You look like a deserter."

"He's riding alone," said the man wearing the hat with the red plume.

"I have fled from Holland," Pieter said. "I am a farm hand and I am looking for work."

"He's lying," the man said and threw Pieter's sword and dagger on the table.

Pieter looked at the man with the red plume and memorized his face. He would pay for all of this. "My home was destroyed by Spanish soldiers," Pieter lied. "My family, killed by them. I am trying to get to Nuremberg."

"I have been around these decrepit wars long enough to know a soldier when I see one," the Hauptmann said. He filled his cup with wine, emptying the flask. "And you speak German and you speak Dutch. What other languages can you speak?"

"I speak English as well," Pieter said.

"You can read?"

Pieter nodded.

"Then you can write, too." He rubbed his chin and pointed to the man with the red plume. "Untie him. Bring me more wine."

The man with the red plume stood still on the spot. The Hauptmann barked at him and he slit the ropes around Pieter's wrists and scurried away. The Hauptmann motioned for Pieter to sit on a stool next to the table. He shoved a bowl containing a heel of bread towards him. Pieter grabbed it and bit off a chunk of dried bread.

"You, boy, are a liar but I can use you. None of my men can read. None of them are soldiers, either."

The man with the red plume came back with two flasks of wine and set them on the table.

"Just a mix of riffraff, ruffians and criminals," the Hauptmann said. "Like this bastard here."

The man grunted like a surprised dog and ran off with his tail between his legs.

"You fit right in," the Hauptmann said. He filled a second tin cup with wine and pushed it across the table towards Pieter. "My name is Schwartz."

"My name is Tanner," Pieter lied again.

"That a Dutch name, boy?" He snorted, leaned back and drank from his wine. "We are marching towards Holland. Under contract to the Catholic Emperor so we are fighting against those heretics of your land. We are to support a Spanish regiment and fight against your Prince of Orange." He emptied his wine cup. "But this is not a war of ethics, boy. We fight for the highest bidder, don't we? Whoever is giving us money."

"Where are we right now?" Pieter asked.

Hauptmann Schwartz hesitated, a sly, knowing grin widening that mustache. He pulled out a roll of parchment from under the table and unrolled it on the table. "We are here, traveling north along the Aisch River and should reach Höchstadt in a few days' time. We will join with von Wittenhorst's troops. They will go on to France and we will head north and join more men along the Elbe. We have a long march ahead of us."

What a spot of luck! It seemed Pieter *had* ridden too far south. No matter now, he could travel with them and defect when they reached Höchstadt.

The Hauptmann shoved his chair back, crossed the tent in two strides and stuck his head outside. "Send me those two Prussian bastards now," he roared.

The two scruffy soldiers from earlier pushed into the tent. The man with the red plume looked uncomfortable.

"You, scoundrel, will not survive the night," Pieter whispered.

"Eh? What's that, boy?" Hauptmann Schwartz said. "You will not flee tonight, Dutchman. These men will post a watch. You will report to me in the morning as soon as you are sober enough to put together a coherent sentence."

Hauptmann Schwartz stood aside. The two scruffy Prussian bastards flanked Pieter's chair, waiting until he stood and led him out of the tent. They approached the outer ring of tents. The rain had stopped. Small fires burned here and there in the open.

A main fire roared in front of a larger wagon packed with ten or so drunken men and women. Around the fire, a good fifty men and women drank and amused themselves. This was the *Tross*, the collection of soldiers' families, marketeers, prostitutes, refugees and stragglers who followed the main troop. Pieter had heard the *Tross* could be bigger than the regiment itself. The more the war displaced and ruined the people, the larger the *Tross* would become, too. The whole crowd seemed to move and flux to the rhythm of the flames. Outside the firelight, figures meandered in and out of view. The light of the cloud-covered moon illuminated their movements and cast eerie shadows. The buzzing din of their merriment echoed back from the surrounding fields.

"I want a drink," Pieter said to the two scruffy men.

They looked at each other dumbly and agreed. "We all want a drink," the man with the red plume said and led Pieter to the main fire.

Pieter found a spot set away from the other soldiers and sat out of the reach of the fire light. The two Prussian bastards came with a ceramic flask and handed it to Pieter. Another soldier appeared next to Pieter and fell, pulling the wench he was dragging down with him. Her blouse had torn and her breast hung freely. The soldier tried to fit her whole breast in his mouth. Pieter looked away.

He tipped the bottle, drank the harsh schnapps and smiled wide at the thought of deserting this damned life. He would leave as soon as he could and nothing would make him live as a mercenary ever again. Was it the heat of the fire, the schnapps and the thoughts of being close to his goal? Pieter fell drowsy. The man with the red plume roused Pieter from a half sleep and helped him stand. They brought him to a tent and shoved him past the entrance guarded by two scruffier-looking men. Pieter let himself fall onto the first mat he came to. He rolled over and just as sleep was to take him, a rise of celebratory howling from the comrades outside his tent jolted him back to reality. The flap flew open.

"We have free passes." A few men laughed.

"They've said we could go into the village. Come with us."

Pieter rolled onto his back. Someone threw Pieter a bottle. He caught it as it hit his head, unstopped it and took a long swig. Pieter stood and swayed on the spot. He took another steadying gulp of the white-hot schnapps and poked his head outside the tent.

"Where are my guards?" he said.

"Ha! They took off with the rest of the men. Come on, before we get caught."

Oh, so they didn't have free passes. But none of that interested Pieter. He was on his way to freedom, even if that meant being hunted for the rest of the war for deserting. He ran after the other men.

Allowing the other men to get farther in front, Pieter slowed his pace, following what little light their torches cast. The path took a slight downhill drop and Pieter looked up. The cloud cover cleared. Even though the terrain in Franconia was for the most part flat, he could see in the moonlight that the camp was atop a rise. The hilltop overlooked a village with maybe twenty houses clustered together.

The other soldiers swarmed down the hill towards the village like vermin on a trail to rotting fruit. Pieter hesitated as he heard voices, whispering and sounds of a small group of bodies scuffling. A shout shocked him and his head cleared from the schnapps. He took a few steps towards the fight.

Closer scrutiny showed that drunken mercenaries had fallen prey to hotheaded farmers. Farmers hated soldiers with good reason. The latter drove the former from their homes whether they were friend or foe. As Pieter looked closer he saw those two Prussian bastards on their knees, a group of farmers surrounding them. Pieter stifled an involuntary laugh.

Two barrels stood a-ready. The farmers grabbed the first soldier. It was the Prussian bastard wearing the black hat with the red plume. He saw Pieter as they carried him towards the barrel. Two other farmers stood with spades next to earthen mounds from the holes they had dug. Pieter could imagine how this scene was going to end. He watched as the farmers stuffed the Prussian bastard feet-first into the barrel.

"Hey, there, help me out of this," the man cried as his red plume disappeared inside the barrel.

Pieter stood quietly and watched the farmers. They were busy with the job they had to do and took no notice of him.

"Hey!" the Prussian bastard squawked, shrill and desperate. "Get me out of…" His words were cut short as they plopped the top on the barrel, laid it on its side and rolled it towards the hole in the earth.

Chapter 14

Katarina

Katarina heard the wagons approaching and ran down the stairs to the front door. Herr Tucher was waiting for them by the open gate. Tanner the Elder had left last week for Nuremberg to fetch the visitors and sent Herr Tucher a coded message this morning that he expected to return with his charges in the afternoon. They seemed to need an air of secrecy around their transport.

Katarina had spent the last week cleaning, clearing and preparing for the guests as best she could. She had vacated her room next to Herr Tucher's and was sleeping down by the kitchen. When Uncle Paul or the Tucher boys visited, she played the part of the maid. Katarina knew her place, yes, and Herr Tucher insisted on discretion when it came to their private involvement. Uncle Paul usually slept in Katarina's room when he stayed for longer periods. The boys would have those in the garret next to Isabeau's.

The first coach pulled into the yard and the second followed close by, driven by a man Katarina didn't recognize. Both coaches stopped and Tanner the Elder jumped down from the first coach. Mud splashed up his leather boots. He opened the door. Two young boys sprang down off the coach. Mud splashed up their boots as well. They both ran to Herr Tucher. Christoph, although the same age as Isabeau, was still a head and shoulders shorter than her. His dark-blond hair was kept short and his movements were adult, trained like a prince. The younger boy, Max, had dark brown curls and features similar to his mother's. Max hugged his father. Christoph shook his hand.

"*Mein Herr*," Christoph said.

"Hello Christoph, no need for formalities here. Welcome to your second home."

Out of the second coach, two heavy-set girls dressed in identical brown dresses hanging loosely over white shifts jumped down. They looked like sisters. A third woman, a gaunt creature with bad posture, climbed out after the other two. She smiled and her teeth protruded from her thin mouth. The smile quickly faded to a frown as she looked down, first at her mud-splattered boots and then around the farmyard. The damage from the last attack was still evident, patched up as best as it could. The gaunt girl moved towards the boys.

Tanner the Elder laid two long wooden boards like a walkway from the first coach towards the house. He took his place by the open door and offered his hand to the last remaining inhabitant. A white-leather-gloved hand covered his. Antique-pink skirts unraveled themselves outside the coach. An elaborate pink and white hat emerged and the gloved hands smoothed over the skirts. The hat tipped back and revealed Frau Tucher's pale, perfect face.

A slim woman of indeterminable age, Frau Tucher was beautiful in a fragile sort of way, as if one smudge to her rouged lips or snag in her costly skirts would ruin the picture completely. She was almost untouchable, a painted ceramic doll. She stepped onto the wooden board and mud slopped over her pink rose-imposed brocade slippers. Her face showed no interest whatsoever. Tanner the Elder led her to where Herr Tucher waited for her. She held her hand up for her husband, who took it and kissed it respectfully.

"*Guten Tag, mein Herr,*" Frau Tucher said.

"Frau Tucher," Herr Tucher said and dropped her hand as if it was on fire.

"I am not looking forward to this stay. We did not want to leave the Hirschelgasse. Paul insisted we leave."

"I will see that your Ladyship and her maids are best taken care of. We have little room but we must all make allowances."

"Paul made promises *mein Herr* will certainly not be able to fulfill. He said I would have my own room."

"Which you may have. Katarina has made up my room for you. I will sleep elsewhere."

"Ah, that woman is still here," Frau Tucher said.

"Katarina runs the household. She will help you settle in."

"She will not. I have my own help," Frau Tucher said. Pointing a lazy, gloved finger at Katarina, she said, "*Magd*, show these young women their quarters. I hope the rooms are cleaner than the last time I was here. Once my women are settled, they will take care of me."

Hot blood flushed Katarina's face. That's why she had to arrange Herr Tucher's room just so and move his things to the small chamber at the end of the hallway. She thought it was because of Uncle Paul. And Frau Tucher traveled with her three maids. Was this the visitor who was staying indefinitely? Why didn't Herr Tucher prepare Katarina for this? He and his wife had always been distant and cool towards each other, addressing each other with formal titles. Katarina had thought Herr Tucher called her a Lady in jest, but the animosity bubbling under every sentence they spoke was palpable.

Katarina nodded and the three maids followed her up the steps and in through the double front doors. She could hear them whisper but could not make out what they were saying. Back in the yard, Katarina heard Frau Tucher say loudly enough for everyone to hear:

"She smells like that horrible oil you brought from one of your trips."

The maids giggled and whispered on among themselves as they climbed the steps. They passed the first landing where Herr Tucher had his rooms and proceeded to climb the chicken ladder to the garret rooms under the roof.

"There are only three rooms up here," Katarina said. "You three will have to share."

"All three rooms are for us," the gaunt, dried-out woman said. "Gret and Gerlin will share, I shall have a room for myself and the boys will share."

"But Isabeau sleeps in this room here," Katarina said as she opened the door to show them the tiny room where Isabeau slept.

"Dörte will have the girl's room," the one heavy sister said, pointing to the gaunt, dried-out woman.

"We'll have this one," the other heavy sister called from the larger room.

Dörte and the one heavy sister gathered Isabeau's blankets together.

"But these are Isabeau's things," Katarina protested.

"I don't want her things," Dörte said. She smiled, her horsey teeth protruding as she piled Isabeau's things together on the bed. "Take them with you. I have my own things. And I spend enough time with children."

Katarina heard floorboards creaking as the sisters inspected their new room. She collected Isabeau's feather bed, her night shirt and a box with her few books and personal things. Arms full, she climbed back down the steep ladder. The three women waited impatiently until Katarina made it to the first landing and then pushed her aside and bounced down the steps. They bounded into the yard and stopped to receive new commands from their mistress. Katarina stopped by the open doors and watched them.

Dörte went directly to the boys. She must be the nursemaid. The two sisters Gret and Gerlin, whichever one was which, fussed over Frau Tucher while she oversaw the unloading of the coaches. Trunk after trunk stood on more of those wooden boards in a row like coffins awaiting the undertaker. A light, misty rain fell. Tanner the Elder and the other coachman dropped one obviously heavy trunk into a puddle with a splat. Frau Tucher reprimanded them for their foolish antics with a squeal. Herr Tucher stood staring absently down the main track as if he'd rather be anywhere than here.

Frau Tucher rounded on Katarina as she saw her standing in the doorway, her arms full of Isabeau's things. "I would like some spiced wine brought up to the sitting room. Immediately. That ride was atrocious. I hope you have the fire burning."

Katarina's feet felt their way down the steps into the kitchen and she dumped the armful of Isabeau's things onto her straw mattress. Any excuse to open a bottle of wine would do her now. She grabbed three bottles of that dark, sour wine standing on the table and opened them, poured the contents into a big pot and added a mixture of cinnamon, anise and fennel. She stepped up onto the stool, retrieved the pot of honey off the top shelf and looked at the jar of arsenic they'd prepared with honey and flour to kill rats. Hesitating, she decided this was not the time.

Katarina set the pot on the tripod over the embers, stirred the spices in and waited until the wine slowly warmed. She filled two jugs and carried them up to Herr Tucher's empty sitting room. The fire blazed and the room baked like an eerie reminder of hell's fury. She set the jugs on his table and climbed back down the steps to fetch some mugs. She ran back up the steps. Heat escaped from the open sitting room door. Frau Tucher had spread herself on the settee. Katarina poured her wine. Frau Tucher accepted the mug from Katarina without looking up. Katarina turned to leave the room.

"When my clothes and shoes have been changed I want the mud cleared from this floor," Frau Tucher said.

Katarina felt her face flush red again. She looked over to Herr Tucher who stood by the bookshelf looking out the window. She walked towards the door to go.

"I haven't excused you, *Magd*," she said.

Katarina set her face into an indifferent mask and looked directly at the woman. Frau Tucher's mean and piercing face was chalk-white, eyebrows plucked to a razor's edge, lips and cheeks painted red. She spoke in a chilling tone:

"The floor will be cleaned. But not by you. I have brought my own maids to tend the house. We need to discuss where we are going to put you."

"I sleep down next to the kitchen," Katarina said looking at the floor.

"I need that room for myself," Frau Tucher said. "To store my trunks. These rooms are so tiny I have no space for my clothing."

Katarina's heart pounded and a lump formed in her throat. "Where am I to sleep?" she barked a bit too hastily and coughed.

"I do not care where you sleep. I have not yet asked my husband where he intends to sleep, either." Frau Tucher shook her head as if she were disappointed. "I've told Paul all along, *mein Herr*, this woman is not the right one to have here at the house. She doesn't know her place."

Frau Tucher watched Katarina closely. Katarina tried to hide it but she swallowed down a lump of anger, fear and uncertainty like a sharp, hard clump of bread. Frau Tucher smiled a small, self-satisfied smirk, just like the one Herr Tucher used to make when Katarina first met him.

"Your duties here in the house are no longer required. My husband tells me you are good with wool." Frau Tucher snorted as if this was nothing to be proud of.

Herr Tucher shifted his weight. "A load of wool is being transported to Herzogenaurach today. The next load needs to be finished as soon as possible."

Frau Tucher sneered at him. "Then whatever is this woman doing here in front of me?" She directed her attention to Katarina, sipped her wine and shook some mud from her skirt. "Get back to work. Your place is with the other farm hands."

Katarina ran back down the steps. Once in the kitchen she poured herself some wine and downed it on one gulp. She heard chains clanking through the paddock door. Isabeau came into the kitchen carrying leather straps and reins hooked to chains that Tanner the Elder used to harness the horses to the coach. She was wet and Katarina could now hear the rain through the open door. Isabeau set the effects down on the stone floor in a clattering heap.

"I'm to oil these things for Tanner," Isabeau said.

"Pick that up and get it out of here!" Katarina yelled and immediately regretted it. Her face flushed hot and a pain shot through her head. "I brought your things down from your room. You need to collect everything that belongs to you. We're going back out to the others."

"What are you yelling at me for?" Isabeau yelled back. "What are you talking about?"

Katarina threw the cup on the floor. It didn't break so she kicked it into the corner where it shattered. "We don't live here anymore. I brought your things down from your room because that spindle of a woman is sleeping there."

A mad tick prickled up Katarina's spine. The thought of stoking the fire to hell's levels and watching the house burn made her mimic that self-satisfied smirk. Damn that woman! This was Katarina's birthplace. For the last ten years it was Katarina's home and now she was being pushed out by these haughty witches. And he wasn't going to stop her, was he? Katarina heard someone coming down the steps. The one heavy sister rolled into the kitchen. The other pushed in behind her.

"We are to help you remove your things," the one sister said.

Katarina pulled herself up to her full height. Gret and Gerlin were still a head taller than she was. Katarina added fuel to her fiery rage and coiled for an explosion. The blood ran hot into her cheeks. She grabbed her poker from alongside the hearth. Soft bootsteps sounded on the stairs. Herr Tucher moved in between the two girls and silently nodded to them that they should leave. They nodded back obediently and scurried away.

He smiled down at Isabeau. "Leave your things here and go back to Albin for the night. Go on, then!"

Herr Tucher and Katarina were alone. He took the poker from her hand and let it clank onto the floor. He put his hands on her shoulders, squared her in front of him, put one finger under her chin and raised her face.

"It's temporary," he said. "Please bear with me. I want to secure a place for my boys. She is just the bad aftertaste."

Katarina deflated like a punctured lung. She looked up at him and tears welled up in her eyes. His soothing words swam like oil on this watery lie. He bent his head and kissed her long and sweet and painful. His kissed the tears from her cheeks. He pulled her to his chest and held her tight.

"I love you," Herr Tucher whispered in her ear. "It's temporary, I promise. Everything will be as it was again."

Katarina heard that gaunt Dörte calling for him from upstairs. She pulled out of his embrace.

"You won't stand up to her," Katarina hissed. "She isn't just the bad aftertaste. She is in command now!"

"Katarina, no. Please. I promise, it is only for a short while. Until they find passage across the Channel."

"This is how it ends, is it?" Katarina disappeared into her little alcove and let the sobs come. She stuffed his journal under the straw mattress and fetched the wooden box that had followed her throughout her life. "Everything I need is in here," Katarina said and left through the stable door.

***

"I hate that boy!" Isabeau said, storming into the kitchen of the workers' house and shoved the door closed with a fury.

Katarina managed to stop the door with her foot before it hit her in the face. "Isabeau, you almost knocked me over!"

Sara and Anna sat at the table, heads together. They stopped their whispering abruptly and looked at Katarina. They had obviously spoken about her.

It had been two weeks since Frau Tucher arrived with the children. Over the years, Isabeau had always been patient with the spoiled Christoph Tucher, who was only a few months younger than she was. When Christoph stayed on the farm without his mother, he was a cordial boy. But Frau Tucher's influence and the intrusion her indefinite stay posed on Katarina and Isabeau was now apparent. Isabeau was used to being Herr Tucher's little girl and had all of his attention. She was not coping with her displacement out of Herr Tucher's daily life any better than Katarina was.

"Would you mind…" Katarina huffed and glared at Isabeau.

"He's horrible," Isabeau ranted on. "He spilled wine all over the kitchen floor and when that thin horse woman came in, he blamed it on me!"

"Then stay away from the main house," Katarina yelled back.

"Herr Tucher called me in," Isabeau said. "He had a book for me. But his wife took it away and gave it to Christoph. Then they left and Christoph spilled the wine. Not me. Then that thin horse woman came in. I would have gotten the whip if Herr Tucher hadn't come back down and stopped her."

"Just stay away from them altogether," Katarina said and sat down on the bench.

Anna quieted Elsbeth's fussing baby by putting her finger in the baby's mouth. "Just keep your head down, do what they say," she said to Isabeau.

Elsbeth's girl Hannah sat at the table and sucked her thumb, her face lethargic, gray and sunken. Sara poured Katarina a mug of tea and turned away.

"Yesterday Christoph wanted to play Executioner again," Isabeau said. "He wants me to kneel down and beg for my soul. He says he's Meister Franz. He said I'm no better than a dirty wench."

Sara fingered the white cap on the table, her face almost pitying. She set the cap on her head and pushed a few of the loose strands of hair back under it. Suddenly her face sparked up as she got an idea.

"Katarina, it's going to be a lovely day." Sara pushed one of the baskets on the table towards Katarina. "Bjarne needs help with the sheep up at the pasture beyond the North Hill. And he needs his lunch. He could use some company, too. Take his bread to him for me. And a bit of meat, too. Get out and get some air."

Sara stood, grabbed a huge knife and sliced a hunk of bread from the round loaf. "Isabeau will stay here. She can go with Albin and help him find some tinder."

"I want to go out with my horse!" Isabeau said, her face red and shiny.

"You have work to do, young lady," Sara said.

Isabeau tried to stomp away but Sara caught her by the elbow and spun her around. Dragging Isabeau behind her, she opened the door and whistled. Albin appeared within a moment. She grabbed the other basket from the table, handed it to Albin, whispered to the two and they ran off.

"That settles that!" Sara smiled, satisfied with herself.

Sara set a thin slab of dried meat on the table and Katarina packed that and the bread into the basket. She filled a jug with beer and Katarina packed that as well. Katarina lifted the basket and headed for the door. She looked back at Sara, who absently brushed some bread crumbs from the table into her hand. Sara's smile was gone and the pitying expression was on her face again. Katarina felt an instant pang of anger.

"What's that look supposed to mean?" Katarina moved back to the table.

"Oh, I'm just so sorry. I know you're upset."

"I can't believe he's doing this to me."

"But she's his wife," Sara said. "You've always known this could happen."

"But why now?" Katarina said. "After all these years."

"Don't act so surprised. You…"

"But that's my house!"

"It is not," Sara said. "You're just his…"

"Say it." Katarina slammed the basket on the table. "Just say it. I'm his mistress. I'm his whore. What else do you think I am?"

"You're his maid, Katarina!"

Katarina closed her eyes and took a deep breath.

"Do you love him?" Sara said.

"Hmpff," Katarina said.

"Do you?" Sara said.

"Do you love Tanner?"

"Of course I do. He's the father of my children. He's my husband!"

Katarina grabbed the basket. She walked to the open doorway and turned back to Sara, wishing she would make this all right again, the way she settled fights between children. Sara just whispered an apology and walked away.

Katarina made towards the North Hill, taking the time she normally didn't have to appreciate the spring day. She had no reason to rush. No one was waiting for her. The day was cool and the birds were twittering and flying about. Pale blue sky struggled to show itself from behind stubborn clouds. Katarina strolled along the path up the hill, observing the changes spring had made. Tiny green shoots peeked through the compressed earth. She picked a twig from a willow tree and rubbed the furry catkin on her cheek. A slight breeze fluttered through the dried leaves that had refused to fall from the trees.

Her heart pounded empty, heavy beats. Of course Katarina loved him! She loved him more than she could allow herself to feel. Her love for him encompassed her and overwhelmed her and the thought of being away from him even for the afternoon made her sick. Now she wanted to wretch. She felt like her best friend had died. Maybe, in a way, he had.

Katarina rounded a few bushes surrounding a small meadow. Sheep bleated and a dog barked. Under a tree, what looked like a cloak thrown in a pile with a hat on top moved in the breeze. Blond curls hung from under the hat. Two scruffy black-gray dogs trotted around the herd, nosing stray lambs back into the group. When the dogs saw Katarina, they bounded towards her, barking. The pile of cloak stirred and Bjarne's sleepy face smiled as he saw Katarina coming. He wiped a dirty hand over his slightly upturned nose. His chin was covered with a coarse reddish-blond beard but the hair refused to grow on his cheeks.

Bjarne and his brother Lasse were still boys when they came to the farm ten years ago. Their father was a Danish soldier and their mother was a German maid. They'd lived in Nuremberg back in the days when Katarina worked at the Stork's Nest tavern. At some point their mother died and the father left the two boys and joined another regiment. The boys scrounged for food and often begged by the Tucher house. Herr Tucher brought them bread or sent them to the kitchens. Eventually the brothers had the idea to ask Herr Tucher if they could work here on the farm.

Katarina sat down next to Bjarne under the tree. He pulled off his hat and shook his head.

"Are you feeling ill today?" he asked.

"I'm fine," Katarina said. "Just fine. Everything is fine."

She gave him the chunk of bread, pulled the dagger from her belt and cut off a sliver of meat. He tore off a corner of bread and handed it to her. She bit into the bread and chewed, wondering if she could get used to a solitary life like Bjarne. He seemed to enjoy it. She wondered if she would have to get used to it.

Katarina heard a hawk calling overhead and turned as something big moved in the trees. Hans-Wolfgang von Untereierhofen, a man the same color as the forest, came out of the trees followed by a horse.

"Good Morning," Hans-Wolfgang said in a hoarse voice. "Have you been promoted to shepherd, Katarina?"

"It's the oldest industry known to man." Bjarne laughed. "Herding sheep."

Hans-Wolfgang smiled at him. "What a lovely day. A wonderful day, as a matter of fact."

He slumped down next to Bjarne and took the jug of beer Bjarne held out. Hans-Wolfgang had not changed in the ten years Katarina knew him. He kept his dark-blond hair cut short and his face showed no signs of aging. Although they were almost the same age, Hans-Wolfgang looked much younger than Katarina, as if his own reclusive life had spared his nerves.

Hans-Wolfgang pulled his brown cloak off and threw it onto the ground. His strong, bare arms glistened with perspiration and the brown leather jerkin and trousers he wore struggled, almost bursting at the seams. He had packed on a bit of muscle this past winter.

"Where have you been?" Katarina said. "I had thought you might be, well, gone."

"You mean dead?" Hans-Wolfgang said. "I'm not dead. I'm fine. But how are you getting by? You don't look well."

She looked at the ground and dug in the earth with a twig. "I'm fine. Wonderful."

"You look awful. Is anything wrong with Isabeau?"

"She's fine." Katarina glared, challenging him. "She's exhausting is what she is!"

"She's a child. And she has always been a confident girl."

Katarina sighed and broke the twig in half. "The master's wife has moved in indefinitely. She's banished us from the main house."

"So where are you living?"

"We're back in the workers' house. With all the others."

Bjarne snorted. "I can't sleep in there. Horrible. Bugs, those boys, the mice…"

Hans-Wolfgang smiled even wider. "How many people are living in that little hut then?"

"Well, Sara and Tanner and Albin sleep behind the stove. Isabeau and I will sleep upstairs next to Anna. Lasse and Bjarne…"

Bjarne laughed. "I've moved into the barn in the hay loft. My brother sleeps with those kids. They drive me to tears. I could never get any sleep after that baby came."

"Have you seen Elsbeth?" Katarina asked.

"I think she's dead," Bjarne said.

"It's very close in the workers' house," Katarina said. "Elsbeth's boys are unruly. The mice make me insane."

"It's time for you to consider a new possibility, then," Hans-Wolfgang said. "I am now the legal tenant of the Eierhofen estates. The complete hilltop. Well, I will, after I sign the papers from the Margrave in Dachsbach."

"You're lucky he hasn't sent an army and cleared you out of there," Katarina said.

"There is a certain *Gewohnheitsrecht* I have: I have always lived here, the Margrave did not force me to leave, hence it is my right to stay. And no protest came from the original landholder. An anonymous source now informed the Margrave that Friedrich died in the collapse of the burnt-out house. I think it was simply too much trouble for the Margrave to fight with me. He has other worries with all these troops." Hans-Wolfgang chuckled to himself. "But he finally realized he could be taxing me. So he will allow me to register as the official tenant."

"Haven't the troops visited the estate?" Katarina said.

"No, not yet. We have been lucky."

Katarina snorted. "We haven't been so lucky."

"Has anything happened to Isabeau?" he asked.

"No, she's fine, nothing has happened to the children. Yet."

Hans-Wolfgang sat up straight. "Katarina, you know what this means? Isabeau is my utmost priority. I must fulfill my obligation now."

Katarina knew this day would come too. One day Hans-Wolfgang would want Isabeau back. Isabeau knew Katarina was not her real mother but the girl knew no other.

"Isabeau can finally come and live with me!" Hans-Wolfgang said.

Now the notion of a solitary life closed in around Katarina, blotting the light of day like the cellar door closing overhead. Not only would she lose Herr Tucher, her entrusted partner and best friend, Katarina would lose the girl as her daughter forever. Katarina sat silently and watched enviously as the hawk took to the current and sailed upwards; wings stretched, the effortless soaring, the freedom, the aesthetic beauty of flight. His wings held completely rigid, he turned two rounds upwards and slowly sailed back towards the trees. Katarina felt no joy in the concept of freedom, only despair and demise. To be alone meant to die.

"Come and live with me," Hans-Wolfgang said. "The two of you. I want what you have had the last ten years. A life with my daughter. You can have your own room. You are the only mother she knows. Come now, or at least, please consider the option."

Chapter 15

Ralf

Ralf knelt in the St. Mary Magdelene church in Herzogenaurach. He finished the last *Vater Unser* and concluded his rosary prayers. His contemplation of the sorrowful mysteries alleviated the melancholy he felt this morning but he still struggled with an underlying loneliness and that angered him. He fingered the rosary that had belonged to his mother. Through all his travels and he still had it. Made of dried juniper berries and silver, this was the only earthly possession he treasured. He sewed a pocket in his robe especially to keep it close to his heart. Mother had taught him to seek comfort in the repetition of the prayers. Today was one of the days he sorely missed his parents. Since Father Marius died, there were days he felt the void left by these important figures and it drained him like losing blood.

Ralf should have grieved enough but Marius' death opened the scarred wounds Ralf had from losing his parents, wounds that had never truly healed. Now they festered, infected with a rage Ralf could not cleanse. He chastised himself because he knew this was Satan distracting him from his true calling. He was here to do God's work and these earthly longings were pulling him away from the tasks he must do. He wiped a tear away, looped the rosary into a tight circle, slipped it into the pocket next to his heart, extinguished the candle and left the church.

From the other side of the cobbled street, Karl, Konrad, Michel and Martin approached the Fehnturm, the square tower that flanked the town's lower gate. Ralf saw shadows of the watchmen conversing in the tower's pyramid-shaped *Scharwachtdach*, the watchman's roof. Ralf led the boys up the street towards the Rathaus.

"We are to meet Sheriff Vogtmann at the hour," Ralf said and showed the boys a roll of parchment. "Dr. Fuchs gave me this written permission of the Prince-Bishop to hand over to him. It is Vogtmann's duty to conform to Bamberg's wishes in legal matters, carry out an arrest and make an example of any culprits."

Dr. Fuchs wanted Ralf to stay in Herzogenaurach until he had audience with the Amtmann von Seckendorff. According to Dr. Fuchs, the only reason von Seckendorff, a Protestant, was still in power in the town was because he was the richest man here. Herzogenaurach, a town comprising of about two hundred souls, was Catholic and belonged to Bamberg even though its distance from Bamberg put it at a disadvantage. During the last century, Herzogenaurach went from being the last Catholic stronghold amid a rising sea of Protestant villages to leading the Counter-Reformation, regaining influence in the surrounding area. Many of the Protestant villages had been re-catholicized but the danger of losing this influence was predominant.

"This decree authorizes us to question the three women traveling with the cloth merchant called Ziegler," Ralf told the boys. "These women were the ones who sold Widow Braun the mandrake root and the cloth that smelled of sulfur. Let's pay them a visit before we meet the sheriff."

Ralf wanted to find Ziegler and his women and make an example out of them. Then the people of this town would know Bamberg was watching. Even here in the province, they were subject to the laws of the church and not that heretic thinking of Nuremberg. They were too close to Nuremberg, having ties with them because of the textile trade. Herzogenaurach was a too-important outpost of the territories of Bamberg to lose to the heretics.

Ralf and the boys walked around the city wall, up the hill to the Rahmberg, the field where the tentering frames stood for drying the fabrics. That's where St. Mary Magdelene's vicar said Herr Ziegler would probably be, and insisted Ralf agree he hadn't heard it from him. Ralf and the students happened by an open door in the city wall. Residents had utilized the city wall as the boundary to their private properties. Beyond this door, a man laughed quietly with three women in his courtyard. One woman exited the property through the door in the wall, greeting Ralf as she passed him by. The other two women pulled an ample measure of fabric from a tub. Ralf recognized them from the market and he waved the students by, a gesture to enter the courtyard.

"May I help you men?" the man said. "I can offer you this fabric, measuring four Nürnberger Elle, finest Franconian wool. We have blue or this lovely green my daughters are working on."

Ralf and the boys stood in a uniform line as if they practiced a military drill.

"Ho, Father, I don't think I have anything in your color." The man chuckled. "But you're not here to buy cloth, are you?"

The women unraveled the large measure of light green fabric and moved away from one another. They twisted the fabric and the dirty water puddled under their feet. Together they carried the still-dripping fabric out of the courtyard. Ralf watched them through the door as they crossed to the adjacent field. Wooden racks were lined throughout the field like fences. The two women gently tugged at the fabric ends and arranged the cloth by hooking the topmost edge to the tenter hooks on the top of the frame. They secured the bottom edge to the hooks on the bottommost rung. Together they stretched the bottom rung until they agreed on the length and fastened the rung securely. Ralf moved away from the courtyard door. He and the boys circled the man.

"Herr Ziegler? Do you sell cloth in Bamberg?" Ralf barked. "With your daughters?"

"Why, sir, I sell cloth in a lot of places," he said. "That's how we live, simple folk we are."

Ralf did not care for the sparkle in this man's eye. Herr Ziegler had a knowing, cunning expression. Ralf felt the man's charisma and it made him feel awkward. But Herr Ziegler would not get the better of Ralf. Ralf knew men usually broke when they watched officials drag their women away. Any man of conscience would. Ralf could rely on this man's arrogance. He'd give these women up, family or not, to save his own hide.

"You were in Bamberg in the last month then?" Ralf said. "With your daughters?"

"Let me think. I do most of my trade in Nuremberg. Sometimes we travel to Bamberg but not often."

"Are you even allowed to sell cloth?" Ralf asked. "What is your status?"

"Yes I am allowed. I am a town burgher."

"An *Äckerbürger* no doubt, a proper provincial farmer's son." Ralf chuckled.

Herr Ziegler led Ralf towards the doorway. He walked out of the doorway, towards the tentering frames and his daughters. Ralf and the boys followed him out. Herr Ziegler stopped mid-stride and turned, stepping aside as the girls returned to the courtyard. Together, he and the girls re-entered the property. Ralf realized too late he'd been escorted from Herr Ziegler's property. Herr Ziegler had the upper hand and Ralf was instantly angry. He'd been had.

Herr Ziegler grabbed a hold of the gate. "I would have to check my books. What is all this about then?"

"*Herr*, one of your women has been denunciated by an accused witch we have detained in Bamberg. She said you and your traveling women were involved in one particularly intense night of feasting in the Hauptmoorwald."

Herr Ziegler laughed, a booming and threatening laugh. "That is rich, Father. Go home to your Bamberg and have your mother clean the snot from your face. Do not come here again."

"You do not deny it then? And, no worry, I won't need to come here again. I have men to deal with these things. Our witch commissioners will pay you a visit. I have only come to allow you to admit what you've done and give you the chance to reflect on your sins and those of your women."

"Good day, Father," Herr Ziegler said and gave the gate a shove.

Ralf stepped out of the way of the swinging gate as it slammed shut with a bang. Ralf's anger peaked and receded as he quickly regained his composure. He still had the upper hand.

"No matter," Ralf said to the boys. "We have an appointment."

Ralf and his four students followed the path around the city wall back to the Rathaus. Ralf burst into Vogtmann's office on the ground floor. The sheriff sat behind a heavy, dark-stained table stacked with books and papers and riffled through a large ledger.

"I demand help from the watchmen," Ralf demanded. "If I do not get your support, I will report you all to the Prince-Bishop for hiding and supporting a denounced witch! If you do not help me, Vogtmann, right now, I will go, by power of the Prince-Bishop, and arrest this man and his whole family and take them to Bamberg. I demand to see the Amtmann!"

"Currently out at his estate in Oberlindach, Father, attending to a serious matter there," Vogtmann said. "There is a war on, by the way, or hadn't you noticed? There are more pressing problems than a man having spit on the Prince-Bishop's road or something."

"Can't you see that these misfortunes, the war, the inclement weather, are all caused by these heretics and their cohorts with the devil? Bamberg is fighting a war here as well and we only want to save the population from the disasters that befall them, caused by these people."

"Yes, Herzogenaurach must always pay the piper for Bamberg," Vogtmann said. "While we are only an insignificant hamlet here at the far outskirts of Bamberg's border, your Prince-Bishop surely comes to call when he needs money. But where are you and your men when we're being plundered and robbed?"

"You will be arrested with them for such heresy," Ralf said. "I have the power to do it and so I shall. This city belongs to Bamberg and Bamberg shall let the verdict fall!"

"Go arrest your witch then," Vogtmann said. "Bring her here and we will lock her in the tower."

Ralf and his men marched back to the house of the Zieglers'. The gate was firmly latched from the inside. Karl and Konrad scaled the wall and unlatched the gate. They entered the courtyard. The shutters were tight across the windows and there was no sound.

"Herr Ziegler come out of your own accord or we will make you come out," Ralf hollered.

Two boys bashed against the door. The wooden door frame made a cracking sound as the wood split. Herr Ziegler flung the door open. Ralf and his students shoved their way into the kitchen. A woman yelped.

Ralf lined up his four students along the wall of the darkened kitchen. "Give me the witch or we will take you all to Bamberg."

Herr Ziegler moved away from the place at the head of the table. He instructed the five women seated around the table to stand and back against a wall fixed with shelves full of wooden plates and mugs. Herr Ziegler's charisma and sparkle had turned to anger and rage.

"Only a simple man would believe that humbug you preach," Herr Ziegler said.

"I know you do not say that yourself," Ralf said. "The devil is at work here."

"This is no devil speaking," Herr Ziegler said. "This is the voice of reason. Of sanity!"

Ralf unfurled his parchment. "Herr Ziegler, in the name of His Princely Grace, the Prince-Bishop von Dornheim, I hereby denounce you and your family of banding with…"

"Stop!" Herr Ziegler grabbed a woman by the hand and pulled her out of the group. "This one," he whispered.

He shoved a thin woman with dark brown hair out of the group towards the middle of the kitchen. Herr Ziegler and the other four women backed away as a whole. Ralf moved in front of the woman and focused his attention on her.

"Are you in cohorts with the devil?" Ralf asked.

"No," the woman said.

"Tell me now. You will save yourself the interrogation. We will find out no matter what. We only want to cleanse your soul."

The woman shook her head, eyes on the floor.

"What is your relation to Herr Zielger?" Ralf asked.

"None at all!" Herr Ziegler boomed. "We picked her up in Höchstadt last week. She said she was a weaver and wanted to get to Nuremberg. I thought I could use her. She's useless, says she's injured, can't work, what do I know."

"Injured?" Ralf said.

"Show him your so-called injuries, Elsbeth," Herr Ziegler said.

Elsbeth gathered the simple, light green skirt and showed Ralf her legs. They were covered in purple, green, yellow bruises and scratches, as if some animal had mauled her.

Ralf grabbed a hold of her skirt and pulled it high. "That is the result of animalistic coupling. We have seen the same marks on other witches," he said.

"That is the work of soldiers!" Elsbeth screamed and pulled her skirt out of Ralf's grasp.

Ralf gathered the skirt in both hands and heaved it up. He scrutinized her legs. Yes, he'd seen this before. Women who had been involved in excesses with the devil at these fests. He could smell her corruption, her vile thirsts. Those drunken women, blind by their own desires, conceiving spawn of the most evil kind.

"Your words belie your lusts!" Ralf said. "There were no soldiers. You are damned, dear, and we will force this devil out of you. You have been denounced by an accused witch, the Widow Braun, of holding sabbath in the Haupmoorwald forest and engaging in the most foul of rituals with the same."

Elsbeth looked to the other women as if she searched for their support. Ralf saw this gesture and quickly pounced on it.

"Who really knows this woman?" Ralf said. "Is she innocent? Who will speak for her innocence?"

Murmurs rippled throughout Herr Zielger and the other four women. They all made negative head-shaking gesturers.

"Soldiers, take this woman to the tower." Ralf rolled the parchment together and left the property.

He marched back along the city walls towards the tower, pleased with his day's work. He wanted no more than to serve his God by defending, in the most forceful way possible, the doctrine that cost his mother and father their lives. The doctrine that saved his life. He was spared the day his parents were killed in the name of the one true religion. A sign from the divine, his life spared, so he could be a soldier in this fight towards a world filled with nothing but passionate devotion.

Chapter 16

Pieter van Diemen

The assembly drum beat out a rhythm that countered the pounding in Pieter's muddled head. Bits of the evening past fell into place as he shook off his drunken dreams. He held his cool hands to his swollen face. His tongue was thick and dry. Scuffling feet pounded past his tent. He rolled back and forth on the hard ground in an attempt to loosen the knotted muscles in his neck and shoulders. He felt like he'd been beaten with a club.

Pieter stood and pulled the muddy trousers over his soiled undergarments. He had stayed out of view last night until the farmers buried the two Prussian bastards in barrels. He then fell in the mud when the farmers heard his rustlings in the bush but managed to slip away and return to the tent unnoticed. By that time serious fatigue dragged him into its depths and he fell into a black and lightless set of dreams and images.

He threw the tent flap back. The camp teemed with an unorganized scurrying back and forth—wagons being loaded, animals grunting as they tugged against tethers, soldiers arguing amongst themselves. The three soldiers nearest Pieter were trying to organize their tents and their belongings in three different languages and their patience was running thin.

Three of the Hauptmann's guard stomped across the camp and lined up in front of Pieter. Two men flanked him, grabbed him by the arms and led him to the spot where the Hauptmann's quarters had been. Here the men talked quietly among themselves as they packed wooden trunks the size of coffins and loaded them on to two separate wagons. Two men stood by feeding and cleaning four bay workhorses. Another four men carried a decorated metal trunk the size of a beer barrel and dropped it onto a wagon causing the wooden wheels to sink. The *Kriegskasse*, the regiment's till.

Hauptmann Schwartz rode up the hilltop on his dapple gray stallion, dismounted and waved his guards away from Pieter. "These are the trunks with the books," he said. "They haven't been filled in for weeks now. We need to count how many men are here. They are assembling now and you can see we still have at least a thousand men."

"I can see nothing of the sort," Pieter said. "Seems there are less soldiers than last night. And more stragglers."

"I don't care how many soldiers are still here," Hauptmann Schwartz said. "You need to record something. I don't even know if I'm going to see any money at all. The till is empty. The books are your responsibility now. When we reach our next camp, you just write down what I tell you."

Pieter climbed up onto the coach box next to the driver whose face was as sour as his smell. From this vantage point, Pieter could see across the hilltop where they had spent the night. The smoke from abandoned fires rose in wisps. The market wagons stood hitched to their horses and were ready to move out. A sad collection of torn dirty clothes, bare feet, blank stares and sunken features formed the motley collection of soldiers.

As a boy, Pieter heard the tales of the proud *Landknechte*, the mercenaries of days gone by, elite soldiers full of ambition and adventure, wearing their doublets and hose of many proud colors, sleeves puffed and slashed. These men here had long ceased to reflect the pride of that guild. This war had reduced men to pillage and plunder for an existence—they had long to wait for pay, if it ever came. Food was expensive and often spoiled. Like Pieter had seen in Mansfeld's camp, more men were dying from disease and hunger than they ever would from battle.

"Oh, Tanner, put on these clothes," Hauptmann Schwartz said. "You cannot travel with me looking like that."

A young boy no more than twelve years old threw a damp, moldy-smelling beige-green doublet and green hose, the same colors the Hauptmann wore, onto Pieter's lap.

The regiment traveled the whole day through. The next morning they assembled before dawn and moved on. A silence fell over the ranks after hours of arduous journey. About midday, Pieter's sour coach driver pointed to a hillside up ahead.

Hauptmann Schwartz rode up alongside Pieter. "Here we are. Just outside of Höchstadt. We will set up camp here until we receive our orders."

Pieter jumped off the wagon. A nostalgic wave of childish excitement welled up in his throat as he fully took in the scene. He walked up the hill and realized he could see the Sichardtshof farm to the other side. He saw no animals in the old farmyard, no people either, no smoke rising from the chimney. The fields where Pieter remembered once planting grain were trampled and muddy. Weeds choked the vineyard on the North Hill.

"There's nothing back there, just that old abandoned farm," the coach driver said. "Help me unload. We will have a look in the village tonight."

The coach driver handed Pieter a ceramic flask and Pieter took a long swig. Could it be his last hope, his only refuge, the one shimmer of light on this dreary day had been stomped, extinguished, dashed? They assembled the Hauptmann's quarters, a methodically laid-out compound. Pieter set up a table in front of the main regiment tent in the late afternoon April sun, opened the regiment book Schwartz had given him and warmed his bones. He had a view of the market girls from here and he could look over the hollow Herr Tucher called the Edelgraben. He had to watch Sichardtshof for any sign of life. There must be someone living there. This was Pieter's last hope. He had to leave this regiment and traveling alone was not an option.

The Hauptmann gave Pieter a torn bit of parchment. "These are my notes. Start a new list on that page. Start with these dates."

"That was six months ago!" Pieter said.

"It doesn't matter. Just make up anything. We need money. We may not see any but we have to try."

Pieter copied Schwartz's notes into the regiment book. His concentration wavered every time he thought he saw movement in the distance. He could have sworn he saw the figure of a woman coming down the North Hill. Foolish woman out alone. The late afternoon sun caught flares of her russet hair. Could that be Katarina? Pieter thought he caught sight of the worker's house overgrown with brambles. Two children ran around the yard and were quickly caught up by a heavy woman in a brown skirt and a white blouse. It must be Sara. She swept the children into the house and closed the door.

Hauptmann Schwartz suddenly appeared in front of Pieter and blocked his view. "Since you are so interested in the surroundings." He chuckled. "Take this group of lousy men, go into the village and try to collect some food for tonight. Another regiment is coming from the west and those greedy bastards will plunder the village if we don't get to it first. You need to be quick. I heard the new regiment will reach Höchstadt by morning."

Hauptmann Schwartz laid Pieter's sword, baldric and dagger on the
table. Pieter hung his baldric over his shoulder and sheathed his sword. He
stuck his dagger in his belt and felt a gripping hatred for authority and a
need to break free. Hauptmann Schwartz grabbed him by the arm.

"I know what you're thinking, boy. I can defend myself and you will
not get near me." Hauptmann Schwartz flung Pieter's arm to underscore
his statement.

The Hauptmann must think Pieter a threat to say something like that.
Pieter enjoyed the moment. Let him think Pieter wanted to kill him. Truth
be told, Pieter meant him no harm, meant no one harm. Like the lamb he
was, he followed the group of lousy men as they slunk away from the camp
and into a knoll of trees. Here the men waited and drank for courage until
the sun dipped down behind the North Hill. Flickers of bad conscience
threatened to make Pieter turn back. He hated what they were about to do.
One more night and he would get out of this damned life.

Pieter had drunk more than he thought and the drink was strong. As
they neared the village, he lagged behind and watched the men separate into
small groups of threes and fours. He walked past two German speaking
comrades as they worked together to get their torches lit. The smell of pitch
surrounded them as they both grabbed Pieter by the arm and took him with
them. They discussed the first farm they approached, their words slurring
and so riddled with dialect Pieter could hardy understand them. As they
entered the yard the two men headed for the barn. Instead of looking for
food, the two went right for the farm implements.

The one comrade staggered and went off towards the house, pitchfork
held straight out. A pale light glowed in between the slats of the closed
shutters. The other, just as drunk as his friend, swayed into the next
outbuilding looking for animals. He could hardly stand. As he crossed the
threshold, he slipped and fell, dropping his torch. The straw on the barn
floor was immediately in flames. A man rushed out of the house. He must
have been watching from the window. The other comrade caught the
farmer with the pitchfork, almost by mistake, and pricked him, knocking
him down.

"Take what you want, just help us put out the fire!" the farmer
screeched.

The farmer's two young farm hands ran out of a small shed. They carried long-handled implements that looked like wide flat rakes and whacked at the fire. Pieter's two comrades jumped on them and began beating the young men with their fists. Pieter left them to it and went into the house looking for food and drink. He shoved a young woman aside who was trying to get past him, wanting to get out.

"Just give me food and I will leave," Pieter said.

"The barn is on fire," the young woman wailed. "You idiot, let me out!"

Pieter's temper flared. He grabbed her by the hair and pushed her to the floor. "Just get me what I want. Don't you understand? Just give me food and I will leave you alone. Don't be stupid and try to fight me."

"Get out of the house before it starts to burn, fool!" an older woman said and shoved Pieter.

Pieter knocked her onto the floor. He walked into the tiny sitting room, grabbed a bottle off the table, uncorked it and smelled the contents. Alcohol. This would do. He took a large gulp. He saw the two women in the hall out of the corner of his eye as they regained their footing and fled the house. The smell of smoke came in from the barnyard. Pieter went upstairs wondering if it was wise with the buildings burning. It wouldn't take long for the house to catch fire.

Pieter grabbed some bed linens out of the upstairs wardrobe and knotted one of them to a sack. He looked out of the window and could see fires springing up all over the village. The sky began to light up. He was sweating and felt sick so he took another swig of alcohol. He walked back down the stairs, drunk, dazed and removed from the situation.

He searched the larder. Of course there was no food. The farmers were used to being sacked and had hidden all their food. He drank the bottle dry and threw it aside. Ceramic cups sat on the table so he smashed them. He overturned the table. He loathed himself for this. Hated this life. He needed to run away now.

Pieter stumbled on a raised board on the kitchen floor. He pulled up the loose board and found two loaves of bread and what looked like moldy, dark brown dried meat. He grabbed all of it, stuffed it in his sack and slunk outside. Of the two comrades, one had the farmer's wife and dragged her away from the burning barn. Pieter could hear her screaming. He took his spoils and fled. He was going to leave this life.

Chapter 17

Katarina

Katarina swept the floor of the sleeping space above the workers' house before she turned in for the night. Her broom scraped softly on the wooden floor. David and Friedrich rolled and thumped behind the hanging linens dividing the open garret space into small private quarters. The shadows the two devil-children cast on the white swaying linens were almost comical. Katarina hoped they wouldn't overturn the tallow lamp. The wooden floor was littered with mouse droppings, clumps of earth and straw from the mattresses they slept on. An overturned lamp would surely burn the house down.

Hannah squealed each time the boys came too close to her. This pitiful loft smelled like mouse urine, child's shit and sweaty woman. A cat wandered across the floor, spied a mouse and pounced. When the mouse got away, he lifted his tail and sprayed against the thatching of the roof. Katarina grabbed the straw mattress where Isabeau slept, heaved it up and gave it a shake. It was crawling with fleas. The winter past had been harsh and according to the *Bauernregeln*, all this vermin should have died. Frau Kuni would have said it came from washing the linens during the phase of the waxing moon. This would cause the fleas to multiply:

Mann soll die Wäsche nicht im zunehmenden Mond machen,
Denn sonst vermehrt sich die Flöhe.

Oh, it didn't matter what they did, the vermin would spend the whole winter reproducing and the whole moon phase too. Katarina dropped Isabeau's mattress on the floor and climbed down the ladder into the kitchen. Sara threw the wad of hair she had just cut from Albin's head onto the fire.

"My legs are open and itching," Katarina said. "And Isabeau is bleeding where she scratched the bites open."

"Albin doesn't have fleas, but his head was itching," Sara said.

Albin squirmed in his seat as she smeared his head with oil. She nodded towards the small ceramic flask on the table. Katarina picked it up and unstopped it. The bitter smell made her recoil.

"Use some of that, it's a tincture of those broadleaf mouse-ear leaves," Sara said.

Sara finished with Albin, grabbed the bottle and slathered Isabeau's head with oil. Isabeau howled.

"It's really crowded up there," Katarina said. She took the bottle Sara held out, sat at the bench and treated her own hair as well. "And if we all have to stay stuffed in that room, we're going to get sick."

"I can't keep the rats out of our stores," Sara said. "They keep chewing their way into what little grain we have left. If I didn't have my own room, I would not want to sleep upstairs."

"Bjarne won't sleep in here anymore."

"Tanner the Elder won't sleep here, either. He sleeps on the hay loft because it's airy and he says the room up there stinks." Sara smiled at Isabeau as she rubbed her legs with a mixture of lanolin and calendula. She finished with Isabeau and sent her to bed with a kiss on the cheek. "What has happened to us? We never had such a bad spell of vermin. We keep things clean. I thought for a while we were prosperous even."

"Frau Kuni would say it was the moon," Katarina said. "I think it's the soldiers. Herr Tucher says it's a normal development of nature. Bjarne says in Höchstadt they blame it on witches."

"Silly superstitions," Sara said.

Katarina said her good nights, climbed the ladder and retired to her cramped garret space. She heard the boys' snorting snores as she sat back on her mattress. From Anna's spot came the sounds of Hannah and the baby both sniveling, coughing, whining.

Katarina woke before the sun came up. Her head was heavy and she felt as if she hadn't slept at all. She slid along the floor on her backside until she felt the opening and the prongs of the ladder and eased her way down the ladder into the kitchen lit only with the last hint of glowing embers. Outside, in the distance, a familiar rumble traveled along the main road. Katarina opened the door and looked down the hollow. There was a faint orange glow on the horizon and the rolling din of approaching damnation. A panic shot up Katarina's spine and she broke out in a cold sweat. She knocked on the wood panels outside Tanner's alcove by the kitchen where the family slept.

"Tanner! Wake up!"

Katarina heard intakes of air and bodies rolling under crispy bed covers. The bed groaned under their shifting weight.

"What is it?" Tanner said.

"They're coming."

Tanner came out into the kitchen, lacing his trousers. He pushed by Katarina, bare-chested and bare-footed. "I have had my fill of this, believe me, Katarina. Get the others up."

Katarina climbed the ladder and pushed the hair back from Isabeau's face. "Come with me. We must get up now. Hurry."

Katarina shook Anna gently by the shoulder. "We must hide now."

Anna sat, weary with understanding, went through the motions of collecting the baby and Hannah like she'd resigned to have this a normal part of her day. David and Friedrich brushed past Katarina and were off down the ladder. Tanner was walking out the door pulling on his shirt as Katarina came back down to the kitchen.

"So, Katarina, help me get our breakfast into the cellar," Sara said. "Hopefully this will be over with quickly. I have so much to do today."

Katarina rushed for the door. "I have to go get something, first."

"Where are you going?" Sara shook her head in panic. "Katarina, don't be foolish!"

"I forgot something at the main house."

Katarina pulled the door open and ran across the farmyard before Sara could object. Katarina had no shoes on, if only to signal she would be coming back quickly. A new wooden door from the paddock into Katarina's old kitchen leaned over the opening. There had been no time or manpower to install it. She pulled it open a slit and slipped in. From the rooms upstairs, brief spurts of a panicked woman's voice reminded Katarina that Frau Tucher was still here. In the kitchen, Tanner barked commanding tones at either Gerlin or Gret. The girl ran up the steps out of the kitchen.

"Katarina, get back home," Tanner said. "Take care of the other women. Please, stay with my wife."

"I left something here," Katarina said. "I cannot leave it here. He asked me to take care of it."

Katarina went into the alcove and pulled Herr Tucher's diary out from under the straw sack. A queasy feeling hit her stomach. She went back out into the paddock. Horses pounded up the main road. She ran flat out towards the workers' house. Bjarne ran at her from the barn and shot on past towards the main house. She heard Herr Tucher shout. Tanner called out, too.

Sara stood in the doorway as Katarina approached. She stood aside and let Katarina enter. The chickens were still outside and they would lose them today, Katarina was sure of it. Bjarne and Katarina had secured the sheep back in the pasture. His brother Lasse was still out there alone with the sheep and the dogs. If Herr Tucher could offer the soldiers no animals, they would be angry. They would demand money. If Herr Tucher had none, the next best thing would be women. Katarina's fear was so immediate she only realized she sat in the cellar when Sara pulled the trap door closed as she climbed down the steps. There was no one to cover it with a rug this time. Katarina sat down on the floor next to Isabeau and laid the diary on her lap.

"I can't breathe," Katarina said.

"Stay quiet," Anna said.

"Where are the boys?" Katarina said.

"Dear Lord," Sara said. "I told them to get down here! Why would they go anywhere else?"

"No one is going to look for them," Katarina whispered.

Katarina hoped, dear *Holla* forgive her the thought, without those boys, the soldiers would overlook the women and the children in the cellar. If the trap door should open, she would pour fat from one of the ceramic lamps on the book and let the journal burn. And destroy the past and the only thing she had left of Herr Tucher. Anna sat quietly on the floor, Hannah beside her, wheezing and coughing. The baby slept, each breath rattling its tiny body. Sara stared at Katarina and hugged Albin close. Isabeau fidgeted with her fingers. Katarina put her arm around Isabeau and she pushed Katarina away.

"What about my horse?" Isabeau whispered.

She had an impulsive, crazy look Katarina could feel. Coupled with Katarina's panic, the look scared her. Katarina saw a rage similar to that she'd seen on Isabeau's father, his determined will, his capable spirit. But Isabeau was a child. She would act rash and get herself killed. What a waste of human spirit. Katarina only hoped Isabeau would get to know her father before that happened.

Clanking boot-falls enter the house. Men shouted. Someone screamed. The trap door flew open. Bright morning light and a chilly spring air flooded the tiny cellar. This was promptly replaced with a beastly stench of sweat, blood and alcohol. The ceramic lamps fluttered in the wind.

A man's guttural command made the women and the children stand up and back against the wall. Three soldiers dressed in dark uniforms with red sashes around their torsos bounded down the steps and planted themselves in front of them. Dark hair hung limp out the bottom of their red fur hats. Droopy dark mustaches spread like mangled curtains in front of their stained, smelly snarls. This lot of soldiers was different than the last. They weren't looking for food and beer. These men meant to extinguish them.

One soldier up in the kitchen hollered in a strange language and waved for the women and the children to come out. The three soldiers led the way. Katarina clutched the book in one hand and Isabeau's hand in the other and climbed the steps. The tiny kitchen teemed with men's bodies. The smell was overwhelming. The soldiers pushed the women out of the house like the frightened lambs they were. They prodded the women and made them line up against the wall.

The horses whinnied. The back of the barn was on fire. The fire would engulf the building in no time if the smoke didn't kill the animals first.

Katarina felt Isabeau's hand tighten around hers. Isabeau's body tensed and coiled like a cat preparing to strike a mouse. She pulled out of Katarina's grasp, but Katarina managed to get another grip on her hand. She squirmed. The horses' whinnies rose in pitch, demanding, desperate. Isabeau tried to break free again but Katarina held her back. One of the soldiers grunted and pointed his sword at the two of them.

The horses shrieked now, audible panic and pain. Man may suffer, but the cries of trapped, injured animals were pure agony. The soldier looked away. Isabeau shot Katarina a threatening glare. Katarina understood. She felt Isabbeau's hand squeeze her own. Isabeau wouldn't let her look away and tightened her grip. Her energy was building. Katarina took a deep breath and gathered her strength.

Together Katarina and Isabeau bolted. Men shouted behind the two of them, all around them. They ran on. Isabeau pulled the heavy barn door open and smoke billowed out of the barn carrying the smell of burning wood, tinged animal hair and flesh. Isabeau disappeared into the barn. One after another, the horses shot out of the door and galloped away. Soldiers ran in every direction after the horses. Isabeau came out with her sorrel mare. She grabbed a handful of mane, jumped on the horse's back and stretched her hand towards Katarina.

"Get on!" she commanded.

She bent down and grabbed Katarina's free arm before Katarina could argue the point. Katarina jumped as high as she could and let Isabeau yank her astride the horse's back end. Katarina adjusted her seat, feeling the warmth and the panic of the horse as the mare readied to run. Katarina looked back at the worker's house and saw the other women lined up against the wall. Tanner pleaded with the soldiers. Herr Tucher ran to his side. Soldiers ran towards Isabeau and Katarina atop the horse.

"Wait," Katarina said.

Isabeau worked the reins and the mare pranced on the spot. "Do you want to stay here?" Isabeau screamed.

Katarina closed her eyes. "Ride away."

A horrible pang of guilt burned an image onto Katarina's mind: her best friends in the clutches of mad mercenaries. This drove the panic of being on a horse's back out of her thoughts. As they galloped away, the guilt faded and panic returned. She opened her eyes. They were riding into the thick of the troop.

A horde of men approached them with drawn swords. They yelled to Isabeau and Katarina and tried to spook the horse. Isabeau slowed the horse to a canter. The horse bobbed and Katarina felt like she would fall off. Katarina grabbed Isabeau around the waist with her free hand, the book wedged in between them. Isabeau slowed the horse to a walk.

"Ride up the South Hill," Katarina whispered.

Isabeau steered the horse away from the encroaching men, kicked the horse's flanks and they jumped into a gallop. They passed up over the South Hill covered by linden trees. Once over the hill, they rounded a bend. In the distance, Katarina could see the sloe bushes that served as a wall around the secret meadow. Katarina pointed and Isabeau understood.

A favorite place of Katarina's where old fruit trees and herbs grew, there was something mystical about the meadow. As they neared the sloe bushes, Katarina saw the covered wagons of the *Tross*: the throng of those who traveled and camped with the soldiers. Made up of everything from families and friends of the soldiers, refugees to marketeers and prostitutes, Herr Tucher said the *Tross* could grow larger than the troops themselves. Smoke rose from inside the bushes.

"How could they camp there?" Katarina said. "This is my meadow!"

"Where should we go now?" Isabeau said.

"I'm not sure," Katarina said.

Isabeau steered away from the meadow and they rode at a walk in a southernly direction. It was now well into the morning. They needed to find cover.

"I have an idea," Katarina said. "Head towards the river."

Katarina pointed to a grass-covered path. Isabeau nodded in agreement and urged the horse forward at a gallop. Katarina laid her head on Isabeau's back. The horse's hooves splashed in shallow water. Isabeau motioned for Katarina to dismount. Katarina slid off the horse's back and waded through the icy river. The horse bounded across the water and Isabeau steered the horse towards a tree stump so Katarina could easily get back on. They galloped on. Katarina pointed to the tree-covered hill where she remembered Hans-Wolfgang lived. The roof of his house had once peeked up over the forest, but now she saw only the trees. There was also no visible way up the hill. Katarina slid off the horse's back and walked along the road at the base of the hill, looking for a path through the trees. Isabeau dismounted as well.

"I was sure this was the way," Katarina said. "I haven't been here for a while."

"I think I found a path," Isabeau said.

Together they picked their way up through the underbrush until they saw the ivy-covered stone wall surrounding the Eierhofen estate. Isabeau had to coax the mare to follow her through the overgrown area. They hugged the wall, their clothes snagging on brambles and twigs, until they saw two large wooden gates in a stone arched door frame. One gate was open just a crack. Its hinges squealed as Katarina pushed it open.

They entered a tidy courtyard. Next to the door frame stood two exotic-looking trees planted in terracotta pots double the size of a wine barrel. The bottom floor of the house was completely built from pinkish sandstone and the upper story was timbered. Small windows with round panes of thick glass looked clean and whole. Hans-Wolfgang had kept the place well and it had obviously never been sacked.

An arrow whizzed over their heads.

Katarina tried to make out where the arrows were coming from. The windows in the upper floors were closed. Isabeau backed out of the gate and took cover behind the stone wall. Katarina ran towards the house. Another arrow whizzed over her head.

"Please don't shoot!" Katarina yelled. "Stop!"

A face looked out from a hole in the red tiled roof. "Oh dear God!" the face said and disappeared again. Promptly the front door opened and Hans-Wolfgang ran out. He pulled Katarina into an embrace and looked at her with an affection she never thought the man capable of. The journal Katarina had in her grasp pressed into her chest. Isabeau walked up behind the two. Her horse snorted. Hans-Wolfgang let Katarina go and stared at Isabeau, speechless for a moment. He had not been this close to her for almost ten years.

Katarina never understood why Hans-Wolfgang wanted to stay out of Isabeau's way, watching her only from afar. She wondered why Hans-Wolfgang hadn't told Isabeau he was her father or why he didn't bring her here to live with him. Now Katarina watched him approach her. It seemed painful for him. Isabeau had grown into a gruff, tough-skinned girl who would have accepted the truth, or so Katarina thought.

"Isabeau, this is Hans-Wolfgang," Katarina said. "We can stay here tonight. He'll take your horse to the stable with his."

He cleared his throat looking for his voice. "Come with me. You can see the stable for yourself so you know where she stands."

Katarina watched the two walk away, Hans-Wolfgang leading Isabeau's horse. He watched Isabeau with a mixture of fascination and pride. They returned after a few moments. He saw the two gates were still open, ran over and shut them up tight, securing them with a large wooden board. He motioned for Katarina and Isabeau to follow him, ran ahead and opened the front doors, leading them into the entrance hall. Two staircases in this tower structure curved to the upper floor around an intricately carved oak door that led to the main hall.

The house had belonged to Friedrich von Obereierhofen, Isabeau's grandfather. Her mother had grown up here. The only surviving family Isabeau had now was her father, Hans-Wolfgang. Up until now, she'd had Herr Tucher as her teacher and mentor and Katarina was the only mother she knew. Isabeau knew Katarina was not the woman who gave her life but she never asked about her parents. As far as anyone else was concerned, Isabeau was the maid's bastard child. Katarina realized Isabeau had no idea where they were. Or who she was.

Isabeau von Obereierhofen.

Hans-Wolfgang walked under an arched doorway to the side of the entrance hall and descended a dark stairway that led down to the kitchen. Katarina and Isabeau followed him into a warm, brightly lit kitchen smelling of sweet spiced wine. Two women peeled root vegetables at a long working table lit by two high windows.

The one woman with thick dark hair braided down her back sipped from a cup. She walked to the wide, low fireplace, a large hearth where a few maids could cook at the same time, and ladled up three mugs from an iron pot hanging from a chain. Isabeau and Katarina each took a mug from her and they drank the warm, honey-laden wine flavored with cinnamon and anise. Katarina finally set the heavy journal down on the table and rubbed the cramp in her arm.

"Five of us live here, including me," Hans-Wolfgang said as he sat down at the bench. "I have the two women: Magdalena…"

The woman with the dark braid set the third mug down in front of him and nodded.

"…And Sieglinde here."

The young blonde smiled, thin lips straining over tiny teeth.

"And we have two farm boys who help with the chores."

Isabeau and Katarina sat at the bench as well. Hans-Wolfgang leaned closer to Isabeau.

"I have known Katarina for a long time," he said. "I have asked her to come here and work for me. For the two of you to come live with me. You could help me with the horses. I would like to start breeding this year. We could cover your mare, if you'd like to have a foal next spring."

Isabeau scrutinized Hans-Wolfgang now, searching his features, trying to figure out who he was and why he was here. Sitting next to him, one could see she had Hans-Wolfgang's piercing blue eyes, the curve of his mouth, the rounded tip of his nose.

"I don't like living there with Herr Tucher's wife," Isabeau said. "She's stupid. Christoph is mean to me and she doesn't make him stop."

"Then it's settled…" Hans-Wolfgang said.

"Nothing is settled," Katarina said. "We'll stay here today and tonight and then we'll see…"

"I'm staying here," Isabeau said.

"I'll show Isabeau to her room. Katarina, you can stay down here by the fire tonight. Rest up. It may be a long night. I hope the mercenaries overlook the house up here. We'll extinguish the lamps. They might think this is but a knoll of trees on a hill."

A young boy, not yet a man, sweat dripping from dark-blond stringy hair, ran into the kitchen, speaking and catching his breath at the same time.

"Slow down, Bubo!" Hans-Wolfgang said. "Give him something to drink."

Bubo waved Magdalena and her cup away and spoke:

"Seems there was some trouble between the soldiers and the Hauptmann who made their quarters in Lonnerstadt. Four soldiers are to be hung tomorrow for their crimes. They must have really caused some trouble last night. Lots of villagers have suffered. The four soldiers are to be made examples of. I'll walk towards Höchstadt to see where the hanging will take place—don't want to miss that."

Katarina stood. "I must go see if anything has happened to Sara."

Bubo took the mug from Magdalena and swallowed it down in one gulp. "You won't be going back just yet. The soldiers are making their camps on the hill by the Alter Hut. They are still out looking for food and spoils."

Katarina took another mug of wine, her hand shaking as she took a sip.

"Just stay put for now," Magdalena said. "You can move tomorrow."

The rest of the day dragged by. Katarina wrestled between thoughts of leaving Isabeau here and walking back to Sichardtshof or giving in to drinking the wine Magdelene gave her. Its effects reduced Katarina's panic to a nagging, anxious dread. The whole night, Katarina sat by the fire nodding off but not finding any peace. The time passed without any intrusions except the sounds of violence in the distance.

The next morning, Hans-Wolfgang finally felt it was safe enough to move around outside. Katarina followed him down the front steps of the Upper Eierhofen house, walking through the cool, morning mist that hung as tangible drops in the air. The foggy damp carried the smell of large animal and spent gun powder. Hans-Wolfgang and Isabeau led their horses out of the barn and tethered them to the wooden wall. Isabeau brushed her mare's flanks in long strokes. Hans-Wolfgang took one of his stallion's hooves in between his knees and scraped it clean.

"I'll be back this afternoon," Katarina yelled over to the two.

Hans-Wolfgang let the hoof down, straightened and waved a hand in response.

Katarina walked out of the yard and down the path towards the Aisch River flood plain, crossing the river and heading towards the mill. The first farm she passed in Mailach depicted the result of the violent, swirling storm Katarina had heard in the night: wooden planks strewn throughout the farmyard; slaughtered animal carcasses that had been picked to the bone; straw and hay covering the ground. The stinging smell of charred flesh hung around the farm like a shroud. The farmer cleared the planks to one side. The farmer's wife stood next to the gate and stared at Katarina as she walked by, as if she was wary of anyone who ventured out today.

"*Scheiss Söldner*," the farmer's wife said.

There was no sign of the damned mercenaries, though. Katarina asked her if the mercenaries had continued on and she said no, they were camping in the villages and had to behave themselves today now that four were to be hung.

Katarina crossed the silent main road and walked along the track back into the Edelgraben, the hollow situated at the base of the low mountain range called Steigerwald. The North Hill, once green with forest was now a rise of burnt brush and trampled mud. To the south, smoke rose from that indigo shadow, meaning the *Tross* still camped in Katarina's secret meadow.

She walked along the string of ponds at the deepest point of the hollow. They were called *Himmelsweiher*, Heaven's Ponds, because they were filled only by rainwater from the heavens. The ponds were stocked with carp but how could the fish survive? The water smelled brackish and a slimy film swam on top. At the end of the track Katarina saw smoke rising from the Sichardtshof farm.

A smoky, burnt smell intensified as she walked into the farmyard. The fencing surrounding the yard had been battered down. The barn where the horses bedded had burnt down completely. Across the farmyard, Lasse led one of the horses to the paddock behind the house. Katarina walked over to him as he led the horse into the stable adjoining the kitchen. He ducked his head to come back out of the door, took off his hat and approached Katarina.

"I retrieved the horses somehow," Lasse said. "They'll have to stand in the vaulted stable now where the cows were." He removed his long leather coat and wiped his forehead.

"Is anyone hurt?" Katarina said.

"No, we are a bit shaken, but…" Lasse said.

"Where is the master?" Katarina asked.

"He left with Bjarne to retrieve the sheep. They aren't safe out in the pasture. The master wants to bring whatever the wolves have left us and keep them here in the farmyard. If any are left at all."

Katarina nodded and took her leave. She walked past the well back towards the workers' house. The loose bushes around the well were charred as was much of the other surrounding shrubbery. The workers' house had suffered no damage by the look of it.

Katarina tried to open the door but it was locked. "Sara it's me."

Sara threw the door open and grabbed Katarina with such an impact that Katarina nearly fell against the wall.

"Are you two all right?" Sara asked. "We saw you ride right into the group of soldiers and thought you'd had it. I am so glad to see you. Herr Tucher is worried sick about you two."

Katarina hugged her tight and they stood silent for a moment. "Is anyone hurt?"

Sara loosened her embrace. "No, Herr Tucher gave them whatever they wanted and they left. I have no idea what. Must have been a lot of something. But Elsbeth's baby died. I buried him this morning. And the boys never came back. Maybe they joined the ranks."

Katarina took her hand. "None of you are hurt, that is the main thing. I came back to tell you we're leaving. I want to fetch my box and a few of Isabeau's things. And my hand cart."

"What?" Sara slumped onto her stool. "I wouldn't blame you if you left, but, Katarina…" Her eyes filled with tears. "Where in God's name are you going?"

Katarina told her about riding up to Hans-Wolfgang last night and the well-kept state of the place. "I have no business here anymore. And I feel Isabeau needs to be with her father. She will learn the truth when he's ready to tell her."

"Funny man, that Hans-Wolfgang," Sara said. "Why hasn't he told her?"

"I wonder the same thing. But she wants to stay there. They are taking care of the horses."

"You must stay and wait for Herr Tucher to come back. He is worried sick." Sara stood and prodded the fire. "Albin! Get me some water, please, so I can start the meal."

"Here, give me the bucket," Katarina said, "I'll get the water."

She went outside with the bucket and walked towards the well. The day was going to be warmer than the last weeks. But any comfort the warmth gave Katarina was quickly stolen away as she took in all the damage around the farm. The charred smell made her nose sting. One bloody night could destroy all the work they had done over the last ten years.

The path to the well was dotted with strange boot prints muddied with blood. Katarina slowed down and looked closer at the loose bushes alongside the well. Something moved inside. That smell of sweat, leather, rancid meat and alcohol the soldiers carried filled her nostrils. Throwing the bucket aside, Katarina pulled the dagger from her belt and prodded through the light-green and black leaves surrounding the well. She saw something metal and stuck her other hand in among the brush. Her sleeve snagged on the twigs.

A bloody hand shot out and seized Katarina's wrist.

"Help me," a man's voice whispered.

Katarina suppressed a scream and she froze, hot with fear, paralyzed. The strong hand, almost twice the size of hers, pulled her towards the bushes.

"Don't call out," the man's voice said. "Help me!"

Katarina spread the leaves with her dagger and saw the man's bloody face. Long curls the color of a stray dog, not quite blond, not quite brown. Menacing blue eyes she remembered as once angelic. A slit over the right eye. Another slit underneath.

"Pieter? Oh, dear Lord in Heaven, what are you doing here?"

"Katarina, help me. Get me indoors," Pieter said. "Please get me out of sight."

Katarina helped him crawl back out from the bushes and steadied him on his feet. He put a rancid smelling arm over her shoulder and together they limped back to the workers' house. He swayed when they got to the door and fell to his knees. Katarina propped him against her thigh.

Sara opened the door and jumped back like she'd been punched in the stomach. "Kata…oh dear God, no…!"

"Sara, be quiet. It's Pieter. Help me get him in."

Together they dragged him through the kitchen and into the Tanners' sleeping alcove. He was about to lose consciousness.

"I need water," he whispered. "Help me get these clothes off. I must get rid of them."

The two women sat him on the floor, wedged up against the bed. Sara shook her head and muttered as she backed out of the alcove. Katarina followed her into the kitchen and poured a cup of wine. She came back to Pieter and handed him the cup. He downed it in one gulp.

"Help me out of this shirt," he said. "Get me onto the bed."

Katarina took his cup, set it aside and helped him onto the bed. She pulled the bloody shirt over his head. He could only raise his arms to shoulder height. His back was covered with fresh, deeply-slashed wounds and red, swollen welts that looked older.

"What happened to your…?"

"No hysterical questions, Katarina," he said.

He staggered to his feet, unlaced his trousers and his legs crumpled underneath him. Katarina abruptly left the room.

"Don't be so shy," Pieter said. "Come back and help me stand up."

She returned to his side and helped him to his feet. He leaned on Katarina's shoulder and pulled his trousers down. He got them over his behind and slumped back down on the bed.

"Help me out of these," he said.

Katarina knelt down and took one of his boots in her hands. She pulled gently.

"No, don't," he whispered.

Katarina tugged his trousers off despite the boots and left him sitting there naked.

"Get me some water," he said, slumping back onto the bed.

Katarina went into the kitchen, grabbed the bucket from next to the fireplace and filled it with hot water. She took a rag that hung by the fire. Sara handed her a ceramic flask with essential oils and she dribbled a shot into the water. Katarina went back to Sara's bed. Pieter was sitting up. She set the bucket next to him and left the room.

"Do you have clothes for me?" he said.

Sara had already gathered a few bits from Tanner into a pile and handed Katarina the clothes.

"Just throw them through the doorway, Katarina," he said.

Bjarne came rushing through the door. "What a catastrophe! You should have seen the hanging. They only hung two of them because one of the soldiers slammed two of the guards and made this spectacular escape. He went right up and slit the throat on two other guards who shot at him. They were trying to reload. Then he just disappeared in the crowd of spectators. The crowd closed around him, like they swallowed him up. He was a bloody mess, too. He won't get far. The villagers hate those soldiers. You'll see his bloody bones hanging from a tree when the farmers get a hold of him!"

He stopped talking and caught his breath. Sarah handed him a mug of beer and he took a long draw.

"Then they decapitated the last soldier, just in case he decided to escape too! That lot won't be bothering us anymore. The Hauptmann made a point to apologize for the soldiers and their behavior."

Pieter leaned in the doorway, dressed in Tanner's things. Katarina remembered Pieter as being quite tall, but he had become massive. He handed Katarina the bucket of bloody water.

"Thank you," Pieter said.

Bjarne stood with his mouth gaping disbelief. "That's him! The soldier who escaped…"

Sara looked sternly at Pieter. "You cannot stay here."

She shook her head like a mother wanting to scold her boy for playing too roughly. Pieter slumped in the doorway and all three of them rushed in as he collapsed. They laid him out on the floor. He was unconscious.

Sara wagged a finger at Katarina. "You're going to need to be very careful."

"Why me?" Katarina said. "He is not my charge."

Katarina had to collect her things and leave before anyone else saw her. She was not taking care of Pieter. She would leave Sichardtshof without saying anything to Herr Tucher. Looking for her handcart, she sneaked around the outbuildings. Once her home, her haven, she now felt threatened and exposed, like someone was watching from the windows, from the hills, from Heaven above. She slipped into the barn where all the farm implements were kept. Her handcart stood on the spot where she'd been attacked. Panic forced her to catch her breath again and again like she was suffocating. She forced back the tears. Voices outside, ones she couldn't identify, made her keep her composure and peek out of the door. No one was about.

Katarina pulled the cart out of the barn and towards the main house. She parked the handcart in the paddock and walked into the vaulted stable adjoining the kitchen. Three horses filled the stable and she squeezed by them. She looked into the kitchen and breathed a sigh when she saw it was empty. Sticking her head through the doorway she looked up the stairway. Animated women's voices cackled in the rooms overhead.

She climbed up the stairs. The voices came from the sitting room. Floorboards creaked as she sneaked along the hall to the small room in which Herr Tucher now slept. The voices stopped. She slipped into his room and stood silent for a moment, breathing in his scent and looking over his things, cramped into the tiny space she had used as her room. The voices in the sitting room chattered on again so Katarina searched for something, anything she could take that would remind her of Herr Tucher. Behind the basin on the table, she found a full bottle of laudanum. She was having that.

"Hello?" one of the maids asked.

Katarina ran out of his room and down the stairs. She slipped back into the kitchen, into the alcove, and climbed over Frau Tucher's trunks. Isabeau's feather tick, her writing things and her bible lay strewn on the stone floor in the corner. She gathered Isabeau's things, climbed back over that woman's trunks and carried her things to the handcart, set them in and came back into the kitchen.

Sara stood in the doorway holding Katarina's wooden box. "I thought you might need this."

"I was too comfortable here," Katarina said. "I should have known this was just temporary."

"I don't know what to say, Katarina," Sara said and set the box on the table. She pulled Katarina close and held her tight. "I will miss you terribly. You won't be far away, you can come back during the day."

The tears threatened Katarina again. "I'm afraid to even move about outside here."

"Oh this can't go on. You'll see." Sara sniffed and turned her face away.

"Who knows how long these soldiers will come through?" Katarina said. "Will we survive this whole thing at all?"

They stood silent for a moment. Sara pulled away, wiped her face with the back of her hand. She seemed to wrestle with herself.

"There's something else we need to settle." Sara stopped and looked away. She walked over to the fireplace and poked at the fire. "It's about Pieter."

Katarina waited for her to go on.

"He can't stay here." Her voice rose in pitch. "He is infested with bugs. He is injured horribly and I'm afraid he has some sort of plague or something. You know what these soldiers are like. He's not the same boy he was ten years ago."

"You can't turn him away," Katarina said.

Sara gave her a disappointed look. "He cannot stay here."

"What are you getting at?" Katarina said. "Do you want me to take him with me? He can't travel."

Herr Tucher came into the kitchen. Katarina's heart jumped up in her throat. He rushed to her side, took her shoulders in his hands and then embraced her.

"Dear Lord, am I relieved to see you are not hurt." He kissed her lips, not caring that Sara stood there. "Who cannot travel?"

Sara came next to the two of them. "Pieter is here, Herr Tucher. He must have been traveling with the soldiers."

"Ah, yes, the boy made it back," Herr Tucher said, releasing Katarina. "I had corresponded with him and then lost contact. How is he then?"

"He's hurt," Katarina said.

"He's dangerous," Sara said. "He can't stay back there with us."

Gret and Gerlin came into the kitchen. "My mistress wants a word," the one said.

"Oh, good God, what doesn't your mistress want?" Herr Tucher said, louder than necessary.

The two girls parted and in swished Frau Tucher. The kitchen was quite full at this point. Katarina turned away, stoked at the fire, took two logs and laid them on the bare embers. Frau Kuni had always said logs burn better when they have a companion. Sara backed up and touched shoulders with Katarina. Katarina watched as Herr and Frau Tucher positioned themselves face to face as if they prepared to duel. Herr Tucher's cheeks burned red with an anger Katarina had seldom seen.

"Someone must take control of the workers and their comings and goings," Frau Tucher said. "I will now regulate this. These women will stay out of the main house unless summoned." She pointed the lazy finger towards Sara and Katarina. "My maid will take care of this kitchen. I do not want these flea-bitten women in my house."

So, Frau Tucher *was* staying here indefinitely. Katarina's forehead broke a sweat. She suddenly felt the need to make a break here and now. Katarina moved to the table, heaved her wooden box and walked through the stable, dropping the wooden box onto her handcart.

"Where are you going with those things?" Frau Tucher's voice resonated from the kitchen. "Whose things are those? This woman cannot just remove things that do not belong to her."

Herr Tucher's voice boomed. "Take my wife upstairs now. I will deal with this."

Their argument droned throughout the house. The din pulsed into unimportance. Katarina took a last look around the paddock, the farmyard, the North Hill.

"Silence all three of you!" Herr Tucher hollered.

"This discussion is by no means settled," Frau Tucher called from above.

Katarina peeked around the stable door. Sure that Frau Tucher was upstairs, she walked back into the kitchen. Sara stood quietly with Herr Tucher. When he saw Katarina, he rushed towards her and put his hand on her shoulder. Katarina shrugged it away, tilted her head back and met his gaze with as much defiance as she could summon. She turned to Sara and hugged her, tears welling hot and explosive in her head. Katarina released Sara, brushed by Herr Tucher and found an old cloak hanging in the alcove. She shook the dust from the cloak, slung it over her shoulders and came to a stop in front of him.

"Adieu," Katarina said to him, her head high.

He said nothing. Katarina walked to her cart and took the handle in her hand. Sara came up behind her.

"What am I going to do with Pieter?" Sara said. "I can't have him there with the children. With my child."

Katarina put the handle down. "What should I do with him? He is bad off and cannot travel."

"Don't leave him here."

"You act like he's my charge. Go ask the master. Or the master's wife, for that matter."

"Katarina, don't do this to us."

"Why are you burdening me with this too?"

Sara gave Katarina an exasperated look.

Katarina growled. "Where is Tanner? Will he give me a horse? And come with me and help me bring Pieter up to the Eierhofen estate? The house is big enough for me to isolate him and try to make him healthy. I'm sure you will all agree this is my task."

The two women walked together through the farmyard and looked for Tanner. They found him in the shed collecting firewood for the evening. As the three walked back towards the workers' house, Sara explained the situation and how she wanted him to take Pieter up to the Eierhofen and away from here.

"I think he should stay here," Katarina said. "Ask the master."

Tanner nodded towards his wife. "Katarina, we can go over the hill by the four lindens and towards the river where you said the water was so low we could pass."

Anna met them at the door. "He is feverish and should not travel. I'll take care of him. He's grown into quite a handsome man."

Sara shook her head. "No, Anna, we'll all get sick."

"Let me talk to him," Tanner said and disappeared behind the wood stove.

He nodded his head as he came back out of his bedroom. "He is barely conscious but he is willing to go. He can't stay here in our room. I'll collect him and get him up there. Please, wife, scrub the room with everything you have after we leave. I will put him on his own horse. I don't want to get close to him. Poor bastard."

After Tanner loaded Pieter over a horse's back, they stood in the farmyard. Sara hugged Katarina and kissed her on the cheek.

Sara smiled. "This is for the better."

"For you, of course," Katarina said.

Katarina looked up at the house, blank reflections from empty windows. Herr Tucher was going to let her go. He had always said she was not his prisoner and it was her decision to stay or leave. She walked through the smashed gate, wishing he would run up behind her, tell her the wife was leaving and beg her to come home. But he wasn't going to, was he?

She never even considered the thought this day could come. He was her dearest friend; for the last ten years, her constant companion. This past decade, Herr Tucher had worn down the guards around her heart, dismissed them and sent them home. Katarina learned to love him completely. When he traveled, she missed him terribly. The longing made his homecoming so much sweeter. She knew he would return and he always did. But this parting was more complete, cutting, interminable. They would not only be separated for days, for months, but forever.

"Come on, Katarina," Tanner bellowed. "Keep up. I have other things to do today."

Part 2

Chapter 18

Katarina

Katarina stopped in the middle of the stone staircase leading to the upper floors of the Upper Eierhofen estate, set Pieter's feet down and wiped her sweating forehead. Tanner, just above her on the staircase, readjusted his grip under Pieter's arms, blew out a puff of air and continued climbing backwards up the stairs, dragging Pieter with him.

The Upper Eierhofen entrance hall was cool and dark; a shock after coming in from the bright afternoon. High windows framed the two stone staircases curving around a massive oak door that led into the main hall. Shafts of muted sunlight shone through the round fist-sized window panes. As Katarina and Tanner struggled to get the unconscious Pieter up the steps, their scuffling and laboring echoed off the stone walls.

"This is one big boy," Tanner said, turned his head and carefully felt the next step with his foot.

One of Hans-Wolfgang's farm boys, the one he called Bubo, pressed past Katarina. He took a place next to Tanner, placing both hands under Pieter's right shoulder. Together the two men supported Pieter's upper half. They lumbered the rest of the way up the stairs and into the hallway. Katarina struggled to keep a grip on Pieter's legs but his heavy feet scraped on the floor.

Hans-Wolfgang came up behind Katarina. "Is that the Dutchman? He's taken a pounding somewhere, hasn't he?"

"Yes..." Katarina panted. "I want to try...to heal him."

"Good," Hans-Wolfgang said. "Another man of his size residing at the estate is an asset." He moved ahead of them all, opened a door to the left and bent over Pieter's unresponsive face. "If he lives."

They carried Pieter into the room. Katarina let his feet drop. The room looked like it was made up for a guest. The window was open and the light breeze carried the scent of freshly washed linens. A gray woven-wool rug lay on the floor and a pitcher filled with water stood in a washing bowl on a table.

"Whose room is this?" Katarina said.

"This is to be your room, Katarina," Hans-Wolfgang said.

"Don't put him on the bed."

Tanner shifted his weight impatiently from one foot to the other. Katarina moved to the wardrobe, opened the door and found a large basin and bed sheets. She shook out one sheet and smoothed it over the rug. Tanner and Bubo laid Pieter down on the floor. Tanner waved to Katarina and, without a word, left the room. The others ran out behind him. Katarina knelt next to Pieter and felt his forehead. He was burning up.

Isabeau walked in and let herself fall on the bed. "My room is nice. Do you want to see it?"

"Yes, but let me clean him up first."

Isabeau knelt by Katarina's side. "Is he going to die?"

"I hope not," Katarina said. "Do you remember him?"

"Why would I remember him?"

"He lived with us when you were a baby." Katarina moved towards his feet and pulled on one of his boots.

"I don't remember what happened to me as a baby."

Pieter's boot seemed to be stuck fast. Katarina was reluctant to pull any harder. An infection of the feet could lose him the limbs. She was not in the position to treat such serious afflictions. She wondered where he had been and if she should be afraid of him. Just like all of them, he probably fell prey to those soldiers or some mob of bandits. She would do everything she could to save him but this could finish him off.

"Could you please bring me some water from the kitchen?" Katarina said.

Isabeau left the room. Pieter muttered in his dreamy, fevered state. Katarina took the basin out of the wardrobe, set it down and knelt next to his head. Isabeau came back holding a pitcher.

"One more thing," Katarina said. "Would you please bring my box? I left it out in my handcart."

Isabeau ran out. A few moments later Katarina heard a thump, thump, thump. Something was working its way up the stairs. Now it was being dragged down the hall. Isabeau appeared in the doorway. She gave

Katarina's wooden box one great heave, carried it across the room and thumped it down.

Katarina opened the box, took out some oak bark and threw a handful into the pitcher. Oak bark had astringent properties and was the only thing she had to treat these infections. "Please have one of the women boil this for a few minutes and strain the tincture."

Isabeau ran out again with the pitcher. Katarina grabbed a spoon out of the box, pulled the full flask of laudanum she found in Herr Tucher's room from her pocket, and poured some onto the spoon. She dribbled just a few drops into his mouth, licked the spoon and laid it aside. She stood, knelt again by his foot and pulled on the boot. It wouldn't budge. Isabeau walked into the room and set the steaming pitcher down.

"Hold his leg still," Katarina said to Isabeau. "Yes, by the knee."

Katarina yanked again and felt something crusted giving way. The boot slid off and the smell of rancid meat made her stomach lurch. Katarina unwrapped the footwrap. The flesh was pounded, chewed and rotten, like the carcass of an animal lying in the forest after being mauled by a predator. But his toes were still red and intact. She threw the boot in the corner of the room, worked the other one off and threw it there as well.

"We will burn both of these."

Katarina fished some dried herbs out of her box, set them in a shallow bowl and handed the bowl to Isabeau.

"Take this to the kitchen and sprinkle some embers over the top. Get the herbs smoking. This smell makes me sick."

Katarina poured the warm oak bark brew into the basin, bent Pieter's right knee and put his foot in. His knee slumped to one side so she supported his leg while his foot soaked. After she dried his foot, she emptied the basin out of the window, refilled it and soaked the other. She applied a tincture of hawthorn soaked in alcohol to the infected skin.

She took a comb out of the box and found a small pillow stuffed with sloe seeds. When Isabeau had a belly ache, she heated the little pillow and laid it on her stomach. Now the little pillow would help prop Pieter's head. She covered the pillow with a rag, set his head down on top and picked through the matted hair. Nits jumbled on the individual hairs close to his scalp. Clumps of hair came out in her hand and the lice scurried across the bare scalp. She took a bottle of broadleaf oil out of her box, poured a handful onto his head and massaged his scalp.

Isabeau came back with the smoking bowl of herbs. She set the bowl on the floor and lay across the bed. She seemed to be fascinated by their new guest.

"Please fetch me some more water," Katarina said. "I'm sorry to chase you so."

Isabeau jumped up, grabbed the pitcher and ran out of the room. Katarina removed all his clothes and threw them aside. She pulled another linen sheet from the wardrobe and covered him. Isabeau came back with a steaming pitcher of water. Katarina washed each limb with clean water. She rolled him on his side and studied his finely-muscled back. The fresh welts on his back burned with infection. He must have been whipped not only recently but, judging by the scars, years ago. Regularly. He seemed more comfortable lying on his side so Katarina treated his back with the hawthorn tincture and let him lie. Good thing he was almost unconscious. If he had felt the pain and protested, she would not have been able to do this job.

Sieglinde appeared in the doorway. "He's a handsome man. Now that he's clean." She had a suspicious glare and a slight sneer on her lips. Her thin blonde hair hung to her shoulders and a few wisps covered her smooth white forehead giving her a weasely look. "Give me his clothes. I will boil them and hang them over the fire. We have nothing else in that size. We certainly have no boots that would fit such a large man."

"Do we have another room for him?" Katarina asked.

She came in, knelt by Katarina's side. "He can stay in my room."

"There's plenty of room here," Katarina scolded. "This is larger than the house at Sichardtshof. He needs his rest. You can see how sick he is."

Sieglinde rolled his brown breeches and the bloody shirt together and left the room. "I'll make one up for him."

Katarina shut the window and laid her hand on Pieter's forehead. He was still feverish but his limbs were cold. She found an extra blanket in the wardrobe, covered him and stood to leave the room. He stirred and tried to say something. It sounded like he said 'thirsty.'

Katarina took a clean swab of linen, dipped it in the fresh water and let water dribble in his mouth. He tried to talk again; delirious mumbling of a feverish man. She found a tattered bed sheet in the wardrobe, tore it into smaller sections, dampened them with water and wrapped his calves to bring down the fever. He mumbled again. She leaned over, pushed a strand of hair away from his forehead.

"Thank you, Katarina," he whispered.

Katarina kissed his cheek, stood and walked to the door. She looked back at the young man she had known ten years ago. Here, quiet and subdued, he looked like that angelic boy of sixteen. He was never an angel though. He had been a complex and serious young man, too clever for his own good, with an inclination to murderous violence. Katarina shut the door and went looking for Isabeau. She walked down the hallway and peeked through one open door and then another. She found her in the room at the top of the stairs.

Furnished with things fitting a young woman of good standing, the room was dominated by a wooden bed, four posts carved with leaves and vines. Isabeau stood in front of the wardrobe carved in a similar fashion. Her face beamed with pride. Katarina had seen that look once before; the day Isabeau received her horse. The doors of the wardrobe were open. It was filled with a young lady's clothes, some just the size to fit her youthful, lean frame. A chest of drawers stood on the opposite wall with combs and little crystal bottles on it. A candle in a brass holder stood on the bedside table.

Katarina went into the room and looked out the window. Here behind the ivy-covered stone wall surrounded by the trees, the Upper Eierhofen estate seemed cut off from the rest of the valley. She thought Herr Tucher would have enjoyed seeing Isabeau in her new room. She suddenly missed him terribly. She'd almost forgotten him with all these new, pressing, life-threatening duties. Herr Tucher would want to engage Hans-Wolfgang in a conversation. He would be impatient, waiting for Pieter to return to health so he could squeeze him for every last detail of his travels. He would...

"Oh dear God, what have I done with his diary?" Katarina seized Isabeau by the shoulders. It was all she had left of him.

Isabeau backed away from her. "He let me draw a picture in that once."

"Where is it?"

"You left it in the kitchen," she said. "I put it under your mattress."

Katarina ran out of the room, back down the hall and threw the door open. Pieter had rolled onto his back and lay noiselessly. She knelt and held her cheek against his face to see if he was still alive. Relieved, she moved to the bed, pulled the journal from under the straw mattress and opened the book.

It fell open to the entry from a trip to Hamburg Katarina and Herr Tucher had made almost ten years ago. Katarina read the poetry he'd written for her after they made love. The rest of the trip was recorded with such care to detail she could hear the gulls and smell sea air. She should tear the pages out, burn the book completely, anything not to feel this void she felt now!

She slammed the journal shut and only then took notice of the tears dampening her cheeks. How pathetic she was—a slave begging for captivity. What had happened to the woman who once ran her own tavern? Katarina put the journal back under the straw mattress. She had made her decision to leave and would attempt this thing called freedom, something she had surrendered intentionally.

"Where is Katarina?" Hans-Wolfgang's voice boomed from below.

The smell of roasting meat wafted up the stairs filling the hallway with a mouth-watering smell. Katarina's empty stomach growled. She wiped the tears from her face, hurried down the steps into the entrance hall and down the steps into the kitchen.

"Set yourself here Katarina and have something to eat," Magdalena said.

Her hearty smile and stubby nose made her look like a fairy. She had her dark-brown curls fixed in a braid down her back. Her broad forehead and dark eyebrows rose and fell as she spooned some pottage onto a wooden bowl and slid it under Katarina's nose.

"How's your man?" she said.

"My man?" Katarina spooned some food into her mouth and savored the wild boar, trying to figure out what spices she had used. "You mean Pieter?"

Sieglinde poured some hot beer and drank from her mug. "What a lovely man. Where did you find him?"

"He must have gotten hurt traveling here from Holland," Katarina said. "He used to live with us at Sichardtshof ten years ago."

"We can use another man here," Hans-Wolfgang said as he came into the kitchen from the open garden door.

Isabeau followed behind him and they both took a seat on the bench. Magdalena set down a plate of food for each of them.

"One that can work," he said. "He's a strong man."

"I bet he carried a pike," Sieglinde said. "He looks like a soldier. They have that look about them. I'd be careful around that one."

The two farmhands came in. The kitchen filled with the smell of horse. Bubo sat next to Katarina and the other boy they called Sepp sat next to Isabeau. Magdalena jumped up and got them some food and poured beer. Their conversation rose and fell beyond Katarina's hazy thoughts. Her limbs became heavy as her stomach filled. She stood, smiled and nodded to the group. Satiated and feeling an unfamiliar loneliness, one she had not felt for a long time, she retreated up the dark stairway to her room and after a quick look at Pieter, she settled onto the bed. In the middle of the night, she jolted awake. She couldn't remember falling asleep. Footsteps padded outside the bedroom. She stood and opened the door. A large tallow lamp hanging at the top of the stairs lit the stairwell. At the other end of the hallway, Katarina saw Magdalena in the shadows as she slipped into the room where Hans-Wolfgang slept.

She shut the door and tried to get back to sleep. Pieter slept uncomfortably and moaned and muttered. Katarina walked into the hallway, lit a sliver of wood from the still-spluttering tallow lamp to light her own lamp. She pulled the journal out from under the mattress, sat on the bed and let the book fall open to an entry written six years ago and a picture of a horse Isabeau had drawn dated 1620.

June 1620

The child Isabeau has just finished her lessons. She is a complex child. Amazing to see her mind at work. Oh yes, I can see her mind at work. I marvel at what the child can do. Propose a problem, like giving the child some meat to chew, and one can physically see her deduce and analyze, swallow and digest. I may never have the chance to work with my own children because the wife insists they only be allowed to interact intellectually with the tutor her family has employed. So, in the spirit of anthropological experimentation, I will see what this girl-child is capable of.

Isabeau asked what I do in this book. She asked if I drew pictures as she does in the dirt with a stick. I showed her my writing and she traced the letters with the finger of her left hand. She wanted to know what my scribblings represented and I read a few sentences for her. I then placed a quill in her right hand and set a fresh piece of parchment on the table. She absently scratched the quill on the paper and quickly tired of the game.

She insisted I allow her to draw a picture in this journal. I at once protested but relented and allowed her the book. I offered her the quill full of ink and as she reached with her left hand, I urged her to use the right hand. She accepted it cautiously but still blotched a great blob of ink onto the journal page. My face involuntarily registered my shock. Isabeau froze as she saw my horror. I caught myself in a heartbeat and corrected the grimace. I smiled. She did so too, laid the quill aside and dipped the forefinger from her left hand into the ink pot.

Her ink-laden child's finger made four swift swipes, incorporating the blob of ill-placed ink. The lines took on the one form she trusted, her most beloved form of all, the outline of a horse, head turned to the side, proud. I quickly grabbed a piece of parchment, set it in front of her and instructed her to repeat the same movements as she had just done. She stood next to the table, wielded that finger like a weapon and drew the same figure, double the size. She added some shadow for the haunch and a curved mark for the strong jaw trained by chomping on grass for hours on end. The image was full of fluid movement and from what I know about art, the image compared to the expertise of a trained artist. I found an empty frame behind my bookcase and showed Isabeau. She nodded in approval and we decided to allow the ink to dry before framing.

I decided to test her new found confidence. I grabbed another piece of parchment and my quill and carefully wrote out the numbers from one to nine, Isabeau's discerning eye watching my every movement. I dipped the quill, shook the excess away and handed it to her. She switched the quill from hand to hand and settled on the left one. She seemed again more comfortable with the left hand and continued to use it, mimicking my movements and writing the numbers quite legibly for a first time.

As quickly as she took to the new skill, she abandoned it, disgusted with how easy it was. She threw the quill aside and stood on the chair, one foot raised as if to step onto the table. I promptly grabbed her wriggling body and set her on the floor. She would swing from the rafters if there was one to swing from. I asked the child to leave, seeing as I must now prepare for my London trip.

Alas, the world is up in arms. The revolt in Bohemia and the installation of the Protestant king Friedrich and his English queen Elizabeth has brought much resistance from the Catholic community. The Catholic Liga has substantial financial support from Bavaria and the storm clouds are gathering. Uncle Paul is supportive of the Protestant cause and what it means to Nuremberg, namely our need to remain independent of the Holy Roman Empire, Bavaria, the Hapsburgs and the Pope. Paul also sees a lucrative business prospect. I am to go to London with a load of raw wool and use his associations to acquire more funding to trade in metal goods and armaments to move into the realm of the Bohemians.

I will attempt to learn some English. I myself will board with a lovely family I met at a public house last year. They are not as those other puritan families we do business with. They know nothing of my family and our businesses and it will stay that way. Because of them, I have developed a taste for the theatre. Crude though that English theater is, yes, but it is entertaining.

Uncle Paul had corresponded with a diplomat named Sir Henry Wotton. I have not yet met the man. Paul knows him from his extensive stays and ties with Venice. He is to be my contact but knowing the way these English noblemen are, I will be meeting the servant of the servant. Still, Paul has secured a safe haven for my wife and boys and they will be spending the summer there, even though I would prefer to have both boys with me. Since the second boy was born, I feel more than ever the need to have some contact with my sons. But the offspring are not mine, they belong to the dynasty.

I am happiest here at my farm. We are far enough away from the city to make us as good as unreachable, at least for whimsical visits. We are still close enough should the need arise. There is no other place for me, no place I feel at home. At home I am, here to stay, to stay with meine Katalein.

Chapter 19

Ralf

Ralf jumped up onto the coach box next to Konrad. The old farm gelding jerked the cart forward and Konrad pulled back tight on the reins. Karl, Martin and Michel settled onto the rotting cart facing backwards. Ralf smiled at the two brothers Michel and Martin as they settled on the back of the cart. The two boys had a special place in his heart. They were orphan boys who were taken in by the Jesuits, much like himself.

"Keep watch," Ralf whispered. "Make sure no one is following."

Konrad snapped the reins and the gelding plodded into motion. Even though the gelding looked like a worn out hack, he seemed to like the work. His shoulders stood as high as Ralf's head and his back end was almost as wide as the coach box. He ate sparingly, could pull his weight the whole day without complaining and also had strong nerves. In the half-light of dawn Ralf needed everyone to keep their wits. Billows of mist swirled around the horse's head as his breath puffed to the rhythm of his labor. The cart rocked slowly to each hoof beat and Ralf felt his stomach lurch. He wished he had thought about food before they set off this cold May morning but he wanted to leave Herzogenaurach before anyone saw them.

They were traveling back to Bamberg after staying in Herzogenaurach days longer than planned. Today, they would reach Höchstadt, a perfect halfway point where they could hopefully spend the night. On the road, they would need to be extra careful. To those soldiers, anyone traveling who might have food, loot or a horse was fair game, no matter which confession they represented.

Soldiers posed only one of the dangers to Ralf and his mission. Other devilish forces striving to thwart him at every turn seemed to be gaining strength. He played over the unusual conversation he had yesterday with the sheriff Vogtmann. Now, all of the sudden, the man was not convinced that Elsbeth, the accused witch, was guilty. Ralf told Vogtmann he wanted

to transport her to Bamberg but Vogtmann refused to give the woman up.
The sheriff finally agreed to keep her in the tower until Ralf filed the
denunciation properly with Dr. Fuchs. Ralf feared Vogtmann would let her
go free. The sheriff seemed to be under Elsbeth's spell and believed her
story about being abused by soldiers. Ralf tried to make him see how he
was being bewitched by the woman's sobs and pleadings, how Satan's
dealings in this case were evident. But no matter, Ralf would have the
woman and the sheriff. If only the people Ralf was trying to help would do
as he said! In the end they were just provincial farmers' sons under the
influence of their misled women.

And then, after his meeting with Vogtmann, the most peculiar thing
happened. Ralf and the boys returned to the inn where they slept. The
innkeeper acted bristled and agitated and told them, all of the sudden, the
inn was full. There was no room for them to sleep. He and the boys could
sleep in a chamber just off the stable with their horse. Then during the
night, they had some intruders. Ralf first thought it was ruffians who only
wanted to scare them. But the men who broke into the dark chamber
intended harm. The intruders were not expecting the Jesuit students to be
so well-trained, prepared to do anything to defend themselves. The
boundary between scaring a man and beating him to death was quickly
overstepped.

Martin, in a half-sleep and backed into a corner, had pummeled one of
the men until Michel had to drag him away. The other intruders fled when
they realized their *Kumpel* was dead. For the rest of the night, he, Martin and
Michel took turns on watch while Konrad and Karl disposed of the dead
ruffian. Who the men were, Ralf had no idea. He feared his welcome in
Herzogenaurach was overstayed. This would all be in his report to Dr.
Fuchs. Ralf would insist commissions be put in place throughout the
provincial villages to strengthen the Catholic presence and further support
the re-catholicization efforts. Bamberg's control over Herzogenaurach was
necessary because of the money the town generated with textile sales. The
close proximity to Protestant Nuremberg was a constant threat to the little
Catholic hamlet and Bamberg had to keep a tight hold over the area.

Even the villages that had not yet fallen to the Protestants strayed
from the correct path. City officials were indifferent and their clergy, inept.
Ralf began to realize the magnitude of his task, this spreading the Word of
God, this saving of the world. One man alone could not protect these

people from their gullible natures and insatiable lusts. The depths these people had already sunk, posing as prey for the devil through the practice of pagan beliefs and superstition was, after all, a simple lack of faith!

Out here in the province, the clergy was just as much to blame for the deterioration of their parishes. They were poorly prepared to teach their people. The Jesuits were the only educators competent enough to take on a task like this. But it was a lot of work and there were so few able bodies. Sometimes, like now, Ralf felt overwhelmed and defeated. Even though he needed to get back to Bamberg, his most pressing task was teaching the people, spreading the word. But how was he supposed to accomplish that? The task was monumental and he couldn't do it from the back of this cart.

The bumpy ride along the rutted road jarred Ralf with every inch of ground they covered. This north-south route was sadly one of the main thoroughfares and the passing troops were leaving it hard-hit, neither sown nor reaped. He remembered this area from ten years ago as a quaint countryside with inviting villages, carp ponds, country inns with kitchens producing mouth-watering delicacies and delicious beer. The waves of troops left little for a traveler, let alone for the people who still lived here. Their traveling was slow going. Ralf could tell he and the boys followed close behind a regiment as if they followed a herd of strange animals. Camps hastily packed and evacuated; forgotten, worthless loot, like torn aprons and dirty, discarded blankets; leftover damp firewood.

They reached the west side of Höchstadt and the Lonnerstädter Tor late in the afternoon, much later than Ralf would have liked. The gate was shut for the night. After Ralf threatened the watchmen with eternal damnation, the reluctant sentinel let Ralf and the four students enter the city. The watchmen pointed them towards the Seelhaus, the town's harborage. Ralf realized he and the boys must look like begging monks in need of alms and Ralf felt this was not a bad thing. They would get some food and wood for a fire. He walked in front of the horse and cart and led the way in the direction the watchmen pointed them in.

Ralf left Martin and Michel at the stable to tend the horse and cart. Martin had developed a cough and looked ill. Ralf thought it would be better to let the two stay in the stable, someplace dry to sleep. Ralf, Konrad and Karl headed for a half-timbered building, central to a steady stream of comers and goers. A fire burned in a metal brazier at the entrance. One man helped another limp through the door. They must use the Seelhaus as an infirmary. A young nun suddenly stood in the doorway and grabbed Ralf by the sleeve of his robe.

"Evening Father, I'm so glad you made it here so quickly," she said and took hold of Ralf's hand.

"Excuse me, do we…?" Ralf protested and tried to pull his hand from her cool, dry grip.

"After that last battle, we have so many injured," she said, her grasp firm as she led Ralf past injured men and boys laying in neat rows on the floor. "The barber-surgeon can't keep up."

The young nun stopped and pointed to a young man lying on the floor. "Over there, Father," the nun said. "That one requested a priest." She moved closer to Ralf and whispered, "He won't make it through the night."

Another nun stopped by the young man's side. A hacking cough rattled her as she knelt down and peeled the dirty dressings from a weepy wound on his middle. Ralf yanked his hand away from the first nun, held his sleeve over his face and looked towards the doorway. He had to get out of this place.

"Did you find me a drink?" the young wounded man said to the coughing nun. "You forgot me, didn't you?"

The nun giggled and coughed. "Have you been a good boy?"

"I'm whatever you want me to be," the wounded man said.

A rat scurried out of a hole in the sandstone close to the earth. The air hung heavy with the smell of blood and disease, feces, urine. Ralf backed away from the nuns and the wounded man, their festering humanity chafing his already raw mood. His path towards the door now blocked by two men carrying a wounded child, Ralf felt a strong grip around his ankle.

"Father?"

Ralf looked down towards the voice and tried to free his leg but the man's grasp was firm.

"Help me, Father," the man said. "Hear me out."

Ralf knelt by the man's side and hoped he could loosen his grip without having to touch him. "What happened, my friend? Have you been hurt badly?"

"Yes, I was hit in the leg just above the foot and the infection almost killed me," the man said. "I will live and I will keep the limb. But my regiment moved on and now I am stuck in Höchstadt."

The first nun came back. "Hauptmann Schwartz, you're not dying, you don't need the priest. Why don't you just settle back here. Be grateful and stop complaining. Father, come with me."

"Settle back?" Schwartz said. "Settle back?"

The man's voice had authority. He looked older than the other soldiers. His steely eye and his air of stern command reminded Ralf of his father.

Ralf ignored the nun and spoke to Hauptmann Schwartz. "Can't you go home?"

"What, go buy a farm, find a woman and start a family? There's no one here, there's no farms. I'm from Rhineland and I would like to get back but I have no money, I have no transport, I have no one. I'm lost."

"Can you walk?"

"I could walk if someone helped me," Schwartz said. "I want to get out of here. See that young thing there, that nun, tending the wounded? She has consumption. Yes, she's a nun but I know she did little favors for the last barber-surgeon for money. And the last barber-surgeon died of consumption. This new barber came with the last troop and decided to stay here. He stayed here because he's tired of walking, he said. I'll be dead if I don't get out of here."

"What would I do with you?" Ralf asked. "I am not a nursemaid."

"Listen to me, Father," Hauptmann Schwartz said. "I want to find the dog who shot me. I'm sure whoever it was, he was part of my banner and he made off with my loot. The regiment has moved on and they took all my effects with them."

"He talks of nothing else, Father," the nun said. "Just leave him and come with…"

Ralf dismissed her with a shake of his head and turned his attention to Schwartz. "I am only interested in doing my service for my faith. Not an easy task with these heretic villages and wayward people we come up against. Now you seem to be only interested in loot and money and I am only interested in doing the work for the Society of Jesus. No two tasks could be further disparate."

"I had a small fortune," Schwartz said. "Those weasels took everything I had. I can help you. I was quartered at a widow's house in Uehlfeld. Frau Hammerl. And she conspired against me with the other devils in my banner. It had to be her. She lives alone and I want to get her back. Like you say about these villagers: there were some strange goings on there!

She's probably a witch. But her house would be good enough for me. If I could have that house, I would cry quits. We'd be even."

"Why don't you just go then?" Ralf said. "What do you need me for?"

"Please, Father, I am not sure if I can walk. Help me out of here." Schwartz struggled to sit up. "And I'll make it worth your while. I hid some grain in a cellar on the outskirts of the village. I'll share it with you. It will help us get to these people and together we can expose this heretic nest. If those women aren't doing anything wrong we should know of, they won't have anything to hide. She will let me live there with her as a service to you and your cause. But if God wants us to have the place, he will give us reason to arrest her."

"What has she been doing?"

"Well, I heard she was giving cows some sort of herbs so they would give more milk. And I heard they do some strange rituals this time of year so the devil helps the crops grow better. Or maybe she's does not want the crops to grow. Maybe she wants the crops to fail. These women are always so jealous of their neighbors. There's more than just Frau Hammerl. I'll show you those people in power who are in your way, and I'll have them taken care of. Just get me out of here. We'll work together, just get me to Uehlfeld."

Chapter 20

Pieter van Diemen

Pieter loosened the blanket tucked around his shoulders and stretched his stiff and sore limbs. Straw poking out of the mattress scratched his back, a pleasant feeling except for where his wounds still smarted. The last thing he remembered was lying on the floor with Katarina hovering over him. He'd been moved to a different room. The skin on his feet pulled. He took one foot in his hand. It was crusted with scabs. He would never put boots on again.

He could not remember ever feeling so weak and drained. He felt even worse than when he got off the ship in Amsterdam. Disgusted with his present state, he rolled himself to a standing position, stood for a moment and slumped back down on the bed. He grabbed his folded clothes on the mattress, pulled on the trousers, limped over to the window and leaned on the window sill. His feet stung like he was walking on splintered glass.

Katarina and Hans-Wolfgang were in the garden. Katarina knelt among the plants and searched through the leaves. She plucked one, handed it to Hans-Wolfgang and he stuck it in his mouth. They waved up at Pieter like they were surprised he was alive at all. In spite of the pounding in his head, he limped down the steps and went outside.

Katarina stood and smiled as he approached. Hans-Wolfgang walked towards Pieter and extended his hand. He said nothing, just smiled as Pieter grasped his hand. Katarina looked down at Pieter's feet.

"Are you in pain?" she said.

"I'll manage," Pieter said. "Lovely garden. I've seen an herb garden like this once." *Yes, when his banner had sacked that monastery.*

"This was Andra-Angela's herb garden," Hans-Wolfgang said. "I've had to do a lot of work to get it back in shape."

"She must have collected the plants from the meadow and replanted them here," Katarina said. "Plenty here but there's still a few plants I need."

"We'll need more spruce to make a soothing bath for your feet."

Hans-Wolfgang nodded at Pieter. "Andra-Angela dug this spruce tree out of the meadow as a sapling and planted it here."

"Yes, the meadow," Pieter said. "I had been there once, too."

"I have the feeling the *Tross* is camping in the meadow. I am afraid to go look at what they might have done to it," Katarina said.

Pieter pointed to a grave topped with a simple wooden cross in the middle of the garden. "Is someone buried there?"

"Andra-Angela," Hans-Wolfgang said. "Isabeau's mother."

"Ah, yes, I remember the story now."

"You do?" Hans-Wolfgang said and looked sharply at Katarina.

"Please don't be angry with Katarina," Pieter said. "She told me the story about you and Andra-Angela. I know Isabeau is your daughter. I was looking out for her back then. I would still look out for her now. I have told no one."

"Isabeau doesn't know," Hans-Wolfgang said.

"She will learn nothing from me," Pieter said.

Hans-Wolfgang pointed to a tree on the other side of the wall. "I grew up in the house beyond that wall."

"Yes," Pieter said. "I remember the house."

"I had to search for Andra's grave here on the grounds. Ralf had not marked it. In the end I moved her remains to the middle of the garden. She would have liked that."

"What ever became of Ralf?" Pieter said.

Hans-Wolfgang scoffed. "He ran away after the battle ten years ago and I have heard nothing of him since."

Pieter walked away, leaving Katarina and Hans-Wolfgang to chatter on. The air made him feel better. The warmth of the day and the safety of this idyllic sanctuary gave him a feeling of security. He had to get comfortable here, maybe consider settling down. He would never feel German, though, or really be able to integrate in this country. If he could only live in Amsterdam, by the sea, grow old and die there. But that would have to wait. He would stay on Hans-Wolfgang's estate until it was safe to move around again. If he was recognized by anyone from Hauptmann Schwartz's banner or those in Lonnerstadt who had tried to hang him, it would cost him his life. If he went back to Amsterdam he would be arrested as well.

Pieter watched two women who carried water buckets enter a wooden door and then rejoined Katarina by the edge of the garden. "Do you now live here?"

"Isabeau and I have left Sichardtshof. I want her to live where she can have the best chance of survival. If such a place exists these days."

"And you are welcome to stay here, Pieter," Hans-Wolfgang said. "We need help. Stay as long as you like."

"I would be happy to work here for you," Pieter said.

"I wonder if the troops overlook this estate," Hans-Wolfgang said. "Because we are hidden in the trees. They have grown to the point that the rooftop is no longer visible from the road."

"If they want to find it they will," Pieter said.

"*Essen!*" the young dark-haired woman shouted through the door. "Don't you want to come in for something to eat?"

"*Wir kommen*, Magdalena," Hans-Wolfgang shouted.

Pieter felt Katarina pull his arm and laid it over her shoulder. He allowed some of his weight to lean onto her. "How long have I been here?" he whispered.

"It's been about two weeks." Katarina helped him hobble towards the kitchen.

Magdalena had laid out dried meats, eggs and some yeasty-smelling bread. She had smeared the hunks of warm bread with lard containing bits of tasty smoked meat. The young Magdalena had a fresh, devilish smile and she handed Pieter a cup of what smelled like weak beer. He could manage a few sips of beer or wine. He would not drink any of those clear, potent alcohols. They were his undoing.

"Sieglinde, bring more beer, dear," Hans-Wolfgang said to the blonde woman and she grabbed a pitcher and left the table.

"So, Hans-Wolfgang," Pieter said. "How can it be you have not been sacked at all up here?"

Hans-Wolfgang bit off a chunk of bread, chewed and washed it down with beer. "Over the years the path through the trees grew over and I never cleared it. When the troops started traveling along the river, I was glad I had done so."

"Have you taken any precautions in case you are attacked?" Pieter said.

"I have my arrows and I have some weapons hidden around the grounds. What more can I do? I am alone with two women and two farm boys."

"May I suggest we teach the women how to defend themselves?" Pieter asked. "How to use a sword. Maybe how to shoot a bow. At least how to stay alive. There are techniques to help small, slight persons fight when they are attacked. I learned some when I was in the East."

"You were in the east?" Hans-Wolfgang asked.

"After my father died. Seems like another life. He died after I returned to Amsterdam. There was nothing there for me so I left and worked on a ship. I went to the east and met a Chinaman who showed me sword play and hand grappling. It doesn't matter how big and strong you are. He was no larger than one of these women here. I learned a lot from that man."

"Is he the one who whipped you?" Katarina asked.

"No." Pieter fixed her with a look and hoped she understood he was in no mood to be provoked. He sipped the beer and swallowed his annoyance, not wanting to alienate her. He needed her and did his best to hide his anger. Pieter watched her, wondering why she was trying to prick him so. She slid her last bite of bread between her lips and licked her fingers. He wanted to understand her, each of them for that matter. He needed them.

"Katarina, let the man in peace," Sieglinde said as she set the pitcher of beer on the table and sat down.

Hans-Wolfgang stood and sat between Pieter and Katarina. "Let's talk about my plans for the summer. I want to cover the mares. I want to plant a bit of grain. I want to fortify the estate here. Pieter, you can surely help me."

"I think we'll also find time to teach the women to defend themselves," Pieter said. "I don't want to stand by a group of screaming women who watch us get massacred."

"Oh, my friend. You are determined, aren't you?" Hans-Wolfgang said. "But is that wise? Then we'll have a group of blood-thirsty women here to tame!" He produced a ceramic bottle from under the table, uncorked it and held it under Pieter's nose.

Pieter pulled his head back. "No, thank you. I am tired. I will probably go get some rest. I am still very weak from my injuries."

"Just one pull, for friendship's sake," he said.

"No, my friend, I need some rest." Pieter stood to leave the round. He was to stay away from that stuff if he was to have his peace in this house. "I would like to start with some training with the women in the morning. We

163

need them."

A beautiful young girl walked into the kitchen. Head held proud, long white-blonde hair, mean blue eyes. She ignored the people at the table and looked around for something to eat. Pieter recognized her at once.

"I could start with Isabeau here," Pieter said.

"What?" Isabeau said.

What a beautiful girl. Pieter looked to Hans-Wolfgang to see if he could discern any similarity between him and his daughter. She had a regal air about her, a strong will and the same look of determination Pieter saw in her father. Like now, when he took a hearty swig from his ceramic flask of schnapps. He handed Pieter the flask. He seemed determined to have Pieter drink with him.

"*Nur ein Schwein trinkt allein*," he said. "Only a pig drinks alone."

Pieter took the bottle from him and drank as deeply as he did. The fruity smell of berries wafted up Pieter's nose as the burning liquid reached a place in his heart and opened the door. The door he wished to keep firmly locked. Pieter took one more swig and handed Hans-Wolfgang the bottle.

"I must retire," Pieter said and left the kitchen.

In the shadows of the entrance hall, the blonde maid Sieglinde watched Pieter as he went by. Pieter turned and she smiled. He bowed and offered his hand. She left with him to his room.

Chapter 21

Katarina

The walls around the Eierhofen estate were wet from early morning dew. Elder bushes full of juicy green leaves hung over the sandstone. Drops of water hung from the unopened elder blossom buds. Faint mists rose as the spring sunshine burned off the fog. The May day promised to be pleasant and warm and summer was not far away. Katarina collected her handcart from the barn and parked it in front of the house. She laid some tattered cloth inside to separate the herbs she intended to collect. Bubo said the troops had finally moved on and she could venture a bit farther today. She wanted to look for the small green knoll behind Gottesgab Hans-Wolfgang had pointed out, where she could find the spruce she needed to make a tincture.

Katarina watched as Isabeau led her mare out of the barn, tied her to a post and combed the mane with her fingers. Hans-Wolfgang led his stallion out and tied him next to Isabeau's. Isabeau didn't notice Katarina wave as she walked out of the open gate. Katarina was happy the two of them got along so well and she hoped Hans-Wolfgang's influence might tame the girl. She wondered why Hans-Wolfgang would not tell the girl he was her father. She would understand. This led Katarina to question where she fit into all this. She never had to define her role with Herr Tucher at Sichardtshof before. Here at Eierhofen, she was neither maid nor mother, caregiver nor concubine.

She followed the path towards Schwarzenbach, the wooden wheels of her handcart crunching on small stones. Most of the forest in this area had been cleared for wood or to create land worth cultivating. A patch of trees this size was unusual. Katarina found some young spruce trees and pinched the delicate new shoots off. Taking only a few handfuls from each tree, she bundled them in bits of fabric. She didn't want to rob the trees of all their new growths. Ground ivy grew by her feet. She bent down and dug the plant out for the garden, rolling it carefully in a fabric swatch, and laid all the bundles into her cart.

A dry rustling in the underbrush caught her attention and she turned towards the sound. It stopped. Leaves suddenly began to flap about and it sounded like someone frantically searched through papers. She picked a path towards the noise and it stopped again. Creeping now over a low thorny growth, Katarina could see the furious flapping fling dead leaves aside. In the tangled vines lay what looked like a pile of charred parchment, grey and brown and white.

From the pile, two black eyes watched, challenging Katarina to come closer. She moved in, unsure of what sort of animal this was. Those black eyes watched her every move. She knelt down and moved some dried leaves out of the way, exposing long white, grey and brown feathers, a yellow hooked beak and yellow feet with claws that looked like they'd have no problem piercing skin. Leather tethers hung from the bird's feet.

Here was the most beautiful creature Katarina had ever seen.

Impulsively, she reached her hand towards the bird then thought of Hans-Wolfgang. He said the beak of a bird of prey was strong enough to break bones, like a woman's finger. Katarina thought better of it and watched those black eyes; deep, unrelenting and proud. She could see back to the beginning of time in those eyes. Something passed between her and this bird and it tugged on Katarina's heart.

Abandoning her herb hunt and her hand cart, Katarina ran all the way back to the estate. Hans-Wolfgang was in the yard, undoing the saddle girth. Katarina reached him, leaned forward with her hands on her knees and tried to catch her breath. He pulled off thick leather gloves, let them fall to the ground and threw the saddle over his shoulder. The horse tossed his head at the sudden motion. Isabeau walked out of the barn and joined him.

"What is it?" Isabeau said.

"A…bird…" Katarina huffed and puffed.

"A bird? What bird?" Hans-Wolfgang said.

Katarina paused for another breath. "I found a hurt bird in the forest. A bird of prey. He's tangled in the underbrush."

Hans-Wolfgang dropped the saddle to the ground, picked up his gloves, jumped onto his bare-backed horse and grabbed a fistful of mane.

"Come, get on. Show me."

Katarina ran over to the barrel next to the barn and climbed on top. Hans-Wolfgang pulled his horse around next to the barrel. Katarina climbed on the horse's back behind him and they rode at a walk out of the yard. Katarina pointed towards the path she had just come from. He nodded. His horse bounced into a canter. Katarina laid her head on Hans-Wolfgang's back and closed her eyes. She would never get used to this means of travel. Isabeau followed them on horseback, the sound of her mare's unshod hooves padding close behind.

"Katarina, where?"

Katarina lifted her head and pointed to the only shock of forest in the landscape. Hans-Wolfgang steered the horse towards the place where she left the cart. She slid off the horse's behind. Hans-Wolfgang jumped down too and the horse dipped his head to feed. Katarina stepped through the underbrush and Hans-Wolfgang followed soundlessly. She motioned for him to stop and they stood listening. Silence. Katarina turned to look at him and he gave her an irritated look.

The furious flapping began again and he sneaked out in front in the direction of the rustling. Katarina heard him speaking quietly like he was talking to a small child, soothing sounds she never heard him make before. She could not understand his words. She took one step towards him and a twig snapped under her foot.

"Stay there," he whispered. "Don't move."

He knelt down and reassured the bird with his voice. Out of his top pocket, he produced what looked like a little hat and hung it on his own ear. Katarina wondered what he was going to do with the thing. He cleared the debris from around the bird's head, took the little hat from his ear and with one fluid movement, slipped it over the bird's head. He pulled a knife from his belt and snipped at the vines and brush, untangling the bird from its trap.

"Katarina, do you have a blanket?"

She unrolled the ground ivy and laid the plant back in the cart. She handed the fabric to Hans-Wolfgang and he wrapped the bird in it. He tightened the little hat on the bird's head by holding one of the thin tethers that hung from the hat and pulling on the other with his teeth.

"It's a gyrfalcon," Hans-Wolfgang said. "Like mine. I cannot tell if the wing is broken or not but it is injured."

Hans-Wolfgang tried to lay the subdued bird in the cart. It squawked like it had been pierced through the wing. Hans-Wolfgang turned the bird upright.

"Hand me that glove," he said.

He pulled it on, unrolled the bird from the blanket and allowed it to climb onto his leather glove.

"He hasn't been shot." He waved Katarina over to him and took one of the falcon's feet between his fingers. "See? His foot is injured as well. Maybe he chased a mouse into the brush and got tangled. Hard to say what happened." He led the horse by its nose towards a tree stump and carefully mounted without so much as disturbing the bird on his glove. "I'm going home. Meet me there as quickly as you can."

Katarina grabbed the handle of the handcart and marched off. Hans-Wolfgang rode at a walk. He and Isabeau would still reach the estate before her. As she entered the estate through the gate, Hans-Wolfgang ran up, took Katarina by the hand and they hurried towards the house.

"Come with me, Katarina. Bring some of your tinctures."

She ran past him and up the steps. In her room, she threw the box on the bed and rummaged through various flasks and pouches of dried leaves. She pulled out some dried boxwood leaves, a flask of propolis and one filled with vinegar. And the flask of laudanum. Deciding to take everything, she threw the whole lot back in the box and slammed the lid shut.

Katarina stopped. She reopened the box, took out the flask of laudanum and shook it. It was still quite full. She opened it, smelled the bitter poppy extract mixed with strong wine and took a few drops on her tongue. To quiet the fiend. She stoppered the bottle, hid it under everything else in the box and closed the lid. She heaved the box and made her way back down to the kitchen.

Hans-Wolfgang stood next to the large working table. Isabeau sat on the corner of the table. The falcon stood on a perch on one foot, the hood still covering his eyes. Handling the bird like a glass statue, Hans-Wolfgang rolled him into a cloth, just enough to expose the injured wing. The falcon began to squawk in a pitch that would drive all the ghosts out of this house. The sound echoed off the stone kitchen walls.

"See, here's an open wound," he said, raising his voice over the screeching bird. "But the wing doesn't seem to be broken at all. He was just so entangled in the vines. But this wound must be treated so it doesn't get infected. And he's crawling with bugs. God knows how long he was tangled there. He is too thin. He must be thirsty. Can we get some water in his beak?"

Katarina dug a dried straw halm out of her box. She filled a mug with water and stuck the straw in.

"Try this," she said, handing Hans-Wolfgang the mug.

He held his finger over the top of the hollow straw, trapping the water within, and allowed the water to dribble into the falcon's open beak. The bird appeared to be drinking. "I need some meat. Ask Magdalena for some raw meat, please."

Katarina found Magdelena out behind the stables preparing a rabbit for the meal. She returned to the kitchen with a bowl of innards, bits of fur and tendons.

Hans-Wolfgang said, "He may have even been sick before this happened. He's haggard looking. I don't know if he'll make it through."

He dabbed the sore spots on the falcon's wings with the aromatic propolis tincture, the strong distinctive honey-like scent filling the kitchen. He treated the wounded foot as best he could and wrapped the bird back up. He collected the bird in his hands and left the kitchen. Katarina and Isabeau followed him up the bowed stone steps, through the entrance hall and up the staircase to the upper floor. He walked to the end of the hallway, pulled a key from his leather jerkin and opened the door. A squawk met them, the same sound the falcon had made.

The room was dimly lit. Boards had been fixated in front of the windows. Tethered to a long leather cord in the corner of the room stood a falcon of the same sort. Acrid dry air and a smell much the same as chicken droppings hung in the doorway like a curtain. The bird squawked in low tones. Its claws scratched on the wooden floor.

"I never saw this bird before," Katarina said.

"I keep him in here at night to keep him safe," he said. "Who knows what animals prowl through our garden? I just haven't brought him out yet today. Luckily I had his hood in my pocket. I was waylaid before I could take him out, wasn't I, Katarina?" He chuckled. "His pen is hidden in the garden. I have to be careful when I fly him."

"Why do you have to hide him?" Isabeau said.

"I found this falcon a few years back much the same way Katarina found hers today," he said.

"Mine?" Katarina said.

"Well, you found him or he found you, however you would like to look at it. He'll be your charge until he's healthy. Then we'll see what we do with him."

"I don't know if I have the stuff it takes to take care of this creature," Katarina said.

"Of course you have the stuff, even if you are a woman. But you and I are not permitted to take care of falcons. That privilege is reserved for those of noble birth. I assume these two birds have flown off from the same owner. I decided to keep mine but if I get caught flying him and hunting with him, I could be hanged."

Hans-Wolfgang secured the tethers of Katarina's falcon on another long leather lead behind a partition on the other side of the room. "He can stand. We'll leave him be for now. Let's go, you two." Hans-Wolfgang showed them out of the room. "Check back on him regularly. They need to be kept apart. They are loners." Hans-Wolfgang shut the door and locked it. "It's a big responsibility. You make a commitment when you have a bird like this. But you live here now so it doesn't matter."

Hans-Wolfgang and Isabeau hurried off, leaving Katarina. Katarina went back to her room. Alone. She wondered if Frau Kuni felt a void, after Katarina left home, like Katarina did now, watching Isabeau grow more independent and moving away from her. Frau Kuni was a reluctant mother figure and Katarina always had the feeling she'd burdened her grandmother.

Katarina watched out the window as Pieter and Isabeau walked into the garden followed by Hans-Wolfgang. Pieter instructed Isabeau to stand across from him and raise her sword. The motions Pieter demonstrated were slow and fluid, like a dance. Isabeau imitated him exactly. She was a natural with a sword. Her movements were precise, athletic and graceful. This wasn't sword play like Katarina had ever seen. He seemed to be repeating combinations, rehearsing them like a theater piece. Isabeau laughed, enjoying the exercise.

Katarina turned her back to the window, facing the empty room in a house as foreign to her as the Slavish language of the mercenary soldiers. Somehow she would overcome this feeling of displacement. Until then, her solitary standing was the lot she'd drawn, her decision, her curse. Katarina pulled her feet up on the bed and opened Herr Tucher's journal. The entry was from six years ago, dated 1622.

May 1622

I have lived at the Sichardtshof farm now six years. The last time I recorded anything in my journal, I now see by reading my last entry, was right after the New Year. The work is mounting and we have seldom time for ourselves. There has still been no reprieve from a damp spring that entered cold and raining this year. Unrelenting rain has made the fields soggy and sowing them is impossible. The horses sink in the mud, the rest of us as well.

I have had a windfall this year with my business and the family has invested considerable amounts in the metal trade. The metals we ship from Nuremberg are desperately in demand. We will be delivering every second week up north. Paul and I have reliable couriers and if all goes well, we will have a small fortune by the end of this season. These businesses are directly related to the unrest over all of Europe.

A few clever deals may bring our family though this time of turmoil. Unnecessary church bells are taken, melted down for the metal. The metal is desperately needed for helmets, breastplates, muskets, cannons. And Nuremberg is known as the Waffenschmiede des Reiches, *Europe's center for the fabrication of mail shirts, cannonry and cannon balls.*

The rains have not stopped since the middle of April. Any trip we embark on takes twice as long, calculating the amount of time we waste sunk in mud. And because we cannot sow the fields, the other farmers cannot either. What good does a small fortune serve us, when there is no food to buy? This year even the rich man will go hungry. The lack of food has sent prices soaring. Terrible to write this, but there are too many people to feed. The country cannot contain them.

Isabeau will be six years old this month and the little sprite is growing like a well-watered sapling. Wiry and long limbed, she is a beautiful child. Difficult to discipline. Hard-headed and determined, smart as anything. She is already learning to write and comes voluntarily every afternoon for her lesson when I have my tea. She still draws, too. She holds the quill like an adult, even if it is with the left hand. I have brushes and pigments for her to paint with. She likes the paintings I have hanging in my sitting room. The Still Life in Muted Tones *by the Dutch artist Lastmann; my favorite painting called* Fruit and a Dagger *by one of Lastmann's students, I believe he called the boy Rembrandt;* Tavern Scene *by another Dutch artist named van Swanenburgh. Isabeau draws apples or horses.*

Yes, Isabeau and horses. We need to be so careful with this child. She is always in the barn and if one doesn't see or hear her when one is harnessing or leading the horses out of the stable, the danger of trampling her is rather realistic. She will run alongside the horses and has no fear, not even a healthy respect.

Her relationship with my son is strenuous, though. I thought they would be playmates, being the same age, but my boy Christoph has inherited too many attributes from Frau Tucher. He has his nose in the air, yes, already at the age of five. He makes remarks to Isabeau, calling her his servant and wanting her to do unsavory things. Paul says this is the boy's place, his birthright, and she should do what he says but I do not want the girl treated this way. She tries to get out of his way but he follows after her. I am glad when the boy comes but I am glad when he leaves again.

I am most content when we are without visitors, without added conflict. I sometimes feel I could be content with Katarina as my only source of interaction. She is the backbone of the animal, if I may phrase it so. Where I always step out of the way of conflict of any kind, Katarina will collect those involved, take the situation to Sara and work though a solution. Where I am not in the position to speak to another, she will relay my message in the proper manner. She runs my household to my liking, knowing when to leave me be, to stew in my cauldron. Yes I know I can be as difficult as a child. I will never be able to offer her the standing she deserves. But she is the only one who can really care for me. All I can offer her is my undying love, my reverence, my eternal gratitude, my heart, my soul. Dear Lord, now I sound like a poet.

Chapter 22

Ralf

Ralf and Hauptmann Schwartz met outside the walled city of Höchstadt. The air was warm, the blue sky and weak sun struggling to appear through layers of cloud. The two men settled together on the back of the cart while Konrad coaxed their gelding to bring them to Uehlfeld. They'd left Karl and Michel behind in Höchstadt to care for Martin who was worse off than Ralf had thought. Illness was God's way of urging men to seek refuge in Him, Ralf told the boys. Only in their faith would they find help for Martin. The nuns in the Seelhaus tried to persuade Ralf to use their teas to cure his maladies. Potions with magic effects from poison-mixers. This would allow the devil entrance into the boy's soul. Ralf had to find another place for Martin, far away from those provincial good-for-nothings. He felt God's spurs digging into his sides, exhorting him to seek refuge in Him the same way a man would drive an ornery horse with whips. And Ralf would drive himself—his body clean, purged and thoroughly chastised—to prove his faith.

They passed through the village of Mailach and the two farms on the main road seemed deserted. Once they cleared the village, Konrad brought the gelding to a canter out along the flood plain. The wind whipped along the flat river valley. As they approached Uehlfeld, Ralf sat up behind the coach box to have a better view but his eyes filled with tears and he couldn't see. His nose filled with condensation so he turned his head to one side, gave a great snort and the liquid flew from his nose on the wind. He pulled his hood closer around his neck. The cart plodded towards a row of young poplars at the beginning of the village. The trees broke the wind and the air was once again warm.

"That row of houses there." Hauptmann Schwartz pointed to a row of timbered houses standing under the shadow of a linden tree growing on the church's front garden. "Frau Hammerl lives in the middle house."

"Konrad, keep moving," Ralf said. "Drive past and turn along that small alley. Yes, there, behind the church. Take us out towards the fields."

They drove past the outskirts of the tiny village and stopped by an empty and broken down paddock. The fields seemed to be void of animal and man, the whole village for that matter. Ralf dismounted and offered his hand to Hauptmann Schwartz who'd taken to wearing dung-brown breeches, a scratchy flax shirt and a simple brown felt farmers' hat. He winced as he settled his weight onto his feet.

"There's the small cellar back here," Schwartz said. "Let's see if they left me anything. I never told anyone what I hid in there."

The road leading out into the fields made a decline before it entered a patch of trees. On both sides of the road, wooden doors were fitted into the sloping, earthy bank. Cellars had been dug into the hillside for the villagers to store food and beer. Judging by the broken and dilapidated doors, some cellars had been plundered and abandoned. Hauptmann Schwartz began removing brush and debris piled up outside one of the doors, pulled the door open with a squeal of rusty hinge and limped down the steps.

"Hurrah." Schwartz's whisper echoed off the cellar walls.

Ralf joined Schwartz and together the two men pulled three small sacks of grain up the steps and let them fall onto the back to the cart. They jumped back onto the cart, Konrad snapped the reins and the cart jolted back towards the row of houses. They parked behind the sandstone church with a *Zwiebelturm*, a tower with an onion-formed bonnet. Schwartz dismounted again and Ralf carried one sack of grain. This would ensure their success at begging a place to stay the night.

A woman of perhaps sixty years opened the door, her eyes widening in surprise and apprehension as she recognized her visitor. "Hauptmann? Are you hurt? I can't, I don't…"

Schwartz tried to push his way into her house with Ralf close behind him. "Frau Hammerl, we need a place to stay."

She blocked their path and kept them outside. "I am sorry, sirs, I have no…"

Schwartz gave her another push. "You see we have something to pay for your hospitality."

She noticed the sack on Ralf's shoulder. "I suppose I could put you up for a night or so."

The door to the neighboring house opened. A small woman with dark curly hair bunched into a bun poked her head out the door.

"Frau Rössler, this is of no interest to you." Frau Hammerl leaned back to Schwartz. "That's the nosy Rösslerin. Pay her no mind."

"I'd like to look in the church," Ralf said. "Is there still a priest there?"

Frau Rössler grabbed onto Ralf's black robe. "I have the keys. My husband was the sexton and now I am. That's a protestant church now, Father. These people don't want to hear any Catholic papist mumblings. They want to hear the bible in German, like our Martin Luther."

Ralf yanked his robe free from the woman's grip. "We will meet with anyone who would like to share a meal with us. We will give thanks and eat together in the name of the Lord. I will conduct my prayers in German, if you wish. I wish to discuss the strength of your faith and those of this village. Can you gather a few others who would like to join in our meal?"

"The church has been damaged the last few years," Frau Rössler said. "The windows are broken. The altar was smashed. People have looted and resorted to burning the wood in their fires."

"It's a house of the Lord, no matter what sort of condition it is in," Ralf said. "You could give the grain to your neighbors or whoever you want to."

Frau Rössler seemed more than happy to help. "Yes, I will assemble a group of neighbors. You can talk all you want."

A man and a woman approached.

"Well that didn't take long, did it?" Frau Hammerl whispered to Frau Rössler. "Look who's coming."

"That Schneider couple are always mixing in everyone's business," Frau Rössler said.

"Frau Rössler, you and I will take this sack of grain and we will inspect the church. Frau Hammerl, please take another sack, assemble the congregation and we will meet at the church in an hour. They can have more when they meet us in the church. In the meantime, Frau Rössler and I will open the church and prepare for the service. Your souls must be starving for the true word of God after all these years as Lutherans. This was once a Catholic church I presume."

"Our Pfarrer Krähmer was a great man, Father, can't say anything against him. After the last wave of mercenaries, he disappeared. We miss him. His wife was badly shaken and after she died he was gone. We never found out what happened to him. Since then, we have had no direction. Sheep without a shepherd you could say."

"Maybe I can help you," Ralf said and took her by the arm.

Ralf and Frau Rössler walked over to the church. He was taking that first small step, right here. If he could convert this group back to the true religion, he could convert more. He could leave Schwartz here to oversee this place and then bring Martin here and have the boy cleansed through prayer. He could travel up and down the river valley and… Oh, what was he doing? Doubt crept over him. And that persistent feeling of being overwhelmed. Was he the right person for this task? The Lord had a way of building him up and then knocking him down. Was this again the devil, seducing him with power?

Ralf got a closer look at the grand sandstone structure and the *Zwiebelturm*. Ralf liked these. They were common in the south of Germany. Frau Rössler turned the iron key in the ornate smithed lock and shoved the oak door open. The damage was not as dire as Frau Rössler said it would be.

"The scoundrel mercenaries smashed the altar," she said. "We burned the wood. No sense in letting it rot. We really needed it. God doesn't mind if we stay warm, does he?"

"Wasn't this a Catholic church?" Ralf asked.

"Maybe a long time ago," Frau Rössler said. "There's been a house of God on this spot since the beginning of time! Maybe not that long, but certainly the last five hundred years. We were married in this church, Sexton Rössler and I. Right after they refurbished the nave. Those were happier times."

Ralf was drawn to the impressive bible lying open on the table standing where the altar should be. The leather-bound cover and wood-cut pages were in perfect condition.

"How have you managed to keep this so well? The soldiers never got to this?"

"Our Luther Bible is our prized possession, Father, you'd agree. We have kept it hidden."

He'd never seen a Luther Bible so he crossed himself and ventured a look at it. "How many villagers are left?" he asked.

"We were once six hundred or so," Frau Rössler said. "Since the beginning of the war, we have been reduced to the half, maybe less. Many have fled, or died. Those soldiers bring disease and have hurt many villagers."

The Schneider couple entered the church and others followed. A group of maybe twenty villagers approached the makeshift altar. The man called Schneider stepped forward and said: "Hauptmann Schwartz spent some time talking to the men and says you will help us rebuild Uehlfeld. Schwartz says he needs men like us."

The men nodded agreement.

Ralf filled bowls and sacks with grain. "Join me, villagers of Uehlfeld. I'd like to teach you the proper approach to God."

"He wants to help us rebuild the cellars and our defenses, too," a squat man said. "Well, we are all for that. All the men will join in our effort here. No idlers, I can tell you."

Ralf held the empty sack of grain aloft. "I feed you for a day with this grain. But allow me to teach you and I will feed you for a lifetime."

"Yes, Father, we will start now," Schneider said. "We have so much work to do, we will come back to hear you speak this evening when the sun goes down."

Head nodding and murmured agreement went around the group. They dispersed as quickly as they assembled and Ralf stood there alone in front of the Luther Bible with Frau Rössler.

"Yes, Father." Frau Rössler bent her knee in a curtsy. "We must use the daylight. I still have to tend to my chickens and my housework. Let me light you a candle and you may meditate here as long as you like."

She mumbled more excuses and left the church, leaving Ralf alone. He bent over the Luther Bible and turned the pages back to the beginning. He read the title page: *Die ganze heilige Schrift: deudsch. D. Mart. Luth.* He riffled through the pages. A hundred-year-old bible printed in Wittemberg. Where did they get this? A prized possession, indeed. Ah, there's the Apocrypha, the books of the bible Martin Luther deemed 'not holy scripture but maybe worth perusing.' How could he think he knew what belonged in the Bible and what didn't? Who did this Luther think he was, imagining these simple folk were as qualified as clergy to interpret scripture? They were not in the position to read this stuff, let alone think they could decide what comprised living by the word of God. This was heresy and had to be stopped. He grabbed the candle, tore at the pages and set them alight.

Chapter 23

Pieter van Diemen

"I've been calling you, Katarina!" Pieter leaned up against the door jamb of Katarina's room and shook his head. "Haven't you heard me? I have some free time and would like to train with you before it gets too dark."

Pieter did not have the patience for this today. The room smelled like spilled beer and musty linens so he crossed the room and pulled the window open. Katarina swallowed hard, sniffed and wiped the tears from her face. As she rolled over, a leather-bound book fell to the floor. She stood and faltered. Her legs gave out and Pieter caught her before she fell to the floor.

"I miss him terribly," she said and pulled out of Pieter's grip.

Oh, no, Pieter thought, affairs of the heart. Well, he was not the one for her to confide in. "I don't know what to tell you, Katarina. But we have work to do."

Katarina bent down, retrieved the book and shoved it under her mattress. She walked to the window. A breeze rustled through the leaves, rippling the treetops and the sheer linen hanging over the window. She wrapped her arms around her shoulders, shivering. Pieter hoped he was not obliged to take her in his arms. He was the one who needed comforting, not her. She should be above this. She had Isabeau to take care of and Hans-Wolfgang and Pieter to think of!

"Come with me," Pieter said. "Let's get out of this room and get you thinking about something else."

She was supposed to be the strong one here. He needed her to take some responsibility for her own safety. He didn't want to have to protect her. These women should pull their own weight. Like Isabeau. The child was willing to learn to do anything to save herself. She was independent and headstrong, not like any other female he'd known. She was quick, intelligent and talked to Pieter like he was an equal. He'd never met anyone like her before.

Katarina ran her hands over her face. "I walked out on him. I hate myself for going. I ruined everything."

"Who? Herr Tucher?" Pieter said. "He's still married, isn't he?"

"He drove me away," Katarina said. "He didn't even try to stop me leaving! After ten years."

Oh, she didn't know what she wanted. Pieter should just leave her wallow but he did owe her for nursing him. And this was not at all like Katarina. He remembered her stronger than this. How love made people weak, he thought, love changed them and diverted them from their paths. There was nothing worse than a rejected woman. Though, from man to man, he owed Herr Tucher the favor of shielding him from Katarina's wrath. He could make himself useful and soften this situation. It was the friendly thing to do.

Katarina was still sobbing. "But I didn't even try, did I? I should have fought for my position, for my home, for my life with him. Oh, Pieter, I can't do this today."

Pieter turned her around, grabbed her hand and lowered his voice. "What you need is to come outside with me and do some physical work. There will be no arguing with me."

She allowed him to pull her away from the window. He could feel her bony shoulders through her scratchy flax shirt. He put an arm around her waist and felt her ribs. She had a skirt on today but he'd noticed she and Isabeau had taken to wearing breeches like men. It made sense, actually. Skirts set something off in a soldiers' mind; the same thing raw meat did to a starving dog.

"You seem to be walking pain free," Katarina said. "I'm glad to see you feel better.

Pieter ignored her, wanting to focus on his lesson. It would benefit Katarina to listen, to concentrate. "I want to start you with some push-pull exercises. Because you are small and weak…"

Katarina's face reddened. "Pardon?"

Pieter reworded that. "…I would like to point out that you are weaker than a full grown man. But still, there are some things you can do so you are at an advantage. Like using the thrust and power of an enemy's attack against him. Say I would lunge at you like this…"

Pieter lunged at Katarina and knocked her to the ground. He felt

Katarina's breath quicken. It was warm on his cheek. He could smell fresh-cut grass and her earthy smell. A sweet intrigue stirred somewhere deep inside him, a welcome diversion. Pieter knew she felt it too. He would never teach her to fight like this. He jumped back up to his feet.

"Katarina, this is serious," he said. "In order to use the power of my attack to your advantage, you can do one of a few things. For example: grab onto my arm and help me continue on by. The thrust of my attack will help you project my weight. Like this. Try to attack me."

Katarina lunged at him like he had at her. He stepped aside and at the same time, grabbed her arm and gave her a simple pull, propelling her further along in the same direction she was going in. With the extra thrust, Katarina was moving uncontrollably. She fell and rolled onto her side.

"Stand up. You try it," Pieter said and lunged at Katarina again before she could get steady on her feet. She only managed to move aside causing him to tumble onto the ground.

"That's a start," Pieter said. "If you can manage to duck and run away and remain uninjured, that's also good. But depending on how many attackers there are, it may be impossible."

Pieter saw Katarina's attention waver as her thoughts drifted. He commanded: "*Achtung!*"

Katarina laughed at him. The pitch of her laugh offended him and his temper flared. She found him comical, did she? He lunged at her. She stepped aside, stuck out her leg like a child would do to another and he tripped over her leg. He rolled onto the ground, hearing her smug, snide ridiculing. He felt his face turn red and he stood, snorted like a bull and lunged again. Katarina stepped aside, grabbing his arm at the same time. She yanked his arm with minimal effort. She was obviously pleased with herself and laughed again. Pieter stood, enraged, unseen threat pushing him towards uncontrolled panic. He had to make her stop. He'd show her who was stronger here. He dove on Katarina with the speed and agility of a wolf attacking some fleeing prey.

"What would you do now?" he hissed.

Pieter bared his teeth and wanted to bite her. He felt her heart pounding, her chest rising and falling, her breath puffing from the exertion. His rage was replaced with the pleasure of imminent conquest, a feeling that surfaced right before he took a life. A tingling desire rose behind his loins until he remembered where he was and who he was with. He willed his tense muscles to relax. She smiled at him. What would happen if he kissed her? He exhaled, cooled his temper and stood up, offering Katarina his hand.

"Get up now," he said. "Enough playing around. Let's start with the correct way to hold a sword."

"Is this the correct way to hold a sword?" Isabeau stood behind them, her arms at her sides. She held the hilt of her sword in her hand. The blade pointed upwards, hidden behind her arm. She slowly raised her arms in front of her, the hilt grasped in her left hand, the blade flat against the underside of her arm. She began the slow series of motions Pieter had taught her. He admired her grace and he moved to her side.

"Yes, child, very good," Pieter said. "You remembered."

"I always forget what comes next here," Isabeau said.

Pieter took his place to Isabeau's right, standing as she had, his feet apart and his arms at his sides. He raised his arms and went through the motions as Isabeau had a moment before. He raised and lowered his arms, bent his knees and dipped his body. It felt sweet, as if he swam through a sea of honey. Isabeau mimicked his movements.

"The Green Dragon Flies out of Water, then, yes, exactly, the Knee Protecting Sword. Close The Gate…very good Isabeau."

These exercises gave Pieter peace. He felt his darkest emotions quieting when he did these movements. The channels of energy he tapped into made him euphoric in a calm, contemplative sense. Back in the east, after a tough session with the master, his mind was still and he would sleep peacefully. If it hadn't been for the master, he would have gone mad, killed someone else or killed himself. Out of the corner of his eye, Pieter saw Katarina turn away and head towards the house.

"Katarina, stay here, you need to learn this too," Pieter shouted after her.

She waved her hand at him and continued walking. He was relieved she was leaving. He'd done all he could for her today and he'd rather train with Isabeau anyway.

Chapter 24

Katarina

Katarina shook herself and wondered what had just happened. She thought Pieter was going to kill her. He was a powder keg. One spark could set him off. Next to the kitchen door, Bubo and Magdalena waved Katarina over and she headed towards them without looking back. Magdalena handed Katarina a wooden cup and filled it with an alcoholic concoction.

"Have a seat here," Bubo said. "Try this, it's made from last year's sloe."

Katarina now noticed a considerable resemblance between the two and wondered if they were related. Their rapport was infectious. Katarina found herself drawn out of her dark mood and pulled into the silly bantering of the two who were indeed brother and sister. They teased each other, poked each other, made convincing impressions of animal noises. Magdalena could honk like a goose, even imitating the hiss. Bubo lay on the ground and mimicked a snail and Katarina found herself laughing. Their private jokes and stories, when mixed with alcohol, were truly entertaining.

Hans-Wolfgang came from inside the house with the other boy, Sepp. Magdalena handed them both cups and filled them from the bottle next to the leg of the bench. This seemed to be the evening ritual. Another bottle was produced; another round drunk. Their laughter rose and fell with the evening light.

"We must enjoy the day, we have only this one," Hans-Wolfgang said. "We may not survive the night."

"I must survive the night," Magdalena said. "I must travel to Höchstadt with Mother in the morning."

"Why would she want to go there?" Bubo said.

"She has no choice," Magdalena said. "The blacksmith from Uehlfeld walked here this afternoon to tell me. He's only just gone. He said, some priest has gotten Mother in a bit of trouble. This priest just appeared in

Uehlfeld, wanted to get into the church, gave her a sack of grain and told her to distribute it among her neighbors, which Mother did. The priest came back the next day and demanded payment or something. The blacksmith says she wanted to pay him but she has no money. She is so correct when it comes to things like this. She thought the grain was a gift. Now she has to appear in front of some council to settle the matter."

Bubo huffed in anger. "Why didn't you tell me this before? I must go with her."

Hans-Wolfgang sat straight up. "A Catholic priest? What was a priest doing in Uehlfeld?"

"Mother wondered the same thing," Magdalena said. "He told them he was a wandering monk and he was just passing by on his way to the north. Said something about wanting to teach them."

"A Catholic priest has a lot of courage to stop off in a Protestant village," Bubo said. "I'm surprised they didn't tear him apart."

Hans-Wolfgang seemed to be working out a puzzle. "I've heard that somewhere before."

Magdalena poured another cup of sloe liquor. "He wanted to gather some of the villagers and conduct a lesson, Mother said. He wanted to talk to the villagers about their beliefs. Said his life's work was for his society. He traveled with two other men and they had grain for everyone. He had Mother open the church for him and told her to invite other villagers to his lesson. Of course they took the grain and divided it up and disappeared. They have no time for lessons or religion! They are hungry and they have to work."

"What was his name?" Hans-Wolfgang said.

"What did the blacksmith say his name was?" Magdalena said. "I can't remember. He said he belonged to some Society of Jesus. Something like that."

Hans-Wolfgang jumped to his feet and grabbed her by the shoulders. "What was his name?"

"I don't know!" she hollered. "Rupert? Ralf?"

Hans-Wolfgang sat down and sunk into himself. Katarina could see he thought hard and furiously. An uncomfortable silence fell over the group and an eerie, late-night wind stirred through the garden.

"I will come with you to Höchstadt tomorrow," Hans-Wolfgang growled and left the once-merry gathering.

But Hans-Wolfgang didn't get past the watchmen at Höchstadt's tower the next day. Or the day after. Days on end, Hans-Wolfgang slunk in and out of the Eierhofen gates, riding out at all times of day and night, coming back each time angrier and unapproachable. Katarina finished her chores, cleaned her falcon, worked in the kitchen and stayed to herself. Magdalena seemed to do the same. A dour spirit settled over the household. This black bile was affecting Katarina's constitution as well. Even though she was taking the laudanum before bed, her sleep was interrupted and fitful. Her legs ached and itched.

Then the situation reached its pinnacle. After a particularly restless night, Katarina walked down the front steps of the Eierhofen house. The unseasonably cold air soothed her burning cheeks but froze the condensation in her runny nose. The sky was clear and blue. A frost had descended in the night like a wave of evil and the damage it left was evident. Elder leaves hung from the bushes. There would be no blossoms this year. If the frost had damaged the bushes under the trees around the Eierhofen estate, what did the fields look like? She'd mark this date, May 27th, 1626, in Herr Tucher's diary.

Katarina could not remember a frost so late in May. Frau Kuni would have a whole slew of rituals and sayings but Katarina couldn't remember any of them either. It took all her composure this morning to battle her feeling of unease. The smell of falcon droppings in the bucket Katarina carried turned her already upset stomach. Katarina dumped the droppings onto the manure pile alongside the barn. She pulled the linen rag from the pocket of her apron and wiped her nose.

Pieter waved her over. "The frost. This is bad."

"Another hunger year," Katarina said.

"I'll see the full extent when I ride out." He tightened the saddle strap on Hans-Wolfgang's heavy gelding. "What is the matter with you? You look terrible."

"I'm not feeling very well," Katarina said, waved her hand and shook her head. "I'm going back to my room."

He prodded the lazy gelding with his heels and pulled on the reins. The horse finally lifted his nose off the ground. Pieter gave him one sharp command and he moved one hoof then another forward. "Try to help Magdalena today. She's in a bad way. They still haven't allowed Hans-Wolfgang to see her mother. I hope they let me in today."

Katarina nodded, turned towards the door, wiped her runny nose on her sleeve and sneezed. She couldn't face anyone this morning and was grateful when she made it to her bedroom door and engaged the handle.

"There you are." Hans-Wolfgang appeared from the end of the hall. "We have things to do this morning."

"When did you get back?" Katarina said.

"In the night," he said.

"Pieter says no word yet on Magdalena's mother," Katarina said.

"Pieter will try to find out today. He is going alone. After my last outburst, the watchmen told me to go home. If I see Ralf he will pay for having Frau Rössler arrested. Pieter thought it best that he take care of this. Magdalena said it was better for her mother if I stayed away. She's worried I made it worse."

"How could Ralf be there? You would have seen him."

"We tried three times to get into Höchstadt and they wouldn't let us in. If they don't let Pieter in today…" Hans-Wolfgang growled, grabbed Katarina by the hand and dragged her behind him down the hall. "Have you been to your falcon?"

"Yes, I swept up the room right after I woke up," she said.

"Fine, hold these," he said and handed her a handful of dead baby birds. "Sparrows. I found the nest this morning and shot it down. This is perfect for what I want to do."

"I'll help you feed them but then I need to lie down," Katarina said. "I'm not well."

Hans-Wolfgang unlocked the door and pushed it open. Slivers of light shone through the boarded-up windows. A wing fluttered and the sound echoed in the otherwise empty room. Talons scraped along the floor. One bird squawked as Hans-Wolfgang pounded across the floor. He opened a wooden crate and rummaged through the contents.

"What you need is to get out of the house," Hans-Wolfgang said. "Get some fresh air. Hold this."

He threw two heavy leather gloves Katarina's way. She held her hands out but the gloves slipped through her fingers. Her head pounded as she bent to retrieve them.

"Hold this," Hans-Wolfgang said and a threw a length of leather tether.

It was wound and knotted into a figure eight and landed with a thud on the wooden floor. Dust rose and sparkled in the slivers of light. Katarina watched the kernels of dust twist and sail through the shaft of light and disappear again. A length of rope with a bird-shaped piece of cloth tied to the end sailed past Katarina's ear and landed behind her.

"That is the lure," Hans-Wolfgang said. "Hold that for me."

Katarina turned and bent to pick it up. Hans-Wolfgang slung a leather pouch around his shoulder. He relieved Katarina of one of the gloves and the tether and the lure. He packed the stuff into his bag and then shoved the dead baby sparrows on the top.

"Pull on your glove," Hans-Wolfgang said.

"I can't do this today," Katarina said.

"Nonsense. Just do it. Pull the glove on your left hand and come over here. That's right. Now bend down in front of the falcon. Hold your fist out. You can do this. It's fine. Now hold your fist like this. Hold it a bit higher than the falcon's feet."

Katarina's fist came too close to the falcon and the falcon squawked. She recoiled and looked at Hans-Wolfgang. Katarina's whole body shook in respect and fear at the thought of touching this majestic creature.

"Watch me." He bent down in front of his falcon. "Just hold your glove a bit higher than his feet and nudge him like this. See? He just climbs on. Now you try it."

Katarina did as he said and the falcon climbed onto her gloved fist. He was surprisingly light.

"Unhook the lead. Grab the tethers and secure them like this." He pulled the tethers under his thumb.

Katarina did the same.

"Come with me," he said.

Katarina followed Hans-Wolfgang as he left the room. He was down the stairs and out the door. Katarina slowly walked down the steps, making sure the bird stayed balanced on her fist, afraid he would fall off. She admired the beauty of the falcon's feathers; grey-brown sprinkled with white. Hans-Wolfgang came back into the entrance hall and shook his head as he saw Katarina gingerly picking her path like she climbed down a rocky terrain.

"What are you doing?" he asked.

"What if he falls down?" she said.

"It's a bird," he said. "He has wings."

He led the way, behind the house, to a break in the high hedge. In the clearing stood two little huts. One was weather worn and the other was light-colored, made of fresh wood by the sight and the smell of it. In front of the huts stood perches about a knee's height. Metal rings had been rammed into the earth. Leather leads were fastened to the rings and draped over the perches. Hans-Wolfgang set his falcon on the one perch and hooked his leather tethers onto the long lead. He removed the little hood. The falcon blinked.

Hans-Wolf came over to Katarina. "Come, let's see how well yours can fly, if at all." He unraveled the long leather lead. "We'll hook him on here so he doesn't fly away."

He walked about fifty paces away from Katarina, holding the other end of the leather lead. "Pull the hood forward and off."

The falcon began flapping furiously and tried to get away from Katarina. She panicked, holding the bird's tethers tight which caused the flapping falcon to slip from her fist and to hang upside down, flapping and flapping. Hans-Wolfgang came to her side and somehow righted the bird on Katarina's fist. She opened her eyes.

"Hold your fist high. Higher. Good. And let go of the tethers."

Hans-Wolfgang moved back into position, held his gloved fist high and wiggled the dead baby sparrow in the air. Katarina held her fist steady. The falcon bobbed up and down, opened his pointy wings, flapped them once and seemed indecisive. Maybe he couldn't fly. Then the falcon spotted the dead sparrow. He lowered his body as if he readied himself for explosive movement and flapped his wings. Katarina let the tethers loose and he flew to Hans-Wolfgang. The falcon grabbed the dead sparrow, jumped to the ground, tore into the baby bird, swallowed a bit and then tore in again and again.

"Well, he can fly," Katarina said.

A life dedicated to the raising and caring of falcons had real appeal. She understood how the beauty of the birds themselves, the awe of flight and the joy having such a creature in one's vicinity was enough to make one commit their life to such a task. Isabeau walked through the break in the hedge and sat on the grass. They all watched the falcon eat. When he was finished, Hans-Wolfgang handed Katarina another baby bird.

"Now hold that up in your glove. We'll see if he'll fly back to you."

Katarina held her fist high and waved the dead bird. The falcon spotted the prey. He flew back to Katarina's fist, alighted and fed.

Hans-Wolfgang walked towards Katarina, winding the leather tether together. "That's enough for today. Give him another bird to eat and we'll let him rest. We don't want to overdo it."

Katarina set the falcon on his perch and hooked his tethers to the lead next to the new hut. She stuffed a dead bird in her gloved fist, knelt down, allowed the falcon back onto the glove. The falcon held the dead bird down with his talon and tore it apart.

"He can stay out here today," Hans-Wolfgang said. "We'll collect him tonight." He allowed the other falcon to climb onto his fist. "These birds need to fly high. When I was younger, we would train them with high-flying kites. But I don't dare fly a kite and give away my position these days. We'll have to be happy training with the lure."

The fresh air had made Katarina forget about her nagging sickness until it began to crawl up her aching legs again. She wondered what was wrong with her. They had all taken ill at one time or another but nothing a tea or a cold compress couldn't soothe. Now she felt a malaise like she'd never experienced before. Katarina watched for a lull in Hans-Wolfgang's falcon activities, a moment she could sneak away unnoticed. Hans-Wolfgang let the lure fall and allowed his falcon to eat the dead baby bird. He called Isabeau over to him, handed her a glove and instructed her to take his falcon. He turned away to get something out of his leather pouch.

Katarina moved out of his range of sight. She slipped around the house to the open kitchen door, hoping she could get by again without anyone seeing her. Magdalena stirred a black iron pot hanging over the fire. Sieglinde held a board with chopped root vegetable and dumped it into the pot. Pretending she was looking for a wooden cup on the shelf, Katarina nodded to the two women, took her time choosing a cup and listened to their conversation.

"I can't go to Uehlfeld today," Magdalena said. "Hans-Wolfgang wants me to stay here, just in case they take me too."

Sieglinde fetched a bowl of beans from the table and dumped that into the pot as well. "What else do you need? I'll walk there this afternoon and pick it up when I get the leg of lamb Bubo's friend promised us."

"Bubo said to have a good look at the farmer before you take any meat from him," Magdalena said. "Plague," she whispered.

"My mother's village had plague. They burnt the whole village down,"

Sieglinde said.

Katarina hurried out of the kitchen and retired to her room without seeing anyone else. Maybe that was her problem: plague. She dug through her box, found the bottle of laudanum and had a spoonful. And another. The aching subsided and her unease quieted.

Ranting voices, huffing and spluttering in the back garden, woke Katarina. The afternoon had passed and Katarina realized she had slept the day away. She stood and looked out of the window. Hans-Wolfgang and Pieter held an excited and heated discussion. Magdalena ran from the house to join the conversation. Katarina understood only 'Ralf' and 'torture,' 'execution' and 'bastard.' Magdalena turned and left them, obviously shaken by the news.

Chapter 25

Ralf

Ralf inspected the straps and chains hitching the caged livestock cart to the two work horses. The chains clanked as the two work horses tossed their heads and tugged impatiently on the ropes tying them to the Höchstadt city wall. Here the sun was warm as it shined against the stone wall. The last night was still unseasonable cold for the beginning of June. Ralf nodded his appreciation to the man on guard and circled around the cart, continuing his inspection.

The prisoners within the bars were quiet, subdued and ready for transport to Bamberg. These were the five women and two men that Ralf, along with his students and Hauptmann Schwartz, had rounded up in Uehlfeld. Among them were the heretic sexton, Frau Rössler, and her neighbor, Frau Hammerl. Their houses in Uehlfeld were in Ralf's possession and Hauptmann Schwartz was in charge. Ralf was pleased with the work he and his Soldiers of God had accomplished in the last few weeks. They split the hive of heretics in Uehlfeld open. These people were now tried and sentenced to death.

Hauptmann Schwartz approached Ralf, still limping and obviously pained. "I am not up for such a long journey today, Father."

"No matter, Konrad and Karl will accompany the wagon," Ralf said. "They will meet with Dr. Fuchs and report our progress in the fight against heretics. He is pleased with our extensive plans to win back this territory for the one true religion and wants regular updates."

"Michel and I will stay with Martin in Uehlfeld," Schwartz said. "He's taken a bad turn in the night."

"He is under attack from this lot here, I'm sure." Ralf dismissed the guard with a friendly nod as Karl and Konrad approached. "This group of *Druden* is just a small sampling of the witches we will find in the whole

Aisch valley, given the time and the manpower. These women have been tempted by the fruits of evil and their men have followed their unwholesome path. I am sure there are others."

"We are ready to leave, Father," Karl said.

Konrad handed a rolled parchment to Ralf. "Here are the protocols, Father, signed by the sheriff."

Ralf unrolled the parchment and read the scribe's careful script from the day before. Karl and Konrad would need the signed paper for Dr. Fuchs and the Bamberg witch commission. It began with the date:

4.Juni 1626 Höchstadt Anna Rösslerin accused of Zauberey

Before exact examination did the woman say absolutely nothing to her defense. She was accused of stealing grain to use at a witches Sabbath in which Satan was feasting with Rösslerin and other women from Uehlfeld.

Head shaved: Hexenmal *found.* Hexenmal *tested with the needle. Pricking the* Hexenmal *brings no blood.*

Stripped Body examined: Hexenmal *between the folds of buttocks. God as our witness, she still knows nothing, will confess nothing.*

Thumb screws: Will confess nothing. Interrogation will not bear fruit.

Leg screws: Rösslerin confesses to sodomy with Satan.

Reverse hanging and whipped with leather: Rösslerin names four other women at the fest. Hammerlin, Schneiderin *and her* husband Schneider, *two other* women…

The protocol continued for each of the people in the cart. Each one had freely admitted their guilt. Ralf never enjoyed these interrogations. Tears filled his eyes as he watched each of the witches in the clutches of Satan's bonds, begging the Lord to save their souls. The pain of the *peinliche Befragung* was never enough to drive the devil from their bodies and they screamed in agony to be saved from Satan's grasp. After they admitted their guilt, they wept with joy, having accepted God's grace and the knowledge that it was the devil all along. They were then ready to tell about all the others involved so they, too, could be rid of this intrusive evil. So they, too, could be cleansed. Ralf would abolish the heretics from this land, drive Satan out of here, the true cleansing achieved by fire!

The frost exposed the witches and their influence in this area. The other witches confessed to spreading the fat of murdered infants onto the fields to destroy the plants and create the frost. This year would be another year even the rich man would go hungry. Ralf remembered the last few years all being the year he went hungry.

Konrad and Karl exchanged handshakes with Ralf. Konrad climbed on the coach box and Karl took his place next to him. Today, Ralf would not accompany them: he was on his way back to Herzogenaurach. He'd received word from Sheriff Vogtmann that the witch Elsbeth was to be interrogated for the last time today. Vogtmann had requested Ralf come and offer Elsbeth her last confession. Today her sentence would fall.

Ralf had borrowed an old nag from one of the farmers in Höchstadt. He took his leave of Hauptmann Schwartz and hopped on the old mare's back, expecting to reach Herzogenaurach by midday. On the way, Ralf passed a lone farm that had been burned to the ground and one quiet village after another. The last troop movements left these Franconian villages wary and afraid like never before. Many hid in their homes or had run away, if they had survived at all. The ride was uneventful enough, the trip being almost void of man or beast. Traveling alone could be seen as folly on his part but he had the protection his unwavering faith.

As planned, Ralf reached the walled hamlet of Herzogenaurach by midday. He met Sheriff Vogtmann at the base of the tower and Vogtmann led him into a tiny chamber and lit by a single torch.

"The executioner has arrived," Vogtmann said. "We can now continue the torture."

"Continue?" Ralf said.

"We are only allowed to interrogate in half-hour sessions. We consider that to be a 'suggestion,'" Vogtmann said. "And no more than three sessions are allowed. But we so oft need more time to get a confession. So, for the record, we just prolong the session. It is a matter of clever record-keeping."

Vogtmann nodded to the scribe. He leaned over his pulpit and scratched out a sentence on his parchment, his bald head shining in the light of his candle.

"The villagers are up in arms since the frost," Vogtmann said. "All of the crops, what crops they have been able to sow, are frozen, *kaputt*. And the weather is still cold."

"At least your townsmen still have their textiles to sell," Ralf said.

"Yes, but most of them have small farms to produce what food they need," Vogtmann said. "The villagers are wary. They know we have an accused witch in the tower. They want us to get rid of her. We want to get rid of her before anything else happens."

Ralf waited in the chamber as the executioner left with a guard to collect Elsbeth from the tower. They returned with the woman, her head shaved and dressed in a dirty burlap sack.

Ralf motioned for the scribe to note his words. "Five Juni 1626. Herzogenaurach. Who are you and where do you come from?"

"Elsbeth Spiess," she said. "I come from Fetzelhofen."

"Elsbeth henceforth known as Spiessin," Ralf said. "Born in…where is Fetzelhofen?"

"A small village by Lonnerstadt."

"The Spiessin is hereby accused of the most serious crime of *Zauberey*…" Ralf dictated for the scribe. He turned back to the woman and boomed, "We have arrested women in Uehlfeld who have told us everything. To save your soul, you must confess your crimes. The crime of *Zauberey* carries the heaviest of all penalties. Tell us who was involved with you."

"What brings you to Herzogenaurauch?" Vogtmann asked. "Did the devil bring you? Who brought you here? Did you cast your spells on our community? Cause the frost?"

"After my village was sacked, I fled to Sichardtshof," Elsbeth said. "When Sichardtshof was sacked I was taken by a soldier. When he got tired of me, he left me in Höchstadt and I met Herr Ziegler. I have told you this, Sheriff. Over and over."

"I know that heretic nest, Sichardtshof," Ralf said.

"Scribe…" Herr Vogtmann pointed to the scribe. "Questioning this woman still bears no fruit. She does not want to talk."

Elsbeth spoke, strained and evil. "Scribe, write down how Vogtmann wanted to prove his manliness by forcing it on me. Only his manhood doesn't work, does it?"

Ralf asked, "Is that true?"

Vogtmann whispered to Ralf, "This woman is evil embodied. It is true. Since she's been here, my manhood won't work anymore. It is her fault. She has stolen my manhood. One of the other guards said it has happened to him as well."

"We will now set the thumbscrew on the accused witch Spiessin," Ralf said. "Confess to us the crime of witchcraft. Your dealings with the devil have caused the frost. You have been stealing manhood."

"We have familiarized the accused with the torture instruments," the executioner said. "As is noted in the protocol, we showed them to her during the last session. We demonstrated their usage and still she would not tell us anything."

"Then put the instrument to use on her," Ralf said. "Do not be too soft."

"Tell us," Vogtmann said. "Who was at the feast with Satan? We know the devil is inside you and we will drive him out. We can help you cleanse your soul."

The executioner positioned both her thumbs in between the iron plates of the instrument and tightened the screw. A simple instrument, the top iron plate closed in on the bottom one and squeezed her thumbs. He continued until Elsbeth winced and grew uncomfortable.

"Tell us," Ralf said. "We want to help you."

Elsbeth was silent and the executioner tightened the screw two more turn.

"I am not a witch," Elsbeth groaned as blood oozed out from under her thumbnails. "Nobody was involved. Stop. Please."

"Set the legscrew upon her shin," Vogtmann said. "I want this woman out of my tower, out of my town."

The executioner fitted the iron boot-like instrument with a nasty serrated edge on the inside against the woman's right shin. He grasped the wide-winged screw on the side of the boot. One, two, three turns of the screw and the shin bone audibly splittered.

"Tell us," Ralf hollered.

"Dear God in Heaven, stop!" Elsbeth screamed. "Please!"

"Tell us!" Ralf hollered again.

"Sichardtshof!" she said.

"Sichardtshof?" Ralf said. "Yes. Tell me who else was involved."

Elsbeth whimpered.

"You know, Elsbeth," Ralf said. "There has been frost in all these communities where you have been known to travel. You could not have been responsible alone. The unseasonably cold weather persists. Who else is involved?"

"Nobody," she said.

The executioner tightened the legscrew one more turn. Elsbeth whimpered, shock and pain driving her close to unconsciousness.

"Who was it? Tell us!" Ralf screamed. "Was it Sebald Tucher?"

Elsbeth was fading. The executioner gave the legscrew one more turn. Her body gave a jolt and she screamed.

"Yes!" Elsbeth cried.

"Are you a witch?"

"Yes!"

"Was it that devil's woman, Katarina?" Ralf said. "Is the whole farm involved?"

"All of them," Elsbeth cried.

The executioner loosened the leg screw. Elsbeth sobbed. Sheriff Vogtmann stood in front of the accused and announced his sentence to the scribe:

"Elsbeth Spiess, you are hereby pronounced guilty of the crime of *Zauberey*. You shall be executed at dawn by the sword and then burned at the stake."

Chapter 26

Pieter van Diemen

Pieter heard Magdalena's melodic, booming voice holler, "*Essen!*" That woman's highest priority seemed to be the regulated, community evening meal and he liked her cooking. Pieter never knew this mealtime ritual as a young lad, never understood the importance. His father was often abroad on business for weeks at a time. Mother was flighty and spoiled. She never cooked. She had a housekeeper named Truyde who was easy to control. She did whatever Pieter wanted. Now that Pieter thought about it, that made him quite spoiled too.

Pieter's mother would often drag both Pieter and Truyde either from one tavern to another, or to some artist's atelier or to some market along the canals. His mother would drink and Truyde would mind Pieter. Truyde would give Pieter food and drink, whatever pleased him. When he became of a certain age, she would *do* whatever pleased him.

Magdalena called again. What wind pipes that woman had.

Pieter set his book aside and opened the bedroom door, wincing as scars stretched on his back. The wounds itched as they healed. Katarina was at the end of the hallway, locking the door to the falcon room. Pieter offered Katarina his arm and together they descended into the kitchen. They were met with wonderful smells. The young Magdalena still managed to take care of the household, Pieter thought, even though she was terrified of the outcome of her mother's impending death sentence. Magdalena still had no word whether the execution had been carried out or not!

The smell of roasted lamb with garlic and parsnip reminded him of a rare occasion when he was together with both his mother and father. It must have been a holiday gathering. That was a long time ago. Tonight he would treat this meal like a holiday gathering. He was alive.

Pieter took in the rest of the group. They were a peaceful group. Hans-Wolfgang smiled as he sat down next to Pieter. He smelled like horse.

Isabeau sat next to her father. She had latched onto him. He was spending all his time with her, trying to make up for the past ten years.

Bubo and Sepp were two skinny, unremarkable, Germanic-looking boys, just old enough to grow facial hair. Sieglinde, Magdalena; two women who if they had no work here would only amount to prostitutes for some regiment. Katarina, Pieter himself; none of them really had any family. What a disparate group they were, belonging nowhere, to no one. Pieter concentrated on Katarina, sitting across the table, holding a cup. She took a mouthful unfitting for a woman and looked like she'd been crying again.

"What a lovely evening," Pieter said in her direction.

The door was open to the garden and the smells of the warm spring evening came in on the breeze. The candles fluttered and the air was cheerful. This was a welcome break after the unseasonably cold weather. Pieter would try to get her out this evening.

Hans-Wolfgang refilled his mug with beer. "Let's just ponder on another day we were given the privilege to enjoy. Please join me in a moment of silence to express our gratitude for this meal and this peaceful evening. And a moment to pray for Magdalena's mother."

Sieglinde sat down on Pieter's other side. All bowed their heads and he felt a hand on his thigh. Sieglinde smiled at Pieter and gave his thigh a meaningful squeeze. She broke into a giggle. Hans-Wolfgang scolded her with a *shush*.

"Thank you," Hans-Wolfgang said. "Enjoy your meal."

"*Pastinaak*, we would call these at home," Pieter said. "Roasted parsnips have always been a favorite of mine."

"I know what else you like," Sieglinde said.

Pieter shook his head, a plea to please be more discreet. His subtle reprimand was wasted on that dim woman.

"Pieter, meet me in the barn later?" she continued. "We'll get some wood."

Sieglinde laughed and filled her mouth with food. She chewed with her mouth open. The sounds turned Pieter's stomach. He watched the others eat. The plates were empty in no time, a method of survival. Whoever ate the fastest had the chance to have more. Pieter grabbed another piece of lamb before it all disappeared.

Magdalena ate by the fire. She had been crying and didn't join in the conversation at all. When the bowls emptied, she filled them all with the rest of the meal. They emptied at an alarming rate. Hours of preparation and all it took was ten minutes until the food was gone. She cleared the table as the boys struggled to lick their bowls clean. Sieglinde stood to help her and bent close to Pieter's ear.

"I'll be in the barn after I round up the chickens," she said. "You know where to find me."

Pieter ignored her. Katarina watched Sieglinde leave the room. Magdalena settled next to Isabeau and Hans-Wolfgang. Isabeau leaned into her.

"Would you like to hear a story?" Magdalena said. She put an arm around Isabeau's shoulder. "Do you know about Sybilla Weiss?"

"Katarina has told me about her." Isabeau said. "But I want you to tell me."

"Here is my story about Sybilla Weiss," Magdalena said.

The room went quiet. Magdalena's melodic voice was perfect for storytelling.

"Sybilla sat behind the ancient willow tree," Magdalena said. "One side of the tree was brown and decayed; the other full of lush grey-green leaves. Its trunk had been split by a lightning bolt one night in the spring when sudden rains had flooded the village. Sybilla peeked around the tree's wide girth.

"She saw a young woman struggling on foot up the path towards the forest. The young woman fell to her knees, tried to crawl on all-fours then stood again. She cupped her massive belly with her two arms and plodded on up the path.

"A white flash of light struck Sybilla from somewhere deep behind her eyes. She could no longer see. This happened so often these days. She'd learned to breathe evenly, relax and let the vision come. The white flash of light took shape. She saw the young woman, a beautiful girl, but sad. She was to deliver a child, alone in the forest. Then she would die. Sybilla could do nothing to change the woman's fate.

"Sybilla had seen many things in the past. She told the villagers of her visions: one day people would travel in wagons that needed no horses; a great plague would befall mankind; there would be a war that would desecrate the land. Her name would adorn history books as the greatest seer of the age.

"The villagers had banned her from her house. They forced her to live in the stone house at the top of the South Hill next to the four linden trees. Do you know the place, Isabeau?"

Isabeau nodded.

"The trees that served as gallows," Magdalena continued. "Her only companion was a black rabbit, old as she herself, and she was generations old. Sybilla could do nothing to change her own fate, either. It was an ancient curse.

"The vision faded and she wiped the sweat from her brow. She peeked around the split willow trunk but the young woman was no longer on the path. She stood and followed the same path, towards the forest, hoping to find the young woman.

"Pounding hooves forced Sybilla to jump down from the path into a ditch. One, two, three, four horses she counted. After they passed, she stood, straightened her white dress and continued into the forest.

"A man's voice shouted. 'I knew you were a witch! What sort of bloody ritual are you performing here?'

"A woman's voice whimpered and sobbed.

"Sybilla caught sight of the man through the trees, his sword drawn and dangerously close to the woman's neck. The woman sobbed and pleaded. As Sybilla came closer, she saw the bloody mess surrounding the young woman that must have been caused by the child's birth. But where was the child?

"Sybilla steadied herself against a young oak as another white flash slowly overtook her eyesight. The white flash took shape and she saw the young woman's newborn baby, quiet and unmoving. But the baby was alive. The baby was a miracle. The baby was destined to be a legend, too. Sybilla must rescue the child. That much was sure.

"The vision faded. She heard a sword swing and a thud. She saw what was left of the young woman crumpled on the ground. Her head lay next to the afterbirth. The men mounted their steeds and rode out of the forest. A hawk cried overhead.

"She ran to the young woman, searching the bloody scene for a trace of the child. Her heart raced as she heard another horse approach. Only one. A man the color of the forest came into view, jumped from his horse and ran to Sybilla's side.

"'She's dead. But the child lives,' Sybilla said to the man.

"He said nothing. A peep like a baby bird sounded from the ground beneath the young woman's cloak. The man the color of the forest bent down, threw the cloak aside and raised the child up high.

"'This is our child,' he said.

"'Take the child away from here. She will have many tasks to perform. She will be detrimental to your life.'

"'Where am I to take her?'

"'If they find you, they will kill you. Get on your horse and ride past the ponds.'

"The man jumped lightly and settled on the horse's back. The hawk flew through the trees and lighted on a tree stump.

"'You will only stop when the horse stops. He knows where to go,'" Sybilla said.

"She wrapped the baby in the woman's light blue cloak and handed the package to the man. The hawk flew off the stump and out of the forest. Sybilla slapped the horse's behind and he bolted in the same direction.

"'Good luck,' Sybilla said.

"That is the end of the story," Magdalena said. "Or the beginning. I wonder why Sybilla didn't interfere. Maybe the woman could have lived too. Are we all subject to such violence at the hand of men who think they are doing the work of a punishing God?"

Magdalena kissed Isabeau on the cheek and excused herself from the table. She stood by the fire, her body shaking from silent sobs. Hans-Wolfgang moved behind her and wrapped his arms around her.

Pieter, uncomfortable with all this naked sentiment, grabbed Katarina by the hand and said, "It's a lovely evening. Let's go for a walk."

He pulled her to the door and had a good look at her face. Her eyes were half-closed, glassy and indifferent, a shroud over her personality. Unsteady on her feet, she tried to shake off the effects of what Pieter believed to be more than just the alcohol she drank. Pieter held tight onto her hand, afraid she might sink to her knees at any point. What was the matter with this woman? Pieter worried he might be saddled with taking care of her.

They walked hand in hand through the main gate and towards the fields behind the estate. Pieter was aware of how delicate this situation was: Herr Tucher was Pieter's most respected friend, almost like a father. Katarina was Herr Tucher's lover who was obviously brooding over the loss of the relationship. What did he think he would accomplish by getting her on his side? Did he want her friendship? All of his presumed friendships with women ended in bed. And Katarina was not the woman Pieter should want to go to bed with. But he wanted to feel her approval, he wanted to feel anyone's approval. Maybe he should try to kiss her.

"I kept in contact with Herr Tucher after I left," Pieter said. "I sent him letters until I went to the East. He was the one who suggested I come back here."

"And it took you all this time to get back here?" Katarina said.

"I had some unfortunate accidents."

"I'm not even going to ask because you get angry with me, don't you?"

"I'm sorry, Katarina. I need to be more patient, I know."

"If you want to talk about it you may. I won't push you."

"What I do want to talk about is more training with you," Pieter said. "Have you learned to ride in the meantime?"

"No." Katarina wrapped her arms around her shoulders.

"Doesn't change the fact that you should learn at least to flee with a horse. But no matter. I have moved the blades on some scythes so we can use them like pikes. I found a small one I want you to learn to handle."

"I don't want to learn to fight," she said.

"You may have to," he said.

Pieter led Katarina down the hill towards the carp ponds around the outskirts of Gottesgab. Katarina pointed at the waterfowl as they swam, dove their heads under the water and kicked their feet.

"Katarina, why did you leave Sichardtshof?"

"Isabeau needs to be with her father."

"Yes, but that isn't why you left Herr Tucher," Pieter said.

"You know why I left. You were there. I told you why."

"I was unconscious for the most part. I don't remember even being there."

Katarina's smile was strained, pained. "His wife has come to live on the farm."

"Surely he didn't want you to leave. You could have stayed."

"He didn't stop me leaving, did he?"

"But you left him."

"No, he drove me away." Katarina turned and walked up the hill.

Pieter followed her back to the path. She pointed to some plants, all trace of emotion gone from her face. She stopped, bent over and pulled up one with roots.

"I don't have this in the garden. It will be a nice accent. Try this." Katarina gave Pieter a small light green leaf and he took it in his mouth.

"Pfew!" He spat the horrible herb out.

"Wormwood. It's a touch bitter, isn't it? It has healing properties when soaked in wine. Or as tea. Good for the stomach."

Pieter felt Katarina take his hand. Hers was cold, damp and trembling. He wondered if she might be ill and if she should be out walking at all.

"I'd like to go and visit Herr Tucher," Pieter said. "Would you come with me? Is Sara still there?"

"You don't remember anything from the day you were there, do you?"

"No, I'm not even sure how I made it to the farm at all."

"I'd wager it would be a good story."

"We could ride there together," Pieter said. "Tomorrow morning."

Katarina took a deep breath. "I'm not going back there."

"You'll change your mind tomorrow. Please come with me." Pieter took Katarina in his arms and pulled her close. "I'll always be here for you."

Pieter squeezed her tight and then released his grip. Katarina took a few deep breaths that were dangerously on the verge of becoming sobs. Please don't cry, he thought. Katarina wiped her face and smiled up at him. They walked through the gate of the estate. A golden glow bent around the buildings as the sun set. Katarina took her leave and went into the house. A few minutes passed and the golden glow darkened to a warm orange as the sun set behind the trees. Pieter entered the dark entrance hall and climbed the stairway. On the landing in the shadows, Sieglinde lurked. She touched Pieter's arm. She breathed words he did not understand but made very plain what her motive was.

***

The next day, Pieter rode out of the Eierhofen yard, down through the forest and across the flood plain. The fields that should have been green this time of year were brown. The innumerable parade of military wagons plodding through here left deep ruts in the mud. This year's unseasonably chilly, rainy weather and lack of vegetation created an unending terrain of mud. He crossed the river, tried to ride up the muddy bank in Mailach and dismounted because he didn't want the horse to break its leg in the mud.

Once through the plundered village, Pieter jumped into the saddle and rode back towards Sichardtshof, up past the ponds. The landscape had changed since he was last here. Ten years ago, the fields grew green in the summer. Waterfowl swam atop the ponds. Sheep bleated and he remembered being able to hear them as he rode up the track, even at this distance. But this year, the fields had not been sown, there were no sheep. The hills to the north and the south were brown. There were no trees around the farmyard, just lots of muddy-brown barrenness.

He stopped inside the Sichardtshof gate, dismounted and tethered his horse in front of the main house. It was quiet. There was no one around. Out by the workers' house he saw an ample woman hanging linens on a line hanging from one tree to another. He walked back towards her.

"Sara! Hallo, how are you?" Pieter said.

Sara stood still. She seemed uncertain, as if she dithered between running away or staying and conversing with him.

"It's me. Pieter," he said.

"Of course, I'll go get Tanner," Sara said and turned to leave.

"Wait a moment, I brought you something." He pulled a flask out of his pocket and showed it to her.

"Thank you," she said, grabbed it from him and put it in her apron pocket. "I'll go look for Tanner."

Pieter grabbed her by the arm. "It's spruce tincture. From Katarina."

"Let me go," she said.

"I'm not going to hurt you, Sara."

Sara wrenched her arm out of his grip. "You look much better, Pieter. Feeling better?"

"Thanks to Katarina," Pieter said.

She finally looked at him. "How is Katarina?"

"She sends her regards."

"Why didn't she come with you?" Sara fussed with her hanging wash. "I understand why she wouldn't come here alone, I wouldn't travel alone anywhere either. But she could have come today with you."

"She is very busy," Pieter lied. "I didn't see her before I left."

"Oh, if I didn't have so much work here I could go up to Eierhofen with you today. But I can't just leave."

Women's shouts by the main house echoed down the hollow.

"Is the master in?" Pieter said.

"Yes, but he isn't easy to find," Sara said. "He's hiding from his wife and those maids of hers. He's very upset. He hadn't realized Katarina left for good. Silly man. He is often out walking, when it's safe, or he stays in his room."

Pieter saw two plump maids milling about in the yard in front of the main house. A thin woman hung out of an upper window, hollered and slammed the window shut.

"You can take yourself to the main house," Sara said. "I'm not going with you. I don't go to the house unless I must."

With that, Sara disappeared into the workers' house. Pieter walked back past the well to the main house. He remembered none of his recent visit here. The one farm boy, he thought his name was Bjarne, stood next to Pieter's horse. He looked like one of the Danish boys who lived here ten years ago.

"You don't mind if I leave him here," Pieter said. "The horse. I can't take him up with me to see the master, can I?"

Bjarne looked at Pieter as if he had just flown down from the highest tree. "You're that soldier, escaped from the hanging..."

Pieter silenced him with his best stern expression. "Would you please tell Herr Tucher I have come to visit?"

Both men turned as Herr Tucher came through the double front doors. Bjarne stood aside, still watching Pieter. Herr Tucher, the master of the house, conversed with someone inside and shook his head. The last ten years had aged him. Pieter assumed he was about forty years old now. His greying hair hung open around his shoulders, he had thinned and his eyes had dark shadows around them. His clothes hung around him and he had a slight stoop Pieter had not seen before.

"She will be the death of me, that woman," Herr Tucher said and slammed the doors shut.

"We have not finished this conversation," the woman yelled from inside the house.

"I am finished," he said. "Done, through, spent, exhausted."

"Hello, sir," Pieter said.

He registered Pieter's being there and shook his head. "Pieter?"

"It's me, sir, and what a pleasant thing to see you," Pieter said and, seeing an old, trusted friend, felt a happiness he had not felt in a long time.

"Fine young man," Herr Tucher said and grasped Pieter's hand. "You have become a fine young man, even if you do look a bit dragged over the coals. Yes, what a welcome change. Come quickly, we will find a spot as far away from this woman as we can find."

Herr Tucher nodded a greeting to Bjarne and laid a hand on Pieter's shoulder, leading him away from the house, past the now completely burnt-down barn. They climbed the North Hill to a walled terrace on the rise that had been planted with currants. Herr Tucher led Pieter behind a knot of bushes and showed him to a spot where a hidden bench stood. As Pieter sat, Herr Tucher kicked the leaves away from a wooden board installed in the earth like a trap door. He bent and opened the door. Out of the hidden hole in the ground he pulled a bottle and two ceramic cups. And a metal box. He handed Pieter the bottle and the cups.

"What else do you have in there?" Pieter asked.

Herr Tucher opened the metal box and took out a pipe and a leather pouch with tobacco. Out of the hole, he pulled a small clay brazier the size of his hand. The brazier held glowing coals. He stuffed the pipe with tobacco, held the clay pipe over the brazier and puffed it until it lit. Pieter filled the two cups with some quite exquisite smelling liquid.

"I spend a lot of time here these days," Herr Tucher said.

"What else can you do during the day? What is left of the farm?"

"Not much left here, Pieter. It pains me to see this happen to the only real home I have ever had. Oh yes, I have had other places to live, but this is the only one I will ever call home. This belongs to me, not something my family built up over the years. I will never be a favorite in our family tree anyway. But enough about me and my troublesome woes. How are you faring? What are you doing these days?"

"I am living up at the estate with Hans-Wolfgang," Pieter said.

"Of course. With Katarina? Is she still there?" he said.

"Yes, of course she is."

"How is she? Is she all right? I would die if anything would happen to her."

"She is fine, never been better."

Herr Tucher seemed pained. "Yes, she only suffered here with my wife."

"She and Isabeau are fine."

"I must say, this last visit from the mercenaries, your troops I would gather, has left us barren. Most of our sheep are gone. I have hidden a few in the stable next to the kitchen, we have slaughtered and dried the meat secretly and hidden the meat in various holes in the ground. Otherwise there would be nothing left. Seems everything I value is hidden in holes."

"Why don't you go back to Nuremberg?" Pieter asked.

"Yes, these thoughts occupy me the whole time. Nuremberg is not the place either. Where is the place? I have the wife here now and we have arranged passage to London. My children are here too and are to travel with her. The wife is in my rooms all day, she can do a bit of needle work, otherwise she cannot move about safely. But a secure route has finally been worked through so she and the children will be leaving in the next few weeks."

"I hope no one was harmed by those troops," Pieter said.

"Wounds heal, Pieter. The terror will live on in our souls, I am afraid." Herr Tucher sipped the liquor. "The maids had dressed my wife in servants' clothing. The soldiers were so preoccupied, fighting over my wife's clothing, shoes and finery. She was left unharmed. So spoiled is she, the fine Frau Tucher, she grumbles over losing her best dresses and shoes. She was left with her integrity and her life. Tanner's wife and our Anna fared much worse. And Katarina. No man could endure what these women must."

"And you will stay on?" Pieter asked.

"We are waiting for Paul to travel with them." Herr Tucher relit his pipe. "Yes, I wonder myself if I should just leave too. Without Katarina, I wonder if it is worth living at all."

"Certainly no woman is the reason to live or die," Pieter said.

"You are too young to know what it is to have finally found the one you love more than any other."

"I don't believe in such undying love."

"I hadn't either, until…" Herr Tucher puffed on the pipe and his gaze traveled with the smoke.

Pieter took a sip of the fragrant brandy. "The death of my parents has left me unable to love, I am afraid. My father died in the winter around the New Year after I returned to Amsterdam."

"Yes, I had heard. We had been quite good friends," Herr Tucher said. "If one can have friends among those we do business with. We had known each other a long time."

"My father died a poor man and left me only debts," Pieter said. "He owned a house occupied by a foreign family and they let it burn to the ground. The house we lived in with my mother had been taken over by the bank to pay off his debts. The year I left and came to Germany with you hurt his businesses. He would have needed me, but when I was sixteen, I was in no condition to help him."

"We cannot blame ourselves for the past, my boy. Otherwise we live in a world of regret, shadows and ghosts."

"Losing my mother had scarred my ability to love but losing my father hardened me. I was offered the position of soldier on a ship and took the chance to run away gratefully."

"You never mentioned your travels in your letters. Please tell me more about them. I expected you to return to Sichardtshof. I must say, this is the most meaningful conversation I have had in ages."

"The tales I have of the East are not satisfying or decorated. And now that I am in Europe, I fear I have traded one war in the East for another in the West. I always think I want a simple life at home, in Amsterdam, but when I imagine such a life, I grow bored, wanting for adventure. I could have found a woman and settled down there but I always seem to get involved with the wrong people. In Amsterdam, I was circling on the verge of trouble the whole time. Until I had no choice but to escape. And work on the ships sailing to the East is plentiful."

"I can imagine traveling on the continent, but to sail the waters, uncharted new lands, savages…" Herr Tucher raised the bottle to refill Pieter's glass.

Pieter declined and waved the bottle away. "The Europeans are the savages, I am afraid. To see what the Dutch and the English are doing in those island countries, for spice, for trade, for money, one sees who the real barbarians are. How they fight to stake claim in those lands, what they do to the islanders who try to deny them, what the Dutch and the English are doing to each other for the rights to these territories! It was not a good place for a sane, feeling man."

"Most successful businessmen are not sane or feeling. But why did you go East at all, Pieter? You could have come back here."

"I would have liked that but after my father died, I had to leave Amsterdam in a hurry. He had left quite a lot of debt. And I tend to escape in the bottle." Pieter had never said those words out loud to anyone. "And, yes the effects of alcohol are worrying me. I have told no one what trouble I believe it gets me into."

"Yes, many men cannot handle its effects."

"Oh, I can handle its effects. Only too well. Others cannot handle me, though, when I am under its effects." Pieter laughed, distressed at how evil he sounded. "My first voyage east was my last. We sailed and made it to the Spice Islands in eight, maybe ten weeks. Although I arrived in good health, many did not. We ran out of fresh water by the end of the journey and lived on salted meat and biscuits. Many were sick with scurvy and dysentry. And when we reached the Spice Islands, there was an all-out war between the English and Dutch over the island Puleroon, a nutmeg plantation.

"I have no interest in traveling to those areas," Herr Tucher said. "Hot and stifling, I have heard."

"Yes, and there is no reprieve from the heat. Tempers flare and it is lawless and fueled by lack of discipline and lack of food. I had some trouble."

"Tell me a woman was involved, Pieter." Herr Tucher chuckled.

"Yes, and unfortunately for me, it was an island woman. So I had not only the wrath of the island natives who demanded I be disciplined. I had also the wrath of my Dutch captain who had been abusing the young woman and blamed it all on me. The captain had the young woman executed before she could speak out against him. I had found the captain as he mishandled the woman and yes, I hit him and threatened to kill him if he didn't leave the woman be.

"I was beaten and imprisoned. Lucky for me I was in a cell and not chained where the Dutch would chain the English prisoners. The English prisoners were chained under the holes where the men would shit and piss on their heads, fed only dirty rice and tainted water. I was in a cell with men they still needed. I can read and write. That has gotten me out of more scrapes than I can tell. They used me as a scribe and locked me up again. I met a Chinaman who supplied officers with opium. That is some stuff you don't want to get involved with. I watched men ruined from that stuff."

"You are lucky to have made it back at all," Herr Tucher said.

"I was released because the Dutch East India Company needed someone to sail on a homebound ship with spice. They let me out and let me leave under the condition I be tried and imprisoned in Amsterdam. Still, when I finally got back to Amsterdam, you know all I wanted was to get back to Germany. After all these years, I have returned."

"And what a state our country is in," Herr Tucher said. "Maybe I could interest you in taking my family to London? The route and the ship across the Channel has all been arranged. Once you get away from Fraconia there are areas of the country practically untouched by these troops."

"I am weary of traveling. I am also not up for such a journey. I am also grateful to be living with Hans-Wolfgang. And I owe my health and well-being to Katarina. I would like to repay the kind services by staying on for the time being and helping Hans-Wolfgang and his *Magd*, Magdalena. I believe someone needs to keep an eye on him. There is talk that Ralf is traveling about the area again."

"Our friend the Jesuit," Herr Tucher said.

"Yes, and he seems to have recruits with him. Because of Ralf, Magdalena's mother had been arrested, sent to Bamberg and is to be executed."

Chapter 27

Katarina

Katarina heard something hit the window frame and drop onto the wooden floor next to her bed. She turned her head towards the sound and watched an acorn roll under the wardrobe. Voices in the garden caught her attention: Pieter and one of the boys. Pieter had returned from Sichardtshof. He and the boy laughed.

The overcast sky teemed with diving, low-flying swallows. That usually meant rain. Katarina lay on her bed, mesmerized by their darting, careless flight. The early evening sky was still bright in spite of the slow-moving clouds. Late spring always gave her so much joy. With summer approaching, this promise of lazy, sultry evenings and warm glowing nights further saddened her and she shut her eyes.

"Katarina, I know you're up there," Pieter's voice said.

She rolled over on her stomach and covered her head with her hands. There were no glowing nights. The nights brought her only haunted thoughts and she seemed to lay either awake or retreat into a blackened state, never able to rest and regenerate. This caused a devil's-circle of sleepless nights followed by lethargic, exhausted days.

"Come to the window," he said.

Something else sailed through the window and clattered onto the floor.

"Katarina, please don't make me come up there and get you," he said.

She rolled off the bed and dragged herself to the window.

"There you are," he said. "I have something for you. Come down here."

Yes, master, she thought. She would obey and come down the steps. She poured some water from the pitcher into the washing bowl, splashed her face with cool water, dried her hands and ventured out. The garden smelled of fresh-cut grass and damp, growing things. Chickens scratched on the manure pile like they were doing a little dance. Pieter and Sepp grappled and struggled in what looked like a serious clench. As Katarina approached, Pieter laughed and shoved him away. They both looked at her. She suddenly felt very exposed and out of place.

"Can you use a knife?" Pieter wiped the sweat from his reddened face and turned his dagger towards Katarina.

"Yes, I always have a knife with me." She pulled the dagger she kept tucked behind her back in her belt.

"But will you use it?" he asked. "It's one thing to cut a chicken or a rabbit, but it's another thing to stick a large animal, like a man."

"Yes, Pieter, I know, the knife will get caught in the bone, the opponent might turn on me…"

Sepp grabbed at Pieter's knife. Pieter let him take it and then turned the boy around and pulled both of his arms behind his back. They scuffled and laughed like two brothers who liked each other.

"Well the biggest problem here," Pieter said, "is when the smaller, less experienced person has the weapon, the stronger of the two can take the weapon away…" He shoved Sepp away, rounded on Katarina and in an instant, pulled her knife out of her hand. "… and turn it on its owner."

He pointed Katarina's knife at her and lunged. She grabbed his arm, gave it a pull and let his body weight thrust him by.

"Very good," Pieter said. "But remember, I am unhurt and will counter. *Sofort*. Without hesitation." He stood, threw the dagger aside and lunged at Katarina, knocked her down and held her with all his weight. "What are you going to do now?" he whispered in her ear.

Katarina was getting fed up with this game. There was another weapon she liked to use. She put her head under his musky smelling curls and felt his neck with her lips and bit down as hard as she could on that strong strand of muscle next to the wind pipe.

"Woman, have you lost your mind?" he screamed in her ear. He jumped back onto his feet, his face a twisted picture of revolt.

"You wanted to know what I would do in that situation!" Katarina jumped to her feet, dove for her dagger, retrieved it and lunged at him. The point of the dagger just missed his stomach.

Pieter shoved her away. "For the love of God, woman…"

She kept her balance and lunged at him again. He grabbed her wrists and the knife popped out of her hand.

"Are we just playing or do you want to teach me some serious fighting?" Katarina's words spat against his chin. "You want to fight? Or just wrestle around? Then you can come up to my room, young man, and I'll teach you a few things!"

He shoved her away. She turned and stomped towards the open kitchen door, adjusting her dress. She wiped the blood from under her nose with the back of her hand. Sieglinde blocked Katarina's path.

"Katarina?" Sieglinde asked, concerned.

Her compassion enraged Katarina. "Move out of my way!"

Sieglinde stepped aside. Katarina stomped on past her, retreated to her room, slammed the door shut and stopped short of smashing the window as well. She looked out at the now-empty garden and then to the sky and then to the bottle of laudanum. Damn this whole life here. She swallowed a mouthful of the bitter potion and threw herself face-down on the bed.

The next thing Katarina knew, the room was dark and a quiet breeze rustled the leaves outside. She rolled over, sat up and sneezed. Her head pounded and her stomach protested. She stood on uneasy legs, undid her dress and splashed her face with water. Herr Tucher's journal lay on the floor next to the bed. She bent to pick it up and something caught her eye. The crack under the door was illuminated from the lamp in the hallway and a sealed letter lay in the glow. Had someone shoved it there while she slept?

She recognized the fine, flowing script. Like a starving child given a hunk of moldy bread, she opened the letter but couldn't read it in the dark. She opened the door, grabbed the burning tallow lamp hanging from the hook and set it on the table next to her bed. She opened the letter.

I can't begin to tell you how much I miss you. I can think of nothing but you the entire day. My nights are cold, my days empty, my evenings unbearable...

Katarina remembered one particular evening the two of them had spent in Herr Tucher's sitting room after a simple but filling meal. Why this particular evening stood out, she could not say. He'd been writing for most of the day and was quiet, reflective and preoccupied. Katarina knew he would share thoughts when he'd turned them into understandable speech. Until that time, he was best left in silence. She also knew his other senses were enhanced when he was like this and she knew how best to reach him—either a sweet pudding or a sensual kiss. She sat next to him, the very air around him crisp with crackling energy, like the sky before a storm. She touched his hand. He took her hand and considered her with reverence, a look he reserved for only her. Their connection was strong, true and unbreakable. No words needed exchanging.

He had kissed her and held her in a thrilling embrace. She wanted to disappear in his arms. He made love to her that night and swore he would love her and care for her until the end. She had believed he truly loved her. Now she felt a bottomless, eternal void and the need for him drained her of every last thread of trust. Oh, fool she was to believe him. Katarina wrapped her arms around her shoulders, trying to hold the wrack of her life together. She feared her sobs would dissolve her to an insignificant drop amid a flowing river, lost in the swirling current.

Somewhere under all those tears, a spark of anger glistened. A drop of water could not fight the current but a strong swimmer could. Katarina was not a strong swimmer, but she'd survived the current once before. She held the parchment against the flame. As the letter began to burn, she lit the wick of her own clay lamp with the burning letter. Acrid smoke from burning fat stung her nose. Her tear-filled eyes could barely discern Herr Tucher's words as the flames engulfed each sentence.

My love, my life, my…

She turned the parchment around.

Please come back to me. Nothing has changed in our life. I promise it will be as it was. Believe me, nothing is as important to me…

Yes, she was the one who left Sichardtshof, her home, her life, her love. She had no place there anymore; nor here at Eierhofen, for that matter. She was truly free. Could she rebuild this life? Could she find her place? Her fingers burning, she finally let the ashen parchment flutter to the floor.

Chapter 28

Ralf

Ralf slipped his leather-bound Breviary under his arm and, with the other hand, grabbed the burning tallow lamp. He went outside the Uehlfeld house, set the lamp on the table next to a single chair and sat down. The evening was quiet, the air pleasant and it was still light even though it was late. A blackbird chirruped on the neighboring rooftop. Exhaustion crept through his bones, a weariness he hadn't noticed before. For the best part of the evening, he had nursed Martin and sat by him, in the same room, overcoming his own disgust at the impurities running rampant in the boy. The illness had again intensified, the boy's skin now yellow. His breath reeked of infection. What little urine he could pass was dark and had an acidic, salty smell. He'd recited the evening prayers for the unresponsive boy, who had only woken long enough to refuse his evening broth and bread.

Ralf heard a rustle behind the house and expected to see Michel coming back from wherever he'd gone. Ralf feared Michel blamed him for the plight of his brother Martin. Ralf had assured Michel that prayer and God's will would take care of the boy but now his condition worsened and Martin was close to death. If God so wanted to call the boy home, Ralf felt he was not the one to stand in the way.

But it was not Michel who approached. Ralf jumped to his feet like he'd seen a demon as the unknown woman sneaked from behind the house. Her thin blonde hair touched her bare shoulders and a few feathers of fringe covered her smooth white forehead. She was dressed like a maid but had the cunning look of a devil's woman.

"Good evening Father," the woman said. "I'm just passing through. Heading back home. I was in the village trying to buy meat this evening."

"I don't think they have a lot of meat here. These villagers are poor and starving."

"Yes, they say that, of course, but there are those who have food. They just wouldn't tell you. Why should they give you food? You have nothing of value to barter. What do you offer them? A prayer?"

"You should think about your salvation, young lady," Ralf said.

"I am going to hell and I don't care," the woman said. "At least I won't starve to death."

From the open window above, Ralf heard Martin's grating, dry cough.

"Ho, there, Father," the woman said. "I heard there was plague in this village."

"That the boy is ill, is the work of these heathen witches," Ralf said. "We have saved a few of them but I fear there are still many about. I am praying for the boy's return to health. And for his soul, should he not return to health."

"I could help you. I have some *Lungenkraut* here and I could brew him a tea."

"That is devil's work, those herbs. You won't heal him. He'll be bewitched."

"*Quatsch*," the woman said. "Father, that is straightforward nonsense. Do you care for the boy?"

"I care everything for that boy!" Ralf yelled.

"Not enough to try to save him," the woman said. "Doesn't your church have enough gold to try to get him some medicine?"

"What do you know about medicine? Devil's work," Ralf said. "Your quack remedies are nothing compared to the strength of my faith."

"I know a little about herbs," she said. "And I can get you the medicine you need. That boy can be healed."

"Where do you come from?" Ralf said.

"Oh, I travel around," she said.

"You need to be careful," Ralf said. "You provoke me and it is unnecessary. Do you know what sort of power I have?"

"Oh, yes, I've heard about you," she said. "The priest who is taking care of them all. Don't worry, I am not one of them. I'm not a witch. But I can help you."

"What's your name?" Ralf said. "Why would I believe you?"

"My name is Sieglinde," she said. "I live over the hill in the house hidden by the trees. There's an estate. You've already executed the maid's mother."

"Of course, the Eierhofen estate," Ralf said.

"There are those who say you and these boys will be held responsible for these executions, no one else," Sieglinde said. "That the real devil's work is the interrogations you perform and that what you do in the name of God is nothing more than murder and the seizing of property. Where are the women who lived in these houses? Where are they?"

Michel appeared in the doorway. "Father, have you said Martin's night prayers yet?"

Michel must have heard the whole conversation. Ralf needed to get rid of this woman. He grabbed his Breviary and his tallow lamp and went upstairs to the boy's room, followed by Michel. Martin lay on the bed, the glow from the lamp giving his sweaty face a waxy, yellow glow.

"What did that woman have?" Michel said. "Did I hear her say she had something that might help?"

"Do not ever listen to these tricksters. They are only the devil in disguise. She is not from around here. I can tell by her accent. She is too cunning to be one of these dim-witted villagers."

"What is going to happen to Martin? He is all I have."

"That pains me, Michel," Ralf said. "I have taught you better. He is in the Lord's grips now. We will recite our prayers and our faith will carry us though."

Ralf startled and jumped to the side when he realized Sieglinde stood right behind him. This woman unnerved him and he felt he was being confronted with a true devil's servant.

Sieglinde held a cup out for Michel. "Here, boy, I have a tea that will help the sick one."

Michel looked at Ralf like he was searching for his approval. "Father, please, let us try this. Otherwise…"

"Otherwise, what?" Ralf said. "Otherwise the Lord's will should be done?"

Sieglinde moved closer to Michel. "Give him sips of this. I'll leave the rest of the herbs on the table by the fire. Make him tea every few hours through the night. The fever should break."

Michel took the cup and Ralf snorted. Michel ignored him and went about rousing Martin. Ralf turned to find Sieglinde gone. He bolted out of the room, ready to chastise the woman for undermining his authority but she was gone. What had he allowed into his house? A dread of fear ran up his spine and he ran outside into the still, dark evening.

Chapter 29

Pieter van Diemen

Pieter knocked on Katarina's door and received no answer. He let himself in her room, prepared for a reprimand. It was, after all, midday and there she lay on the bed, on her stomach, dressed in her day clothes, her face covered with her hair. Pieter bent over her motionless body and watched her ribcage slowly rise and fall. He reached out a hand but was unsure if he should touch her or not. A few days had passed since she last came out of her room, taking her meals alone and conversing with no one.

He put a hand on her shoulder and rocked her gently. "Katarina, come have something to eat. I want to talk to you."

She rolled over and the leather-bound book fell to the floor. She put out an arm and pushed herself to a seated position, her movements like a newborn foal.

"Have you been drinking?" Pieter said.

She leaned forward, grabbed the book from the floor and lost her balance. She caught herself and shoved the book under her mattress. The mattress puffed a cloud of dust as her body fell back down onto it.

Pieter grabbed her hand and pulled her back up. "Come, stand up, we'll go get some tea."

"Just leave me here," she said.

"If you don't walk by yourself, I'm going to carry you," he said.

Katarina slumped down on the bed and Pieter sat beside her. She tried to pull out of his grasp but he pulled her in even tighter.

"Isabeau doesn't need me anymore," she said. "She has her father. Herr Tucher has his wife. I've lost my home, my family, and now I am losing myself. There's nothing left…"

"Stop with this nonsense, Katarina. You know that's not true. There is no reason for you to be saying any of this. Don't force my hand."

"I cannot go on," Katarina said.

Pieter hated this talk. He'd heard his mother threaten to end it all often enough. It was always her selfish attempt to get Pieter to feel guilty and do whatever she wanted. And that behavior always stemmed from heavy bouts of drinking. He was not going to play this game.

"And your plan is to end the suffering?" Pieter said. "Then do it. End it. I have other things to do today, Katarina."

Pieter stood up and chanced a glance at her. The lost and frail woman sitting on the bed evoked such pity. He held out his hand and she took it. Together they shuffled out the door and down the steps to the kitchen.

"What is wrong with her?" Magdalena said. "Is she ill? Fever?"

Pieter helped Katarina sit onto the bench. She leaned her elbows on the table and her face disappeared into her hands.

Magdalena held a cautious hand on Katarina's forehead. "I'll give her some tea and bread. After she's eaten I'll take her upstairs and check her over. If she is ill, I want to keep the others away from her. None of us should breath the same air. She smells sour and dirty."

"I don't think she's ill, I think she drank something too strong. You know, something out of that box of hers."

Magdalena set a wooden board with a slice of bread smeared with fat on the table in front of Katarina. Katarina bit into the bread and tried to swallow but the solid food seemed to gag her. Magdalena handed her a mug. Katarina accepted it and took a hearty swallow. She continued to gnaw on the bread carefully, like she was afraid of being sick.

Magdalena touched Katarina's arm and Katarina flinched, like Magdalena's touch pained her. "Let me check under your arms."

Katarina shrugged her away and glanced at Pieter.

"I'll wait until you're finished eating and we'll go upstairs if you don't want Pieter watching," Magdalena said. "I need to make sure you don't have any swelling."

Magdalena handed Pieter a piece of bread. "Since the market in Lonnerstadt on the first of May, there have been new cases of plague. Some say it is because there were so many peddlers from out of town," Magdalena said. "Sieglinde says the people she meets in Uelhfeld are afraid. I don't dare go there. Since mother…" She drew herself up and stood straight. "Since mother was unjustly tried and…executed, I am considered touched by evil, therefore I could be blamed for spreading disease. Everyone is looking at each other, like they're carrying the plague or in league with the devil—even if they don't look sick."

"I know," Pieter said. "I travelled with the troops last winter. Hundreds were dying every week of dysentery."

Katarina set her mug down and buried her face in her hands again.

"Up you go." Magdalena grabbed her arm and pulled her up. "Let's get you upstairs."

Pieter took the other side and together he and Magdalena helped Katarina up and out of the kitchen. They led her to her room and laid her on the bed. Magdalena pointed Pieter towards the door, instructing him to leave.

"Pieter?" she called after a few moments. "Look at this." She held out a small ceramic bottle. "Smell this."

Pieter sniffed the bottle and recoiled, shaking his head. "If the plague doesn't kill her, that stuff will."

"She doesn't have plague," Magdalena said. "She has no fever and no boils under her arms or around her groin."

Katarina had rolled onto her side.

"It smells bitter, like some tincture with opium," Pieter said. "Let her sleep it off. I still have work to do."

Pieter was relieved to see Bubo next to a large pile of wood that needed splitting and stacking. Pieter smiled, took the splitting maul from Bubo and got to work, his mind quieting with every fall of the heavy axe. Bubo stacked the split logs and Sepp brought more wood. This work with the two boys gave him a real sense of serenity. The reward was then the evening meal together with Magdalena and the others.

"What a fine meal," Pieter said to Magdalena after eating a simple pottage of beans and onions with a mouthful of chicken.

The early evening sun cast amber hues on Magdalena's face. She cleared the rest of the bones into a large iron pot over the fire. She smiled and set a mug of beer on the table in front of Pieter. Sieglinde appeared in the open doorway carrying a basket full of eggs. Her blouse was torn and exposed both her shoulders.

"The smell of that fine meal will attract all sorts," Sieglinde said. "Attract soldiers quicker than a whore spreading her legs."

"Horrid woman," Magdalena said.

"Go outside in the courtyard and take a deep breath," Sieglinde said. "Everything smells like food. I remember once we were traveling for days.

The smell of bread brought us to a village. We just followed our noses. That bread got a lot of people killed."

Katarina shuffled into the kitchen. She sat on the bench.

Sieglinde laughed. "See what I mean? Attract all sorts." She plunked her basket on the table, came up behind Pieter and ran her fingers through his hair. "All sorts."

Magdalena set a bowl in front of Katarina. She ate in silence. Sieglinde bounded towards the door and almost collided with Isabeau.

"Where is the comb for my horse's mane?" Isabeau said and stood behind Katarina. "The one I got from Herr Tucher. I had it at Sichardtshof."

"I never saw it," Katarina said quietly, not looking at the child. "Didn't you bring it with you?"

"You packed my things."

"I only grabbed what was in your room."

"Why didn't you bring that, too?"

"I am sorry, I only took what I thought was necessary."

"I want my comb!"

Katarina jumped up from the bench and grabbed the girl by both shoulders. Pieter was surprised she could move so quickly. She pushed Isabeau up against the stone wall and bellowed into her face, "You want the damn thing? Then get on your damned horse, ride there and get it yourself."

"It's your fault we had to leave in the first place!" Isabeau screeched.

Katarina raised her hand and slammed the girl with the back of her hand. Isabeau fell to the ground. Pieter had to intervene now. He jumped up and pulled Katarina away. She turned in spite of Pieter's grip on her, lashed out with her other arm and whacked him with the back of her hand. Pieter tasted blood. His lip smarted like he'd been cut with a razor and he saw red. Holding her two wrists together with one hand, he raised the other, prepared to club her. She wrenched herself out of his grasp just as he swung and ran out of the kitchen. Pieter was relieved she had gotten away. He would have hammered her. Magdalena knelt by Isabeau, who sat on the floor.

"A wonderful Good Evening to you all!" said a very merry Hans-Wolfgang as he came in with Sepp and Bubo. Sepp plunked three bottles on the table. Hans-Wolfgang grabbed four ceramic cups and slammed them down next to the bottles. "I took advantage of a great deal today. I sold the two old work horses. Bought some seed and some chickens. And for a really low price. If we remain untouched up here this summer, we will have enough to eat. Hopefully some good weather. I thought seed would be impossible to come by."

He poured the men all a drink and held his cup high. "Maybe our luck is changing. I will entertain this thought tonight and drink with my men to better times ahead."

Pieter huffed and tried to shake off his anger. That woman would not ruin his evening. Yes, maybe their luck was changing. He grabbed one of the cups and downed the strong, fruity schnapps. A hint of apple maybe? After two and then three drinks, he knew he could handle it. Living here had changed him. He could drink like anyone else.

The three bottles empty, Sepp stood and staggered out of the kitchen and returned with one last bottle for the night. He uncorked it, slopped their four cups full and they drank deeply to loves lost and new frontiers. That was the last thing Pieter remembered.

Chapter 30

Katarina

That evening, Katarina read in the diary until her heavy eyes refused to stay open. She punished herself with these readings, hoping to find reasons to be angry with Herr Tucher. In the end, she only loved him more and missed him terribly. She would not end it all, as she had said to Pieter. She was ashamed she'd even said the words. That talk came from one place: fear. She was afraid she had nowhere to go, no place to call home, no family. A woman could not just strike out on her own. She had no money, no means and she was exhausted.

Autumn, 1624

Christoph has been at the farm for weeks now. His visit should have come to an end but when his mother and Max rode out to fetch him, he refused to go. His mother, my wife in name only, who is again not speaking with me, stayed one overnight and left yesterday. Christoph is still here. I truly enjoy my time with the boy. I wished the younger boy would stay on as well. She had also hoped Max would stay here but when he learned his mother would be leaving, he would not stay. He needs to be with her. Oh, how she babies that boy. Christoph seems to rule the roost and Max is her baby, her Nesthäckchen.

Christoph will stay on until the weather makes it imperative for him to travel back to Nuremberg for the winter. I will winter out here on the farm again. I need to oversee the farm. I try to teach Christoph some of the values I live by but it is very hard. My wife and uncle are training him to be great and greatness can be dominating, formidable, overbearing and downright harsh.

I tell myself I truly enjoy my time with the boy but as his body and intellect grow, I find it more challenging to relate to him. I found him out in the barn this morning with Isabeau. Yes, she is difficult as well, but she is delicate, intelligent and very perceptive. Christoph had her tied to a post in the barn and was playing Henker. *He had taken the role of the judge in this case. Yes, it was play, but he was ordering his 'play' executioner to flog the poor girl. In Nuremberg we may be spared the witch trials so prevalent in other Franconian cities, but the cases of young women accused of killing their children are numerous. I feel this is less the number of young women killing children, but more the instance of young women with illegitimate or stillborn children they are afraid of sharing with their families and no comprehension of what to do or where to turn.*

As was the case of Appolonia, a young girl who had once served in the Tucher household. She worked for my uncle for two years, as is the custom, and had earned enough money for her dowry, which my uncle paid. She was already engaged and my uncle assumed she would be married. But her father would not consent to the marriage. I believe he took the dowry money for himself. Well-known was the fact she'd been maltreated by father and brother. When she inevitably turned up pregnant, she was verbally denounced. When she was found with a stillborn child, she was punished, flogged and banished from the city. The father degraded her, calling her a whore, even though we all believed the child to be his. Hers is not an isolated case. Many of these poor girls lack the understanding of their situation or are too ashamed to confide in anyone. They would be punished for telling the truth as well, that is, if any one would believe them.

I reprimanded Christoph for his dreadful game and sent him to his room. He had no comprehension why I would take Isabeau's side. I brought Isabeau into the sitting room for some tea and her lesson, something I fear further alienates the boy from me. Christoph then came out of his room and stomped into my sitting room, enraged, and called her a 'Bastard Child.' I asked him where did he ever learn such a term. He's seven years old, going on eight!

I tell Katarina none of this. She has enough to do now in the autumn. We are getting stores together and bedding down for the winter. We will have enough to eat and it should be a pleasant winter. We number 12 souls here on the farm and have a nice group. If I told Katarina, she would never leave Isabeau alone again. I am planning a Hamburg trip for the next spring and I need to have her with me. Paul and I are already planning another London trip for the summer and I must suffer the travel without her, if the circumstances allow us to travel at all. It is becoming dangerous to travel.

I severely dislike traveling without Katarina. I want to spend every waking moment with that woman. We can go for weeks cooped up together in a coach and never once cross words. I never tire of her presence. As with all other people, I can take only so much and then I want to retire alone. But not so with Katarina. Even to hear the melody of her breathing is a balsam soothing my weary soul. I love the scent her every warm breath carries and each one landing on my cheek is a gift from the heavens.

I find when I travel with Katarina, I record none of the trip. I am so engaged in our conversation. It's like seeing the world for the first time, traveling with a woman so full of wonder and joy. She will point to things and comment on passing landmarks I never would have taken notice of before. The bird song is music in her ears, the world is full of wonderment and we never stop talking!

Katarina calls to me now. I smile. I will continue this entry later.

Katarina extinguished the lamp, lying in the darkness with the window open. The men had quieted, their merriment coming to an end. One man hummed outside in the garden, relieving himself with quiet splashing sounds. The kitchen door closed and someone latched it with a click. Bare feet padded on the steps and they proceeded along the hallway past Katarina's room. She looked for her dagger and realized she'd never retrieved it from the grass in the garden. She must remember to get it tomorrow. It was that silver dagger with the silver and bone inlay handle Herr Tucher had given her.

A door opened and closed along the hall. Katarina wasn't sure whose door it was. She stood and looked out the window. It was already June and she had given no thought to Isabeau's birthday in May. She was now ten years old and she was impossible. What would she be like at sixteen? Isabeau would surely never trust Katarina again. Katarina had never hit the child before.

The moon was waning. The blue light was cold and eerie. Isabeau had spoken the words that kept Katarina awake at night: *It is your fault we had to leave in the first place!* Katarina's thoughts raced and she realized she would never get back to sleep now. She felt restless, uneasy and a creeping sense of panicky fear. She thought about Sara who would be angry because Katarina declined Pieter's request to visit them. Katarina missed her and her grounding sense. But Sara made no effort to contact Katarina, either.

The same door opened and closed again. Bare feet sounded along the hallway towards Katarina's room. Who would be wandering in the middle of the night? Those drunken men should just get to sleep.

Katarina's thoughts settled on Pieter. What would she do with him? He meant well, but sometimes he acted so young and confused. She wondered what he was thinking. She wondered where he had been. He was always a bit of a mystery, but now even more so. He was born on the first Christmas holy day. *Rauhnachtkinder*, people called them, children born during the twelve days between the Christmas holy days and Epiphany. They were all strange in the same way. Feet on the ground but head in the clouds. Intelligent but stupid. Wise but foolish. All at the same time.

Katarina found him intriguing but exhausting. She took a mouthful of water and gagged on it. She sat back down on the bed, that same sickening nausea at the pit of her stomach. The skin on her legs crawled like she was covered in fleas.

Suddenly, her door flew open and slammed against the wall. Dirt sprinkled down from the ceiling and dusted Katarina's head. She could only see Pieter's outline in the eerie blue moonlight. The hairs stood up on the back of Katarina's neck.

Pieter's voice lulled some unintelligible words in a demanding tone. Katarina froze in terror as she watched him sway on the spot. He slammed the door closed, staggered towards the bed and let himself fall onto the mattress with a thud. An almost tangible, nose-stinging cloud of schnapps surrounded him. He sat up and ranted on. Katarina understood none of what he said. She was trapped. The dread of impending pain and abuse forced her to retreat to that sacred refuge beyond fear.

"*Doe je kleren uit!*" he said.

She would try to speak to him. "I don't understand you. Pieter it's me, Katarina."

"*Het heeft geen zin om te weigeren.*"

She would never be able to defend herself against him. Pieter stood, tore his shirt off and removed his breeches. He garbled on and Katarina thought he must be speaking Dutch. Then he lunged at her and lay on top of her and she could feel how aroused he was.

His hands groped under her nightshirt. He pushed the light fabric up and pulled the nightshirt over her head. Using all his weight, he forced her back on the bed and straddled her, penetrating her with one swift motion. Katarina lay still and her thoughts slowed. She tried to retreat into her place beyond fear, where she'd always dampened the pain of the punishments— from Farmer Hanson, from the soldiers—but her feelings intensified. A petition to *Holla* escaped before she could stop herself: *Deliver me from this and I will do anything!*

He was finished as quickly as he started. In the blue moonlight reflecting off the walls, he looked at her as if he just realized where he was. How foolish Katarina was to think him harmless; how naive and childish. All she wanted to do now was drown. Pieter rolled off her, turned his back and began to snore.

What had happened to Pieter? What had she done to make him hurt her? The night breeze chilled Katarina's skin. She stood, closed the window and pulled an extra blanket out of the cupboard. Then that dread exhaustion crept over her. She grabbed her nightshirt off the floor, pulled it on, rolled herself in the blanket and lay down on the floor. Hidden in this cocoon, she felt beaten, spent, unable to move or fight back.

Now someone was shaking her. It was morning. Terror slowly rose within her as she woke from a black, dreamless sleep. This curse had just started the last few weeks. Waking from these blackened states in the Eierhofen house was frightful enough because she couldn't remember where she was. But now Pieter hovered over her. The incident from last night came back to her. Katarina bolted upright, her person at the ready, all senses spiked, expecting a backhand from the man. A cold sweat beaded on her forehead. She brushed the damp hair out of her face. His face folded in what could be anger or terror.

"Katarina, are you hurt?" Pieter said.

She jumped up onto her feet, moved away from him and looked out the window. Pieter tried to touch her but she ducked away from him. She sat back on the bed, ran a hand over her tatty nightshirt and crossed her arms over her breasts. Pieter knelt down on the floor in front of her. He was bare-chested and held his torn shirt.

"What is it?" Katarina said, her arms tight around her chest.

He took Katarina's chin in his hand. "Are you hurt?"

"No, Pieter." She would do nothing to provoke him.

"Did I hurt you?"

"No, Pieter." She would say nothing to provoke him.

"I can't drink that stuff anymore. I never know what has happened. It was at its worst when I was on the ship."

"Were you on a sailing ship, Pieter?"

"Yes. After I went back to Amsterdam."

He turned, sat back and leaned against the bed frame, his face turned away from her. She wished she could trust him but he terrified her. She tightened her face and gripped her own shoulders, praying he would say his piece and leave.

"My father was very sick when I got home," Pieter said. "When he died there were only debts. The only place I found a job was on a ship. I was in the Spice Islands for a few years. Got into some trouble there. You've seen my back."

Katarina sat still and allowed him to continue. He turned, knelt again in front of her and sat back on his haunches. She felt very exposed in her nightshirt and wished he would face the other way. She sneezed, nausea building in her stomach.

"It's the only way to handle being on those ships. And there was nothing else to drink, except schnapps, rum, wine. I am tall and had to walk hunched over all the time. Under the deck it is stifling hot and smells foul and the men are all sick or drunk. The voyage took three months to get there and we never had enough stores. Or the stuff was rotten.

"While we were sailing, I was fine. I had a job to do and had to keep my wits about me. But when we got to the Spice Islands, I saw the massacre, the natives being taken as slaves. The rich getting richer. I was torn between two worlds. I began to drink heavily."

Katarina watched him intently as he spoke. This seemed to make him uncomfortable and he talked faster, his eyes darting towards the door like he was waiting for someone to come and arrest him.

"One night, I was at a tavern drinking with a friend," Pieter continued. "We saw our captain as he dragged a well-dressed native woman out of the place. She was probably a prostitute. I thought of my mother. I have no recollection whatsoever of what happened next. I only hit him once, they said. Well, broke his jaw, actually. But the man was my superior and they thought I needed to be taught a lesson.

"I was thrown in prison. I should have been hung for it, but for some reason they didn't. I spent five years in that dank hole. It's a wonder I lived through that. Especially after the whippings. The infections almost killed me.

"But I met the Chinaman in the prison." Pieter smiled, the memory obviously a fond one. "At least I called him Chinaman. I don't know where he came from. He was in there for cheating some officers in a card game. He was not hanged because he would keep them supplied with opium. So the two of us were kept alive. He taught me his strange fighting style and I taught him some Dutch.

"Once back in Amsterdam, I thought my problem was solved. I wanted to come back to Germany, even with the rumor of war and all the atrocities. Herr Tucher asked me to come back. He told me you still lived there and things were well. I joined a regiment who seemed to be on the move south towards Germany and I thought I could hide among their ranks. I changed armies a couple of times, just trying to get far south enough to desert."

He tried to take Katarina in his arms. She flinched and drew her knees up to her chest.

"Pieter, please don't worry. I'm fine. I need to be alone." She sneezed and felt she would retch.

"Please let me explain," he said, kneeling again in front of her. He tried to take her hand but she pulled away. "You're the only one who can help me. What is happening to me? In Lonnerstadt, the same thing. All I remember was the frenzy of destroying the homes and I awoke with a guard pointing his musket in my face, saying I was to be hanged during the hour. I had been whipped beyond pain. I felt nothing, just numb. But I refused to be hanged. Something like a white light exploded in my head and I attacked that guard. The next thing I knew, I was at Sichardtshof. With you. You saved my life."

He seemed to wait for Katarina's approval. "I promise I'll never drink that stuff again."

She searched his face and saw pride and humility, courage and fear. She felt he would tell her anything to keep her on his side. A coughing sound in the garden made Katarina jump up and look out the window. A hooded figure walked through the garden with the gait of a woman. She carried a full basket, its contents covered in cloth. Katarina motioned to Pieter to come have a look. She put a finger to his lips to keep him quiet.

He snorted. "Sieglinde, that bitch. Where is she going?"

"Go after her," Katarina said.

"You're coming with me." Pieter grabbed Katarina by the arm and pulled her towards the door.

"I'm not dressed."

Pieter opened the wardrobe and threw Katarina her dusty cloak from Sichardtshof. She caught it.

"Come," he said and pulled her behind him. They ran out of the room, down the stairs into the kitchen and out the back door into the garden. "There's only one way out of the garden and that's over the wall. I can't imagine her climbing that."

He led Katarina towards the garden wall and spotted a place where the stones were worn and low enough to climb over comfortably. "Come on Katarina." Pieter climbed bare-footed over the wall and Katarina did the same. "Look at this path. Someone comes and goes here quite regularly."

They followed the path and it headed westward across a grassy field towards the bit of forest where Katarina found the falcon.

"If anyone is in that forest, they will see us coming," Katarina whispered.

Pieter broke into a jog and Katarina struggled to keep up with him. He let her go when they reached the tree line.

"Listen," Pieter said.

A man laughed. A horse snorted. Another man spoke but they couldn't hear what he was saying. Pieter crouched down and Katarina knelt beside him. The men's voices were coming closer.

"There. See her?" Pieter whispered.

Katarina saw the cloaked figure of Sieglinde conversing with three young official-looking military men who were leading their horses. An older officer limped into view, a tall, steely-looking fellow, and Sieglinde handed him the basket. He uncovered it and transferred its contents to his saddle bag; bread and eggs and something wrapped in cloth. Katarina wondered if Sieglinde thought to cook the eggs first. Standing seemed to pain the steely-looking fellow as if he'd been recently injured.

"I know that man," Pieter said. "Hauptman Schwartz."

The four men mounted their horses and rode off. Katarina and Pieter sat quietly and watched them ride towards the south. Sieglinde sneaked on foot in the direction of the Eierhofen house.

"We need to get away from this place," Pieter said.

"Who was that officer, Pieter? What will he do to you?"

"Nothing because he won't get a hold of me."

Chapter 31

Ralf

Ralf brought two chairs outside the Uehlfeld house. He could not bear to sit in that fetid, dank room any longer. Martin struggled but he was on his feet and he hobbled to the chair. Ralf eased the boy onto it and threw a tattered blanket around his shoulders to ward off the slight chill. What they all needed was fresh air and Martin seemed to feel better for it. Still, Ralf was not convinced that the boy was getting healthy. Inside the house a pot clanged and he heard Michel talking to Sieglinde. Cutlery clacked together and ceramic bowls were being laid out. The woman had magicked a meal, he supposed. He was wary of anything that woman did.

He wondered why Martin's illness was so stubborn and unrelenting. He'd given quite a lot of thought to the direction of his mission as a whole. The witch Elsbeth from Sichardtshof had been dealt with and the farm was officially denunciated and under investigation. He had acquired the Schneider's house in Uehlfeld and here he lived with his students and Hauptmann Schwartz. He'd managed to get rid of that Rösslerin. She was the mother of Magdalena, the *Magd* from Eierhofen, he'd found out from his new 'friend' Sieglinde. The rest of the heretics had been dealt with. Surely there should now be a reprieve!

Sielginde appeared in the doorway carrying a ceramic bowl that smelled salty with a hint of chives and handed it to Martin. The boy took it and the wooden spoon and dipped in greedily. From her skirt pocket, she produced a heel of dry bread and handed it to him. Ralf thought the boy ate like a starving beggar under a dangerous spell.

Sieglinde had stopped offering Ralf food. He accepted nothing from her and preferred to scrounge for himself. He still had access to Hauptmann Schwartz's stores and he would produce some grain and beans after Sieglinde disappeared. Ralf watched Sieglinde as she doted on Martin, her face full of falsities. Martin was smitten with her, too young to understand the danger of this power she had over him. Ralf was unable to decipher her true motivation so he held his tongue. If he protested her presence, he could alienate Michel and Martin and they would flock to her. He would have to get the boys out of here before it was too late.

Yes, the signs his work was finished here and he and the boys should return to Bamberg were too numerous to ignore. He could no longer disregard the rumors of the approaching troops, of their hatred of Catholics and the danger this imposed on Ralf and the boys. Sieglinde had mentioned it in passing, almost in jest. Karl and Konrad had voiced their concern since they'd returned from Bamberg, but today the brothers were adamant. They had gone to prepare the gelding and the cart in secret, without Sieglinde seeing them. The boys wanted to leave this afternoon while the weather was mild. Ralf was reluctant to go with them, even though he knew he should.

Sieglinde stopped doting on Martin and a smile spread across her face. Three young officers atop three sleek warmblooded black bays rounded the corner at a walk and approached the house. She skipped over to meet the men. Ralf had an unsettling feeling, watching her flirt and talk so intimately with them. He did not recognize the men nor did he recognize their uniforms. Sieglinde whispered with the men, glancing over her shoulder at Ralf until she finally brought them over to meet him.

"These men are scouts for General Mansfeld," she said. "He is expected to travel though these parts in a few weeks. They are securing quarters for him. It seems the General is quite sick and needs some care. I have told them they could stay here."

"General Mansfeld?" Ralf asked. "He fights for the Protestant forces?"

"It doesn't matter who he fights for," Sieglinde whispered. "He has money. They have money and will pay us to keep him here."

Hauptmann Schwartz appeared in the doorway and limped towards them. "General Mansfeld? I am the Hauptmann in these quarters. I will see to the General."

Ralf drew back from the group. The officers seemed already acquainted with both the Hauptmann and Sieglinde. As Ralf looked on, the uneasiness spread. He hoped Konrad and Karl would see the officers here and wait until they were gone before they appeared with the horse and cart. Then the boys would have to move immediately. As the officers rode away, Ralf joined Sieglinde again. She was conversing in low tones with Schwartz.

"That's a stroke of luck, Father," she said. "We will have a great chance to better ourselves with the General."

Ralf shook his head. "I will not work with the Protestant forces and I will not be the General's *Knecht*."

"There's a mass of troops traveling up the river right now. You don't want to be dressed like a Catholic priest with those Jesuit boys. They will massacre you. If they don't, the villagers will. The force that is coming will be too much for you."

Sieglinde giggled and Schwartz followed her into the house. The clanking of the ladle in the soup pot echoed in the hallway. From the kitchen, their quiet conversation murmured. Those two would pay no more mind to Ralf and the boys.

God bless the cunning of Konrad and Karl! As if summoned, the two sneaked around from the back of the house and without a word, Karl gathered Martin in his arms and carried him away. Michel waited by the cart, holding the reins and Karl eased Martin onto the straw-covered loading bed. Ralf's decision was made and he got in the cart with them.

The main north-south road to Bamberg, an old trade route, was sure to be full of troops so they headed towards Demandsfürth and would try to cross the Aisch at the point Ralf hoped the water was low. A lesser-traveled road parallel to the river was accessible there, the better option to continue their journey north. They would also pass by the forest and the path that led to the Eierhofen estate. He would have to be careful: Hans-Wolfgang was always sneaking around in the forest. Of course, he was not afraid of the little stocky brute. In truth, Ralf wanted to meet up with him and settle that base battle they never had.

They traveled along the road to Demandsfürth, crossed the river and followed the road to Weidendorf. Ralf knew the path to Eierhofen was in that knoll of trees; the estate atop the hill. He had loved his life there. He started working for Friedrich von Obereierhofen when Andra-Angela was but a girl. White-blonde hair and a thirst for knowledge, the girl was a joy to teach. She challenged Ralf's superior intellect even when others bored him. She was clever in many ways, lived by scripture and was a wonderful companion.

Seeing a path that could lead up to Eierhofen sparked an anger he'd not felt in years. It burned as if he grabbed a hot iron he'd thought had cooled. His hands balled to fists like they were tightening around Hans-Wolfgang's neck. Ralf imagined the battle, knowing he was the stronger swordsman and the all-round predominant fighter.

Hans-Wolfgang was the only reason his Andra-Angela fell from grace. He alone was responsible for her downfall. She was a beautiful girl who'd suffered for his carnal passes and Ralf believed that Hans-Wolfgang had raped her. She would still be alive today, God willing, if Hans-Wolfgang had not insisted on bewitching her. The girl believed she loved that little brute. She wanted to marry him! After they were sure Andra-Angela carried Hans-Wolfgang's child, Ralf secured a place for her in the Bamberg convent. They would have taken her with child and she and the child would have been raised by the nuns there.

Over the years, Ralf searched himself to discern why he so vehemently opposed their marriage. Were his reasons impure? Did he have carnal lusts for Andra-Angela? Was that his objection, simple human jealousy? No, he assured himself over and over, he knew what was best for the girl. A life in the convent and a life of God—celibate and chaste and pure—was the only life for her. He could not bear the thought of any other man having her. Did he say any other? No, he meant he could not imagine this pure child of God being held and defiled by any man. She would not have wanted that, he swore, he knew her better than anyone!

Ralf jerked out of his reverie as Konrad hollered and pulled the cart to an abrupt halt. A sorrel horse had bolted out of the forest and now reared up in front of them. Ralf stood as that same white-haired girl brought the horse under control, jumped into a gallop and rode past. Dear Lord in Heaven! This time he got a good look at her. It was Andra-Angela! What witchery was at work here? But it couldn't have been. He was there when that soldier killed her all those years ago. And Ralf stood by and let it happen. Oh, he was no better than the murderer, no better than Hans-Wolfgang.

Konrad fought with the reins as the gelding pranced and grunted. The cart jerked again and Ralf fell to the ground. Then he found out what the girl and her sorrel horse had run from. A group of about seven young men and boys charged out of the forest and spooked the gelding. The gelding shrieked, jumped to the side and reared. Konrad and Karl managed to jump free as the cart toppled over. Martin fell and rolled to his side, Michel landing on top of him.

By the grace of God, the gelding stopped on the spot and Konrad spoke soothing words to calm him. Ralf was unhurt and rushed to Konrad's side as he inspected the front axle of the cart. It was splintered clean through.

"The bed is *kaputt*, too," Karl said.

The boys slit the leather straps, releasing the flustered horse from the battered cart. Konrad gathered the long reins in his hand and stoked the gelding's mane. He jogged away urging the horse to a canter. The horse limped and would put no weight on his front left hoof.

Michel knelt over Martin, who was dazed and not capable of sitting up by himself.

"What do we do now?" Michel asked.

"Here we are, no cart, a lame horse," Konrad said. "We must carry Martin and try to walk back to Uehlfeld."

Chapter 32

Pieter van Diemen

Pieter and Katarina agreed to say nothing to Hans-Wolfgang about Sieglinde and the officers for the time being. Hans-Wolfgang was wont to emotional explosions and Pieter feared he would ride off in a frenzy to look for the men and thereby compromise their hidden position up here in the trees. Pieter also worried there would be implications with Hauptmann Schwartz in the area. The thoughts had robbed him last night's sleep; not to mention the lack of drink. He was grateful that Hans-Wolfgang had a strenuous task for him today. He needed to get out of the house and do some hard work; exhaust himself so he wouldn't be able to put one foot in front of the other tonight. Sleep would come easily. He'd meant what he said about the drink. He would never touch a drop again.

Hans-Wolfgang was in high spirits and Pieter wanted to keep it that way. Pieter needed to burn excess energy and Hans-Wolfgang was happy to work and not talk. Together, they harnessed up Isabeau's mare and Hans-Wolfgang's stallion and they both set off to the field Hans-Wolfgang wanted to plow. Birds in the forest squawked and flew away as the men approached. The sunshine burned the misty, morning fog away from the fields and a steamy, fresh smell invigorated the horses.

The field was plowed by early afternoon. Pieter led the horses to a trough filled with rain water at the edge of the field. They dipped their heads and drank. Pieter scooped water from the trough as well. Sepp and Bubo let themselves fall on the soft grass and opened the basket Magdalena had packed.

"Bread, dried meat and two flasks of beer?" Sepp said.

"Na, then," Bubo said. "What are you going to eat?"

"Catch, Pieter." Sepp laughed and threw a hunk of bread to Pieter.

Bubo handed Pieter the flask but he declined. "Right, you drink with the horses."

Pieter sank onto the grass alongside the boys and they shared their food. They finished eating and got to the next smaller field. This one would go fast and with the harnessed animals in place, Pieter set the plow against the earth and whistled. The animals jerked into motion, only slower now. The two farmhands sowed the seed and Pieter plowed alone, the animals obviously tired. They finished late in the afternoon, unhitched the plow at the field's edge and drove the horses home.

Once in the yard, the three men stripped the wet leather harness from the team. The two boys led the horses to the water trough. The horses drank and didn't come up for some time. Pieter was thirsty himself and hungry as a bear. He went to the well, pulled up a bucket of water and washed his hands, his face and poured the remains over his head. Wanting only food, clean clothes and his bed, he went to look for Magdalena. She'd said Isabeau's grandfather's clothes would fit him and she would take care of the few alterations.

Pieter walked into the entrance hall and stopped short before he climbed the steps to the rooms above. He smelled the air. Nothing. No food cooking. Strange. This time of day there was always cooking going on. No women's chatter came from the kitchen either. He walked down the steps into the kitchen and no one was there. He walked back up to his room and found the clothes on his bed. Dressing quickly with the door opened, Pieter listened for sounds of anyone moving around in the house. A door in the hall opened and urgent voices whispered and hissed.

"What are you going to do?" Isabeau whispered.

"Go look for Hans-Wolfgang," Katarina hissed. "He must decide what to do."

Pieter walked into the hallway and met Katarina. "What happened?"

"Magdalena is sick," she said. "Hans-Wolfgang must come and look at her."

"What does she have?"

"Horrible head-splitting headache, she says. Now fever. She collapsed in the kitchen with the headache and we brought her up here. We need to know what has made her ill before we all get sick."

"It's the cold spring weather," Pieter said. "It'll be the death of all of us."

"She's been so sad since her mother…. And afraid to go anywhere. Maybe the melancholy. I don't really know who else she sees." Katarina lowered her voice. "She sleeps with Hans-Wolfgang. Maybe that has something to…"

"Where is she?" Hans-Wolfgang bellowed down the hall as he hurried towards them.

Pieter stepped aside. Katarina opened the door and went in first. Pieter followed the two into the room. Hans-Wolfgang knelt next to Magdalena's bed, took her hand and smoothed her hair away from her sweating forehead. She smiled at him and said something. He spoke a few gentle words that Pieter couldn't hear.

Hans-Wolfgang glared at Katarina. "What is the matter with her? Katarina, do something. Help her."

"I want you to tell me what to do," Katarina said.

"She says her head hurts," Hans-Wolfgang said. "Maybe you have a potion for that." He grabbed Pieter by the arm. "We will leave the women alone. Katarina, find the reason for her unease."

Hans-Wolfgang motioned for Pieter to follow him down the steps into the kitchen. He grabbed a bottle from the shelf and set two cups on the table. Pieter declined immediately.

"You have to drink something," Hans-Wolfgang said.

Hans-Wolfgang downed one cupful and poured himself another. Sepp and Bubo came in from the garden, dumbfounded looks on their faces as they considered the cold kitchen. They grabbed cups off the shelf and sat next to Hans-Wolfgang, who filled their cups with schnapps.

"Where is that wretched Sieglinde?" Hans-Wolfgang asked.

"Haven't seen her. Haven't looked for her, either," Bubo said. "Where's Magdalena? I'm hungry."

Hans-Wolfgang said nothing and rubbed his thumb and forefinger over his brow. His hands were still dirty, his face dusty. He smelled like horse.

Katarina came into the kitchen. "I think you should look at Magdalena. She has swelling under her arms. If she has the plague, we have to get her out of the house."

"Is Magdalena sick?" Bubo said. "What does she have?"

"I don't know," Katarina said. "I'm not a doctor!"

"I won't banish her from my house!" Hans-Wolfgang yelled.

"We can't have her in here," Katarina said. "It could be plague but I can't be sure. She has a high fever. Her poison breath will ruin the air for all of us. We'll all get sick."

"You treat her, Katarina. You'll think of something."

Katarina shook her head. "I am not a doctor, Hans-Wolfgang. I can treat diarrhea or simple wounds but not this. Nobody lives through this. Everyone just gets sick."

"Think of something to help her, for the love of God," he shouted and left the kitchen.

The two farmhands got up and left, too, looking at Katarina like it was she who was poisoning the air with her foul breath.

Pieter felt a stab of guilt, a feeling he couldn't quite explain. Katarina swiped a strand of hair out of her face with the back of her hand. She looked helpless and lost and this made Pieter very uncomfortable. Katarina and women in general were there to help him and to make him comfortable. There was nothing he could do for her. Pieter turned away and watched a fly climb up the wall.

"What about that officer we saw?" she said. "What happens when he finds you?"

Yes, he had thought about that. He'd thought about it the whole day while he was plowing the field. Meditative work, it was, the tearing at the heavy ground with massive, muscular animals and hearing nothing but the rustle of wind in the trees, birds calling, the horses snorting, chains of the harness clanking and the excruciating work ripping his muscles but calming his mind.

"I had no chance to consider any of it," Pieter said. "We were working all day in the field. Don't you have anything to ease Magdalena's pain? It would be the friendly thing to do."

Katarina's eyes filled with tears. She turned her back. Pieter got up and left the room, left her there to figure out this problem. He walked up the steps and escaped to his room. He sat on the bed, thought he'd just put his head down for a moment.

He awoke when he heard Isabeau screech in the kitchen. Day had only just broken. He'd slept the whole night through. Isabeau's voice was raised, high and frantic. He went down the steps and entered the kitchen. Isabeau hollered at Katarina.

Isabeau turned when she saw Pieter. "Hans-Wolfgang has fever now too. And she won't do anything about it."

Katarina looked helpless. "I am not a doctor. I can't cure diseases. I've made them both calendula tea and chamomile compresses. That's all I know. I don't know what you expect me to do."

"Help him get better," Isabeau said.

"I'm trying," Katarina said. "I can only give them the remedies I know about. Pieter, help me! Sieglinde has come back. She's out collecting firewood."

Pieter had to find out about Hauptmann Schwartz and Sieglinde's acquaintance with him. This could cost him his freedom, could cost him his life. He trusted Sieglinde as much as he trusted a wolf to watch his herd of sheep. These other problems were for Katarina to sort out. Pieter looked at her with a mild annoyance and it seemed she read his mind.

"You can't leave me alone with this situation," Katarina said. "The farmhands have gone and want nothing to do with this. I don't know what Sieglinde is up to."

"It is your task to see to Hans-Wolfgang and Magdalena," Pieter said. "You can't let them alone."

"I don't know what to do," she said, undid her apron, threw it on the worktop and stomped out the back door.

"I'm starting to hate her," Isabeau said and stomped out of the kitchen as well.

Chapter 33

Katarina

Katarina's thoughts rushed in a cluster as she bolted down the path from Eierhofen and out of the trees. She headed towards the secret meadow, hoping to find any herbs she could have forgotten, ones that could help Hans-Wolfgang and Magdalena. Judging by the state of the trampled flood plain, thousands of men had marched by. She picked a careful path through the mud and then found a well-traveled path of stones and boards in the river where she could cross.

She'd given Hans-Wolfgang and Magdalena all the herbs she had on hand. The onion and the garlic tinctures she made should have helped with their fevers, but these illnesses were lethal. She was not a doctor. How many times had she said that today? She could try the laudanum, but would it help? She hardly had enough for herself. Watching the contents of the bottle dwindle made her body panic in a way she'd never experienced before.

This time of year she would certainly spot something growing that would ease headaches and fevers. The season was close to the solstice, *die Sonnenwende*, daylight lasting long past its welcome. The body tired but the daylight urged one to continue working. Usually she would plan a celebration, a midsummer bonfire. But common sense told her a bonfire would only lead the evil to them. Soldiers would see the smoke from far, far away.

She ran up the river bank towards the Mailacher Weg. No one was about as she made her way through the fields, towards the sloe bushes forming a sort of wall around the meadow. Had the *Tross* destroyed the meadow on the evening she and Isabeau rode past, the night they escaped? Katarina walked around the periphery, looked for a way in and began a second pass. About half way around, she spotted a small hole, like a tunnel. She got down on her knees and crawled through the thorny brush.

There were no signs that soldiers had slept here, or hacked the trees, or set fire to the whole place, like she imagined. It was as if nobody ever entered. The fruit trees stood just like nothing happened. She thought they would be fruitless. It was a warm day and the smell of elder blossom filled her heart. There had been no frost here. Like a blessing. Maybe she would find her luck, bring some herbs back and everything would just be fine.

She cursed, realizing she'd left without a basket to transport any finds. She sat down on the grass in the sun, stretched her legs, closed her eyes and dipped her head back to bask in the warm rays.

"She will try to save his life," a voice said.

Katarina looked around and saw no one.

"She will attempt to save Hans-Wolfgang's life," the voice said.

Now she was hearing voices. "Pardon?" Katarina said.

"Hans-Wolfgang knows this. That is why he keeps Isabeau near. He will not let her die for him."

Katarina tipped her head back again. A shadow passed in front of her eyelids. She opened her eyes to see an old woman dressed in white standing over her. A long white braid fell over the woman's shoulder along her left breast. She looked ageless.

"That's not why he keeps her near. He loves her," Katarina said.

"He loves her because she looks like Andra," the woman in white said.

"He loves her because they are so much alike. She needs to stay away from him now. He is ill."

"Do you realize how much she needs you right now?" the woman said.

"Me?" Katarina said. "I am nothing to her. I am not her mother. I am not her friend."

"She needs you."

"Hmpff," Katarina scoffed.

"Isabeau is your charge. She is the most important thing to you."

Guilt racked Katarina. Her inability to control the girl brought tears to her eyes. Had she lost Isabeau's respect? She had failed. Did every mother feel this way? Katarina closed her eyes, the bright outline of the tree-trunk woman in white still impressed on her eyelids. This was her second encounter in the meadow with the great seer they called Sybilla Weiss, the woman in Magdalena's story.

"You have not failed," Sybilla said. "Why should you be different than any other parent?"

"What do you know about children? I have failed the girl, I have failed Magdalena."

"The maid does not have plague," the woman said. "Her blood carries a deadly infection. It ravages her body. But the swellings are not from the plague. Still, she will die. If you do not help Hans-Wolfgang, he will die as well. You can still save Hans-Wolfgang."

"That's why I am here," Katarina said. "Looking for answers."

"I can see why you are here," Sybilla said. "You are enveloped in your own thoughts."

"I have my own problems," Katarina said.

"Help the others and you will see how to solve your problems," she said. "I promise you. Wallow in your muddy, dark hole and you will never find your way out."

Katarina lay back on the warm grass. "I am always helping others. Just makes them more prone to blame me."

"Take your basket and collect some elder blossoms," Sybilla said. "They should have elder tea during the day. At night they should have tea from hawthorn. Set up a tincture of columbine this afternoon, let it soak overnight and begin with a few drops in the morning."

"What basket? I don't have a…" Katarina said, sitting up with a jolt.

She was alone. A few birds chirped. A light breeze rustled the leaves. By her feet stood a basket.

Katarina never doubted Sybilla Weiss's existence. She seemed to be watching over Hans-Wolfgang. Katarina stood and walked through the meadow, reciting the names of the herbs growing wild and unruly. She found the columbine, plucked the flowers and dug out some of the roots. Hawthorn bushes grew strong and were blooming white. She cut whole branches off and would chop it all—twigs, flowers, leaves—and cook it. She finished filling the basket with elder blossoms and looked for the way out of the meadow.

On the other side of the sloe bushes voices rose and fell. Katarina ducked down, her first instinct to hide, even though no one could possibly see through the thick bushes. But the voices, more distinct now, belonged to children, not men. No soldiers then. A woman grumbled quietly and a child groaned. This calmed Katarina. She walked again around the periphery and searched for the way out. The tunnel she'd come through was no longer passable.

Katarina saw another hole in the bushes on the other side of the meadow. Katarina could just fit her shoulders through the hole, like a rabbit going down a hole. It actually went down a bank and at one point Katarina thought she was tunneling underground. It was difficult to pull the basket behind her and she checked to see if her herbs were falling out. She wondered if she could get out at all. Again she heard the woman's voice. Katarina inched through the bushes and finally poked her head out the other side. There in the field beyond digging for roots was Sara.

Katarina lay still for a moment, reluctant to attract her attention, almost afraid of Sara's reaction. She prepared herself for a reprimand. This was silly. Sara was her best friend. Katarina wriggled her way free of the bushes, pulled the basket out of the hole and stood, waiting. Albin saw Katarina emerge, squealed and came running over.

"Where's Isabeau? Is she here, too?" Albin said and hugged Katarina around the waist.

Katarina smoothed the hair on his head. "Hallo, young man. My, you are so big!"

"What a surprise," Sara said. "Hallo Katarina. You're still alive, I'm happy to see."

"Hallo," Katarina said sheepishly.

The situation felt so awkward. Sara had a scolding tone in her voice which made Katarina apprehensive. Katarina loved Sara dearly but Katarina was still angry. She was angry at herself for leaving home, she was angry at Sara for letting her leave, and, she was ashamed to realize, she blamed Sara for Pieter.

"We miss you, Katarina." Sara embraced her.

"I miss you, too," Katarina whispered, trying to fight back the tears.

"She won't be here much longer. Frau Tucher, that is," Sara said. "He's secured her passage across the Channel. They have acquaintances in England and she is to leave within the next few days. He offered the job to Pieter but Pieter doesn't want to go. Uncle Paul is going to travel with her and the boys. All very secretive, when and how they travel. You didn't have to leave. You could have stayed in my house and stayed out of her way. We have so much work to do, now even more because you aren't here. I've taken the children to help me wherever I can use them. Evenings we need to spin the wool."

"I don't know if I can come back. But I can't stand it up at Eierhofen, either! I wish I could just leave once and for all."

"Oh, Katarina, sometimes I could slap you." She waved her hand in front of Katarina's face, scolding Katarina like a five-year-old. "Your place is here with us. Collect your things and come back. Frau Tucher needn't see you. She never comes back to our house and rarely crosses paths with any of us. Isabeau has her father. Let her stay with him."

"We have been arguing," Katarina said. "Isabeau and I." Sybilla said Isabeau needed her. Without Katarina there, Isabeau would do something foolish. Katarina loved the child no matter how difficult she was and had to set her own feelings aside. No, she couldn't just leave Isabeau.

"How did you get into the meadow?" Sara said. "I haven't found a way in. I tried to cut a hole in the bushes. I'd been in once this spring. When I came back the next day, the hole had grown shut."

"Hans-Wolfgang's *Magd* is sick. Deathly ill, actually. He is sick, too. I found these herbs. I hope they help. I am afraid they won't make it through the night."

"Don't come back here if you get sick," Sara said.

"I've been drinking Herr Tucher's tincture. I wonder if it is the plague, like they are all talking about. Or just a fever."

"Either would finish them off. In Lonnerstadt, fifteen people have died from the plague."

Hannah cried out. Both women looked on as Albin punched her on the arm.

"Stop that fighting!" Sara shouted at them. "Hannah is not well either. And David and Friedrich never came back. We never saw them again."

"How is he?" Katarina said quietly.

"Who?" Sara said, shaking her head, puzzled.

Katarina whispered, "The master."

"Oh." Sara nodded, understanding. She came closer. "He misses you terribly. Come back to the house with me this afternoon. Just for a few moments."

"No, I can't. I have to take care of Hans-Wolfgang and his *Magd*. I need to make a tincture out of this."

"You'll have to make some for me, too. I can't seem to find any of the herbs I need."

"I'll make sure you get some." Katarina gave her a kiss on the cheek.

"I really need to leave." She smiled and hurried away.

***

After Katarina spent the afternoon brewing herbs and caring for her patients, she came back to her room and opened the journal at random. The pages held a passage where Herr Tucher had witnessed the aftermath of one of Christoph's nasty games with Isabeau. Katarina never knew of these things. Is this why Herr Tucher gave Katarina this journal to read? To tell her things he could not speak of? She laid the journal aside on the bed. Her abrupt action made the candle flicker and it almost went out.

Katarina watched the treetops sway outside the open window. Humid and laden with storm, the air had taken on a solidity and hung like a sodden curtain, refusing to enter the room. Voices whispered in the garden. Katarina stood and cautiously peeked out the window. She could see Pieter speaking with the hooded figure of a woman. Sieglinde. Their voices were cordial and quiet. Katarina could not understand their conversation.

She turned away from the window, tipped a few drops of laudanum onto a spoon and licked it clean. What would happen when it was all gone? The few drops did nothing for Katarina anymore, only gave her a slight relief from this sickness that plagued her. She put the flask back into her box, changed her mind and slipped it into her apron pocket. She grabbed the candle, left the room, shutting the door. Voices echoed up the stairway so Katarina blew the candle out and sneaked down into the kitchen. Thunder rumbled in the distance.

She pulled an empty bowl from a pile by the fire, filled it with warm water and dropped swatches of cloth into the bowl. Compresses for Hans-Wolfgang's and Magdalena's calves should bring down their fevers and make them healthy too. Sieglinde pushed the door open. The smell of wet grass and the pattering of rain brought a chill into the room. Katarina thought the grey clouds against the darkening sky framed Sieglinde's hooded form like the backdrop of an eerie painting. Sieglinde dropped her armful of wood onto the floor right by the open door and a shiver ran up Katarina's spine.

"Nothing you do is going to help them," Sieglinde said.

"You are free to take over whenever you like," Katarina said.

"I've seen this before. They have *typhos*," she said. "Ship's fever."

"Well, what do you suggest I do?"

"Get out of here now." Sieglinde chuckled. "Just a warning among

246

friends."

Katarina did not trust this woman at all. "And you know a better place for me? Yes, you know all about the world."

"Yes, I do know the world." Sieglinde threw a log on the fire. "Soon you will have no place here, Katarina."

Katarina waved Sieglinde away and then lit her candle, grabbed the tablet with the bowl of compresses and the tea and carried it to the room Hans-Wolfgang now shared with Magdalena. As she pushed the door open with her foot, she was relieved Isabeau was no longer there.

Isabeau had insisted on staying by his side the whole afternoon. Hans-Wolfgang barked at her so fiercely, insisting she leave. The girl finally listened. Katarina told her he was seriously ill and he wasn't being mean, he just didn't want her to get sick. Whether the illness was caused by their personal beliefs, the air in the room or the constellation of the planets, Hans-Wolfgang said, he wanted Isabeau far away.

"*But you go in there*," Isabeau had said to Katarina.

"*Nobody cares if I get sick, do they?*" Katarina sneered back.

Hans-Wolfgang and Magdalena now looked so serene, lying there in bed, covered in white bed linens that took on a warm glow in Katarina's candle light. She set the tablet down on the table next to the bed. She lit their candle from hers, set hers on the table and opened the double window. Katarina hoped the fresh air would dilute anything foul she was breathing in.

This room looked out over the main courtyard. From here Katarina could see the front gate. The rain continued in a steady, light stream. She turned back to the room. This was obviously the master's room. Her room was only a quarter of the size. The walls were lined with dark-stained wooden panels. Portraits hung on the wall next to the door, the subjects' eyes illuminated by the candle light.

Hans-Wolfgang stirred and muttered in his delirium. Katarina took the lukewarm fabric and wrung the extra water out. She rolled the feather tick back to expose their calves and wrapped them in the damp fabric. Nothing worked better than this for breaking a fever. Hans-Wolfgang gave a relieved sigh. Holding a cup, Katarina quietly asked him if he wanted tea.

"Have you anything stronger?" he croaked.

"Would you like some schnapps? I can put some in your tea. Sit up and drink this first. That's good. I'll go fetch a bottle."

Katarina grabbed her candle and went down the hall to her room. She set the candle on the table and grabbed the schnapps bottle she'd hidden under her bed. The candle light flickered on the belly of the upturned spoon on the table. The laudanum weighed heavily in her pocket. Her hand was in her pocket gripping the bottle. She uncorked the bottle, put another few drops on the spoon and licked it. Maybe she should give Hans-Wolfgang a few drops of this in his tea. It might be worth keeping him quiet. He'd sleep like a baby. But how long would this bottle last? Katarina turned to see Pieter standing in the doorway.

"Are you trying to poison him now?" Pieter said.

"No, he'd like something to help him sleep. And this will ease the stomach cramps."

Pieter took the bottle from Katarina and smelled it. "Bitter. Horrible. I've seen what this does to people." He corked the flask and returned it.

"It keeps me healthy," she said. "You're not sick, are you, Pieter?"

"No, I just can't sleep. I hear things moving outside. I hear wolves."

Katarina offered him the flask again with a nod of her head. He declined. She dropped it into her apron pocket, grabbed the schnapps and left the room. Magdalena muttered and woke when Katarina entered their room and lit another candle.

Magdalena sat up, her face sunken and ghostly. She cleared her throat, a dry broken cough. "I'm so thirsty," she said.

She was still burning with fever so Katarina removed her compresses, rinsed them in the bowl of water and re-wrapped her calves. She dribbled a few drops of laudanum into their cups and filled them with tea. She handed Magdalena a mug. Hans-Wolfgang snored sitting up but Katarina woke him by trying to help him recline. His head was still hot, but not nearly as hot as Magdalena's, and Katarina re-wrapped his calves as well. The breeze picked up and the rain came through the open window. As Katarina closed it, the wind slammed it with a bang.

"Are you thirsty?" Katarina asked him.

He held out his hand and she gave him a mug of tea.

Magdalena's smile faded and she looked sleepy. Katarina touched her forehead with her fingertips. Her head had cooled. She took the mug from her, removed the compresses and helped her to lay back. His forehead was cool, too, so Katarina removed his compresses. Katarina blew out their candles and left the room.

The door to Katarina's room was open and the warm, creamy light of a candle lit the doorway. Pieter sat on the bed, one leg crossed over the other, one finger twirling a strand of hair, reading the journal. She leaned on the door jamb, folded her arms in front of her chest and frowned at him. She wondered if he was violating some private element here.

"I'm sorry, Katarina," he said and pointed to the passage in the beginning of the book. "But he wrote about the time he came to Amsterdam and picked me up. Remember that? He was sitting in the breakfast room at an inn on the street I grew up on. He was waiting for my father to arrive and he wrote almost the whole conversation between my father and himself."

He paused and smiled, flipped to the next page and pointed to a three-stanza verse in fine flowing script. "Did you read this? This poem he wrote? He wrote this other poem there, too. He must have been there a few weeks. He was sitting in the breakfast room. He describes the room and everything. It's like being there. I don't think the inn is there anymore. Most of the street has burned down. I've been gone so long. I loved Amsterdam."

Katarina came in the room and sat down next to him on the bed. "I've read the whole thing through now and I've just started over again. Tell me about Amsterdam. I never got there. I was in Hamburg over the years often with him, but we never went as far as Amsterdam."

"Amsterdam? So much has changed since I left. And I only lived there a total of about two years in the past ten. I think we all have a soft spot in our hearts for our childhood homes. Though living there never seemed to live up to my memories of the place." He smiled, laid the journal aside and said, "Enough of my silly stories. I'll let you get to sleep. You must be exhausted."

He leaned in and kissed Katarina on the cheek. Startled, she froze, a prickling fear warming her and flushing her face. Would she react like this every time a man came near her? Would she expect them all to hurt her? Would she always await the forceful hand expecting her to hold still, the same hand that would hit her for holding still? And then be called a whore for doing so? Should she let him have his way and then try to forget what he'd done, thankful he didn't kill her? Pieter slowly reached up, slid one hand behind her neck, under her hair, and pulled her close. He kissed her deliberately on the mouth. She waited to feel if he was going to pull away or not. His one arm then his other pulled her even closer and the tip of his tongue played on her lips.

Katarina wanted to know what he was thinking. She pulled her lips away from his and tried to discern what he wanted. A breeze caught the candle. It flickered and went out. Katarina stood and moved away from him, towards the window. He stood, pulled off his shirt and caught her in the middle of the room.

"Do you hear that?" he whispered.

A chorus of wolves sang in the distance, their howling mournful and beautiful. It sounded like two animals and then a third joined in harmony.

"May I?" He slid her blouse down over her shoulder and tugged at her skirt with his other hand.

This would end here. He was not a man she wanted to lay with. He was not a man she wanted to love. He was not going to violate her.

"No, you may not," Katarina said. "I won't let this happen again."

He kissed her on the cheek, collected his shirt and hurried out of the room.

Chapter 34

Ralf

As Ralf walked back to the Uehlfeld house from the community oven, he savored the aroma of the fresh bread in the basket he carried. After the last few weeks of what seemed like being held captive in the Uehlfeld house, Ralf took advantage of this lull today to move about freely. With each passing regiment Schwartz was required to quarter in the house, the soldiers seemed to become steadily more desperate and degenerate. They did not know friend or foe. Ralf had not been able to find the means to move the boys back to Bamberg. They were required to work to keep the soldiers. Even when the regiments had passed, stragglers followed for days on end: deserters, sick or injured; homeless families, broken folks, children.

Ralf pulled the basket closer to his chest, aware of the enticing smell of yeast and wheat, and quickened his pace. He could lose his life because of this bread. As he approached the Uehlfeld house, he was met by Karl and Konrad.

"What is it, boys?" Ralf said and handed Karl the basket full of bread.

"Sieglinde is upstairs," Karl said. "She came back with those officers after you left. They don't want us here when the General comes. They said he would have us hanged because we are Catholic. We want to try to finally leave."

Ralf nodded vigorously. "The plan was they would clothe us as farmers and we could stay here until they went up and took over the Eierhofen estate. Then the officers would all leave and we would be permitted to stay here in peace until Martin was better."

"Father Ralf." Karl looked sheepish. "They are up to something. They locked the room and have been in there since. They made us leave the house. But Martin is too ill to move."

Ralf stepped through the front door and looked up. "I hear nothing."

"Father Ralf," Karl said. "Konrad and I are worried. We cannot trust

251

them. Martin is worse again but if we stay they will kill us all anyway. We should make a break for it."

Konrad stepped up next to Karl and squared his shoulders. "We don't know how much longer we can hold here. Let us get Martin back to Bamberg now. We'd like to make a run for it."

Martin's sickness had come back full force. The herbs Ralf so unwillingly allowed the boy to have made him better but that was all just a trick of the devil. The cough had subsided but now he was just as weak as before, if not worse. As much as he loved the boy, he was pleased to see that he was right about those devil's-remedies.

Ralf agreed with the two boys. "We shall leave today."

"Two weeks have passed and Martin is not better," Konrad said. "I agree, we should leave today because it is quiet, we may have a chance of getting out of here with our lives."

Ralf laid a hand on the boy's shoulder. "Now, how do you propose we do this? We have a lame horse and the broken cart. Should we walk?"

"We are moving out now." Schwartz stood in the doorway of the house. He wore a new uniform much like the ones those other officers wore, even though it looked used. He set a wide-brimmed black hat with a flowing white plume on top of his head.

"Where are you going dressed like that?" Ralf asked. "Where did you get that uniform?"

"I am the officer in charge," Schwartz said and patted the hat. "I am still a Hauptmann. The others said we will ride out now and I am to accompany them to meet up with the General. I will get a promotion for securing that estate for the men. This house is ours as well. I have been instructed to allow you to leave now or have you executed when the General sees your papist ass."

"You will get a promotion?" Ralf said and tried to appeal to the man's better sense. "I brought you here and you throw me out? Take the General to Eierhofen and leave us here. You said this house was beneath him. We'll move out when it's up to us."

"Father, let him have the place," Konrad interrupted. "We belong in Bamberg with the Prince-Bishop, not here under these soldiers."

"We are not here to stuff your *Pfaffen Beutel*," Schwartz said. "Our mission is to save the world from filling the church's coffer."

"Go with God, my friend," Ralf whispered.

"No one would have found the way were it not for me," a woman's voice said. Sieglinde walked down the down the steps and stopped in the doorway behind Schwartz. He stepped aside and let her exit the house. She wore a clean, dark green skirt and a jacket made of cream-colored silk embroidered with green foliage. A pearl necklace with a heavy, carved golden clasp hung around her neck and Ralf could not help but stare at it. Sieglinde was going places; straight to hell, probably, but she would cover a lot of ground on her way there. The two officers came down behind her.

"We thank you whole-heartedly, gentlemen," the one officer addressed the whole group. "But we will not be needing your services anymore. Schwartz, you are to return to your regiment."

"That's Hauptmann Schwartz, *Bübchen*." Hauptmann Schwartz's face turned red with anger. "This is my command."

"Here is a horse, Schwartz." The young officer pointed to the back of the house and the lame gelding. "If you leave now, we will not hang you for desertion. I suggest you get a move on. You are dismissed."

Sensing a storm about to break, Ralf backed away from Schwartz and the officers. Karl and Konrad stepped back to join Ralf who whispered to Konrad: "Have they been arguing among themselves?"

"They were quiet upstairs. We never asked what they were discussing," Konrad said.

"I am not leaving!" Schwartz said. "I am going to the estate and working with the General!"

"We will take care of the General," the officer said. "Sieglinde comes with us." With that, the two officers and Sieglinde turned towards the back of the house. Ralf assumed they'd secured their horses in the barn. Hauptmann Schwartz spluttered and stammered as they left.

"We will begin our journey back to Bamberg where we belong," Karl said.

"We think we can use the gelding if we go at a walk." Konrad nodded. "Father? Do you agree? We think we can fix the cart."

Ralf knew it was time to leave but he wanted to try to see that girl again. Truth was, if he left now, he would forfeit all his chances of ever learning the child's identity. Could this be Andra-Angela's child? Was she living with that heretic Hans-Wolfgang?

"Father? You seem preoccupied."

Hauptmann Schwartz puffed his chest. "I am going to Eierhofen and I am going to claim my promotion." He marched away from the house in the direction the others had gone.

Ralf turned his back on them all and went into the house for a moment to reflect, feeling alone and abandoned. A shiver ran up his spine. No fire burned and the house was chilly despite the warm day. He sank to his knees and held his face in his hands. He was a fool to think he could make any difference in the province, trying to reinstate the Catholic faith to these heretics. This whole undertaking had gone completely awry, diverted from the original goal, and he would be ridiculed, a failure. But it seemed unimportant. All he could think about was Andra-Angela and the daughter who looked just like her! What was his purpose here? Could it be, he misinterpreted his mission all along?

He pulled the rosary from the pocket by his heart and rubbed the smooth juniper berries between his fingers. This action centered his soul. He heard Father Marius' voice: *look to your God in your most troubled hour, and you will be triumphant,* as he made the sign of the cross. *In the name of the Father of the Son and of the Holy Spirit. Amen.*

Ralf heard voices, stood and walked to the front door that still stood open. A group of seven stray boys he recognized as the ones from the forest had gathered around Karl and Konrad. Michel had joined them. Karl broke a loaf of bread and divided it between the whole group. At first Ralf wanted to reprimand Karl for wasting their last bread until he saw a few of the boys held knives at Konrad's soft middle. Ralf also heard the urgent and passionate tone the stray boys spoke with. They were quite angry. Ralf let the fiery and fierce anger wash over him, drawing him into the conversation.

"That bit of bread won't feed you all," Ralf said. "I've been waiting days for this bread. It is only because I demanded it with brute force."

The wiry-looking boy of about eighteen years who spoke for the group answered, "Your talk won't feed us, but that bread will."

"Maybe it's time we work together," Ralf interjected. "You can help us. Together we can find a common goal."

"There's a small group of us in the hills by Sichardtshof. We're all hungry."

"Oh, really." Ralf was calculating, planning, his thoughts running ahead of the conversation.

"And another group lives behind that other estate in the woods up on the hill."

"Eierhofen?" Ralf guessed.

"I don't know what it's called," the wiry boy said. "They have food and horses. There's a pretty girl with light blonde hair that lives there. She has a horse and I want it."

"Up at Eierhofen?"

"Yes. She's out quite a bit. Strange girl she is. We've tried to catch her but she's a good rider."

"I know her," Ralf said.

All of Ralf's worries cleared and his thoughts coagulated. His memory of Andra-Angela had become a fond but cruel memory, one full of loss and rejection. Fond nonetheless. So long ago it seemed that Ralf had lived at Eierhofen with her and her father. So long ago, her affair with Hans-Wolfgang. Andra-Angela had misread Ralf's intentions. She thought Ralf wanted her as a man wanted a woman. He never wanted a woman like that. Those feelings had never, not one time, occupied his thoughts. Sinners and novices alike were in awe of his superiority to the call of the flesh. He remained unimpeded by the egoism of the family. He wanted nothing more than to accompany her on her journey as her mentor. That he had desired the Eierhofen estate for his Jesuit School had been a mistake on his part. He was fully aware of that now.

That moment of chance meeting with Andra-Angela's child was divine intervention, there was no other explanation. He now allowed himself to accept the rehearsed conversations he'd had with her the last few days. He'd even grown fond of her, though he'd never made her acquaintance. This was God's will, he was now convinced, and he saw a way to make right what he had done all those years ago. He would save that girl, set her on the correct path and he now saw a way to accomplish that.

"How many are you all together?" Ralf asked the wiry boy.

"Oh, it changes every day," he said. "Some days we are thirty, some days we are fifty. Women, children. I am the strongest."

Ralf's eyes widened. "That many? And they are hungry?"

"If you give them food they will work for you. Give them something to look forward to. Give them hope, like a promise of food or loot. These people will do anything for food and loot."

Hauptmann Schwartz stomped back to the front of the house. "Bastards. The lot of them. What's the plan?"

Chapter 35

Pieter van Diemen

Pounding on the door awoke Pieter. He heard Bubo and Sepp snickering. The boys scuffled, thumped and shoved one another in the hallway.

"Pieter, dear, time to wake up," Bubo sang.

"Pieter, let's go," Sepp yelled. "We have work to do."

Something large bumped against the door. Pieter heard the boys muttering but could not make out what they said. The boys would want to go straight out to work and he could sneak out with them. He threw his clothes on and hoped to avoid Katarina this morning. What sort of problem did she have? He said he wouldn't drink anymore and he was doing that. She should be proud of him and want to help him. Yes, he had to admit he'd only wanted yet another mindless romantic romp, and maybe Katarina wasn't up for that. It was better nothing happened. He couldn't face another woman who felt jilted after a casual tryst.

"The weeds are choking the vineyard," Sepp said. "Hans-Wolfgang said we have to clean it out today. We want to get done before it rains."

The three sneaked down into the empty kitchen. The sun had risen, so early this time of year, but no one was moving around yet. Sepp blew on the ash in the fireplace, exposed glowing embers and laid two logs on top. They exited though the back door, grabbed their hoes from the outbuilding and left on foot. There was still a chill in the air but it looked like it would be a fine day.

"It's not going to rain today," Pieter said.

They walked up the hill that overlooked Gottesgab, to the tiny vineyard that stood on the only field there that got the sun. Tiny white grapes hung under wide green leaves. Sepp pulled the leaves off to expose the grapes to the sun and collected them in his fist.

"We'll take the leaves for Magdalena. She'll want them. These vines need to be cut too." Sepp grabbed the new growth that grew over their heads. "But Hans-Wolfgang wants to do it himself."

"He told us to pull weeds, that's it," Bubo said. "He'll take care of the vines."

The wind changed and a smell of damp and cold came up over the hill. Pieter looked up and saw the black cloud closing in on them.

"How did you know it was going to rain?" Pieter said.

"In my bones," Sepp said.

"It will only rain once today," Bubo said. "All day."

Light misty rain seeped through Pieter's shirt and he found himself shivering. When they finished their weeding, the three walked back to the house in silence. Pieter followed Bubo and Sepp into the kitchen, its warmth like a loving hug. Hans-Wolfgang, awake and surly, growled from his place at the table. Isabeau sat down next to her father and Katarina flitted from the fire to the table, making them both food. Katarina glanced at Pieter and got back to her work. Her face was flushed. Hans-Wolfgang barked at her. She poured boiling water into a large pot and Hans-Wolfgang shot her another reprimand. Pieter could not understand what they were arguing about.

"You're not doing enough. Why am I better?" Hans-Wolfgang yelled at Katarina. "Make sure you give her some of that tincture, too."

"I'm doing all I can," Katarina said. "She doesn't have your constitution. I've already said that I'm not a doctor."

"I don't care what you are. Make an effort, Katarina."

Katarina put a flask of tea, a cup and some food on a tray and left the kitchen. Pieter sat at the table, took a hard piece of old bread from the basket and pulled the knife out of the ceramic pot full of lard.

"Magdalena is still very sick," Hans-Wolfgang said. "I don't understand it. I am well. Katarina is not sick. What is she doing to my *Magd*?"

Pieter smeared his bread with lard and licked the salty fat from his finger. "Katarina is doing all she can. Don't blame her."

"Katarina is acting so stupid today," Isabeau said.

"Should I see to Magdalena?" Pieter asked. "Can I help?"

"You could help Katarina with the falcons," Hans-Wolfgang said. "Maybe you and Isabeau could take care of them. And help Isabeau with the horses. I can stand and walk but I feel much too weak to do any real work. That would be a fine gesture."

"Come, Pieter!" Isabeau said and grabbed him by the hand.

He allowed her to drag him out of the kitchen, shoving the last of his bread into his mouth on the way. The rain covered his face with cold mist.

"I want to show you how my mare gives her hooves," Isabeau said. "I taught her." The child's face beamed despite the beads of mist. Her cheeks glowed pink and alive, her eyes cunning and deep. "Tanner helped me. But she listens to me."

Pieter held the barn door open for Isabeau. "We've let the training go the last few weeks. We really need to get back to it. You never know when you have to defend yourself."

"I practice on that dead tree in the garden," she said. "And with Bubo. He's strong but he's clumsy."

"Do we have time this afternoon?"

"I'm going to ride first. Come with me!"

Isabeau's horse stood still and allowed Isabeau to slide the halter over its head. The girl laid the lead from the halter over the horse's withers, threw the bridal and reins over her own shoulder and walked out of the barn. The horse followed. Pieter was impressed. Whenever he tried to do anything with the mare, she would protest and ignore all of Pieter's commands. When Isabeau stopped outside the barn and tied the lead to the barn wall, Pieter chuckled.

"So, you do have to tie her to the barn to clean her hooves," Pieter said. "She's not that well behaved, then."

"Only here in the yard. She's always hungry and she loves that bush over there. The leaves on this side are all nibbled away. Crone did that."

"Crone?"

"Her name is Crone," Isabeau said. "I named her after that old woman in the stories from Magdalena."

"I hope Magdalena gets better," Pieter said.

"If she doesn't get better, she will be free," Isabeau said.

"What do you mean?" Pieter said. "Do you think Magdalena will die?"

"She could," Isabeau said. "We all die."

"Are you saying you believe in God and Heaven?" Pieter asked.

"No," Isabeau said. "We don't believe that. Magdalena says she is a spirit like a tree and will grow into a beautiful flower or flow like the river or float like a cloud. Katarina says we return to the earth when we die.

Katarina says I should believe what I want to believe. She says I should be strong and think for myself."

"I wish Katarina would think for herself," Pieter said, more to himself.

"Katarina is worried about everyone else," Isabeau said. "She wants us to do what she thinks we should do. She forgets about herself."

"That is just foolish," Pieter said.

"She says she cares for me. That's why she tells me what to do. But she won't let me care for her. She hates when I try. She hates when I tell her what to do. That's the way she is. I can't change her."

The straightforward wisdom of a child, Pieter thought, what brilliant simplicity. The girl was alive with wonder and beliefs that had not been corrupted with manners or doctrine or the art of euphemism. Life had not yet pounded the honesty out of her and she still had a magic twinkle in her eye. He would like to harness some of that innocence. Isabeau's spirit was confident and untouched by the world. Such an untainted soul. He watched her brush the mare with a regal dexterity and calm composure. Where Katarina was always watching other people and seemed afraid she would do something to displease them, Isabeau had a disinterest for what others thought of her.

"Katarina should go back to Herr Tucher," Isabeau continued. "She wants to, you know. I hope I don't ever act so stupid just because I don't want to admit what I want."

"I think it's something adults do," Pieter said. "They are worried about what they should do and they stop listening to what their heart says."

"I do what I want," Isabeau said. "Why would I do something that I didn't want to do?"

"Some of us have been forced to do things to survive in the past," Pieter said. "We have had to do bad things or suffer being tortured or killed."

"I would rather die," she said.

"Don't say that. You must fear death and hold onto your life with everything you have."

"Why is everyone so afraid to die?"

"I don't know. We are just afraid."

Isabeau shook her head. She released the halter from the mare's head and let it fall. The horse stood patiently and waited for Isabeau to slide the bridal over its head. "Let's go for a ride," she said.

Chapter 36

Katarina

Katarina shifted the tray with Magdalena's evening tea to her free hand. She thought Magdalena had looked better this morning and allowed her to sleep through the afternoon. She should be awake now. Katarina pushed the door to Hans-Wolfgang's room open. A tell-tale fetor of rancid meat hit Katarina like a physical assault. Dropping the tray, her heart raced. Magdalena's face was peaceful in the evening light. Sorrow for Magdalena's passing was instantly replaced by fear. She rushed to the window and tore it open, as if airing out the room could get rid of the dead body. Hans-Wolfgang would kill Katarina. He would hold her responsible.

Katarina shook her head as she found herself sneaking out of the room so as not to wake the woman, even though she was obviously dead. The dusky hallway and stairwell took on an eerie air now that death had come to visit. The fire in the kitchen cast ghostly shadows on the walls and the cupboards. The door to the garden stood open. Katarina peeked out, searching for Hans-Wolfgang and wanting to remain under cover. Katarina walked back into the kitchen and then up the stairs and out into the front yard.

Pieter and Isabeau stood next to the barn and cleaned the two muddy horses. Bored and bound, the horses tossed their heads. The stallion knocked the brush out of Pieter's hand with his nostrils. Isabeau let off a delighted howl and Pieter joined her until the two were almost in tears. Their laughter was easy and genuine. Isabeau could be so free with Pieter. This worried Katarina sick. She knew what he was capable of. It was fine if Pieter didn't drink, but how long could that last? What happened if Katarina was no longer here and he blacked out and attacked Isabeau?

Hans-Wolfgang came out of the barn, walking slowly with a slight bend in his back. He looked old today. Katarina had to tell him. And she'd rather tell him with others present. She swallowed hard, afraid of his reaction and approached the three.

"Hans-Wolfgang?" Katarina would not look at him. "Something has happened."

He stood still and waited for her to continue.

"There was nothing more I could do for her."

Face tense with rage and accusation, he turned away and went into the house. Katarina followed him without looking at Pieter. Isabeau whispered behind her back. Katarina caught up with Hans-Wolfgang outside his room as he opened the door.

"I'm sorry," she said.

"We'll leave her lay here." Hans-Wolfgang coughed. "Give her something to drink. She may not be really dead."

"Of course she's dead!" Katarina heard her own voice, raised and shrill. "We can't leave her body here."

"Give her something to drink!" Hans-Wolfgang yelled. "And clean her up. I saw this happen with my own mother. They all said she was dead, but she wasn't. When they wanted to bury her, then they noticed she still lived. She did die a few days later, but they would have buried her alive. I can think of no single other horror that should ever befall me. With that in mind, should I ever die, then let me lay a few days until I am truly dead. Decaying and so on."

He left the room. Katarina did as she was told and almost retched as she tried to change the bed linens and clean the, in her opinion, very dead woman. Katarina dribbled tea into her open mouth, her jaw now stiffened. She shut the window and left the room, shutting the door behind her. The sound it made resonated in Katarina's mind. It was the closing of a chapter of her life, the ending of an era. She suddenly found herself no longer able to remain in this house. Her decision to leave this place was made.

An unusual calm gripped Katarina. She walked back to her room, grabbed her wooden box and went downstairs into the garden behind the kitchen. No one was around. There stood her handcart. She put the box in, went back upstairs, gathered her feather tick together and the journal. Katarina reached into her pocket for the flask of laudanum. She dripped the last drop onto her tongue, wiped her nose on her sleeve and sneezed. She walked back downstairs, out into the garden and loaded her things, relieved she could get out of the garden tonight without the others seeing her.

There was one last thing she needed to do. She forced herself back up the steps, walked to the end of the hallway, unlocked the door and went into the dark room with the falcons. Katarina's falcon was in the room alone. Hans-Wolfgang's bird must be in the garden. She grabbed a discarded glove and pulled it on, unhooked the falcon's tethers from the lead and allowed the falcon onto her gloved fist. She walked back to her room with the bird.

She opened the window and looked out into the night sky. The moon hid behind the clouds. The falcon bobbed twice on her fist, expecting her to let him fly. She turned her back to the window and ran her hand over the bird's back, the taut feathers covering the delicate, slight frame. His black beady eyes were impenetrable, unrelenting, resolute. This bird was proud, designed for one task and one only. He was built to survive: fly, eat and procreate. He needed no man. Did men believe they could tame such a creature? This bird would never be tamed, would never partner any endeavor with man. Tethered, he was a captive.

Katarina found herself again faced with the elusive nature of freedom and wondered if anyone was truly free. She wondered if anyone really cared and if freedom even existed. Magdalena was free. Or was she? Oh, if Katarina could only live the life of the falcon, its purpose and focus clearly defined, its path marked, its life planned. Free to hunt, free to fly, free to die. She pulled on the tethers around his feet. One was loose and easily tore off. She pulled on the second one, undoing the symbol of slavery. It fell to the floor. She held her fist high. The falcon readied himself, flapped his wings once and flew into the night sky.

As Katrina walked away from Eierhofen, out of the forest and through the flood plain, the little handcart betrayed every movement she made. *Squeak, squeak, creak, creak,* echoed all around her as the cart bundled along over the rutted field, Katarina stopping from time to time to yank it through the mud. Even though no one came to call her back, she felt like she was being watched from every corner. Was this the price of freedom? Was this the fear of being truly alone or the healthy fear of a woman alone in the dark?

She made it to the river bank and stopped. She hadn't thought about how she was to get her handcart across the river. She had not thought about where she would go for the night. Did she want to go to Sichardtshof? If she did even get to the farm tonight, would they let her in? Everyone was poised for an attack and no sane people were out milling around alone in the dark. Panic set in and she stood by the river bank rooted to the spot. Her forehead beaded with sweat. That damned sick feeling with stomach cramps came in waves. Had she contracted their disease? *Liebe Holla* should come and take her home.

"Where are you going?" Sieglinde's hooded figure came out of the dark. "Have you finally had enough?"

Katarina had not heard her approach. "Where are *you* going?" she croaked.

"I am going back to Eierhofen for the night. I have no desire to sleep in that tavern in Lonnerstadt again, even though there is money to be made."

Katarina slumped down, fell onto her hands and knees and vomited.

"Oh, dear, have you caught their wretched disease now too?" Sieglinde said.

"I am cold, then burning, then sweating. I am sick all the time." Katarina vomited again. "I need more of this. It's the only thing that makes me better." Katarina handed Sieglinde the little flask from her apron pocket.

Sieglinde opened the flask and sniffed. "Oh dear, Katarina, not you! I know this stuff. This is what is making you sick. Come we must get under cover."

"I can't leave my handcart here," Katarina managed to say.

Sieglinde rummaged in the handcart. "I'll bring your feather tick. You carry this old book. The rest can stay here for tonight."

Sieglinde led Katarina over the point in the river where the stones were high and the water low. Katarina slipped on a large stone and water slopped all over her low shoes. The water was icy cold and her thoughts cleared for a moment. She allowed Sieglinde to pull her up the other riverbank and they entered a darkened farmyard.

"This is abandoned," Sieglinde said. "There was no one here left alive. I've stayed in this place myself." Sieglinde led Katarina to a corner of the barn strewn with soft hay. "Lay here. You are in for a rough night but you need to sweat this devil out of yourself. Promise me you will not drink that stuff anymore!"

"I'll do anything you say." Katarina would have traded her soul for a reprieve right now. "Are you going to leave me?"

"I'll stay by you tonight. We'll see if you even want to go to

Sichardtshof in the morning."

"Where else would I go?"

"I have been on my own for years," Sieglinde said. "I grew up in Baudenbach. My father died long ago. I never knew him. My mother had a string of men who paid our way but only until she didn't please them anymore. Then I had to do whatever my mother said with these men. That's how we got money. I left home because I didn't want to support my mother anymore. I've been roaming ever since. Come with me. We can travel with the soldiers until we find a nice place like Eierhofen to live and work for a while and when we tire of that, we can leave."

"Isn't it dangerous?" Katarina said.

"What's dangerous? Living with Hans-Wolfgang and waiting for the mercenaries to come and burn the house down and rape us? Or to travel with the soldiers and at least get paid for working. Traveling with the troops is like riding on the top of a wave. We can see where it's going instead of just waiting for the wave to drown us."

Katarina groaned as the next wave of nausea hit her. "Oh, just let me die here."

"Yes, this is a good spot to die, this little run down barn in Mailach. But, sorry to say, you will not die tonight. You will wish for it though! A few days of this and you'll be back to normal, I promise."

Chapter 37

Ralf

Ralf splashed his face with water from the rain barrel and dried his hands and face on a stiff, scratchy linen cloth. He pulled the linen shirt over his head. It was also stiff but smelled like fresh air after hanging the whole morning outside. He tied the shirt string into a neat bow and slung his black monks' robe over his arm. The day was much too warm. The birds were singing and it was hard to believe there was a war on. Somewhere in the distance, a hammer pounded. The gelding snorted and he heard children playing. Days like this gave the farmers and the other villagers hope that their lives could return to normal.

Hauptmann Schwartz limped towards him. "I don't trust this lull in the marching troops. Do you think we are getting comfortable here? We should move out now."

"You act too rashly," Ralf said. "And, yes, I don't trust the quiet for a minute. Even though it has been a joy. Now, man, your smell precedes you. We move out after you've washed yourself."

Karl and Konrad had done everything to ready the lame gelding for travel. After days on end of packing the horse's leg with healing mud and taking him on short walks to graze on healing herbs, the lame hoof seemed to be giving him less trouble. They patched the cart with whatever they'd scrounged in the village. Now the cart was finished and the horse could walk.

"I don't trust those exiles." Schwartz mopped the sweat from his brow and flinched as he set his weight on his good leg. "Those stray boys seem to have an eye on us, all the time. They keep company with a small group of men who speak some Slavish language. They might be Calvinist."

Ralf noticed the Hauptmann was in considerably more pain than he had been. Konrad had offered to pack his leg with the mud they used for the horse, but he'd refused and said he was not livestock.

"They have offered to help you claim command at the Eierhofen estate," Ralf said. "It is up to you to accept it. Today we will travel together in that basic direction. You may continue on to Eierhofen and the boys will continue on to Bamberg. The two brothers are now so ill but at least they will get back to Bamberg to have a proper burial. This place is hexed and we must leave no matter what."

Martin was still alive but just barely. Last night, Ralf offered to hear his confession but the boy faded in and out of consciousness and was unable to speak. After Ralf anointed the boy, Michel collapsed from exhaustion and was now laid out on the pallet next to his brother with the same symptoms. As Ralf folded up Michel's robe, he found a bundle of twisted herbs in Michel's pocket. Sieglinde must have given him some sort of talisman to ward off the disease. The talisman had no healing powers, quite the opposite, and the boy would pay now with his life and soul. Ralf upbraided the boy and offered to hear his confession but the boy was so ill Ralf could only anoint him as well.

Ralf wondered if he should be performing an exorcism instead of last rights. The two boys were obviously under an evil influence. Karl and Konrad wanted to rush back to Bamberg in the hope that they could still save Martin, and now Michel, from the clutches of the devil. Ralf hoped the boys would make it to Bamberg at all, before they were executed as papists.

Ralf himself was in no hurry to reach Bamberg. He would travel with the boys and the cart until they reached the road that swung by Eierhofen. He wanted to test this thing 'divine intervention.' A dangerous game, he was well aware. If he met the fair-haired girl, he would know the task of bringing her to the light was his divine responsibility. If he managed to take her to Bamberg, to save her, he would be righting what he allowed to happen all those years ago. Ralf could send Schwartz in first, to scout the estate, hiding until he was called to move out or move in, his involvement in this task completely up to God. He would lay in wait, prepared to accept his role as God's instrument. No rash act of ego, no emotional outbursts. Pure divinity.

Karl and Konrad carried a sick boy each and loaded them onto the cart. Ralf and Schwartz sat down on the opposite side of the cart. Ralf held the sleeve of his robe over his nose, the decomposing smell of death catching in his throat. Karl and Konrad jumped onto the coach box. They moved out towards Demandsfürth, the same route they'd traveled the last time, crossed the river and continued towards the forest.

"Karl, careful!" Ralf whispered. "Stop the cart here."

At a bend in the road, on the edge of the forest where they'd met the fair-haired girl before, four horsemen started up the path. They hadn't seen Ralf and the boys. Hauptmann Schwartz sat up and looked like he wanted to shout out.

"Stay still, you fool, you oaf!" Ralf hissed.

"Father?" Karl said.

Ralf had a flash of an idea. He patted his robe, the pocket just by his heart. "My rosary! It's gone." He pointed to the trees. "Pull the cart into these trees, there is a cove, just big enough for us." Ralf jumped out of the cart. "I must retrace my steps. I will catch up."

Schwartz jumped off the cart as well. Karl and Konrad whispered among themselves. Ralf realized Konrad did not believe him.

"Father, we must leave now," Konrad said.

"Sorry, boys, I have to settle something," Ralf said. "I must return to Uehlfeld and look for my rosary."

Karl stood. "We cannot wait."

Ralf waved. "Head towards Bamberg. I will catch up with you. Just get the boys home. That's the most important thing."

Without resistance, Karl pulled the cart away.

Ralf turned to Schwartz. "Let's go."

"I am not walking back to Uehlfeld," Schwartz said.

"I am not either." Ralf pulled the rosary from his pocket to show Schwartz and started up the hill. "Oh, look what I found."

Hauptmann Schwartz was forever the oaf, Ralf thought. He did not understand what Ralf was doing.

"Obviously, I've sent the boys away," Ralf said. "They know that. They will be angry with me. No matter. There is another property in these trees, an abandoned one. I want to have a look. Are you coming or not?"

Ralf and Hauptmann Schwartz climbed the narrow, rocky path, well-frequented and well-hidden. Small, soft feet had traveled here—by the look of it, a small man and a child. No sign of soldiers' boots.

"No horses on this path, either," Schwartz whispered. "It looks like someone comes and goes often."

The path opened up onto a clearing that had once been a homestead.

"It looks like a workers' dwelling or servants' quarters," Schwartz said.

"Nobody lives here. Just rubble."

Ralf knew this had been Hans-Wolfgang's childhood home. The large, wide hedge to the left separated this property from the Upper Eierhofen estate. Ten years had passed since Ralf had been here and the flood of emotions rendered him speechless. He noticed how quickly his present convictions and his adult reasoning slipped into the childish, ego-driven fallacies he'd succumbed to years ago. He fingered the rosary and entertained a mixture of shame and pride, a greedy indulgence. He was ashamed for how he acted all those years ago but his pride spoke up, urging him to avenge the wrongs he felt Hans-Wolfgang had done to him.

"Father," Schwartz whispered. "What is this place?"

Ralf snorted. "Another man's ruin, obviously. Let's have a look through the building. I want to know if anyone lives here."

"There is no building left, just rocks," Schwartz said.

"Look here," Ralf said. "Someone has used the stones to make a shelter. They light a fire and often. These rooms, if you want to call them rooms, are clean and swept. Someone uses them like a *Zufluchtort*, and hides here. And they visit the Eierhofen estate regularly by the look of it."

Ralf pointed to the hedge and a little passageway large enough for a man to crawl through. His rosary dangled from his wrist.

"Looks like some large rabbits use that hole, don't you think?" Schwartz said.

Ralf wound the rosary around his wrist, knelt down and crawled into the hole. His knees dampened and he stuck his head out the other side. An older mounted officer arrived at the gate of the Eierhofen estate, followed by a younger one. Two women joined another cloaked woman. He saw it was Sieglinde and snorted. Schwartz's voice droned on behind him:

"What do you see? Are they there? Who's over there?"

Ralf grew more and more annoyed with this Hauptmann Schwartz and decided to send him away, like he did with the boys. He needed to be alone to carry out this last stage of his journey. He crawled back out of the hole in the hedge.

"See here, Schwartz, your officer friends are just arriving," Ralf said. "Why don't you go over and offer your service? You are dressed like them, you speak like they do. I'll continue on my way and catch up to the boys."

"Are you sure you want to be alone, papist ass, on the road by yourself?" Schwartz said. "No horse, no nothing?"

"I am fine by myself. I want to reflect. Say my rosary." Ralf looked at his hands. The rosary was gone. He patted the pocket close to his heart. It was empty. "Holy Mother of God!" He instinctively searched his immediate surroundings, his head darting to and fro.

"Ha," Schwartz let off a booming laugh. "Bad luck, Father, you lied to the boys about losing that rosary and now you really have lost it." He laughed and laughed. "I'm off to join my ranks. *Gute Reise.*"

Schwartz left the yard, returning to the path they'd originally climbed. Ralf sunk to his knees and peeked into the hole in the hedge. He had the rosary when he crawled in here before. Oh, dear God, the one thing he valued, his only prized possession now that, too, was lost. He would retrace his steps from the point he first entered the clearing, back to the beginning.

Chapter 38

Pieter van Diemen

Pieter watched from the window in his room as four horsemen rode into the Eierhofen yard. Two young pages, boys maybe a bit older than Isabeau, followed the horsemen on foot. Three of the horsemen dismounted; one burly officer wearing a black hat with a brown plume and two younger, trim-looking fellows in fine uniforms. The two pages took their horses into the barn. The three officers looked around the property, nodding to each other in affirmation of what good luck they'd had to find such a manor. The three officers reported back to the fourth officer, a small, sickly man with a mustache and pointed beard on his chin. He looked like a rabbit.

Two officers helped the sickly one dismount. A page led his horse away. All four officers stepped up to the front door and out of Pieter's sight. He heard them pull on the locked door handle. Someone kicked the door, hollered an oath in German and demanded admittance.

Pieter pulled back from his window, grabbed his sword and sheathed it, throwing the baldric over his shoulder. He left his room and crossed the hallway to the room on the other side of the house, the room where Katarina had slept. All her belongings were gone. Pieter reached his hand under her mattress. The journal was gone. She must have sneaked out in the night. He cursed her for running away. A pang of guilt swelled and he extinguished it as fast as it came. She was old enough to know what she was doing.

Pieter looked out the window from her room to the garden. It was empty. Sepp and Bubo were still out in the fields with both horses. He went back to his room, looked into the yard and saw the officers standing in the middle of the yard in conversation with themselves. The two younger officers were those he had seen in the forest with Sieglinde.

Hans-Wolfgang had not yet shown himself, then. Pieter paced back and forth in his room, wondering how he should go about this. What would the officers do if they saw him? Pieter was a deserter. Would they try to recruit him? Would they know he was once a soldier? He had no desire today to be taken prisoner or to be hanged for desertion. Even given the choice of being made a soldier again would not please him.

Pieter heard a gruff barking and looked back out the window to the yard. Hans-Wolfgang stood alone, questioning the officers. They seemed to be in negotiations. Pieter could not leave Hans-Wolfgang to this alone. He rushed down the steps and through the kitchen, out the back into the garden then around to the front of the house. Pieter would not be the one to open the front doors and allow the officers to gain entry.

"We need quarters for roughly seven days," the burly officer said. "We march south towards Hungary and are tired. The foot soldiers are taking quarters in the villages surrounding this hill. But we are in need of better accommodations. As you can see General Mansfeld is not well."

So that was General Mansfeld? Pieter had marched with his army but had never seen the man. A small, rabbity looking fellow, the General's face was a yellow-green and, no, he did not look well at all. The one younger officer was supporting him. Judging by the manner of the older, burly officer, his impatience with Hans-Wolfgang was mounting, his gestures demanding entrance to the house.

Pieter stood by and watched as Hans-Wolfgang struggled with his own stubborn head. Hans-Wolfgang never allowed anyone to tell him what to do. Now he knew he had to give in. Pieter could see Hans-Wolfgang's face twisting as he calculated all possible angles of this problem. He was certainly thinking of Isabeau. Pieter was. She was now the only woman left on the farm and would have to be doubly protected.

"The Dutchman will tend to your horses." Hans-Wolfgang nodded to Pieter and Pieter nodded back.

Pieter moved towards the barn to tend the horses, grateful that he could take cover.

Hans-Wolfgang spoke. "My *Magd* will not take care of the accommodations. She is my mistress and is not to be touched. Is that understood? We can arrange for other women."

"That won't be necessary," the burly officer said. "We have women following us in another wagon. They approach now."

Pieter stopped short. A covered cart pulled by a small horse and driven by one woman came into the yard. Two women peeked out of the back.

The cart stopped and the two women jumped out. One was that wretched Sieglinde.

"Hello Pieter," Sieglinde said as she approached him. "We suggested this place when the men said they wanted to stay somewhere comfortable. We knew you wouldn't mind."

"Pieter, take care of their horse as well, please," Hans-Wolfgang said.

Pieter unhitched the horse and the women took care of the cart. He brought the horse to the barn with the others and gave it a pile of hay. He stood by the barn door and searched the yard and the surrounding hedge. He wondered where Isabeau was.

"We will take care of the meal, Hans-Wolfgang," Sieglinde said. "These men are very thirsty. And the General is not well. He needs care. It would be appropriate to bring out your best beer."

Hans-Wolfgang struggled to keep his temper. His face was flushed and he said nothing. Pieter knew that this was a bad sign. Pieter could imagine how Hans-Wolfgang was planning to turn this situation around to his own benefit.

"Of course, Sieglinde," Hans-Wolfgang said. "Bring the men to the kitchen and I will fetch a barrel of beer. The back door is open."

The three women walked around the house towards the garden. The two younger officers followed the women. The burly officer fought to keep his hat on his head and support the General as he laid the General's arm across his shoulder. Together they limped away. After they all disappeared behind the house, Hans-Wolfgang motioned for Pieter to come to him.

"Isabeau is behind the hedge on the Lower Eierhofen side," he said. "Bring her up to my room. Please get her something to eat and tell her to stay there and wait for me. Take some of her things from her room and bring them to her, too. Lock her in."

Pieter found a break in the high hedges that separated Upper Eierhofen from the Lower Eierhofen property. The ruins of the Lower Eierhofen house, the house Hans-Wolfgang grew up in, stood empty and foreboding. Pieter whistled to attract Isabeau's attention and she answered with the same whistle. She came out from the forest with a dour look plastered on her face.

"Katarina is gone," Isabeau said.

"I know."

"Where has she gone?" she said. "Why did she leave? She left me here."

"Isabeau, I don't know why she left." Pieter steered her towards the bushes. "She didn't say a word to any of us."

"You know why. I want her to come back."

"She has probably gone home, to Sichardtshof."

"I want to go home, too. Who are these men?"

"Hmm," Pieter said and looked away. "This will be a bit of a problem. They are officers of the troops moving through the area. They have set up quarters here. Hopefully they will soon be gone. We have to tolerate this."

"Hans-Wolfgang told me to stay here. I could get my horse and go home."

"I'll take care of your horse when Bubo and Sepp bring her back."

"I'm sick of hiding. I feel like a deer. We were hunting today. The deer were smarter, though."

"I'm to bring you to Hans-Wolfgang's room. You are to stay there and wait for him."

"Why? I don't want to go to his room."

"Just do what Hans-Wolfgang says. We can go through the front doors. The officers are back in the kitchen."

Pieter grabbed Isabeau by the hand and they made their way back to the front yard. Pieter opened the now-unlocked front doors. The men amused themselves in the great hall behind the massive carved oak doors. Their merry voices were the exact opposite of Pieter's mood. He tightened his grip on her hand and led her to Hans-Wolfgang's room.

"I will bring you something to eat and drink." Pieter shut the door, went to Isabeau's room, collected a few of her things and brought them back to the room.

"Am I to sleep in here?" she asked.

"It's temporary. Just until the men leave." Pieter assumed he wanted the men to think she was his so that they would leave her alone.

"Am I to sleep in his bed with him?"

Pieter said nothing as he shut the door, locked it and went to the kitchen to get some food and drink for Isabeau. Sieglinde fired order after order at the two women. She picked up a tray loaded with two bottles and cups and moved towards Pieter.

"Pieter, play along for now." Sieglinde shifted the tray to her other hand. "I'll be right back."

Sieglinde left the room. The other two women sniggered behind her back as she went out. Pieter looked at the two of them and shook his head.

"I need food for the girl," Pieter said. "Our food."

"I'll make you something for her," the one woman said. "Would you like me to take it to her? Where is she anyway?"

"Just give me something and I'll take it to her." Pieter grew annoyed.

Sieglinde ran back into the kitchen. "The General is hungry. He is very sick. Pieter, it is so important that you play along for now. For the sake of Hans-Wolfgang and the girl. The officers won't be here long."

"Are you traveling with the officers now?" Pieter wanted to hit her.

"They abducted us on the road." Sieglinde pushed strands of hair behind her ear. "Isn't that right, ladies? We had no choice so we brought them here. Pieter, you and I, we can control them. Let the three of us help you so they don't do any damage. We're on the same side, you and I. They are well-behaved. Just do as they say, give them something to drink. You'd rather have the officers here than the other sods."

Pieter shook his head and tried to control his temper.

"It will only be a few days," Sieglinde said. "Then they should move on. Now where is Isabeau?"

Chapter 39

Isabeau

Isabeau pulled the door. Pieter locked her in! She looked out the window. She was up too high to jump out. Why would he lock her in here? How long would she have to stay? She trusted Pieter, she still did, but she was angry. He should have told her what he was planning. She would understand! She wasn't a child!

The men were loud in the great hall. Isabeau sat down on the bed. It was still light out so she took the book of verse from Herr Tucher and opened it up. He wrote these poems himself. She read the one she liked best. *The fiery girl upon her steed.* She wondered if he was writing about her.

She's up again, she's off again,
The fiery girl upon her steed.
Come what may and every day,
She'll save us with a daring deed!

Isabeau missed Herr Tucher. She liked Hans-Wolfgang because he could ride so well. He didn't say much though. He liked to do the things Isabeau liked to do. But she missed painting. She also missed writing. Hans-Wolfgang didn't like to read or write. He liked horses.

Katarina was acting stupid. Katarina should have taken Isabeau with her! Isabeau would never understand her difficult moods. And Katarina had those moods all the time anymore. Katarina called Isabeau her daughter, but if Isabeau was a mother, she wouldn't act like that. Katarina would never talk about why they had to live here. Why had they left Herr Tucher? Katarina was angry when Isabeau asked. She was angry all the time, like it was Isabeau's fault. Isabeau wondered if Katarina loved Pieter. Isabeau thought Katarina loved Herr Tucher! Katarina didn't know who she loved. Stupid Katarina. They should have stayed with Sara.

Isabeau heard footsteps in the hallway outside. A key turned in the lock. The door opened. She was angry. She wasn't afraid. She was angry.

"Hello Isabeau."

It was Hans-Wolfgang. He came in, shut the door and locked it with the key. Isabeau saw him put the key in his leather tunic. He took the tunic off and hung it on the wooden chair and pushed the chair under the table.

"Isabeau, you will sleep here with me."

Isabeau gave him an angry look. "I don't want to sleep here. I want to sleep in my room."

He came to her, sat on the bed. Isabeau backed up. She didn't understand what he meant.

"I'm not going to harm you. Oh, Isabeau, please, don't think…You don't think I would…?"

Isabeau said nothing. She pulled her legs up and sat like a little package on the bed.

"Those men must think…No, those men can never find out…"

Isabeau still said nothing.

"It is time I told you, then."

"You are acting stupid like Katarina," Isabeau said.

"Isabeau, I have kept something from you too long now. I want to tell you a story."

Isabeau had no time for a story. She wanted to get out of here. She knew where he had the key. She could try to get it and get out of here.

"Listen to me," he said and touched her on the knee. She backed up. "There was once a beautiful woman. Her name was Andra-Angela. I loved her very much."

Isabeau yawned. The story from Magdalena. Only Magdalena was dead. Isabeau was tired and this game tired her even more.

"Andra was the daughter of the man who owned this house. She lived here. The room you sleep in was once her room."

Yes, it was a nice room. Isabeau liked the room she slept in. That was why she wanted to go back there!

"Andra's father was, how can I describe him? A good man, but he didn't act upon the wishes of his daughter."

Maybe he locked her in her room? Maybe he acted stupid?

"Andra's father wouldn't let us get married. And we loved each other very much. No wait, let me finish. Look at me, Isabeau. Let me tell you my story, child."

Isabeau sat still and stared at him.

"Andra was going to have a baby. Our baby. But I didn't know because her father wouldn't let me see her. Yes, she had the baby, but something terrible happened. She was killed but the baby lived. I found the baby, our baby, I found the baby in time. I took the baby to Sichardtshof…"

Isabeau buried her face in her hands.

"Isabeau, don't cry, it's so important that you understand…"

Isabeau held herself tight and hummed. He should feel guilty for telling her this.

"Listen to me. Isabeau, look at me!"

She looked up. She was going to explode like a musket.

"I took the baby to Sichardtshof and gave her to the *Magd* there. She would raise the child as her own. You must understand. I couldn't keep you here. Andra's father would have harmed you."

She rocked herself and sunk her head onto her knees again.

"Isabeau, I am your father. Your mother was Andra-Angela von Obereierhofen. This was her house. This is your house. But we need to keep this from those officers. If they find out, they may use it against me. They may try to harm you to get to me. Do you understand?"

Isabeau rocked and rocked and rocked.

"They must think you are a maid and my mistress. I believe the men will leave you alone then."

She whimpered. It just came out.

"Oh, silly girl. I would never harm you! Believe me, you are safer with me than with any other man. I will never let anyone harm you. Until they leave, you will either be by my side or somewhere where they cannot get to you. Isabeau…"

She looked up at him. He smiled at her. She smiled back.

"Come here. Give me a hug. I love you, my daughter."

Chapter 40

Katarina

Katarina thought two days had passed, maybe three since she ended up in the abandoned barn in Mailach. The march back to Sichardtshof was the longest one she'd ever made. When Sara saw the sad, sick state Katarina was in, she almost turned her away. But Katarina explained to Sara why she was so sick and Sara allowed her to stay. Katarina crawled up the ladder to the upper floor of the workers' house and stayed until the evening. Later that night, she finally sneaked downstairs and sat by the fire, unable to sleep. Dawn broke and she hid herself upstairs again, hoping to avoid the others as they stirred.

It was late in the morning when Katarina opened her eyes. With a start, she sat up. The curtains separating the spaces where the workers slept swayed in the gentle draft. She had slept soundly, even if it was only a few hours. The musty sleeping space had the familiar smell of straw, mice and damp wood. Bjarne and Tanner yelled outside, birds chattered and flew in and out of the thatched roof, Sara's voice scolded.

Sara told Katarina she would be very busy today. Katarina hoped she would have no time to think and prepared herself for an onslaught of questions as she dressed and climbed down the ladder to the kitchen. Sara was washing those early yellow apples and wild plums. Anna ignored Katarina and chopped the fruit, put it in large ceramic pots and covered it with clear liquid.

"Herr Tucher gave us all this schnapps to conserve fruit in," Sara said. "He even gave me some sugar. Here try this."

Sara gave Katarina a spoonful of sugar. She put it in her mouth.

"Sweet, but I like honey better," Katarina said.

Sara handed her a piece of bread with a hunk of dried meat and a cup of peppermint tea. "I have plenty for you to do. Let me know when you're ready."

Katarina ate hastily and swallowed the tea. She wanted to get to work, to go outside. She wanted to see if she could get a glimpse of Herr Tucher.

Sara seemed to have read Katarina's mind. "He's not here. He went with Lasse somewhere this morning. He said they wouldn't be back until the evening."

"I don't want to see him," Katarina lied.

"That will be easy. We have so much work, you may not see him for days."

Sara was right. One day melded into the next. Katarina was up early with the others, they worked steadily the whole day, taking a short break once in the morning and again early afternoon. The paddock was full of sheep, replacing most of those that had been stolen in the spring. Two cows stood in the vaulted stable adjoining the kitchen and numerous chickens clucked and scratched all over the yard. Bjarne seemed to be giving orders and he would wave Katarina over, setting her to task after task. In the afternoon, she helped him with the new outbuilding they were constructing. Towards the evening, Katarina was exhausted but it was a good feeling.

She made a point to fetch Sara's evening water, hoping to get a glimpse of the master. One evening, as she pulled up the dipper bucket, she heard horses approaching up the track. She stopped and watched two men on horseback ride into the yard through the open gate. Tanner the Elder met them and held the reins while the two men dismounted. They walked to the house without looking around the yard. It was Herr Tucher and a man Katarina didn't recognize.

The next morning, Katarina insisted on fetching the water again. A coach stood in front of the house, hitched to two horses and ready to go. The same man came out of the house and jumped onto the coach box. Katarina asked Sara who it was.

"Frau Tucher is leaving today," Sara said. "She is finally taking the boys and Dörte and meeting Paul in Calais. It took so long to secure their ship to cross the Channel. That's all I know."

Bjarne yelled for Katarina and she followed him out of the yard. She never got a glimpse of Frau Tucher but that evening her absence was noticeable. After the meal, a relaxed atmosphere had settled on the farm. Their light conversation soothed Katarina.

Tanner and his father had taken to smoking the pipe. The smell of tobacco filled the room already reeking of onions, roots, beans, herbs and sweaty men. Katarina poured herself another mug of watery beer, sat back at the table and watched the tobacco smoke swirl above the candle flames. Katarina was grateful for the distractions. She had no time to read, no time to fret, no time to do anything. She wondered about all the new acquisitions. Was it worth rebuilding, just to have more soldiers come and tear it down again? Or was the fighting over? Who was paying for all of this? Uncle Paul? At the end of Herr Tucher's book, the last entry written in the spring, he had said he was badly in debt.

There had been no news from Eierhofen and Sara forbid her to go back there. She was sick to death about Isabeau but tried to shut those thoughts out of her mind. *"She's with her father, Katarina,"* Sara had said.

At least two weeks had passed since she came back to Sichardtshof. Time was moving so quickly and Katarina was no longer sure what day it was. The solstice had gone unrecognized and uncelebrated and Katarina thought it must be early July. These late, light evenings usually meant one could get work done that in the winter went unfinished. The men worked in the fields until the sun went down, so their meals were always late.

Sara and Anna finished the cooking and Sara sent Katarina for more water before they settled to eat. As she approached the well carrying two wooden buckets, Katarina saw Herr Tucher sitting on the front step of the main house reading and smoking a pipe. Was this their new crutch? Katarina liked the smell of the tobacco they smoked but had no desire to pull smoke into her lungs. These men should spend more time in the kitchen, tending the fires. That would cure them of the desire to smoke.

Katarina stopped and stared at him, willing him to look up. As if personally invited, he put down his pipe and looked up from his book. He slowly stood when he saw her at the well. She froze and just stood still and stared at him. Her heart opened up and all the blood poured out of it. She wanted to scream, to sob uncontrollably, to rush into his arms and kiss his lips, to turn her back on him, wound him, forget him.

Katarina turned her back on him. He allowed her to leave him once before. If he wanted her, he would have to come get her. She was not running after him. She walked back to the worker's house, resisting the urge to turn around and see if he was watching her walk away. Her heart would have shredded to bits if he was not.

Katarina set the buckets down outside the workers' house. The men were coming in from the fields. Sara scurried in and out of the house, laying the table with simple fare of bread, butter and cheese. Anna carried two bowls of boiled beans garnished with greens. Katarina came to the table and poured some wine.

Sara scrutinized her face. "Have you seen a ghost?" she said.

"No, why?" Katarina said and downed the wine in one gulp. "I'm fine."

Sara grabbed a bottle of wine from the table and refilled Katarina's cup. "You may need this. Don't turn around now. The master is coming."

Katarina froze. She sipped the wine and resisted again the urge to turn around. Her heart now void of blood closed upon itself and turned to stone. But a woman's shout caused them all to look towards the South Hill. Down the steep path from the four lindens, Sieglinde ran towards them. She looked like she had been crying. She gasped for air in between words.

"Up there…Hans-Wolfgang…horses…soldiers!"

Tanner stood and put an arm around her shoulder. "Take some deep breaths and tell us what happened."

"A few officers on horseback. They have taken over the Eierhofen house," Sieglinde said.

Herr Tucher walked over. "I heard there was another regiment in Höchstadt," he said. "This time with General Mansfeld himself. I heard them to be well-behaved."

He tried to meet Katarina's gaze, but she couldn't look at him. She twisted her fingers together.

"This is a small group of officers who want to live in a better house," Sieglinde said. "They've decided to take over Eierhofen as their quarters. But I'm worried about the girl."

Sara came up behind Katarina and laid her hand on Katarina's shoulder. "There's nothing you can do," she whispered.

"May I stay here tonight?" Sieglinde asked Sara.

"We need help in the morning. You may work for your keep," Sara said and waved the group to come to the table and eat.

The simple meal of beans and bread tasted heavenly to Katarina. It was the first meal she was able to keep down. She and Anna cleared the table and the men dispersed, to do whatever men do after a meal. Sieglinde had excused herself and said she was going to sleep. Slowly the men congregated back at the table. The evening was warm so Sara brought clay lamps, lit them and set them on the table. The men lit up their pipes.

"I need to get Isabeau out of there," Katarina said.

"The officers will move on, Katarina," Tanner said.

"I think we should let them get on with it," Sara said. "That's her father. He knows what's best for her."

Katarina twisted her fingers as her thoughts came fast and frantic.

"More wine, Katarina?" Sara said. "You look so pale."

Nein, danke. She shook her head. She'd had enough. The days of having the devil torn out of her soul had left her drained and weary. And wary about letting the devil back in, even in the guise of Bacchus.

Herr Tucher sat down next to Katarina. She refused to look at him. Every inch of her skin crawled with self-consciousness. She felt like he was watching her every move. She had forgotten this cat-and-mouse trait about him. The men continued discussing the events of the day.

"We have too much work to do," he said. "And the deliveries for grain and wool and whatever must be fulfilled. I cannot be late with my deliveries. Like Tanner said, the men will move on."

"What about Isabeau?" Katarina said again.

"He brought her here once before when he needed someone to take care of her. He'll bring her again," Sara said. "Or he can send Pieter. Think about it, Katarina. Don't worry about her. She is his daughter!"

Katarina took her leave and climbed the ladder upstairs in the workers' house. She wanted to sleep. Sieglinde had bedded down on the floor next to Katarina's straw sack and breathed quietly. Katarina listened to the voices outside rise and fall and finally disappear.

"Katarina, are you asleep?" Sieglinde said.

"Yes. Be quiet," Katarina said.

"So that's the master. Tell me about him. Is he kind to you?"

Katarina snorted and rolled over.

"Tell me a story about him. He is handsome in his own way."

Katarina said nothing.

"Does he fill you up? Can he please you? Some men know nothing about lovemaking, foolish oafs. Now the Dutchman, now he is insatiable. His touch makes me…"

"I don't need to hear this, Sieglinde. Go to sleep."

"He was getting on my nerves."

Katarina let out an impatient sigh.

"He could never get enough. Even after I satisfied him, he'd try to stick it in my mouth…"

"Go to sleep, Sieglinde!"

"Then he would just satisfy himself, with me lying there and…"

"Enough, woman! Would you just be quiet?"

Sieglinde prattled on and on. She talked about Hans-Wolfgang's gold. She told Katarina how Magdalena had been stealing from him when he slept. Katarina would not be sleeping now. Sieglinde asked questions about Herr Tucher; who he was and where he came from. She wondered if he was rich. Katarina avoided answering by asking Sieglinde more questions. This proved informative because Sieglinde seemed to like to hear herself talk and chatted on indiscreetly. She told Katarina about the officers staying at the Eierhofen house. They had been there the last two weeks.

Katarina sat up. "And you come here now? After all this time? What about Isabeau?"

"Oh, the girl will be fine. She can take care of herself."

"What about those officers?"

"They can be controlled, just like any man. I traveled with them before I came to Eierhofen. They abducted me when I met them on the road." She chuckled. "Oh, come now, Katarina, I couldn't just walk into the farm and tell you they came two weeks ago! Now your men will help me if I need it." She feigned an anguished expression. "Poor Sieglinde."

"Why don't you just stay with the officers, if you know them so well?" Katarina wondered what Sieglinde was really after and would be careful what she said.

"They bore me. Sometimes I have enough of those louts."

Katarina lay awake for a long time, worried about Isabeau. When she finally slept, she dreamed about Herr Tucher. They had met each other perchance and sat across from each other, but there was a boundary between them. Katarina loved him so deeply but could not get near him, could not speak with him or touch him. She woke before dawn, exhausted. Sieglinde lay next to her, her snoring dainty and feminine. Strained whispering in the kitchen gave Katarina more cause to worry. Tanner and Sara stopped speaking when Katarina climbed down the ladder. Sara's brow was creased with fear and distress.

"There are some stray people wandering in the forest up on the North Hill," Tanner said. "There was, at first, a band of six or eight men and women. I've been watching them the last few weeks. But their numbers are multiplying. There are now children with them. I may have to talk to them today and see what they are after. Food, no doubt."

"We don't have enough for everyone, Katarina." Sara shook her head. "We need to hide more of the stores we have standing around today. You and I."

Katarina nodded in agreement.

"This pains us," Tanner said. "I only wish we could feed them all. But they are wild. We should post watch on the cellars at night. But who should do that?"

"What does that woman want? Sieglinde," Sara said. "Is she going to stay here?"

"She seems to be in service to the officers at Hans-Wolfgang's house," Katarina said. "I cannot imagine she'd want to stay here. I think she's after something."

They heard the floorboards creak as Sieglinde moved about upstairs.

Sara held her finger up to her lips to silence Katarina. "My only wish is to live in an age where I can trust my counterparts."

Tanner grabbed his hat and opened the door. It was still very early but light enough to walk outside without a torch. He walked out of the house, shutting the door firmly behind him. Sara held two buckets out to Katarina. She smiled at Sara, took them without a word and left the house to fetch water. As she walked towards the well, her early exhaustion faded. Katarina pulled the dipper bucket up out of the old wooden well. She'd heard plans were in place to rebuild the well with sandstone and install a pump, but all their plans seemed to dissolve in ash and ruin.

It promised to be a fine day. The back door of the main house stood open. Light from the kitchen, Katarina's kitchen, flooded into the stable. The one heavy maid—Gret or Gerlin, Katarina never knew the difference—bustled out of the house and came towards the well. Proper and much taller than Katarina, she plowed forward as if she meant to push Katarina out of the way.

"I need water for the master," the maid said. "Out of the way."

Yes, it would have been wise to back up and let the woman have the right of way. Katarina looked at her, sunk the dipper bucket back into the well and continued her task. She was not wise and was not going to back down.

"Out of the way!" the maid commanded.

"I am not finished," Katarina said, her voice a whisper. "You will have the chance once I am done."

"The master must have his tea by sunup."

"Or he'll turn into a frog?" Katarina laughed.

"You will be sorry for that remark."

"He is already a frog, then?"

The maid threw down her bucket and stomped back to the house. Katarina smiled. When she worked in the house, she always fetched the kitchen's water the night before, so she could set it on the fire first thing. Katarina learned that from Frau Kuni, God rest her soul. Frau Kuni was difficult, very hard to live with, a downright nasty old bitch at times, but she taught Katarina to work efficiently.

Katarina filled both buckets, taking her time, and returned to the workers' house. She stood in the kitchen as Anna and Sara scurried back and forth, attempting to divide the rationed food amongst the kitchen full of people. Tanner, Lasse and Bjarne grabbed hunks of dry bread from the basket on the table and stuffed it into their tatty fabric bags. Sieglinde clambered down the ladder from above. She stood on the ladder until the men left the kitchen.

Anna cursed as Hannah refused to feed herself. "See if you can get her to eat," Anna said.

Anna set the bowl of runny porridge on the table. Katarina sat down, pulled Hannah onto her lap and offered the girl a spoonful. The girl took the porridge in her mouth and made a sloppy *baa-baa-baa* sound with her lips. The stuff dribbled out her mouth. Hannah thought this was grand, pressed her lips together and forced air and porridge into the room at large.

"Good God, don't let her do that!" Anna said. "She has regressed the last few weeks. She doesn't talk anymore, she has stopped walking. She had been sick and after the baby boy died, she started acting like a baby herself."

"It's getting late, my dears. Time to get to work." Sara pointed to Sieglinde. "Take care of the chickens we have left. Every night we seem to lose a few. I think it's the forest people."

Sieglinde laughed, bit at her bread and left the kitchen.

"Katarina, when Sieglinde brings the eggs, take them to Gret and Gerlin up at the main house. Then you and I are to start digging in the cellars until Tanner gets back. He'll be back before midday."

Katarina stood in the doorway and watched Sieglinde walk away. She could just see Herr Tucher sitting at a table in front of the main house, drinking from a wooden cup and looking at a large book. Out of the corner of her eye, she saw Sieglinde sneaking off, up the South Hill.

"Sara?" Katarina said and pointed after Sieglinde.

"Where's she going? That wretched woman." Sara handed Katarina an empty basket and smiled. "Please see if she left us any eggs and bring them to the maids at the main house."

"Oh, no, I'll bring them back here and you take the eggs up the house. I think it's better I don't go up there."

"Don't be silly." She shoved the basket into Katarina's hands and let go, almost causing the basket to fall. "Off you go."

Katarina found a whole basketful of eggs and took the lot back to Sara, who gratefully relieved the basket of the half of them. She pointed Katarina in the direction of the main house. Katarina walked towards the house silently praying no one would see her. She entered the stable through the paddock door, past both cows standing tethered to the stone wall. Katarina walked into the kitchen and set the basket of eggs on the worktop. Her worktop. Her kitchen. One of the maids glared at her.

"There you are," the maid said. "You certainly took your time, didn't you? Gather some firewood, too, I don't have enough."

Katarina said nothing and turned to leave.

"Are you deaf? Or dumb? Or just stupid? I said…"

Katarina walked out of the kitchen into the vaulted stable. One cow mooed and the other answered. The maid scolded behind her but Katarina walked away. She reminded herself she was free to leave. Every day here could be her last. She had no charge, no child, no commitments. Fear, she had enough of that, but not for this woman. Those that invoked fear were not far away and she felt them moving closer every day. As for these women, their petty troubles would no longer worry Katarina. Suddenly, Herr Tucher appeared in the doorway. Katarina stopped and waited for him to move aside so she could go out into the paddock.

"Good morning," he said.

Katarina smiled, her first genuine smile in a long time. "Good morning, sir."

He stepped aside and allowed Katarina to pass. She heard the maid behind her garble some sort of complaint as she walked back to the workers' house.

Sara waved for Katarina to come over. "Tanner has a task for us."

Katarina followed Sara into the kitchen. They heaved a sack each of what felt like dried beans and went down into the cellar. Back behind new shelves that looked like Tanner's woodworking, sounds of digging scraped in the dirt. Tanner peeked from behind the shelving and went back to his work, talking in between breaths and shovelfuls:

"They will have to get through us, kill us if you may, to get to this. We can't just hand out this food that took all our blood and sweat to accumulate."

"Did you meet any folks up in the woods?" Katarina asked.

He stopped working, removed his cap and wiped his brow with his scarf. "Yes. What a collection. A few deserters, some farmers with scythes, but most are unarmed. Elsbeth's boys, David and Friedrich. They won't come near me. There are women with children. Some children the age of Isabeau and Albin who look like they've been living in the wild for quite some time now. They don't shy from me. They want food, a dry place to sleep, anything they can steal. They surrounded me like a pack of wolves. Most uncomfortable feeling."

The shovel scraped again then stopped. He set the shovel aside. Sara handed Tanner a sack and he set it in the hole.

"I don't dare give them anything," Tanner said. "If they see they get something, they won't stop begging. Alms for the poor is one thing, but those children are dangerous. They are desperate. Dangerous are those who have nothing left to lose."

One by one they stacked the rest of the sacks into the hole. They would have to stretch these stores or no one would make it through the winter.

"I don't know what I'd do if they tried to storm us. You know, they are unarmed." Tanner slammed the shovel against the hard, dry earth. "What should we do? Fight them? Kill them? There are children! One of the women said they are trying to get to Nuremberg. They will try to be admitted into the city. Quite a task these days, especially if they look at all sick. But they are watching the farm. Chickens are disappearing. They see there are horses here and sheep. One sheep could feed them for a few days. It is hard to say how many people there really are."

Tanner covered the hole with a board and stomped the earth flat. "I won't sleep well tonight."

Chapter 41

Pieter van Diemen

Pieter heard that burly officer yell. He slammed his axe against the chopping block and poked his head out from the stable door.

"Where is Sieglinde?" The officer paced to and fro in the yard outside the Eierhofen house. He seemed to be in charge and was called Major Bärstecher. Pieter ducked back into the stable and *psstd!* to Isabeau who filled her handcart with horse manure. He held a finger up to his lips to signal Isabeau to be quiet. She nodded and pulled on the leather cap over her fair hair. From the stable doorway, Pieter watched Major Bärstecher take off his black hat with the long brown plume. He wiped his brow with the sleeve of his jacket.

"Sieglinde!" the Major bellowed again. "Where is that woman?"

Pieter watched as Sieglinde came running from the garden.

"Just collecting flowers, Herr Major." She held a bunch of wildflowers she'd picked from Andra's garden under his nose.

Major Bärstecher held a folded bit of parchment and led Sieglinde towards the front door. "A few men will be arriving this evening. A reinforcement regiment is to accompany us on our way. You tell the other women and I will tell the General."

Hans-Wolfgang would be furious. His patience was running thin as it was. He'd mounted his horse in a huff that morning carrying his falcon and had been gone all afternoon. Pieter had been instructed not to let Isabeau out of his sight. These officers had said they would be spending a few days. Now they said the General was too ill to travel and more men would be coming.

"*I have to hide my falcon away,*" Hans-Wolfgang had said. "*I can no longer keep him here. Katarina's falcon is still missing.*"

Pieter grabbed Isabeau by the hand. "Let's follow that wretched woman into the kitchen to see what she's up to."

Together they sneaked around the back of the house and walked into the kitchen through the garden door. A cheery fire burned in the hearth in the middle of the room. Steam and appetizing smells rose from the huge iron pot hanging from the iron rail over the open fire. The two other women, Ursula and Ronda, stood next to the working table under the high windows in a huddle with Sieglinde. Their whispering was frantic and excited. Pieter could not understand their words. All three women turned when they realized Pieter and Isabeau had entered the kitchen.

"Sit down, Dutchman," the woman named Ursula said.

Pieter stood still, wary of the woman. Ursula grabbed two wooden bowls, filled them with the savory-smelling pottage and set the bowls on the table. Isabeau pulled off her cap and sat to eat. This was, of course, food from the Eierhofen stores. The war financed the war, they said. The officers would use the common man's stores and move on. The horses would feed on the common man's forage. It was the only way to keep mercenary troops sustained. The other woman named Ronda filled a tray with wine and cups and left to take the drink into the hall upstairs.

"The officers don't dine in the kitchen with the help," Ronda said.

She returned with the empty tray, filled it with food and carried it upstairs. She returned and both women joined Isabeau at the table. Pieter finally sat down with them.

"Sieglinde thinks she is better than us," Ursula said.

"She allows me to serve her and she acts like a queen," Ronda said.

"Sieglinde speaks often of the Dutchman," Ursula said.

"Fond memories," Ronda said and laughed.

Pieter tried to ignore their teasing and chortling. He could feel the heat rise to his face. Isabeau's complete indifference to the two women unsettled him. She was normally more forward and this new, silent Isabeau scared him. He watched her out of the corner of his eye.

"Sieglinde says you were once a soldier, too," Ronda said.

"Strong lad you must be," Ursula said. "Why aren't you a soldier anymore? I heard the war is only over for the soldier who dies in battle."

"Did you find your fortune and leave the army?"

"Or did you fall in love with the princess here and save her from the wolves?"

"Tell us a story of your travels. We can get so bored."

Pieter had heard enough. He wanted to shove the bowl away in protest but the food was delicious. Instead, he swallowed the remains of his meal. Isabeau had done the same and had pulled the cap back over her head. Together they got up from the table and left the kitchen. Pieter wanted to find Sepp and Bubo as soon as they came back from the field they were working on and bring them to the kitchen before all the food was gone.

Together, Pieter and Isabeau walked out into the front yard. Even though it was much too warm, Major Bärstecher insisted on wearing the black hat with the brown plume. Sweat dripped down his saggy face as he sat on the step by the front door and puffed on a thin, wooden tobacco pipe. A man's voice boomed and the Major turned to the direction of the voice. Pieter saw a military man walking from behind the house flanked by Ronda and Ursula.

"Major, a visitor," Ronda said.

The military man stood in front of Major Bärstecher and said, "*Hauptmann Schwartz meldet sich zum Dienst.*"

"What do we have here?" the Major said. "Have you come from our reinforcement regiment?"

"Yes sir," Schwartz said. "I am reporting for duty."

Pieter pulled Isabeau aside and whispered, "You must hide now. Run, don't look back. I'll take care of this."

"Who is that?" she asked. "Pieter tell me! I'm not going anywhere."

"He can't see me. He mustn't see you. Just run, Isabeau! Do as I tell you!"

She ducked back into the barn just as Major Bärstecher stood and waved to Pieter. He and Hauptmann Schwartz made eye contact, just a split second. Pieter ducked his head and followed Isabeau into the barn, turned and peeked through the slats of wood. Isabeau had disappeared.

"Fine," Major Bärstecher continued with Schwartz. "How many are there of you? Will we need to quarter you here? No, that won't do. You and your men make camp by the river. We will be moving out as soon as we can move the General."

"You will need me here, Major." Hauptmann Schwartz moved closer to the Major's already-red face. "I have assessed the situation. I have been watching you. You want to heal the General yet you prolong his suffering by staying here. This area is teeming with witches. You travel with them and live with them in such close quarters! Have you ever questioned Sieglinde? Did you know there has been a Catholic priest hiding around this estate for weeks now? What is he planning to do to the General?"

Pieter saw Hauptmann Schwartz point to the barn. He boomed: "That Dutchman is a known deserter."

Pieter searched the shadows in the barn. "Isabeau, are you here?" Maybe the two of them could get back into the garden. He remembered a secret tunnel in the cellar behind the kitchen led to an escape hidden in the forest.

"Isabeau," Pieter whispered.

"My hired hand is not a deserter!" Hans-Wolfgang's voice boomed in the yard. Pieter peeked through the slats in the barn wall just as Hans-Wolfgang jumped from his horse. "Where is he?" he demanded.

"Your hired hands are here to serve us. The men and the women!"

"Where are my women?" Hans-Wolfgang hollered.

"We have them all prisoner!" Schwartz drew himself up to full height in front of Hans-Wolfgang.

Hans-Wolfgang flung himself at the Hauptmann who was a head and shoulders taller.

"Isabeau?" Pieter whispered. She must be in here somewhere.

His eyes tried to adjust to the dark barn. A few birds shot in and out from a hole in a wood panel in the upper part of the wall. A *swoosh!* and the sound of wood thunking caused him to turn just in time to see Sieglinde swing a wooden plank.

Part 3

Chapter 42

Katarina

Excited chickens squawked and flew against the coop as Katarina snatched one out of the air. Feathers flew and stuck to her sweaty brow. She brought its screeching, feathery frame to the chopping block and Sara removed the chicken's head with one practiced chop. All the other chickens were immediately quiet, afraid to be the next in line. Katarina grabbed the second one from the perch and Sara ended its life. Together in the corner of the coop, they trapped the third chicken who was not going down without a fight. The two women then settled in front of the worker's house in the late afternoon sun and plucked the birds for the evening meal.

"Any word from the master's wife?" Katarina asked in an attempt at unconcerned conversation.

"The last I heard, they arrived in Calais and are waiting for passage over the Channel."

"The weather has been good for traveling," Katarina said.

Sara blew at a feather on her upper lip. "I hope these were the three chickens that weren't laying eggs."

"We had them isolated long enough, didn't we?"

"Yes, we did. Still, chicken stew will do us all some good."

Katarina pulled another handful of feathers off and stuffed them into a sack. They could save these, wash them, cut the sharp quills off and sew them into pillows. Although the sun was shining and it was a quiet afternoon, she had to suppress an underlying agitation bubbling in her chest in spite of the pleasant warmth and weather.

"Did you see Sieglinde?" Sara asked. "Did she come back?

"Was she here at midday with the men?" Katarina said. "I thought I saw her."

"Damn woman. She only seems to come when it's time to eat. I asked her yesterday to bring me a bowl full of oak bark. I showed her where the oaks are. I need that bark for Hannah. The rash on her behind is getting worse since she wets herself all the time. I could make a bath for her with oak bark and it will soothe the rash."

"Should I fetch it for you?" Katarina said. "Where are the oaks? Those up the North Hill?"

"Oh, would you? You could bring me a sack full." She pointed. "See that knoll of trees. There are a few oaks among them."

Sara went into the house and brought back a small sack and a blunt rounded knife. "You have a sharp knife with you, don't you?" Sara asked.

"Yes, I always have it with me."

"Take the blunt one, too. You may break your pretty little dagger on the hard bark."

Katarina took the sack and the knife. "I'll be right back."

"Be careful," Sara said. "I'm glad to have you back here where you belong. I don't want anything to happen to you."

Katarina walked up the North Hill towards the knoll of trees, pleased to get a walk after sitting hunched over the chickens this afternoon. Sara made the best chicken pottage and Katarina was grateful there would be something to eat this evening. She would hunt for some herbs they could use as well. As she walked up the hill under the cover of the trees, she enjoyed the cool air, the warmth from the forest floor and its resiny, soothing, herbal smell. A gentle breeze played among the treetops.

Something else played among the treetops. High up, a strange animal call echoed. Only it was not animal. That was human. The same call sounded from the distance and Katarina wondered if she was being watched. She stopped walking. A short distance away stood the few massive oak trees Sara had showed her. Good thing the men had left a few standing. In the last ten years Katarina had lived here, the trees had fallen like soldiers. The need for wood and land to cultivate was so great, large tracts were completely tree-free. Almost every last shock of forest had been harvested for firewood and the lands turned into farming fields.

Katarina chopped at the massive tree and collected the bark chips into the sack. Oak bark had tanning acids that would help the baby's skin heal from the rash. After she filled the sack half way, she tied it shut, relieved she had no visitors nor heard any more strange calls. She left the forest and walked towards the path. Down the hill in front of her, a boy and a girl stood hand in hand next to the path. They were both about the age of Albin and Isabeau. These must be the children Tanner spoke of.

"Hallo," Katarina said to the children.

"What have you got there, Ma'am?" the boy asked.

"We're hungry," the girl said.

"Nothing edible. Oak bark. For a baby's bottom."

"You'll bring us something to eat, won't you? The man who sees us here won't."

"Please," said the girl. "A hunk of old bread. The master won't miss it. Or his fat maids. And the lady is gone."

They had been watching the farm, hadn't they? Katarina felt guilt twinge at her heart. What if this was Isabeau and some woman wouldn't give her anything to eat? This could very well be the lot of them if another wave of soldiers came through the valley. Katarina saw no harm in bringing them a bit of old bread. She had retrieved old bread Gret and Gerlin wouldn't eat from the kitchen this morning and soaked it in milk and eggs to make a pudding. She didn't use all of it. The last few hunks were to be soaked in water for the chickens.

"Wait here," Katarina said and ran off towards the workers' house.

The workers' house was empty. The smell of cooking chicken filled the air around the house. Katarina grabbed the basket with the few dried hunks of bread off the table and ran back into the yard. The children had followed Katarina here. She had told them to wait but they followed her. The smiles on their faces were not those of gratitude. Katarina had been tricked. She feared she had made a grave mistake.

The two children grabbed the basket from Katarina's hands like wild dogs and ran away. That strange call echoed behind the barn. And another from up the hill. Katarina realized there must be more people with them, hiding among the bushes along the path. A shrill scream from the South Hill set Katarina running for the main house. She had to warn the others!

Chapter 43

Ralf

Ralf walked down and up the path a third time. He'd been hiding out here at the Lower Eierhofen homestead for two weeks now and had not so much as gotten a glimpse of the girl. Or his rosary. He made a point each day to search the path and circle the whole periphery. And each day, his attachment to the material world lost another crumb of interest. He wasn't even fond of saying the rosary. It was something his mother had done, something she taught him to do and something that made him feel like she was near.

These last two weeks, he'd truly immersed himself in the contemplation of matters of the spirit. And for the first time in his adult life, he felt his parents near. He realized they had always been a part of him, imbedded in his very being, a part of his soul. This quiet time, the trees, the birds and, most importantly, the lack of companionship, had brought him nearer to his spirit, to his God, to his real calling. He had his travel prayer book, spent each day properly praying the Office and wondered why he had never made a pilgrimage before. Any anger or regret he had felt was now gone. He decided when he found the girl and righted his wrongs, he would retreat and live the life of a hermit, spending his remaining days in prayer and quiet meditation. All matters of the world and the ego would no longer clutter his life. He'd found true peace.

This would be the last time he crawled into the rabbit hole to search for the rosary. He sank to his knees. The amount of time he'd spent kneeling on the damp earth these last two weeks was symbolic. As he crawled into the hole in the hedge, he heard a faint gasp, the sound of a startled child catching her breath, and jerked out of his reverie. He knelt face to face with the fair-haired girl. What a beautiful creature.

"Pardon me," Ralf said. "Did I frighten you?"

Andra-Angela had been a bit older than this when he first moved to

Eierhofen. The similarities between her and this child were startling. The child was afraid, Ralf could tell. He wanted to reassure her, comfort her.

"What's your name, child?" Ralf said. "Come, let us back out of this hole."

"My name is Isabeau," the girl said, following him. "I want my horse and I want to go home."

"Where is your horse?" Ralf said.

"Bubo and Sepp took her to work the field today. They haven't come back yet. I think I know where they went though."

"Well, let's start off in that direction. We can catch them up and get your horse back. Then I'll take you home."

"You don't know where my home is."

"Yes I do," Ralf said. "I've known you since you were a baby. I knew your mother, Isabeau."

"I never met my mother," she said.

Ralf took the girl by the hand. She was strong and trusting. They left the yard and started towards the path leading to the flood plain.

"The field the boys were working is back here." Isabeau pulled Ralf the other direction, towards Gottesgab.

In the distance, Ralf saw two boys together atop a sorrel horse approaching. Isabeau pulled her hand from Ralf's grasp and ran off towards the two boys. He followed her. The two boys dismounted and the one boy handed Isabeau the reins. The two boys ran off in the direction of the Eierhofen estate. Ralf reached her and stopped her before she swung up onto the saddle. He took her hand again.

"You don't want to go back to Eierhofen with the boys," Ralf said. "It is dangerous."

"I want to go home," Isabeau said. "I don't need you. I have my horse."

"Where is Hans-Wolfgang?" Ralf asked her.

"The boys will tell him where I have gone."

"I will accompany you home," Ralf said. "I'll see to it you get where you belong."

Chapter 44

Pieter van Diemen

Pieter slowly tried to raise his head. He moved his mouth and spit out straw. His hands were tied tightly behind his back. Excruciating pain shot through his shoulders. He lay face down in the straw in the barn next to the horses. They stood quietly. Pieter rolled onto his side. Curse the damned wretch that tied his hands together. He counted the horses: all four of the four officers' and Hans-Wolfgang's stallion as well as the nag that pulled Sieglinde's wagon. Isabeau's mare was not back yet.

Excited women's voices chattered in the yard. Pieter rolled himself to a sitting position. He tried to bring his hands to the front of his body. There was no way. They were bound too tightly. The voices were coming closer. He fumbled with the bindings.

"Untie me!" Pieter yelled and added under his breath, "if you dare."

A man's angry voice throbbed under the women's. The barn door flew open. The sky was dotted with inky clouds and the light was subdued as the evening set in.

"Leave us alone for a moment," Sieglinde said to someone behind her. "I will hear him out."

"Give me a few moments alone with Sieglinde," Pieter said. "I would like to thank her for her company."

"The General's reinforcement regiment will be here in the morning, Dutchman," Hauptmann Schwartz said. "General Mansfeld will have you dealt with when they arrive. Sieglinde, he is your charge, then."

"Help me up onto my feet, Sieglinde." Pieter was at a disadvantage with his hands tied. "Untie me. You know I won't hurt you."

She helped him up and untied him, an unexpected gesture.

Pieter rubbed his wrists until the blood flowed into his hands again. "Where are the others? Where is Hans-Wolfgang?"

"He's in the hall with the General, tied like you were. The General is very sick and needs attention. He has told Hans-Wolfgang he is demanding a healer or a doctor to make him more comfortable. He won't let me touch him anymore. Schwartz told him I was a witch and was making him worse and he believes it. He usually travels with an astrologer and they are waiting for him to come. Hans-Wolfgang is supposed to set off and look for Katarina."

"How did he manage to take Hans-Wolfgang?"

Sieglinde shook her head. "He had help from the two young pages. And Hans-Wolfgang is a fool. Schwartz told him his daughter is being held captive."

"Have they taken Isabeau?" Pieter attempted to push past her.

Sieglinde grabbed his arm. "You are just as much a fool. Until Hans-Wolfgang started spouting about you, his hired hands and his women, Schwartz didn't even know Hans-Wolfgang had a daughter! They surrounded Hans-Wolfgang and Schwartz knocked him unconscious. Schwartz is playing him for a fool and threatens to kill the girl if Hans-Wolfgang does not obey. Schwartz hasn't even seen the girl."

"She is his daughter. He loves her."

"Love." She snorted. "Even if it was true! Schwartz is making it up! Don't you see? You fool. Even if he had the girl. Hans-Wolfgang could have more children. He'll lose everything now. He'll lose his property to the General."

"Where is the girl?"

"Nobody has seen her. As long as she stays under cover, Schwartz's ruse will work."

"Why did you untie me? I could kill you right now, you lying little wench."

She came up to Pieter and put her arms around his waist. She smelled like wildflowers. "You won't kill me. I can get you out of this mess, can't I? They're going to hang you for desertion but I can help you escape."

Pieter broke away from her.

"But you won't escape, will you?" Sieglinde said. "You'll try to find the girl instead of saving yourself. I can see you love the girl as much as Hans-Wolfgang. You love her more than he does, I would say, judging by the way you look at her."

"What do you get out of this? A place as whore for all the officers?"

"I want to survive, like anyone else. Together with these men, I can travel freely, with better accommodations. I get money and food. Why do we do anything, Pieter?"

Pieter snorted.

"Where would I be otherwise?" Sieglinde continued. "On a farm like Sichardtshof, as the master's whore? My mother used to let them all have me. I wasn't much older than Isabeau. She let those men have me because she was tired of fucking them herself. There were plenty of times I wished I was dead instead of enduring those years at their mercy. I'll never go back to that life."

"But you could leave the country. Maybe have children of your own."

"Where, then? Go to Holland? I have heard about German women who go to Holland. To Amsterdam. Women fleeing the war are destined to be maids or whores and endure the same hardships they would have here. Nobody marries women like me. You the least of all."

No, Pieter thought. No one would ever marry this bitch. He wondered what he should do to her now. Slap her? Kill her? Take up her offer to escape? At that moment, Hans-Wolfgang rushed into the barn. He pulled a knife out of his boot when he saw Sieglinde.

"Wait, Hans-Wolfgang," Pieter said. "Don't hurt her."

"Because of this woman, I have lost everything." Hans-Wolfgang spat.

"No, because of that bastard child, you have lost everything," Sieglinde said. "Your property is gone anyway. But you can easily escape too. The two of you. Just stop worrying about the girl. Schwartz is lying."

"Are you mad, woman?" Hans-Wolfgang yelled. "He says he has Isabeau. I cannot risk such a thing. Have you no loyalty?"

"Have you seen the girl? She is not here. How many times must I tell you this!"

"Where is she then?" Hans-Wolfgang asked.

Sieglinde shook her head. "I do not know."

Hans-Wolfgang snorted and turned to Pieter. "We must summon Katarina. Pieter, take my horse and ride to Sichardtshof. Even if you can't get Katarina, maybe Tanner and some men can come and help us. Sound the alarm. We may still be able to save my daughter. Get Katarina on the horse. Bring help back tonight. Please don't waste any time! I am going to find Isabeau."

Pieter tied a rope around Hans-Wolfgang's sorrel's nose and jumped on his back. He rode towards the river but turned on the road before Mailach towards Lonnerstadt. He crossed the river there and rode up to the highest point on the North Hill. Here his regiment had camped in the springtime but today it was deserted. On a clear day, one could see for miles around: the looming peak in the south, its sides cut from the legendary *Zuggeist*; the *Walberla* rise in the north, rumored to witness witches' feasts. From here, Pieter could observe the goings on in the whole Aisch river valley. Behind Lonnerstadt, smoke curled from scattered fires. Troops camping. There seemed to be another camp in the north, too, behind Höchstadt. Down the hollow in the direction of Sichardtshof, smoke rose from the chimney of the main house and from another spot behind the trees.

Dotting the North Hill in an offset marching procession, Pieter noticed burning torches, just a few. It seemed a small group moved towards Sichardtshof. Pieter heard a musket shot. And then another. Something was amiss. Pieter struggled with himself. Here he was with a fresh horse. Even though it was getting dark, he could ride in any direction and stop somewhere after midnight. No one would know he was gone. They might wonder where he was when he didn't show tomorrow or the next day. He could finally put all of this behind him. He could go to Holland, like he wanted, and move to another city where no one knew him.

That was fear talking. Another strange feeling came over him, one he had never known: a sense of obligation and responsibility. He could not leave. Isabeau's life was at stake. He would do what Hans-Wolfgang asked of him. Isabeau had a hold over Pieter he could not explain. He wanted to serve her. He had to make sure she was safe no matter what. There was something superior about her, great even. Greatness was a timeworn concept, something he'd never encountered. But here it was. He knew what direction his life would now take and he knew what he had to do.

Another two shots rang out. Pieter kicked the horse's flanks and he jumped forward. He would ride to Sichardtshof, collect Katarina and find Isabeau.

Chapter 45

Isabeau

"We can't cross the river there," Isabeau said.

She wanted to get to Sichardtshof before it got too dark. The clouds were low and threatening rain. And this fellow was not as familiar with the area as she was. If only he would listen to her! He insisted on holding Crone's reins and wanted them to walk towards Lonnerstadt even though she said Sichardtshof was the other way. She'd be home by now if he'd let her ride.

"The water is too high," he said. "We need to follow the river to the north before we can cross."

"I know which way to go. We should go back there. I know this area like the back of my hand."

"Yes," he said. "But you could get hurt."

"No I won't. I can take care of myself. Maybe I should be trying to take care of you?"

"That's funny," he said. "Yes, maybe you should be taking care of me. That is funny, Isabeau."

Isabeau wondered what the man was thinking. "Where are we going?"

"Isabeau, I feel I have cheated you of many things," he said. "I am going to tell you a story."

Oh, no, not another story. Isabeau was getting fed up with all the stories people told her. If people believed in what they did, they would not lie and tell stories. How much breath they would save if they just told the truth!

"I secured a life for you and your mother, with God. But I did not fight hard enough for you. Now I think I have cheated you of the life with your mother. As I felt I have been cheated. A man took my mother's life in a brutal way. Was this because of her conviction? Because of her religion? Of course it was. And, still, I have wanted nothing more than to see this

302

religion, the one true faith, the Catholic faith, liberate the world. I still feel this is the only way to save the world from the terrible fate that is yet to come."

"We need to cross the river back there," Isabeau said and pointed.

"The last remembrance I had of my mother went missing. I know now she is a part of me, as your mother is a part of you. That I cannot lose. That last thread I clung to, my only connection, those beads on a chain. And I have lost them."

"These beads on a chain?" Isabeau said and held out the chain she found in the hedge.

"You found my rosary." The man laughed and thought this was funny too. "That is a sign, my child. My goal was to be instrumental in saving the world. A noble cause, yes? But a futile one. The world doesn't want saving. But there are single souls worth saving."

"Look, there is a path leading to the spot where we can cross," she said.

"We're heading north for a spell," the man said. "We'll just continue on here. This is a good path, I say. I am back to my original quest, the one I had as a young man. To truly find peace. That is a life as God intended, a life in spirit and worship. It's all I've ever wanted. I want to be like Father Marius. But first I must save a young one from herself. I will give back the greatest gift ever given to me. That was the gift Marius gave me when he rescued me and took me to Würzburg, to the Jesuits. That life my parents could never have given me."

The man grabbed Isabeau's hand and she stopped walking. Crone snorted and stopped as well. Her ears were facing front and she was unperturbed by this strange fellow. He held Isabeau's arm up and looked at the chain she had found. He laughed again. Isabeau took in the surroundings. She knew exactly where she was in the flood plain, judging by the bend in the river. Sichardtshof was just a short ride from here.

"I want you to have the chain. It is a rosary and belonged to my mother. It is my most treasured possession. And while this will never make up for your loss, I hope it is a token of what your mother meant to me and how sorry I am she is no longer here. I want to honor her by taking care of you now. You will come with me and I will take you to the convent. You will thank me. The place you should have gone all those years ago. There you will grow up and be safe and not have to run wild like you do here. You won't have to live this base existence with these farmers."

"What about my horse?" Isabeau asked.

"Oh, you won't even want to ride around on that horse anymore. You will grow in the love of God and study Scripture and be surrounded by the blessings of a daily life of prayer and worship."

"But all I want is my horse. I want to ride. I'll never grow out of riding."

"I have searched myself long and realize fully now. I may have cheated you of a life with your mother. But I will save you from this damned existence with a heretic father and the bastard maid, the witch Katarina."

"You aren't listening to me." Isabeau was tired of this conversation.

"Yes I am," the man whispered. "You are a child and you don't know what you want. You are young. Believe me, I know what's best. Let's continue on this path, shall we?"

Chapter 46

Katarina

The darkening sky was overcast with heavy clouds. Katarina felt Sara's back against hers, damp and searing hot. She shivered as a chill went down her spine and tightened her grip on the scythe Tanner had modified. Instead of the usual bowed blade, he'd turned the blade so it stuck straight out. She was to handle it like a pike. From Katarina's position in the middle of the yard, she saw Herr Tucher come out of the house with Tanner the Elder. They both held hand muskets. Herr Tucher fired a warning shot into the air and it seemed to set the forest strays into motion. Outside of the ring of light shed by Sara's clay lamp, Katarina could see nothing. She could only hear people scurrying around the outbuildings.

In the middle of the yard, Tanner rammed a large torch into the ground. Sara lit the torch from her clay lamp and the outbuildings sharpened in the flickering light. The mob called to each other from their hiding places, a strange mixture of an owl's hoot and a wolf's howl. The hair on Katarina's neck stood up. The calls echoed from behind the barn, from behind the well, from everywhere.

Lasse approached carrying a pitchfork. "I could tell the forest mob was becoming more brazen. Maybe I should have anticipated an attack. I saw a few strays by day and heard them at night. I noticed animals were missing and there were signs people searched through the buildings at night. But I never thought these people would try to charge the farm!"

"After Herr Tucher fired that shot," Katarina whispered, "he must have gone back into the house to reload."

"Listen, it sounds like a pack of wolves howling," Sara whispered.

"They're behind the workers' house now," Katarina said.

Bjarne ran up next to them holding a pitchfork in one hand and a dagger in the other. "Anna is upstairs with Albin and Hannah. But they'll be trapped if they set the house on fire."

"Maybe we should split up and patrol the grounds in pairs," Tanner whispered. "Sara come with me. Katarina, you go with Lasse. You two go around the main house. Bjarne, stand by the master."

Katarina walked towards the main house, her legs jiggling with fear and anticipation. Bjarne ran ahead and joined the master. Herr Tucher had a row of loaded hand muskets in front of him.

"It takes so long to load the things, it is better to have few ready," Herr Tucher said to Bjarne.

The strange call came from the paddock again.

"They will break into the kitchen," Katarina said. "Are you worried about them getting in?"

"The door is locked with a massive iron lock from my Uncle Paul," Herr Tucher said. "I am more worried about you."

Katarina stood rooted in front of the main house next to Herr Tucher. The torch illuminated the figures as they hushed in and about the buildings creating unnerving and menacing shadows. It was impossible to count how many there were.

"Come. We'll check around the back of the house," Lasse said.

The tell-tale clopping of hooves in the distance came up the main track. She pointed to the track but Lasse pulled her by the hand. A swishing in the underbrush caused her to stop. Someone ran away up the South Hill. Katarina wished for daylight so she could see. The sound of hooves continued up the track at a rattling pace.

"Lasse, stop! Listen," Katarina said.

"Someone is coming and they are not wasting any time getting here," Lasse said. "Come! Follow me!"

They hid behind the large spruce tree, invisible in the absence of light. Katarina could not make out who the rider was but she could tell it was a man, a good rider. The horse sped towards the open gate. The rider pulled on the reigns and the horse slowed to a trot. Katarina recognized Hans-Wolfgang's stallion, ridden by Pieter. Why was he alone? Was he bringing bad news? Katarina threw down her scythe and jumped out from behind the tree. The horse stomped and snorted, Katarina's rash movement startling him, but Pieter had good hold on the reins. He looked relieved to see Katarina.

"You must come with me," Pieter said. "Collect your tinctures and get on the horse."

"Pieter, be quiet." Katarina held the rope around the horse's nose as he dismounted. "Listen. We're surrounded."

She held her finger to her lips. Ghostly figures hushed in, out and around the outbuildings. Pieter shook his head, like he did not understand what was happening. Tanner the Elder silently took Pieter's horse and led him away. Katarina motioned for Pieter to follow and she led him up the steps to Herr Tucher.

"Hello, Pieter," Herr Tucher said quietly. "We need your help. We have visitors. It may be a long night."

"I need to take Katarina back with me. The General is sick and demands a visit from a healer." He turned to Katarina. "You must return to Eierhofen with me. Now. With your tinctures. We think they have Isabeau."

Wolf's howls sounded from all around the farm.

"Who are these people?" Pieter said.

"I am not sure," Herr Tucher said. "Tanner met them up in the forest. It is a mishmash of all sorts. Simple men, farmers, women, children. They seek refuge and seem to want to travel to Nuremberg. They are desperate. Nothing is more formidable than a man who has nothing left to lose."

Katarina looked from one man to the other. Herr Tucher needed her here but she had to return to Eierhofen with Pieter. She slipped away from the two men and ran back to the workers' house to fetch her tinctures. She broke into a run as a howling call boomed behind the well. She squinted against the darkness to discern shapes or movements in front of her. Sara and Tanner moved from behind the workers' house and met each other by the front door just as Katarina approached. Tanner knocked and the door cracked open. Just a glow from the fire in the kitchen illuminated Tanner exchanging a few words with Anna. She nodded at whatever he said and quietly closed the door again.

Suddenly, a wave of people rushed from behind the house, out of the surrounding bushes, like a flood from the hills. Terror muddled Katarina's reasoning as she watched the vagabonds envelope Tanner and Sara. Tanner hollered as a man pulled the scythe from Sara's hands. Sara screamed. Pieter pounded past Katarina, almost knocking her flat.

"Katarina, help me!" Pieter yelled over his shoulder.

Katarina drew her dagger and walked towards them, fear stiffening her legs. Tears welled in her eyes. Tanner beat his fist against the desperate people and held Sara tight with the other hand. Pieter swiped with a large dagger, clearing the immediate space in front of himself. From Katarina's standpoint, she counted twenty men, women and children in the group. They pushed towards the workers' house. A few men sliced with knives willy-nilly around themselves. Some of the women held torches. Katarina feared they would set the house on fire with Anna inside, like Bjarne had said.

The sounds of shots popping from the main house distracted the whole group. Katarina turned back and a woman's threatening face came right up to her own face. With one hand the woman held a torch. She grabbed Katarina by the hair with her free hand. Otherwise she was unarmed.

"Just give us and our children something to eat and we'll leave!" she hissed.

Katarina struggled to get her hair out of the woman's grip. Pieter came up behind the woman. He set his dagger against her throat and Katarina ducked away. She heard Pieter give a great huff of effort and then a gurgling, gasping sound from the woman. Katarina turned back as the woman dropped the torch and fell to the ground. Pieter gave her body another push and she fell on her face.

"Next time, finish her off before she gets you!" he yelled.

"She was unarmed!" Katarina said. "How can I kill an unarmed woman! She is hungry, desperate."

"If you don't want to be in her position, I suggest you defend yourself!"

"Pieter, I can't…"

"Try to get to Sara!" he screamed.

Pieter ran off in front of Katarina and sliced his way to Sara. Katarina watched in horror as the group slowly backed away from Sara, their pitchforks and implements aimed at her. Another woman charged Katarina. Katarina grabbed her by the arm and gave a yank. The woman lost her balance and tumbled away, just like Pieter had taught her. A young, disoriented beggar boy stood next to Sara. A man threatened the boy with his pike. The boy ran to Sara and she clutched him behind her back to shield him. Would they actually kill one of their own?

"Stop this madness!" Sara cried.

The group tightened its circle around Sara. More shots rang out back at the main house. Feeling rushed, Katarina knew not where to turn or whether to flee. She started towards the main house until a shout in front of the workers' house caused her to twirl back like a hunted rabbit. She watched in horror as the man with the pike advanced on Sara. He held his pike waist-high, swung it back like a battering ram and jutted the blade through Sara's belly. Tanner cried out and ran to his wife. The man pulled his pike back and the boy behind Sara fell motionless to the ground. Sara remained standing and clutched her bloody belly. Tanner held her and looked desperately around.

"I'm going to see my Falk again," she said to Tanner and fell to her knees.

Tanner laid his wife down on the ground, on her back, and called for Katarina. She rushed to his side. Sara inhaled one last deep attempt at life and exhaled as her soul left her body. Katarina felt that same chill up her spine like when Frau Kuni died. A musket shot, then two, then three rang out within the group. The forest people dispersed as quickly as they had descended.

It started to rain.

"Oh, dear God in all of Eternity," Herr Tucher said as he ran up and saw Sara lying on the ground. "Had I gotten here sooner. We had to shoot numerous poor beggars."

Tanner wept at his dead wife's side. Katarina knelt down and touched Sara's cheek. Rain dripped from Katarina's hair and mingled with tears. She thought about what Hans-Wolfgang said about his mother and Magdalena. Maybe Sara still lived. For a moment, a sliver of hope hovered just beyond her grasp. She stood again, knocked on the door and silently asked Anna to help her. Together they pulled Sara into the kitchen, laid her on a blanket next to the fire and covered her. Albin saw them come in, squeaked like a mouse and sat down on the floor next to his mother.

Pieter ran through the doorway, stopped at Katarina's side and put a hand on her shoulder. "We need to get to Eierhofen before the next casualty is Isabeau."

Katarina climbed the ladder to the sleeping quarters, grabbed the tinctures out of her box, put them in a leather pouch, climbed back down and knelt next to Albin. "Keep an eye on her until we come back. I don't know if she will live through this, but you tell her how much you love her. She'd like that."

Katarina slung the leather pouch over her shoulder and went outside again. Those strange calls howled and cooed under the muffling of the rain. The mob had retreated but only to regroup. She wiped the tears from her cheek and held her dagger at the ready. This was not yet finished.

A shot rang out. A man screamed. Katarina ran behind Pieter towards the sounds, her anger coming to the boil. The vagabonds had assembled alongside the barn, armed with torches that sputtered in the rain and farming implements like picks and forks. The group of about twenty men and women were trying to gain access to the horses. Tanner, Pieter and Lasse held them at bay with drawn swords. Herr Tucher aimed his musket, shot the man in the front of the mob, the one who seemed to be the leader. He fell. Those standing close by grabbed their ears after the ear splitting bang. Herr Tucher threw the musket aside and drew a sword. The crowd murmured uneasily amongst itself.

Someone scurried up behind Katarina. In the dark it sounded like more than one person. Katarina's head snapped back as someone pulled great handfuls of her hair. Katarina spun sharply. Her wet hair slid out from the person's grasp. Katarina grit her teeth and closed her eyes. She jabbed her dagger and struck nothing. She stretched her arm and with a broad sweeping movement, swung the knife along the horizontal plane in front of her. A sharp, feminine intake of breath told Katarina she had struck.

Katarina opened her eyes wide, jabbed the knife forward and upward and struck what felt like the woman's breast bone. The knife stuck in the bone momentarily. As Katarina pulled it back with an effort, the softness of a breast touched her hand. The woman put her hands in front of her chest and then grabbed Katarina again. A second woman charged from behind. The second woman grunted and panted as she grabbed Katarina by the shoulders, enveloping Katarina's smaller stature in her embrace. Katarina stretched one hand up and grasped the first woman around her throat and with the other, jabbed the dagger into her soft underbelly. The second woman squeezed Katarina's head.

Katarina heard Pieter in the back of her head: *"Finish her off!"*

Katarina thrusted the dagger deeper and upwards towards the first woman's rib cage. Warm liquid washed over Katarina's hand, chilled from the rain. The woman went limp. The second woman released Katarina's head. Katarina pulled the dagger back and looked around for the second woman. She had disappeared. Pieter stood nearby, in clenches with a round, stooped man. Another man with a pike sneaked up behind Pieter's back. Katarina ran towards the sneaking man, surprised him and stabbed him in his side, right into his soft innards. Pieter finished his opponent off and grabbed Katarina by the arm.

"We must think about getting away from here. Look at Lasse and Tanner. Most of the mob has drawn back." He dragged Katarina towards the two men. "Come with me, we'll tell them we are going."

The trembling in Katarina's legs spread to her hands and her face. The terror of having just taken a life, the stark meaning of the act, threatened to render her stupefied. Lasse and Tanner stood discussing something in a heated manner. Tanner gesticulated in an almost hysterical manner and jabbed his sword in the direction of the ponds. Katarina followed his gesticulating and saw there were at least ten dead bodies around the ponds.

"We need to get those bodies out of there," Tanner said. "Those ponds are stocked. We need those fish! If I catch one of those marauders within ten miles of this farm, I'll, I'll, well, I know what I am going to do. I'm going to set traps though the woods tomorrow." He stomped off towards the ponds.

Lasse turned to Pieter and Katarina. "Well, the two of you are still in one piece. Herr Tucher is unharmed and Tanner the Elder is checking on Anna." He lowered his voice. "You saw what happened to Sara."

"Lasse, we have to leave," Pieter said. "Isabeau is in danger. I'm riding with Katarina up to Eierhofen."

"Do what you must," Lasse said. "Be careful, you two."

Pieter grabbed Katarina again by the arm and dragged her behind him. "Let us go look for Hans-Wolfgang's horse. I hope he is in the barn. I didn't see where Tanner the Elder took him."

He opened the barn door and they were greeted by the anxious whinnying of horses. The excitement had agitated them and they were wide awake. Pieter found Hans-Wolfgang's horse, untied him and led him outside.

"You are going to ride," Pieter said.

"Yes, Pieter."

The rain had let up. Pieter mounted and walked the horse to a bench next to the barn. Katarina stepped up onto the bench. Her trembling legs buckled under her but she caught herself and slid onto the horse's warm, dry back. She fitted herself against Pieter's back and wrapped her arms around his middle. Pieter was a good rider and this was going to be fast. One steadying breath and a prayer later, he kicked the horse's flanks. Katarina almost fell off as the horse sped away, slipping on fresh mud. She could feel the horse's haunches propel them forward, his hooves searching for a sure hold in the wet earth. Katarina pressed her head against his back and breathed in the smell of his leather vest and the scent of his hair.

The tears came now silently, painfully, and her chest burned with the scorching reality of this new void. Losing Sara not only opened a fresh wound, she was also faced with the grief over all those she had lost in the past. She'd never mourned any of them properly. Was there such a thing as mourning properly? Sadness flowed over her in searing waves. Anew, she mourned losing her grandmother at the hands of soldiers, Sara's boy Falk, too. She cried for her own miscarried child and the subsequent children she would never have. She would miss her closest and best friend, Sara, the one steadying influence in her life.

She cried for the violation she suffered at the hands of those soldiers. She missed Herr Tucher and wondered if she could ever find a way back into his life. She seethed when she thought of the life Isabeau must endure, because of the war. All this lost innocence, wasted life, wasted time. A rage fired inside like she had never felt before.

"Don't fall asleep back there," he said.

"Please hurry, Pieter."

"We will win, Katarina."

Pieter slowed the horse to a walk as the hooves sunk into the soft earth next to the river. In the dark, Katarina could hear the rushing water. Even though her eyes had adjusted to the dark, she could barely see the river bank.

"Where can we cross here, Katarina?"

"Let me down so I can look."

He stopped and slid off the horse's back. He grabbed Katarina around the waist and helped her slide down, too.

"We need to find a safe place to cross," he said. "The horse is sinking into the mud. I am thankful the rain has stopped. Otherwise we would never be able to cross."

They walked along the river. The riverbank was muddy and slippery. A flock of waterfowl flew off quacking into the dark night.

"Stop here for a moment." Pieter seemed to be listening. "I hear the water splashing over rocks. Let's try to cross there. Hold on to the horse's tail. He won't kick, I promise. I've seen Hans-Wolfgang pull on his tail with all his weight and the horse does nothing."

They waded across the shallow water. Katarina still slipped on the slimy rocks but she had a good grip on the horse's tail. They reached the opposite bank.

"Stop. Give me your hand. It's muddy here." Pieter pulled her up the bank. "Let's get going."

Pieter grabbed Katarina around the waist and set her in the front astride the horse's shoulders. He jumped up, sat behind her and grabbed the reins.

"Pieter, I smell smoke. Look, up the hill."

The sky suddenly swelled red in the distance. Katarina pointed to the knoll of trees surrounding the Eierhofen estate. Pieter whispered an oath in his own language and kicked the horse. He leaned forward and urged the horse with his legs to gain more speed. Katarina thought she might suffocate as Pieter's body pressed forward. Sleeping birds in the trees awoke and flew away. The orange glow burned brilliant. They stopped before they entered the trees. Men shouted—among the trees, at the top of the hill and on the main path.

"Pieter, veer to the right," Katarina said. "We can take the path to Hans-Wolfgang's ruins. We can see what is happening from there."

They rode up the path, into the Lower Eierhofen yard, to the ruins that were once Hans-Wolfgang's family's house. Pieter tethered Hans-Wolfgang's sorrel stallion to a tree and together they ran towards the hedgerow separating the two estates. He ducked down and looked for the crawlspace leading to the Upper Eierhofen house. Then they could see who was yelling and maybe get a glimpse of Isabeau and Hans-Wolfgang.

Behind Katarina, among the ruined house, someone whistled. The signal for Isabeau.

"Come here," Pieter hissed.

He ducked down and entered a crawl space in the bushes. Katarina followed. They crawled through the thick bushes and peeked out the other side. Smashed furniture and other oddities were burning in a heap in the middle of the yard. A good twenty or thirty foot soldiers stood ready. What a ragged looking bunch. Horses harnessed to carts stood in the yard. More ragged men packed the carts. It looked like they had emptied the house.

An unfamiliar officer and Sieglinde strode around the middle of the yard. He seemed to be giving her orders. Sieglinde called, two other women joined her in the yard and they disappeared from Katarina's sight. The officer continued overseeing the pillaging process. Two soldiers came out of the barn carrying a large, heavy trunk. Another officer on a dun-colored work horse rode into view and gave them orders.

"There's Hauptmann Schwartz," Pieter whispered.

Hauptmann Schwartz bent from his horse and said something to the officer in a low tone. Both men nodded. Hauptmann Schwartz kicked his horse into motion and sped out of the yard.

The whistle sounded from the tree again and Katarina realized it was Hans-Wolfgang. "Pieter, I think he is here. Hans-Wolfgang. Among the ruins. I hear his signal."

The three women came back into Katarina's sight and helped a sickly, small man into a carriage pulled by two horses.

"That is the General," Pieter said. "He is very sick,"

She crawled back out from the hedgerow and walked cautiously among the ruins. Trees had grown up among the foundation of the burned out barn. The faint smell of charred wood still lingered even after ten years. Pieter followed behind her and took hold of her arm. Katarina tried to whistle their signal, low and quietly. Someone grabbed her other arm and pressed a hand to her mouth.

"I need my horse," Hans-Wolfgang said. "They've taken the others out of the barn and have taken them away already. Isabeau is not here."

"Should I come with you?" Pieter asked.

Hans-Wolfgang swung onto his stallion's back, the arrows rattling in the quiver on his back. "No need. You won't be able to keep up."

With that, he shoved the bow up onto his shoulder, kicked the horse to a gallop and sped out of the Lower Eierhofen yard. Katarina followed Pieter at a run. It was almost completely dark in the trees and Katarina's breaths came in huffs as she tried to keep up with Pieter and not fall down this steep path. They came out of the trees onto the floodplain. Katarina could now see her hand in front of her face. She heard Hans-Wolfgang's whistle. Across the flood plain, Katarina saw the regiment with their General. His carriage moved slowly across the river, followed by the remaining horse-pulled carts, laden with spoils from the Upper Eierhofen house. The parade of bobbing torches and mercenary soldiers trundled along behind them.

"They are going…to join the rest of the regiment…" Pieter said, out of breath. "They have their quarters behind Höchstadt. I heard them say they travel towards Hungary."

Pieter grabbed Katarina's hand and they ran towards the river. Katarina heard Hans-Wolfgang's whistle.

"Stop! Quiet!" Pieter whispered. "There he is. Come! Hurry!"

They ran along the river bank, staying close to the rushes growing there. The soft, damp earth slowed them considerably. Just then, a rider sped past them at full speed. It was Hans-Wolfgang.

"There she is!" Hans-Wolfgang said. "Ralf has her!"

Traveling north close to the river bank, a bit farther along, Katarina could just make out the dark form of a horse moving in front of the light growth of rushes. It looked like a grown man walking, leading a horse and a child along the river bank. They must have left the path to travel unseen through the flood plain.

"Hurry, Pieter," Hans-Wolfgang hollered.

Pieter and Katarina ran after Hans-Wolfgang. She heard his raised voice and focused her attention on running, her lungs burning. Hans-Wolfgang had reached Ralf and Isabeau and his horse stamped. As Katarina reached them, she leaned forward and tried to catch her breath.

"Isabeau go to Katarina," Hans-Wolfgang yelled. "Now."

Pieter approached cautiously, leaving them room. Isabeau did not move.

"Leave us be Hans-Wolfgang," Ralf said. "You will allow me to leave right now with the girl who is rightfully my charge. She is going to have the life her family would have wanted her to have. Then my debt to the family and Andra-Angela is paid."

"How dare you speak the name of Andra-Angela?" Hans-Wolfgang dismounted and stood in front of Ralf. "Isabeau, go to Katarina."

Isabeau shook her head. "When the man gives me the reins, I will go to Katarina."

Ralf scoffed. "What sort of life does she have ahead of her? This existence you have damned her to live? She will live a heretic with your Protestant upbringing. Raised by Katarina in a witch's household. I taught her mother, I raised Andra-Angela, I prepared her mother for a sacred life of prayer and contemplation, with a healthy fear of God."

"God should not be feared," Hans-Wolfgang said.

"In your case, He should!" Ralf screamed. "You led Andra further into the life of sin and debauchery! As her teacher, I was patient and nurturing. I suffered her teasing and insinuations and the constant taunts and flirts. Once you had her, she was lost to your vulgar conventions. Still, even carrying this child, I could have brought her to the convent in Bamberg. The child would have been raised there as well. Damned is the soul of Andra-Angela. Damned is this Isabeau!"

Ralf grabbed the girl. "Don't come near us, Hans-Wolfgang. Let us leave."

Katarina was afraid of what desperate measures Ralf might take. This was more than a fight over property and religion, she thought. This was the personal war of wounded men. Pieter jumped forward just as Hans-Wolfgang did the same. Ralf jumped into the river with Isabeau.

"No!" Katarina cried at the same time she heard water splash.

She ran to the water's edge. Ralf had landed on the rocks in a shallow pool, on top of Isabeau. The girl's legs thrashed about. Hans-Wolfgang strung his bow and fired one shot. Ralf yelped and sat up, the arrow lodged deep in his side. He tumbled onto his back. Hans-Wolfgang ran down the bank and knelt by Isabeau's side. As he gathered the girl in his arms, she coughed and spluttered. He carried her up the bank and set her down in front of Pieter.

Hans-Wolfgang whispered, "Please take her home. I will make sure this is finished once and for all."

He slipped back down the river bank and stood over Ralf. The monk lay, unmoving, eyes open, fully aware. Katarina thought he looked peaceful, his arms waving to and fro in the shallow, flowing water.

Katarina watched as Hans-Wolfgang drew a dagger. She heard Ralf's whisper: "All I wanted was to save the child. If anything happens to her, you have yourself to blame. I have done my job, I am finished."

She did not look away as Hans-Wolfgang plunged the dagger into Ralf's throat. Ralf would move no more. Katarina looked over at Isabeau. She had watched too. Pieter put Isabeau on her horse, took the rope and led her away. They would go back home, to Sichardtshof. Katarina followed in silence.

Chapter 47

Pieter van Diemen

Water boiled in the pot on the fire and there was plenty of wood stacked. Pieter was in charge of the Sichardtshof kitchen this morning. He'd taken some early unripe spelt Sara and Tanner had harvested and dried, soaked it and set it on the fire to boil for porridge. He heard the paddock door open and the swishing of feet through the straw covering the floor of the stable.

"Who is there?" he growled.

"It's me," Katarina whispered.

Pieter stood aside as Katarina moved to the hearth, grabbed the poker and played with the embers. She had not slept well by the look of her. Pieter slipped into the stable, shut the door and pull the heavy iron bolt across the door again.

"Would you like a drink?" he asked as he came back into the kitchen.

He motioned towards the cup and ceramic jug on the table. She declined with the wave of a hand and grabbed a hunk of old bread.

"It's peppermint tea," Pieter said. "I just made it."

She poured herself a drink and sipped at it. "I find myself formulating all the things I want to tell Sara. She had been my constant companion for ten years."

"I am truly sorry. That should have been avoided." He hoped she wouldn't start crying.

Herr Tucher came down the steps and into the kitchen. "Welcome home, both of you. For as long as we can call this home."

"Thank you," Katarina said. "It's very good to be home."

"Pieter will be staying on, won't you?" he asked.

"As long as I can, sir," Pieter said. He felt strangely settled, content even.

Herr Tucher put his hands on Katarina's shoulders. "Do you still have my journal?"

Katarina nodded, smiling.

"You do?" Herr Tucher seemed surprised. "After all this and you still have it? Is it here?"

She nodded. "Under my mattress in the workers' house."

"Good work, Katarina. Did you read it?"

"All of it," Katarina said. "Some of it twice."

Pieter thought all of them seemed strangely content and calm, almost happy. The desire to have this feeling go on forever brought a slight twinge of uneasiness.

"Is it wise to stay here?" Pieter asked.

"I am not ready to leave," Herr Tucher said. "According to our information, this was the worst of it. At least until next spring. This season was heinous, the violation against us all irreparable, but let us linger one more winter. I am not ready to give up. We cannot give up."

"Is there anything left after that attack?" Pieter asked.

"In my opinion, yes. We still have a lot to do. These attacks have set us back. Such a waste of time. But there is much to salvage. We must empty the carp ponds. And prepare the fish. Tanner is funneling his grief into his work and I want to keep him as busy as I can. My uncle is coming out again this week and needs to take provisions back to Nuremberg. I am afraid we may see more scenes like what we experienced last night. The soldiers are bad but these displaced people are worse. They welcome death if they are starving and do not seem to care who they take with them."

"What about your children?" Katarina asked.

"My wife is staying in London. She wants nothing to do with the traveling mercenaries. I'd never seen her unsure and scared, but when the regiment sacked us the night you ran away, she became quiet and subdued. And my children are her charge. I have nothing to say about that. Isabeau is welcome to move into her old room, if she'd like. No, on second thought, I insist on it. I can keep an eye on her, too. If she is out in the workers' house, she can easily slip in and out. I will resume Isabeau's lessons tomorrow," he added. "She and I must get back on a schedule. I will try to keep her busy."

"I need to find Isabeau," Katarina said. "Have you seen her?"

"She was up quite early," Pieter said. "She said she was going for a ride. That was a while ago. Surely she has returned. She must be in the barn."

"Dear Lord, you let her leave by herself?" Katarina said and ran for the barn.

Pieter ran after her. Out through the door to the paddock, he took in the destruction of the last evening. A nasty odor hung over the farm; spent gunpowder, spilled blood, human and animal waste, burning hair. They met Lasse outside the barn.

"Where is she?" Katarina gasped.

"Who?" Lasse said. "Katarina, slow down. What is the matter?"

"Where is Isabeau?"

"She left on her horse," Lasse said. "She said you told her to go to the meadow and look for something for the master."

Katarina shook her head and snorted.

Pieter chuckled. "Headstrong, that girl. Don't worry, she'll be back. She can take care of herself."

"Pieter, she is ten years old!"

"She doesn't look it or act it."

Katarina shot him a poisonous stare. "She is a child."

"Katarina, set your mind at ease. She'll be back."

Katarina covered her nose and marched towards the workers' house. Pieter followed her. The door to the workers' house was open. Anna flitted back and forth in the kitchen. She had taken on the role of the house mother.

"Tanner will build a pyre for his wife today," Anna said. "He is at the task now. Would you two take this flask of beer to him, please? Katarina, don't wander around by yourself."

Katarina took the flask and Pieter followed her out behind the house. They followed the sound of a chopping axe followed by thunking logs and found Tanner in the field beyond the paddock. He'd built a low platform and was now stuffing it with straw. He grabbed a few logs and threw them onto the pile with more fervor than necessary. Katarina called out to him. He watched Pieter and Katarina approach and took the flask of beer she held out for him.

Tanner thanked her, uncorked the flask and drank deeply. "Please gather the others and come back at midday. I'll start the fire then."

Pieter and Katarina returned to the house to collect the others. They met Lasse on their way.

"We burnt the other bodies this morning," Lasse said. "Tanner didn't want them anywhere near his Sara."

Pieter joined Herr Tucher and the others gathering in front of the worker's house. They were going to pay their last respects. Pieter touched Katarina gently on the arm. "Are you ready for this?"

Katarina nodded and they walked out to the field beyond the paddock where Tanner had built the pyre. Herr Tucher followed Lasse and Bjarne. Anna held Hannah by the hand. Albin stood by himself. Tanner and Lasse set the shrouded body on the wood platform. Isabeau approached at a gallop from across the field, dismounted and came to Katarina's side.

Tanner touched his burning torch to the pyre.

The finality of that gesture evoked a feeling Pieter had not expected— one of gratitude. The time they had been given was precious and fragile and must be appreciated like costly wine. The only sin one could commit was to throw that away. Each day was a gift and their time together hung from the finest filament, to be cut off at any time. The straw under the pyre's platform ignited fast and burned with a fury. Fire, the sustainer of life, the taker as well, the final expunction.

They would burn the dead and keep their memories alive, through song, stories and the written word.

Chapter 48

Excerpt from the Journal of Sebaldus Novellus
September 1626

Today marks the first entry in the second book of the Sichardtshof journal. My wife had brought this new, blank, leather-bound exemplar from Nuremberg on her visit in the summer of 1626. She threw it on my writing table with a turned-up nose.

"Your uncle asked me to deliver the book you desired. Befitting of you. It is completely blank." She snorted with a smirk on her face. "It may take you all summer to read." She laughed. She amused herself.

I purposely wrote nothing in it. Everything I wrote this summer I burned. I wrote poetry and burned it. Everything. Now I regret it. The only piece I shared with another was the letter to Katarina. I must ask her if I may have the other journal. I would like it back. Even if it is just to burn it myself.

But today, I begin this journal, this beautiful leather-bound book. The wife is gone. My farm is somewhat whole. I still possess the woman I love. The events of this past summer will live on for posterity because I will now record them. Desperate times cause us to cross the line. Extreme angst brings out the best, and the worst, of many people. And I fear the worst is yet to come.

I heard a few footsteps in the hallway early this morning. I rest assured. Isabeau has taken up residence again in the main house. How I missed that child.

The air turned icy cold already. Matthäuswetter hell und klar, bringt guten Wein im nächsten Jahr. *If the weather on St. Matthew's is bright and clear, it'll bring a good wine next year. I only welcome the icy winter because the troops will seek out winter quarters and will give us a few months of peace. I continue to monitor their movements. It seems they travel without plan and settle wherever there is food and money. I am sorry to say this is a rich area and with the sale of weapons we will continue to have enough money. Though, the farm and all the food I am sending to Nuremberg is costing me dearly. I take out loans, I lend the food for little or no money and it is a downward spiral. I can give next to nothing to the Margrave, even though he demands some of my crops and some of my chickens. I find it more important to pay my farmhands, even if it is only in food.*

But here at my side, even if it is cold, I have my Katarina. She has changed, she is quiet and reflective. She is getting older, as I am too. Maybe she feels her mortality more than before, as I do.

Chapter 49

Isabeau
September 1626

Isabeau wanted to check on Crone tonight and feed her some hay. What she didn't want was Katarina to baby her. Whether Katarina liked it or not, she would sleep in the barn again. Isabeau heard the door shut as Katarina went into Herr Tucher's room for the night. She wouldn't hear Isabeau sneak out anyway. Tanner's father slept in the barn with the horses so she wouldn't be alone. Isabeau liked when he stayed with the horses at night.

Katarina said Isabeau should spend more time with Albin. She spent enough time with him. He would be crying and sad no matter how Isabeau tried to cheer him up. She tried to teach him to fight, like Pieter would do. She told him there was no more time to be sad. There was a war on. She had heard those officers in the Eierhofen great hall speak. She never thought about war before. She never had to. But now she did. The war just came home.

Tanner's father left a lamp burning in the barn every evening because he knew Isabeau was coming. Isabeau found her bucket with Crone's brush and the comb Herr Tucher had given her. Crone nosed her shoulder as she tried to pull the comb through her matted mane and then carefully picked at the tangles with her fingers. Horses didn't cry when their mates died, did they? Would a horse be sad if their companion was gone? Maybe they would.

Isabeau wondered why Ralf would say she was damned. What did he mean by that? She thought he liked her. He was nice enough. But all that religion did not make him a good man. It certainly had made him a dead one. Maybe he was free. She pulled the rosary from her pocket and rubbed the beads, like Ralf had done. She wanted to learn the prayers from the book she had found in her room at Eierhofen. There was a picture of beads like these. She would show Herr Tucher. The book was in Latin, like many of the books Herr Tucher had.

Isabeau liked the Sichardtshof farm but she liked her new house too. When she met Hans-Wolfgang this morning, he said they had plundered what was left and burnt the house badly. He said there was a painting of her mother but that had burned too. He was still living there and was hoping to clear Isabeau's room so she could come back. Until then, she should stay with Katarina. Maybe Katarina would stop treating Isabeau like a baby. Katarina wanted to know what happened when she was with Ralf. Isabeau wouldn't tell her. He didn't hurt her but Ralf talked to her. He said he wanted a better life for her. He said she was a child and didn't know what she wanted. She knew what she wanted: nobody would ever make decisions for her again. Isabeau promised herself.

Hans-Wolfgang told her how he got away. He said he knew something was wrong when Pieter and Katarina were gone so long. He told the General he had an herb garden and could make teas, too. He collected herbs and made the General a tea. But when the General drank it, it made him throw up.

"*Heilerscheinung*," Hans-Wolfgang had said. He told the men it was a sign the tea was working. The officers didn't believe him. Then the General had a fit. All the officers ran to help the General. That's how Hans-Wolfgang had escaped.

Isabeau settled into her nest in the hay for the night. She was sick of this war. She wanted to ride her horse tomorrow, every day, but they would make her stay close to the farm and help rebuild Sichardtshof. Why rebuild when the soldiers were coming in the spring again? She would sneak out. They couldn't stop her anymore. She'd find more weapons for her collection. And she would stick with Pieter. Pieter knew how to play this war game.

ABOUT THE AUTHOR

Laura Libricz was born and raised in Bethlehem PA and moved to Upstate New York when she was 22. After working a few years building Steinberger guitars, she received a scholarship to go to college. She tried to 'do the right thing' and study something useful, but spent all her time reading German literature.

She earned a BA in German at The College of New Paltz, NY in 1991 and moved to Germany, where she resides today. When she isn't writing she can be found sifting through city archives, picking through castle ruins or aiding the steady flood of musical instruments into the world market.

Her first novel, *The Master and the Maid*, is the first book of the Heaven's Pond Trilogy. *The Soldier's Return* and *Ash and Rubble* are the second and third books in the series.

www.ingramcontent.com/pod-product-compliance
Lightning Source LLC
Chambersburg PA
CBHW072127250626
47159CB00007B/2595